MIDNIGHT LOYALTIES

MIDNIGHT
LOYALTIES

L.K. LATHAM

L.K. Latham

Contents

For my family and friends whose support means so much to me.

I

Sleeping Beauty

The pool closed an hour ago. The alumnus hosting the party paid for the bar to stay open until ten o'clock. After that, the players, the players' girlfriends, the players' friends, and the players' hangers-on left. The non-players stayed another half hour to be polite. By then, the alum grew tired, and the faculty had eaten the last of the food. All were ready to go home after a successful back-to-school welcome party for the football team. The staff removed the remnants of the party and turned out the lights, but the mirth and life on Fifth Street continued to sprinkle life on the rooftop lounge.

Harry crouched on the ledge above the pool, surveying his city, remembering when dust floated from the scuffle of young male collegiates gathering on street corners, when small-town politicians hustled between homes and brothels to make names for themselves in the burgeoning capital, and when visions of a rose-colored dome dominating the city first took flight in the dreams of visionaries. He remembered the lovely ladies of old Pecan Street dancing under the red lights, and he remembered the hate and the apathy for those who were not wanted but were always needed. He listened as the blues swelled out of Antone's, mingling with the jazz, rock, and country music, floating in the breezes from Fifth Street as new adults drank with newfound freedoms and pressures to excel and experienced the joy of independence. He grinned. *In the morning, they'll experience the crush of reality as headaches and cottonmouth trap them behind doors of tiled palaces.* The lotus of lights crowning the cityscape glowed, unchanged by the revelry below. Everywhere, the lights and sounds of Austin exhaled. Life flowed through its streets as blood through its veins. And mixing with the booze, food, piss, and smoke rose the essence of being. The hairs in his nose twitched with excitement.

Above the den of life, he remembered lives long gone and lives budding new. Her voice echoed past and future, calmed souls, and sent bedlam and mirth stirring. He smiled to hear the voice flowing with the life of the city.

Tonight begins again, what long ago was.
Walk into the future with eyes opened to the past.
Let not the dreams of dawn hinder shadows crossing in the night.
For upon my brow the glittering night crowns what my eyes claim.
Fear not the passing of the day, but welcome moonshine's blinding rays.
Dance the dance of life and love.
Where my voice lingers, warriors gather for the fight.
Death walks your streets tonight.
Live or die, I will always be.
You're listening to Mary Midnight, online and in your mind.
Will Austin be the city of night or the dream of what was?

She arrived as a shadow to stand beside him. He reached his hand, frail, white, and strong to hers. She placed fingers paler than age into his palm, allowing him to move her hand close to his lips.

"How I have missed you, my dearest friend." He kissed fingers glazed with long red nails but no embellishments and gazed into the depths of eyes pale-black, deep, and knowing.

"If I hadn't stayed away ..." Her voice sang the saddest of music but faded away as her gaze turned to the life below.

"Don't be sad. It's time, and there is no one I would rather leave this to. I like your new name. It suits you, but you'll always be my Duchess."

"Names change." Her voice, always smooth, flowing, commanding, whispered in his ears. "Our hearts remain unchained."

They walked hand in hand along the streets and alleys of the city saying nothing, observing, breathing in the essence of its life.

The revelry of the young gave way to the realities of life. Two men with long hair and beards stirred against the cool concrete on the veranda of the Long Center. A German shepherd pup nuzzled close to the older of the men. Neither was old nor young, only lost and hungry. One woke but did not see the shadow of the couple standing above them, gazing at the city reflected in the slow-flowing river.

"Are you certain?" Her voice floated on the first breeze of dawn as it slipped around them, though the sun was still far away.

"Yes. I would never have let them disturb you as they did when I was young. I've lost touch."

"Once, no one would have dared challenge even your name, but the young today have different ideas. We grow with the times, or we fade."

"Thus will you survive." He kissed her hand, held it close to his chest. "I'm so sorry about this summer—"

"Don't!" she interrupted. "We all underestimated them, but I left the city once again in balance."

"And you will set it right here, once I am gone. War is upon us."

"Live just a little longer, my dearest. Love, one more time. Leave us all the richer for having you among us."

She kissed his cheek before turning her gaze to the drowsy man and his sleeping partner. "Dinner?"

*****

"Why is it that working out on a Friday night feels so good?" The elliptical machine beeped. The screen flashed: *cool-down starts now.* "Ten more minutes, and we're done."

"Feels good for who?" Stacy slammed the stop button on her machine and grabbed her water bottle.

"For whom. It's feels good for whom."

"Whom, schmoom." Stacy put the water bottle to her lips and gulped it down. "I thought you said the whole who/whom thing was going away."

"It is. It's just not gone yet."

"And why do you think I give a shit if it's gone or not?"

"You pay me to make sure who and whom are used correctly. Just making sure you get your money's worth."

"Watch it, Grammar Kitten. I'll have you editing one of my romance novels."

"God, no!" Kitten wiped her forehead with her towel as the elliptical machine beeped and slowed, again. "Anything but that."

Stacy refilled her water bottle at the dispenser. "What's on the agenda tonight, Kitten? Gary in town, or taking a walk on the wild side with some dark and handsome mystery man?"

Kitten's machine beeped and slowed once more. She paced herself to the too easy torque, staring out the windows and watching the lightning far to the north of town dance its way toward them. "Nah. It's going to be a hell of night. See the lightning? You're not getting me out on the roads tonight."

Stacy reached over the control panel of Kitten's machine and punched the stop button. "You're too young to run so slow, and you're too young to be such a fuddy-duddy. Come out with me. Dwayne has some absolutely beautiful roommates who would jump at the chance to go out with a pretty thing like you."

"No way. Last time I agreed to a double date with you, I had to listen to every play the hunk of meat had run since he became a Longhorn. I doubt he'll ever understand why he didn't turn me on enough to have sex with him."

"Oh, Dwayne's not a football player. He just got his PhD from Stanford and started teaching here. His expertise is the Tudor period." Stacy sighed and gazed out the windows without seeing anything in particular. "You should hear him on the evolution of postmedieval sword techniques. He's fascinating."

"Tells a good story, no doubt. Is he your latest consultant for your next historical romance?"

"Damn straight. A pretty face, a degree, a professorship at UT. I can make a fortune off of him. I didn't build Hearts and Minds Publishing sitting at home on Friday nights. Come on, Kitten. It'll be fun." Stacy began her "girlfriend I'm begging you" voice. "You need to get out more. Gary's never in town. Think about what you're missing."

The two women walked along the picture windows overlooking the river on their way out of the gym. Although the gym was in the basement of their condo building, the wall of windows offered a full view of Lake Austin. It was one of the last buildings permitted in the Lake Austin community. The builders made use of every inch of space on the steep hill, placing the building so every room offered a perfect view of the Colorado River. Kitten loved the views. The second reason she liked the building was the large, manicured common garden. The gardeners worked overtime ensuring flowers bloomed year-round. As the two women approached the doors out of the gym and into the garden, images of a night out enticed Kitten, but as they opened the doors thunder cannonaded from the north and rolled its way over the hills toward them, reverberating through her.

"I know exactly what I'm missing, and no thank you. Look." Kitten pointed toward the lightning flashing across the northern horizon. "It's going to be storming and flooding. We'll all be drinking, you'll be making love to Dwayne all night, and I'll be stuck with some starstruck historian who thinks I'm going to get his latest theory on the fall of the Roman Republic published. No, thank you. Besides, you will have more fun with me not there." A gust of wind rushed past them. "Smell that rain," said Kitten, filling her lungs, "the summer drought is over."

Stacy stopped walking and took in the north wind. "It'll be one hell of a storm. I just might have to stay all night with Dwayne." Stacy smiled.

Kitten redirected their conversation as they made their way to the elevators. "Didn't you tell me one of your moneymakers is coming into town, one of your Lovelaces or Smittens isn't it? A wine, dine, and get-her-to-sign sort of thing? This week?"

Stacy switched to business mode as the wind picked up. "Vivian comes in Sunday. Needs an impressive editor, usual drill. Throw around a few literary terms. Let her know she's special. Can your old-lady self handle being out on a Sunday night?" Stacy always hit the call button for the elevator as though it were her enemy.

"Want to bet which one of us is late to the office Monday? By the way, which one is it so I can look her up."

"Vivian Love, vampire romance."

"You told me vamps were passé?"

"Keep with the times, woman. She's hot right now. Her latest heroine left her vampire lover for a werewolf, but he's no good." In the time it took them to ride the elevator to the second floor where Kitten lived, Stacy had outlined the arc of the Vivian Love Vampire Romance series. "Of course, the heroine wants to go back to her vampire lover, but she thinks she's pregnant. You would make a good editor for her."

"Spare me, please!" Kitten grimaced as the thought of editing a romance novel sent shivers down her spine. She got off the elevator as soon as the doors opened. "Call me tomorrow, and let me know where you want to go Sunday. Have fun tonight."

"Toodles, Kitten."

"And don't get arrested." Kitten yelled her favorite dig at Stacy as the doors closed. Stacy never got caught doing anything she could get arrested for, but her dates sometimes required bail.

Even as she walked the long, open corridor out of the direct path of the encroaching end-of-summer tempest, the electricity of the storm tingled Kitten's imagination. She stopped at her door, took in a long, slow breath. Her shoulders relaxed.

*****

Kitten looked out the window from the couch where she lounged reading and sipping her glass of wine. "This is why working out on a Friday night feels so good," she said to no one. After the gym, she'd heated the last of the minestrone her mother sent her earlier in the week. She loved her mother's minestrone. It reminded her of the days when they lived hand to mouth in Vegas. They practically lived off minestrone. It was cheap to make, and Mother always made a huge pot as the girls in the chorus inevitably made their way to their house after shows. Mother would give her a bowl as she changed out of her costumes. But when Mother put on feathers, glitter, and one of her big shiny hats, Kitten purred with excitement at her beautiful mother.

A sudden loud crack burst into Kitten's living room, sending a shock wave through her body. The room went dark. "It had to happen eventually." She rose and opened the French doors leading to her large, covered patio.

The bold north wind dwindled to a pleasant, constant breeze. Lightning still cracked and danced in the sky, but the thunder mumbled on distant horizons. Only a misty rain interspersed with short-lived showers fell now, filling the air with freshness. The damp earth glistened as security lights flickered and spit until their reserve power kicked in and they glowed like beacons in the night. Her condo building and the houses across the lake were dark.

"It was a dark and stormy night." Kitten laughed as she took in the wet night air. It was too early for bed, and the protagonist in her novel was about to find out who killed his friend. The small, shiny, battery-powered reading light her mother had given her last Christmas sat clipped to the back of the lounge chair. "But that doesn't mean I have to go to bed early."

She'd bought this condo because of the patio. It was huge, far larger than any of the other condos. Most of the second-floor condos had large patios, but her unit had an extra-large patio wrapping around the corner of the building. Beneath her, the first floor and basement housed administrative offices, meeting rooms, a theater room, a gym, and game rooms—none opened onto patios. The east side of the patio even had a small stair leading to the ground. Her father didn't like the stairs. He worried someone could jump the gate with ease and enter his princess's home while she was sleeping. So he bought a large gate and attached a security system to it along with a video camera. She didn't protest. Besides, he owned the building, and it gave him pleasure to take care of her. "Sometimes, it's easier to let Daddy be Daddy," her mother would say. And she was right. Since moving in after graduate school, no one had tried to enter her condo uninvited.

She cocooned herself on the lounge chair, turning on the reading light. Planters of tall bamboo hid her from her neighbors to the west. From her position, slightly lower than the molded concrete railing, she felt isolated and safe. Plants in large and small pots surrounded her. She pulled and tugged her fluffy white robe to sheathe her body from wandering eyes and settled in with one more glass of wine to finish the chapter before bed. She could just make out the houses across the water, especially the old house with the large eyebrow window and multiple dormers. It wasn't actually across the river, only the little inlet her condo building aligned itself with.

A large white cat with black ears and long, fluffy, wet fur meowed. Kitten shook. She was drifting to sleep. A new veil of rain crept in from across the river. Lightning danced across the sky in silence. The sound of the rain pinging the still waters of the river, the moist earth of the garden, and roofs of homes in the area hypnotized her. The cat sat on the railing of her patio, licking its paws, trying to stay dry. She didn't recognize the cat. Then again, she was finding it hard to concentrate. Maybe it was the sound of rain, or the smell of rain, or the third glass of wine, but Kitten realized she was drifting further and further into sleep.

"Stupid to sleep on the patio," she mumbled reaching for the glass on the floor beside her, but instead of grasping it, she tipped it over. "Damn it. Now, I have to clean it up." She didn't move. She lay still, focusing on the cat, but her eyes wandered into the surrounding darkness. The cat stared back at her while continuing to preen. The power was still out. The reading light clipped above her head faded and finally flickered to darkness. "We should go inside," she told the cat. Neither of them moved. Kitten's eyes tried to focus but sleep consumed them. "At least we're not sitting on the roof of our house. That's a really stupid thing to do on a dark and stormy night."

*****

Detective Renaldo Sanchez stood and typed notes on his phone. He looked again at the body of the girl stretched across the pavement. Her naked torso, bruised and slashed, gleamed white against the black, oiled running path next to the river. Weeds tangled around her toes as though they wanted to squeeze the last of the moisture from her flesh. Red hair tangled with rocks and sticks to hide her face. Where her neck should have been, a gap spaced her head too far from her shoulders. Only a sliver of connective tissue kept the head close to her body. Perhaps a few drops of blood matted in her hair, or it could be mud from the river. He'd wait for forensics to tell him.

Renaldo looked to Frank Jarvis, his new partner. When he moved from the Valley to Austin, he thought he'd get stuck with an old, dickwad. Frank was sixty if he was a day. The Stetson on his head matched the gray curls mingling with black across his cheeks and chin. Only the bushy mustache remained free from gray. Not even the oversized eyebrows escaped the signs of age. Frank said nothing. He wasn't the old, dickwad Renaldo expected him to be.

Renaldo looked through the notes on his phone one more time. "Looks like the one we found last week in the warehouse district."

Frank nodded. "In what way?"

"Lack of blood." Renaldo nodded to the forensics team to take over before moving to stand next to Frank. "Both are young, naked, took a beating, probable sexual assault, and both dumped in a public place."

Frank scratched the hair on his chin. "Public?"

"Well, practically public. The bodies aren't staged, and they're not out where just anyone will see them, but they were both easily found."

"So it seems." Frank looked up and closed his eyes. "Still hot, but not as bad. You've almost convinced me. What else?"

Renaldo pulled his phone back out and reviewed his notes.

Frank shook his head and signaled to the coroner's assistant to move the cover off the body. "Don't depend on notes for everything. Take another look. What do you see?"

Renaldo put his phone away and walked back to the body. He rolled his eyes as soon as he was in front of Frank, then regretted it when he noticed Carmichael, the coroner's assistant, pointed to the neck of the victim. Renaldo knelt, bending as close as he could to the body. "Clean cut," he said.

"Like the kid from last week?"

Renaldo jumped up, "Exactly! It's a signature. Perfectly clean cuts that don't go all the way through."

Frank folded his arms. "That's it?"

Renaldo put his hand to his chin and squinted his eyes. "The kid we pulled from the lake three weeks ago. His throat was cut almost through."

Frank leaned over the body. "It's the *almost through* that's interesting. If our killer is good enough to make such a clean cut, why not cut all the way through? Put the head and body in different places?"

Renaldo paced back and forth in front of the body as the forensics team continued to process the body.

"Slow down, Sanchez," Frank put his Stetson back on his head. "Let's leave forensics to do their job. Plenty for us to do."

"But," began Renaldo, then shrugged his shoulders, put his hands in his pockets, and said, "You're right. I'll start looking through missing persons."

Frank nodded and pulled his keys out. "You drive. I need to think. Drive through for coffee on the way back."

*****

David reclined in the wild grass and weeds forming the fields along the banks of the river. The smell of last night's storms still sweetened the grasses and briars. Stars lit paths to distant worlds in the deepening blackness of evening. And there, Jenny, his moonshine, cascaded along the edge of the river, unafraid of onlookers. Her sinewy albino arms led her torso as she stopped to twirl her skirt as her feet splashed along the shoreline. Her long white hair flew with the breeze and glittered like the stars. Passion swelled in his core to caress, embrace, possess this woman no one could ever possess. And yet, she loved him with all the passion that was hers to give.

He felt Mary's presence before he saw her shadow floating toward him. His heart raced with dread, but her voice, calm, sinewy, commanding, held his attention. He no longer saw Jenny on the shoreline.

Mary stood before him shadowed by the moon. "You like it here," she said.

"Yes," he replied.

"If you want to stay, you must take a side." Her words floated between them half threat, half promise.

"This is a good place."

He didn't see Mary's smile, but something nibbled on his bare toes. He looked down as a German shepherd pup charged his feet, jumped away, then returned to lick his other toes. When David looked up, Mary's shadow had drifted away with the stealthiness with which it arrived. Jenny walked up the hill to him.

"He's beautiful," she squeezed and sat on the ground wrapping the pup with her arms.

David sat beside her reaching for the paw of the playful puppy. The dog licked his fingers, then lifted its eyes to gaze at Jenny.

"Not yet twelve weeks. Full blooded."

"Can we keep him?" Jenny's pink eyes laughed as the dog licked her chin.

David scratched the dog's ears. "I think we're meant to. We've taken a side. You were right; troubles are coming."

Jenny laughed and kissed David's lips, pushing his hair behind his ear. "We'll manage, my love."

"You haven't been in a war. Once it starts, we'll be bound. We must do everything for one purpose."

Jenny leaned into David's open arms, setting her mouth close to his ear. "Everyone should know our pleasure." She kissed his neck, and they made love on the banks of the river under the stars.

*****

"No." Kitten no longer hid the annoyance in her voice.

"She's one of my most successful authors. You would get a cut of each unit. It would double your salary in less than a year, and it wouldn't take more than a few weeks of work."

"Stacy, please." Kitten's annoyance changed to desperation. Stacy was more than her friend. She was her boss. At some point, Stacy might insist Kitten do this editing job, and Kitten didn't want to lose a good friend. "Let me stick to editing grammar books written for school children. I love grammar. I love education. I love good literature and the occasional who-done-it. Your best sellers all tell the same story and are just this side of smut. Nothing I can do will change what they are."

"My books are never smut, but the closer they are to smut the greater the sales. Listen," Stacy enjoyed defending her favorite genre to the most elite literary snobs. "They don't all tell the same story. The good ones open new windows into love, relationships, romance, and sex the ordinary reader will never explore, let alone live. You got your education's worth of fine literature. Barbara and Beau are proud of you, but most people will never experience the levels of romance my books offer."

As much as she tried to hide her emotions, Kitten's face always betrayed her.

Stacy quieted her voice. "I'm not saying anything about you riding on a high horse, but you are a bit of a lit snob. All I'm asking right now is for you to consider these books as a challenge. Think about the good you'll provide the genre." Stacy leaned back in her chair and took another sip of her latte.

"You're right. I can be snobbish. However, I don't see how I could help your Vivian. I read her latest before we went out Sunday. I had to force myself to read the whole thing, but I won't deny the writing was sound."

Stacy stopped mid-sip as the edges of her lips turned up into a huge smile. "You're right. You're too good for Vivian. I know the perfect project."

"Do not plan any projects ..." Kitten did not finish her sentence.

"It's a brilliant idea. Only just forming in my head, right now, and you are going to absolutely love it. Let me get my thoughts together. We'll talk later."

Before a hint of the brilliant plan escaped Stacy's lips, her phone's alarm beeped. "Shit! Meeting. Gotta get back upstairs. Don't forget you're driving me home. Don't leave without me." Stacy dashed out the door as though death nipped at her heels, as she always did.

Kitten sipped her coffee to gather her thoughts. The bigger Stacy's idea, the more dangerous. The week had been busy with complaints about not enough books in stock for this or that school. Her authors complained to her, but there was little she could do. She forwarded the complaints to the shipping department and tried to reassure her authors the books would make it to their locations, and they would get paid. Mostly, she wished they would just leave her alone. Her authors clung to her more than they did to their agents.

She got up grabbing the watering can from the shelf in the corner closet. "I'm too fucking nice," she said to the large fern near her desk. "Stacy always says so. Mommy always says so. It's going to be the death of me." Moving to the windows, she sighed, staring over the sprawling capitol building and its parks. Many of her coworkers left when Stacy bought the publishing house, rebranding it, *Hearts and Minds Publishing: Books to fill the head and flutter the heart*. The smart ones, like Kitten, realized what was happening and did well after the sale. Kitten now headed her department. Leigh Brown, who used to share Kitten's office, edited for several romance writers and enjoyed the fast pace and increase in pay. Kitten missed the long talks she and Leigh used to have and research, books, and life, but she also enjoyed having the office to herself. She liked having plants around her. She also liked it when Stacy came down to share an espresso and talk business with someone who wasn't trying to take over the company.

"What is Stacy's brilliant idea?" It worried her the rest of the afternoon. Watering the plants did little to relax her, nor did turning off email notifications and correcting sentence diagrams in the newest textbook she had to edit, and diagramming sentences always relaxed her.

*****

If Stacy intended to tell Kitten what her great idea was on the way home, she didn't. From the moment they met at Kitten's car, Stacy ranted on the evils and incompetence of auto mechanics. Instead of dropping Stacy off at the auto shop, Kitten navigated the usual traffic congestion toward Lake Austin and Stacy's incoherent tirades. Kitten pondered which was worse: the traffic or the loud rants of her friend.

As soon as Kitten parked in her usual spot and turned off the engine, Stacy let out a long, shrill scream.

Kitten shook her head to clear her ears.

"Sorry. Thought I should let it out before we opened the doors. The whole scream therapy thing really works. I feel much better." Stacy smiled a large, relieved smile. "Is it weights or cardio tonight?"

"You should do yoga to relax but only after a couple of glasses of wine. You're too wound up."

"Maybe it's time for a new car." Stacy contemplated various luxury cars as they made their way to the mailboxes near the elevators.

"Go electric. You'd like all the luxuries in the new ones, and they're green. Set a good example for the rest of us, and you could offer us parking spots with charging stations—"

"Tesla doesn't make the roadster anymore, and you know how I like to drive. What's that?"

Stacy's eyes bored onto an envelope in Kitten's hand with the contemporary arts logo embossed on the seal.

"Looks like an invitation. Probably nothing I'd be interested in."

"Open it." Stacy's eyes widened as Kitten closed her mailbox and put her keys in her purse. "Hurry! I'm sure I know what it is."

"What?" asked Kitten.

"Will you just open it, woman!" Stacy nearly leapt to grab the envelope.

"You're right. It's an invitation. Shit. It's this Friday. Nothing like waiting till the last minute ..."

"Oh my god! How did you manage it? I'd kill for this. Who did you kill to get it?" Stacy grabbed the invitation from Kitten's hands stopping only long enough to catch her breath. "Do you realize how rare these are? You've got a plus-one. Tell me I can be your plus-one. Please, please, please, please, please."

"Fine. But what's it for?" Kitten pried the invitation from Stacy's hands to see what she was committing to. "Who's Harry Reign? Is he any good?"

"Get your head out of textbooks, Kitten. He's only the most elusive and exclusive new artist of the twenty-first century. The hottest thing on the art circuit, and Anthony Mugello is hosting this as a fundraiser, and he's the most eligible and wealthiest bachelors in the world."

"The banker?"

"The *banker*? She says. He owns more banks than your daddy ever did."

"Thought the name sounded familiar. That explains why I got the invite. Daddy's done business with him. At least I've heard him use the name. Daddy probably asked him to invite me."

"Whatever the reason, you've got to take me. It's *the* place to be Friday night. Tell me you're going to take me. Please."

"This Reign any good?"

"Seriously? Of course he's good. And almost never does public showings. Oh my god! We'll have to go shopping—something new for this thing. I'll email Carol tonight and have her adjust my schedule. Let's take a long lunch to shop tomorrow. We'll get our hair done after work Thursday. We'll leave the office early on Friday for nails. I'll have Carol make the appointment."

"There's no need—"

"Do not tell me you've got something to wear. I've seen your best dresses, and none are good enough for this event. Black-tie and diamonds only."

Kitten walked to the elevator too fast for Stacy to stop her. She already regretted agreeing to go to the event.

*****

Madeline didn't like him; too damn Catholic. To make him even more unbearable, he was a West Point officer. She hated soldiers. She hated officers even more. Still, Yasushi trusted him, and she trusted her brother. She would tolerate young Lieutenant Manny Diggers for the sake of Yasushi.

She sighed heavily, making sure Yasushi heard her. He kept his head bowed and continued praying with Officer Asshole in front of the sanctuary, but she noticed the ever so slight shifting of Yasushi's shoulders, assuring Madeline her little brother knew she did not approve of such a long prayer.

The group belonged to no particular church. Yasushi believed God guided him in the fight to rid the world of demons. God specified no particular dogma, so he required none from the group's members. Still, meeting in churches felt like a requirement for her brother. She didn't like to see their Catholic upbringing popping into his everyday actions. She believed he would be a good priest, but she'd see hell freeze over before she allowed him to do that. At this moment, sitting in the padded but still uncomfortable pew, Madeline wished he would pull the faith part out of the group. The whole god thing irked her to no end. There was too much to do to spend so much time praying. Yet, they still waited for the others to arrive; the night was young, and they had time.

She closed her eyes, breathing in the cool, air-conditioned stuffiness of the pale church. The Lutheran Church covered a good portion of the city block, but the sanctuary of the sanctuary closed in on her. It lacked the glamour of some churches she had been in. She opened her eyes to try again to find something of beauty in this rather bland house of God. The creamy yellow walls matched the pale brown brick, making the room too mellow. Even the elaborate woodwork dulled Madeline's eyes. The stained glass windows, however, provided meditative inspiration for the church's members on Sunday mornings. She tried to imagine the window with the Tree of Life in full sun. The emerald greens and ruby reds glowing with life. The leaves of the tree waved to her like the waves from the sea surrounding her home in the Philippines. Despite all the evils there, she missed the tropical air, the smells, the sights, the tastes of home. She told herself that's why she liked her floral dresses with their bold patterns and bright colors. They contributed to her sense of being. Despite the pain that began on the island, she longed for the bright, yellow sun and cool ocean breezes. Sweet papaya tickled her tongue just as the memory of the darkness they had run from flickered in the shadows of her memories.

The heavy door to the street opened, startling Madeline back to the moment. She sensed the three stoics before she saw them. Still, Yasushi and Officer Asshole prayed.

"Madeline," the oldest of the three men greeted her and sat beside her. The other two sat behind him, separated by enough space to imply to anyone watching they were strangers. The habits of infiltrators stuck hard.

"Roger," Madeline nodded her head. She liked Roger. His demeanor never faltered from logical, thoughtful, and resigned. He was as gray on the inside as he was on the outside, but his gray eyes conveyed a drive to live Madeline could understand. He always approached Madeline with the greatest of reverence, and if she admitted it, she would see the fondness he had for her.

"That Diggers?" Roger's arms stretched out on the back of the pew. He lazily pointed his chin toward the young man kneeling next to Yasushi.

"Yah. His information is good. Brother thinks he has a lot of promise." Madeline didn't bother to hide the contempt in her voice as she spoke of Diggers.

"Noticed Banes and Carson locking up their bikes outside. They'll be in soon, and we can get started." Roger sighed but kept it quiet.

Bane and Carson walked in from the street. From a small door on the side of the sanctuary, a young man walked in carrying a wooden vase. His thumb polished the gold band inlaid into the side of the vase as he walked without seeing. He stopped. Surprise flashed across his face at seeing people in his church. The vase thudded on the plush carpet and rolled till it hit the edge of a pew.

Yasushi's head turned before Madeline could say anything. His hand reached out and grabbed the vase as he twisted to stand in front of the young man.

"Pastor Pete, good to meet you at last." Yasushi lifted his voice to sermon level. His deep bass tones bounced off the walls, comforting everyone in the sanctuary like a warm blanket.

Madeline enjoyed watching the faces of people meeting her brother for the first time. His enormity met them first. Pastor Pete's eyes widened as he watched the man whose ethnicity no one could guess approach him. Yasushi had been kneeling in prayer when the pastor entered the sanctuary. Released from his meditations, Yasushi extended himself to his full height, easily towering over Pastor Pete. With an unexpected grace, he extended one hand into Pastor Pete's to shake. With the other, he handed over the wooden vase.

"Reverend Brown? I've been looking forward to meeting you." Next to Yasushi, Pastor Pete looked like a schoolboy standing in front of his headmaster. Even his dark golf shirt and khaki pants looked like a school uniform. Madeline didn't bother to hide the smirk on her face. "The synod told me you'd be here. Is there anything I can get you?"

The look on his face as Diggers crossed himself and rose made Madeline shake with laughter she struggled to hold in.

"I can't tell you how pleased I am that we could meet here tonight." Yasushi continued shaking Pastor Pete's hands at the same time turning him back to the door he had entered. "We won't be any bother. Just a few old friends getting together for some prayer and planning. Just waiting for one more now, a woman from your synod, Anna Leitz. You know her? No? Well, I'm sure she'll be in to see you when we're done."

Like a scolded schoolboy, Pastor Pete left the sanctuary looking sullen and chastised. As he opened the side door to leave, the front door opened. A woman in a navy suit with short hair and a self-important stride entered.

Lieutenant Diggers whispered into Yasushi's ear and walked down the long aisle, passing the woman in the navy suit, giving her the slightest of head nods. He left saying nothing to anyone in the group.

"Let's get started, everyone," began Yasushi. He pulled chairs from the front into a semicircle near the vestibule where musicians played during weddings and funerals. "Ms. Leitz, I'm pleased to meet you."

"Anna, please," said the latest to arrive in the church. She sat in the chair to the left of Yasushi.

Madeline took her usual place to Yasushi's right. Her demeanor remained impassive and unreadable to anyone other than Yasushi and perhaps Roger.

"Anna, it is," began Yasushi with his pastoral grin and introduced the members of the group. "Roger Morgan, former marine and our chief planning officer. You'll find when it comes to planning, he's the man with all the details. He's been with us from the beginning."

Roger nodded to Anna. He didn't smile, keeping his face neutral. He trusted no one until they proved themselves. "Anna," he held out his hand to shake hers. "And once a marine, always a marine."

The two men next to him, Torres and Woods, both let out a quiet "ooh-rah," respectful of being in a church.

"Phillip Torres and Derek Woods, also marines," said Yasushi. "Phillip, weren't you with Roger in the Philippines? You joined us sometime later."

"Yes, sir. The captain recruited me then, but I had another eight months on my tour. Derek joined us much later after the Corp let him down. He wasn't in the Philippines with us." There was nothing to distinguish Phillip from any other marine except his left eye, pale blue, with a scar running over the lid contrasted with his light brown skin and dark brown right eye. "The eye is from shrapnel," added Phillip, noticing Anna staring at it.

Derek leaned forward in his chair. "Ma'am" was all he said as he sized up the newcomer with his piercing dark eyes under thick brows. Unlike Morgan and Torres, he didn't look like a marine. He had the build, long, lean, and strong, but the tattooed sleeves, large gold rings hanging from his ears, and flowing dreadlocks displayed non-military.

"Phillip and Derek are our offensive team. And next is Catherine Carson. If you need a little electronic surveillance done or a little one-on-one surveillance, she's the one to go to."

"Everybody calls me CC." CC bounced out of her chair to shake hands with Anna. Her red curls floated around her freckled face and beaming smile. "Glad to have you on board. And glad to finally have another girl on board, rev. It's about time."

"Indeed it is, CC." Yasushi motioned her to sit and pointed to the man next to her. "And this is James Earl Banes. Thanks to you, he's no longer our newest member. He's our principal hacker. Don't let him near your phone, or he'll track all your movements from last week to next."

James Earl was the plainest man in the group. His baggy pants and wrinkled T-shirt suggested sloth, but the bulges peeking out underneath his sleeves indicated a man fit for a fight. His only ornaments, aside from a large red plug stretching his earlobe, was a Starfleet insignia carved into his scalp. He looked up from his phone to Yasushi. "I can already tell you where she's been this week."

Yasushi and CC laughed out loud, while the others, except for Madeline, tried to hide their laughs behind coughs and sudden interest on the floor. CC playfully punched James Earl in the arm. Anna straightened the lapels of her jacket and cleared her throat.

When CC and Yasushi stopped laughing, Yasushi's smile transformed into reverence. "This, of course, is my sister, my right hand, and my driving force, Madeline." Yasushi took Madeline's hand in his and squeezed. Madeline didn't acknowledge Anna. "I hope you don't mind, Anna, but we'll forgo the long introductions and your story for now. Although they are all important, we have information essential to discuss with everybody."

"Of course." Anna nodded, smiling with all politeness. "Let's get to work."

"Madeline met Lieutenant Manny Diggers, US Army, and the rest of you saw him here earlier. His obligations prevent him from joining us now. We have Lieutenant Diggers to thank for the information about the army's failed attempt to tame one of the demons over the summer."

"Tame," mumbled Madeline and rolled her eyes.

"We could have told them it was impossible," continued Yasushi. "They tried, good people died. But three good things came of it: the demon they captured died, and we now have an inside man to help us track the others. Diggers."

Yasushi stared hard at each of his team members. Each one sat straight in his or her chair with eyes glued to Yasushi.

"You said three good things." James Earl, ever logical, kept the conversation on point.

"We know our prey was there."

Madeline turned her head quickly to look at her brother.

"Proof?" Roger raised his eyebrows. "I read the same reports as you did."

"Not all of them." Yasushi said, allowing the information to sink in. "Diggers obtained a copy of an unofficial report from the scientist who led the attempt. The generals chose to ignore most of it. The colonel in charge of security in Galveston signed off on all reports except this one. It varied from the colonel's in one important detail: a shadowy figure appearing during the attack and seemingly in command. It matches the description of the demon Madeline and I remember."

"Why wasn't this in the original report?" asked Roger.

"The colonel retired as soon as he filed his final report. He's highly respected. Most of the generals take his version of events as truth."

"Typical!" Madeline spat. "No one wants to hear the truth."

"But now they have to at least consider it." Yasushi squeezed

Madeline's hand. "I'll need to talk to this colonel. Roger, do you think your contacts can help?"

"Doubt it," replied Rogers. "He retired and married. From what I hear, he's closed the door to military connections."

"Well, do your best. I'll make some phone calls too. The scientist is out of the picture. Diggers says the army is hiding him." Yasushi sighed. "But now news everyone will be excited to hear."

Madeline could see Yasushi commanded everyone's attention, even hers. He always could command a crowd.

"The demon we seek is in Austin." Simply spoken, but the impact rippled through the circle of Hunters like a shock wave.

"Here?" Madeline felt her face pale. She pulled her hand away from Yasushi's, rubbing it with her other hand.

"Yes. He's here. And I know where he'll be tomorrow night."

Yasushi reached into the black bag at his feet. He pulled out an invitation in a thick, embossed paper envelope. "A charity gala tomorrow night at an art museum."

Madeline stared at the envelope, almost reaching for it.

"Roger and I will attend." Yasushi spoke the words slowly, allowing Madeline to comprehend. Her face reddened, and her eyes narrowed, but she said nothing.

"It's a gala benefiting the museum. A famous artist is showing his work."

"Famous is an understatement." James Earl's fingers stopped tapping on his phone. "Harry Reign is world-famous, Anthony Mugello even more so."

"The banker?" CC turned her head to look at James Earl who nodded. Her voice shook for a moment but steadied before continuing. "I remember his name coming up in old investigations. Nothing was ever found on him. What's he got to do with this?"

Derek let out a long whistle of astonishment. "Mugello is big time. If he's connected with the demons, we're going to need help."

Madeline no longer paid attention to the discussion. Her hands stroked the flowers on the lap of her dress.

"We know our target is a leader. It makes sense for him to place himself among prominent people, which doesn't mean they know what he is. CC, James Earl, we'll need surveillance and communications for the event. Roger, will you see they get what they need? And Anna, do you have intel on this Mugello or any of the other guests at the gala?"

"Mugello's rich with connections everywhere. He's never been a suspect. If he's involved, he's being used."

James Earl almost laughed at Anna's description. "Mugello's richer than God. Comes from a family of bankers. No one knows how rich he really is."

"And he's generous." Anna started again. "He actively supports the arts, children's hospitals, multiple charities in multiple cities, states, and countries. We'll have to be careful. We need hard proof to get support to go after him. He has friends everywhere."

"As do we," added Yasushi. "The rest of you will be on the outside of the event. Everyone be ready to move whether to follow or—" Yasushi closed his eyes. "This is the day I've prayed for. With luck and our wits, we'll have him."

"Amen," said Torres, who bowed his head.

"Yes," Yasushi sighed. "Brothers and sisters, let's pray for the strength we need to finish this."

Yasushi's hand smothered Madeline's. She had no choice but to take the hand of CC and bow her head with the others. She squeezed Yasushi's hand as tight as she could. "Get on with it," the squeeze implied. "We have work to do."

*****

Maddy rolled her eyes as she slouched against one of the stone columns of the old house. "Tell me what's so fucking great about being at such a stuffy party on a perfectly good Saturday night when all the clubs are open?"

"You didn't have to work tonight, Maddy." Tasha sighed, wondering how much more Mrs. LeBrere would take before firing her cousin. Tasha needed the job. Maddy did too, but Maddy hated working.

"And miss a chance to brush against a rich old man with a wandering eye? I don't think so." Maddy turned the silver platter she was holding over and used it as a mirror to check her lipstick and unbutton another button on her blouse.

"You know Mrs. LeBrere likes blouses buttoned to the collar."

"What's she going to do? Fire me during a party like this? She needs me here. I can wrap her 'round my finger anytime I want." Maddy snapped her fingers in Tasha's face. "Don't you worry about me. Oh, look at that one."

Tasha turned to see the man Maddy pointed at. He was old, with more gray hair than their grandfather, but he wore an expensive-looking suit. "Too old," she said and turned to grab a tray of Champagne glasses. "I'm going to work. Maybe you can afford to lose your job, but I can't. I got two more semesters to pay for."

"And what's a degree going to do for you a rich old man can't do? Let me show you how to get a sugar daddy."

Tasha watched Maddy carry a small tray of glasses toward the old man in the gray suit. She saw Maddy trip in front of the man, sending her tray of glasses scattering in front of him. The man's eyes narrowed as his lips thinned. Tasha loved her little cousin, but she wouldn't cover for her anymore, and she didn't want to watch Mrs. LeBrere fire her.

*****

"It's not like you're new to this. So, why so nervous?" Anthony Mugello ran his hands along the lapel of his tuxedo. The fit wasn't what he liked. It looked good, but the left and right shoulders felt uneven. He missed his Italian tailor.

"Not sure how you convinced me to do this. I hate being in public and letting people see me." Harry Reign continued to look around, staring into the shadows and listening to the talk of the serving staff making their final checks as the first of the guests arrived.

"I'll let you know who should see you. Conceal yourself from the rest." Anthony gazed into the silver punch bowl on the buffet table they were standing next to and adjusted the diamond lapel pin, his favorite, in the shape of a large tear. "You could have at least dressed for the occasion. The who's-who of Austin paid a lot of money to be here tonight. They expect to be wined, dined, and spoiled. In turn, we raise a great deal of money for the arts. Ironic, considering all the politicians who will be here tonight who take funding away from the arts whenever they get a chance. You agreed it was a worthy cause. Let's make them bleed. We'll lick it up, and they'll never know it."

"That doesn't mean I have to enjoy being here."

"Of course it does. I'm paying for this little shindig. You're a brilliant artist, Harry. Roll with it. I want a few people to say they met the great Harry Reign. That's how I'll get more money out of them. It's all for art, Harry." Anthony followed Harry's eyes to the entrance, again. "Who are you waiting for? Is there someone I should meet?" He raised his eyebrow. It was dangerous to pry into Harry's life. He almost had the nerve to ask again when he heard his name called out from a woman with a light pink dress walking toward him with two other women.

Anthony turned on his most charming "I love you" expression. "Helena. Ravishing as always."

Helena Stalward blushed as Anthony took both her hands into his and kissed her cheeks. Her gray hair, pulled back with a large diamond comb and wrapped into a tight bun, framed her plump and just starting to sag face. The light pink dress showed off a figure that, for a woman in her sixties, was extraordinarily firm if well-rounded. "Anthony, I can't tell you how much it means you've set this up. Everything is perfect. The gardens have never been more beautiful."

"No expense is too great for art, but the gardens can't compare to you." Anthony gleamed sex appeal as he eyed Helena and the two women behind her.

"Anthony. You flatter too much." Helena's blushes turned brighter than her dress. She took a moment to catch her breath.

"This is Dr. Winifred Kane." Helena turned to introduce the middle-aged woman beside her with the large corsage on her lapel. She ignored the pretty, young artist beside Dr. Kane.

"Dr. Kane, it's a pleasure to meet you. I admired your work at the Sculpture Gardens in Houston and was delighted to hear you were coming to Austin." Anthony caressed Winifred's hand and looked to the young woman behind her. "And you are Maria Toledo, the newest artist in residence." Anthony smiled and made love to each woman as easily as they blushed.

"How do you do it, Anthony," began Helena. "You know everything about everyone. Will I ever surprise you?"

"Helena, my dear, I wouldn't be here today if I didn't know everything about everyone. I especially keep up with all the talented new artists." They laughed as Anthony took Helena's arm to lead her to the entrance where they could personally greet the guests with the largest bank accounts. None of the women seemed to notice Harry Reign. "Now come, ladies. We have money to make. Maria, use that charming gleam in your eyes to make the men bleed. The budding artists of Texas are depending on us. And Dr. Kane, we need to talk about the residence program and how we might expand it."

Anthony caught the nod of approval from his mentor, Harry. When Anthony Mugello held court, he got what he wanted. Tonight, he wanted philanthropists and artists to add to his collection. He moved among the crowd smiling, shaking hands, making love, and taking money. Harry had trained him well.

*****

The crowd grew as the lights scattered about the gardens glowed in the shadows of the sun's twilight. Tuxedos and jewels sparkled from the lights hanging from the trees and placed along the paths of the gardens. Musicians played baroque from a tent near the veranda of the old mansion. Neatly groomed waitstaff maneuvered unobserved but always in the right place with trays of Champagne, caviar, and canapés. Docents, some in jackets too large and some in jackets too small, stood around the gardens twitching and adjusting lapels. They waited with flashlights to guide guests along the paths to the sculptures prepared with memorized lines meant to dazzle guests about the artist and the sculptures.

Harry moved in the shadows, stopping to listen as a gray-haired docent explained how Harry Reign began his career in the steppes of Mongolia. The former communist regime recognized his talents and educated him in Moscow and Paris. Having achieved international success, he left Europe for the United States where he lived in seclusion until found by the renowned art philanthropist, Anthony Mugello. Now, he is showing his work, although he seldom makes public appearances.

"Mr. Reign is here tonight. You may get to meet him if you are lucky," said the man trying not to examine the cleavage of one of the young women he was speaking to.

"Is Mr. Mugello here too?" asked the natural blond woman standing beside the woman with cleavage amply displayed.

"Yes. In fact, he is the principal organizer behind tonight's fundraiser." The docent, disappointed but not surprised, sighed.

"Can you point him out to us?" asked the bleached blond with cleavage.

Harry resisted laughing. He slid among the shadows until he stood under a tree near the entrance. Close to him was the serving tent where chefs removed the lids from silver chafing dishes, lit the flames under omelet pans, cracked eggs, and stirred batter while others poured oil into sizzling skillets and began stir-frying meats and vegetables. Guests gathered with their drinks, waiting for their evening meal. Harry frowned, wishing he had not come when he saw Kitten walking in with another woman.

He had seen the other woman before, sitting on Kitten's patio drinking wine. She was older than Kitten, handsome, well-to-do, elegant without being fussy, but she had a loud voice he found annoying. Harry never liked loud voices in women. It made them too masculine, but such were the times. A woman of her generation had to be feminine on the outside and masculine on the inside to succeed. He was glad Kitten didn't have a loud voice. Her voice was soft, steady, yet held authority when she wanted it to. Tonight, she wore a simple, black dress which followed her curves. The square neckline modestly revealed just enough of her generous breasts to tantalize without taunting. Her dark curls, neatly folded into the modern version of the pre-war coif so popular these days, framed the plumpness of her face, making her dark eyes the first thing you noticed about her. From her ears hung blood opals styled in modern Art Deco matching the necklace wrapped around her throat.

"So, that's why you're so nervous." Anthony spoke with deference into Harry's ear. "I never imagined you would be nervous about a woman."

"I thought you were schmoozing." Harry kept his focus on Kitten. Anthony never teased Harry. Harry liked Anthony better than most, but Anthony had just discovered a secret. "What do you want?"

"Wanted to let you know Leonard finally showed. He's in his element at this type of thing, and Cesar brought David. There won't be any trouble here."

"Three bodies, Anthony." Harry turned to look Anthony in the eyes. "There's already trouble."

"I know." Anthony lowered his face. "We'll find out who's doing this." Anthony looked up, pinching his lips tightly. "It's not one of my people. I wouldn't allow someone so stupid in the city. You know that."

Harry placed his hand on Anthony's shoulder. "I know, il mio giovane amico. Remain diligent and trust no one. One body can be explained, even excused in the right circumstances. Three bodies expose us. I don't like it."

Neither spoke. Each knew the danger of exposure.

Anthony broke the silence as laughter erupted behind them from a group of men standing near the bar. "I came to see if I could get you to meet a few people." Anthony looked back at the entrance where Kitten and Stacy separated. "She is lovely. I thought you had imagined her."

"Don't be ridiculous. I'm a realist. Now, let's meet who I need to meet." Harry turned away from Kitten.

*****

"I'm so sorry," Maddy said, batting her golden brown eyes and puckering sweet brown lips into a perfect heart. She had everything planned. Her cutest twang sprang from her lips. Her sweetest smile perched on the corners of her mouth. Her eyelids batted at the perfect pace to scream charm, but none of the practiced charms emerged. The moment a drop of Champagne touched the man's cuff, an anger and fury Maddy had never witnessed swooped over her.

The man's steely fingers gripped her throat, lifting her from the ground and into the shadow of a clutch of live oaks next to the path. Her mind said scream, but her breath choked back any voice from her shrinking voice box.

The man's eyes burned with fire and hate. It only took a moment to die, but she felt the cold consume each fiber in her limbs. She saw the shadows of death dancing into her eyes. She felt her life flow out of her and into the raging man.

*****

"I told you you'd like it." Stacy wore her smuggest grin.

The gardens at Laguna Gloria were always beautiful, but tonight with the lighting, the sculptures, the floral arrangements, and all the beautiful people, they radiated elegance. On the lawn, sculptures, strategically placed and perfectly lit, grew majestically out of the ground. The lighting along the paths hinted at more delights awaiting those who ventured into the gardens.

"Look. There's Ted from Pearson. Let me go burst his bubble. I'll lay you odds he paid a pretty price for his invite thinking he could have the legislators to himself. You ok on your own?" Stacy walked away without waiting for an answer.

Kitten watched Stacy creep behind Ted as he stood talking to the lieutenant governor and a dashing, older man in a gray silk suit. He wasn't a politician and looked far too sophisticated for an ordinary businessman. In the twilight, his olive skin glowed beneath slick salt-and-pepper hair. Next to him, Ted and the lieutenant governor looked hokey. She watched as Stacy maneuvered Ted into introducing the man to her. Stacy created opportunity. Whoever the man was, he was about to encounter the full force of a woman on a mission. If he could aid her publishing house, he would be the end of her evening. Stacy loved these events and would find her own way home—if not with the striking man in the silk suit, then with another good-looking someone.

Kitten strolled along the closest lit path, sipping Champagne and admiring the play of electric lights and night's darkness on the leaves and tall grasses around her. The path turned to the right, revealing a large sculpture growing from the ground. Two lovers cast in stone swirled in passion's embrace. Arms entwined, grasping and caressing hands ignited the fire of each lover, and their faces, both obscure and distinct, flashed lust, love, and loss.

Kitten wandered, oblivious to everything else as she walked around the statue enthralled in the detail and obscurity with each new angle. As she moved around the sculpture, the smells of earth, trees, bushes, flowers, wine, and people tainted her experience with *The Lovers*. They were on fire or ice depending on the smell. She breathed in each scent and let it guide her feelings.

"Perfect," she said to no one as she returned to where she began. She bent over to read the nameplate. *The Lovers' Touch*. Harry Reign. An ease swept over her body as she realized the evening would be enjoyable examining the work of this artist.

Before she turned to follow the path to the next moment of examination, a couple standing behind *The Lovers' Touch*, deep in the shadows of an old live oak tree, caught her eye. That she didn't notice them when she walked around the statue didn't surprise her. The work enthralled her, but the woman's extraordinary looks would catch the eye of most people. Her wraith-like figure almost swayed in the slight breeze of the river with her lacy, white dress, long white hair, and whiter than white skin. Kitten didn't want to stare, but an almost albino woman (she had a wide streak of black hair) could not help but be noticed. The woman didn't care if anyone stared. The man standing next to her blended with the growing shadows of evening. His tall, powerful physique contrasted with the almost albino woman. The gentleness and care with which they stood together blended into the garden's background. Kitten wouldn't have been surprised if the almost albino woman sprouted wings and flew away with the fairies while the man, Oberon, glided along moonbeams to follow.

Kitten turned, allowing the path to guide her. She examined more sculptures in silent contemplation before she turned back to the couple in the shadows. Instead of seeing the man and woman, she saw *The Lovers' Touch*. She smiled imagining what such a passion felt like.

The number of people in the gardens grew. She could no longer contemplate each piece in silence. The farther she walked along the path, the more people stopped to look at her and point. At first, she thought she imagined the stares, until a funny-looking man with a bright red bow tie and thick glasses stopped her.

"I'm so pleased to see you in person. Harry captured you deliciously, and to be so prominently exhibited must be exhilarating. You must be enormously thrilled." He reached for her hand, but before he could say anything else, a voice from behind her called, "Kevin. There you are. You're needed over here, darling."

"Do excuse. I must answer a friend in need. Don't leave till we've had the chance to talk properly." As suddenly as he approached Kitten, Kevin left.

Kitten's mouth twisted as she stared at his back moving away from her, but the smell of spices sizzling with herbs, meats, and vegetables called her. Stacy had insisted they get their hair and nails done before the party, which left no time for lunch or dinner. Now, food enticed her away from the art and the sweet scents of nature.

The path made a sharp turn to the left. Kitten followed the turn and saw the pavilion and the food ahead of her. She also saw people stopped at an alcove on the right. She assumed she would see another sculpture. Instead a large crowd blocked her view of the display.

Instead of a sculpture, an oversized oil painting suspended with heavy gold ropes from a large tree branch filled the small alcove. Floodlights on the ground and in the tree lit the surface of the painting. The generous format and frame of branches and flora created the illusion she could step into the world of the painting. In that world, a woman lay sleeping on a divan under a canopy of rich red and gold fabrics surrounded by an elaborately carved concrete railing. Outside the canopy, lightning and darkness battled for preeminence. Surrounding the sleeper, small demons, some shadow, some black, some red, scurried around her. The sleeper's right hand fell off the divan knocking over a glass of red wine. Two demons laughed, licking the wine, while a third pushed on the bottle to knock it over. A cat with long, wet, white hair and black ears sat grooming itself and staring at the demons.

A woman in the crowd pointed to the demon and asked her Kitten, "Is it watching them deciding which one to eat or guarding the sleeper?"

Kitten tilted her head from one side to the other. "Good question," was her only answer.

Something about the demon and the sleeper were familiar. The sleeper wore a large white robe. Her left leg crossed her right leg. This opened the skirts of the robe to her thigh stopping only as it kissed her hip. A demon who looked familiar to Kitten despite the pointed ears, oversized grin, and fanged teeth sat on her chest. The right lapel had slipped to expose abundant cleavage but stopped before exposing her nipple. The demon's fingers twitched and clicked his long nails as its hand hovered over the lapel. His eyes stared into Kitten's eyes. He wanted to slide the robe away. *Will he?*

"Sleeping Beauty." The voice beside her resonated over the humming of the crowd and the music and the river running with stillness through the garden. The man stood behind her. He wore a large-brimmed, floppy hat hiding the upper portion of his face. His clothes from the high-necked T-shirt to his oversized jacket to his baggy trousers were black. He even wore black gloves. Only the silk scarf around his neck had any color. The royal purple suited him.

"It's yours?"

Harry Reign fit the description Kitten had read: old, ugly, and reclusive. The man standing beside her could only be him.

"Yes. You don't mind, I hope. But when I saw you sleeping on your patio during the storm, I couldn't help myself. I had to paint you."

"That's not me." Kitten studied the sleeper. The sleeper's figure curved perfectly in the divan hidden only by the white robe. Dark curls fanned her face in a breeze. "There's no resemblance, other than the robe." Her face burned as she realized she was the woman in the painting.

"It's you. I apologize if I caused you any embarrassment but not for the painting. I'm afraid Mr. Vasquez cornered you before I could warn you."

"Vasquez?" quizzed Kitten.

"Kevin Vasquez, the art critic. Red bow tie. He's hard to miss. So far, I've managed to elude him."

"Ah! This is what he was talking about. I had no idea. I assumed he was just a drunk with a bad come-on." They both laughed. As ugly as Harry was, beneath the dark, intense eyes hidden with pointed, bushy, gray eyebrows, Kitten found him charming, even alluring. "How do you explain painting me with such detail?"

"It was the night of the storm that broke summer, just a few weeks ago. You fell asleep on your patio."

"That was you I saw sitting on the roof! I wasn't dreaming. You saw all of those details from the roof across the water?" Kitten imagined Daddy's security gate and cameras. Her spine tingled with a sudden chill, her face still burned, and Daddy's fears for his little princess raced across her mind. "No way you could make out all those details."

"I've seen you on your patio many times. It's my house across the inlet from your building, and I have excellent eyesight. You're not offended, I hope."

Kitten tried to look into his eyes, but the hat, the eyebrows, and the darkness of his eyes made it impossible. She recognized concern in his voice even if she could not confirm it in his face. Something about him was both predatory and defensive. His nature confused her. "No. I'm not offended." The heat from her blush drained from her face. A smile lifted the corner of her mouth as she realized the compliment of being painted by a true master.

Harry reached out his hand, "Harry Reign, an admirer." He bowed his head and kissed her hand.

"Kitten Carlisle. I've always hated being called Kitten, but as you've painted me, it seems right that you call me by my given name and not one of the nicknames people give me." She looked around and wondered when they had moved away from the front of the painting and into the shadows near the path. They stood to the side, just out of the lights of the path and the painting.

"Thank you for letting me call you Kitten."

Kitten took a slow, deep breath to steady her pounding heart and stared behind him at the trees. "You're as brilliant an artist as I heard you were. *The Lovers' Touch* is my favorite, although I should reconsider now that I've seen this. Did you have models for it too?"

"Yes. They're very much in love and don't care who knows it."

Kitten blushed again as she recalled her own desire to feel a passion like the fairy couple she watched earlier. Her cheeks glowed more as she noticed Harry looking away from her blush.

"I'm particularly pleased with this painting. When I saw you sleeping on your patio during the storm, I knew right away I had to paint you as my Sleeping Beauty. I began work that night and didn't stop till it was done. Do you like it?"

Kitten stared at Harry. "Very much. It's beautiful and frightening at the same time. I wanted to step into that world." She realized Harry Reign was a true realist despite all the fantasy. "It is me in there."

"And all modesty, I promise." Harry smiled sheepishly, and Kitten looked again at the demon on the sleeper's chest. This time, Harry stared back at her.

"Prepare yourselves." A familiar voice boomed over the soft noise of the crowd. "When we turn this corner, you're going to see the apex of this collection. Harry Reign turned to sculpture and away from painting over ten years ago, but he just created perhaps the best oil on canvas you'll ever see."

"Shall we?" Harry offered Kitten his arm and turned them toward the pavilion.

"Please." Kitten looked back to see Kevin Vasquez leading a small party toward the painting.

"This is Romance in the Twenty-First Century." Kevin Vasquez's authority echoed in the alcove as he explained the details and importance of the painting to those who could not understand it like he could.

Harry guided them toward the buffet, but the closer they came to the crowd, the more people wanted to talk to Harry and stare at Kitten. Kitten watched as he shook hands, thanked the people for the compliments, and withdrew into himself. The whole time he kept her hand on his arm as a shield. She found herself pleased when Harry introduced her as his model and didn't mind when Harry passed to her the responsibility of pleasantries. Harry appeared receptive and personable without having to say more than a few words and all under the direction of Kitten's guidance.

The grumbling in her stomach distracted Kitten from Kevin Vasquez's approach. Harry tried to nudge her away, but it was too late.

"Harry Reign. I'm so delighted you are making an appearance tonight. I can't tell you how much I've looked forward to meeting you and your lovely new model." Kevin had Harry's hand locked in a handshake and reached his other hand to Kitten. The man was a skilled hunter.

"Mr. Vasquez," began Harry, conveying no emotion. "Ms. Carlisle."

"Delighted. Delighted. Of course, we met earlier. How is the most talked about lady of town?"

"Quite hungry. We were just about—"

"Now Harry, you know I'm writing a book all about your work. When are we going to get together for an interview? We have so much to talk about."

Kevin stopped speaking when one of the most handsome men Kitten had ever seen walked up to them. He placed a hand on Kevin's shoulder,

"There you are, Kevin. We've been looking all over for you. And Harry, I hope you'll introduce me to your model."

"Kitten Carlisle, Anthony Mugello."

Harry kept his eyes on Anthony Mugello.

"I'm pleased to finally meet you. I assumed Harry's portrayal of you was exaggerated, but I can see he is, as always, true to his art." Anthony's alluring expression changed as he spoke to Kitten. His best *I love you and I'm taking your money* grin changed to genuine interest and charm.

Kitten allowed her hand to remain in Anthony's cool, soft hands. "Daddy speaks highly of you."

"Does he?" His right eyebrow arched allowing the twinkle in his eye to shine.

"Beau Parker, from Dallas. When I received the invitation for the gala, I assumed Daddy asked you to invite me." She turned to smile at Harry as Anthony released her hand. "I know better now."

"Anthony," a voice called from near them.

Kitten recognized the dashing gray-haired man in the gray silk suit from earlier in the evening calling to Anthony. "The philistine is now offering to invest in the art as though he were shopping at some bargain basement art dealer's shop. And Kevin,"—the dashing man took hold of Kevin's arm—"he just said the piece would look good hanging over his living room couch."

"Gads!" Kevin puffed himself up, gaining several inches of height. "Anthony, Leonard, we have a duty to protect young artists like Toledo from investors. What is our plan of attack?"

"I leave you to educate the man, but let him invest. No, make him contribute dearly to Toledo's future." Anthony's expression had returned to its previous bloodthirsty gleam.

"And who better to lead the charge than you, Kevin." Leonard said, never faltering in his too smooth grin.

"It was a pleasure to meet you, Kitten. Give my regards to your father. I enjoy doing business with him. He plays his cards close. Always makes me pay for the privilege. Harry," Anthony deferred to Harry. "We'll speak later?"

"Of course." Harry watched the three men walk toward a balding man talking to Stacy and a young woman with dark hair painted red and orange.

Kitten watched as Anthony maneuvered Kevin to the balding man, a Texas banker by his navy suit and burnt orange tie. Kevin shook hands with the banker and began talking as much with his body as with his mouth. Stacy stood too close to Leonard as the artist stared into the headlights of Kevin Vasquez's personality. Kitten could imagine the chastisement the banker was receiving from the energetic art critic.

"Anthony is a good friend. Shall we leave while we can? There is a coffee shop down the road."

"Perfect," said Kitten. "Who's Leonard? My friend seems interested in him."

"Leonard Bellini. Afraid your friend is too old for his taste." Harry turned to lead her away from the crowd, not hiding his dislike for Leonard. "He's working for Anthony now, but I don't think it will last long."

"Shame. He's good-looking, and she could do with someone closer to her age. Maybe it will work out, but I doubt it. She likes her companions young." Kitten intended to laugh, but Harry's grim face removed the grin from her face.

"Not as young as he likes them," spat Harry.

"I know the coffee shop you're talking about. It's good for a cup of coffee, a simple sandwich, and quiet conversation."

From the corner of her eye, Kitten noticed a crowd gathered on the patio of the house. The governor held court there with a small group of men in suits standing around him. A large man stood near. His size alone made him stand out, but even from a distance, Kitten watched as surprise, disgust, shame, and hate emanated from him as he looked onto the crowd.

* * * * *

"A sow in a silk tutu would fit in better with this crowd than I do," said Roger under his breath.

Yasushi lifted the edges of his mouth, wanting to laugh out loud, but sensing Roger's discomfort, reduced the sound to a snicker. "You fit in exactly as you should."

"Don't be so damn smug," Roger mumbled while adjusting the knot of his tie. "I knew I needed a new suit. I just didn't think it would have to be like this." But the suit allowed him to fit in with the posh crowd of the charity gala at Laguna Gloria. No one seeing him would suspect he and the large man with the blue dog-collared shirt were not exactly what they appeared to be.

"It's worth the price, Roger. We have the funds, so stop looking for excuses. Everyone who is anyone is here now. *He* must also be here."

Roger scanned the surrounding crowd. Diamonds, tuxedos, hats, and Champagne meandered around the gardens like the river. He studied each face, but he only had a general description of their prey. Yasushi has seen the face.

"Time to mingle," Roger slowed his pace to let Yasushi move ahead of him.

Yasushi commanded attention wherever he went with both his dynamic essence and his enormous size. His smile, always genuine, and his greeting warmed the hearts of everyone he wanted it to. He flowed into the crowd, and it parted around him until he saw someone to greet.

"How does he do it?" he asked.

"Do what?" replied the voice in his ear.

"Make himself so visible and likable without trying."

"He's the rev. I think preachers are taught to do it at birth." Derek didn't sound like he was joking. He seldom found any reason to laugh or joke with anyone about anything.

"Don't be smart. I'm going to mingle, and I don't need you gabbing in my ear. Marines didn't train us to do this, did they?" Roger immediately regretted adding the part about the marines. Derek would always be a good marine to Roger, despite what the Corps said.

"No." Derek said nothing else.

According to Yasushi, it was essential they be here tonight. His connections were limitless, and one of those connections assured Yasushi their prey would be here. If he was, Roger's discomfort with the fancy suit and the large crowd would be worth it. *Where did he get his information?*

Roger remained on the edge of the crowd, hands in his pockets and eyes following Yasushi as he strolled along with the crowd, stopping at art pieces and chatting with guests before moving on to the next group. If anyone noticed Roger, he looked like any recalcitrant husband of a society wife bored with too much art. Yasushi made his way with the crowd toward the main pavilion where lines formed for food.

Roger idled his way toward the bar farthest from the crowd. It backed to the staging tent.

"Club soda, twist of lime, please." Roger placed his cash on the bar and leaned against it. Few gala guests meandered toward this bar, preferring the larger ones close to the food tables.

"The little cunt!" A woman's voice exclaimed loudly from inside the staging tent.

"Mama! Please. You're always getting onto the staff about swearing. Be what you want them to be. You're always telling me to." A younger version of the same voice answered her.

"Oh, well. Poo! I swear I've had it up to here with that girl. What am I supposed to do now?"

"I'll serve, Aunt Jasmine. I don't mind." A young male entered the conversation.

"You most certainly will not, Marcus," the mother/aunt replied. "I told you, sweetie, we're serving alcohol, and you're not old enough to serve it. No exceptions. I know you're trying to help out and all, but there are rules. You'll have to settle for cleanup duty."

"Yes, ma'am." Young Marcus, obedient and disappointed, sighed.

"I'll take over serving." The young female voice was fresh, alert, determined, and enormously respectful. "Don't worry, Mama. I don't mind. Like you always say, it's all part of running a business. I've got a white shirt in my bag. You can fire Maddy when you see her, if she bothers to show her face to you."

"What would I do without you, Lisa." Mama's voice calmed with relief and pride.

Roger smiled to hear ordinary people solve ordinary problems. It reminded him of the importance of his mission. It reminded him to return eyes to Yasushi. He turned his gaze toward the house and the gathering of politicians on the patio. Yasushi casually walked to them and spoke with them all. Even the governor shook hands with Yasushi and conversed casually with him. Roger wished he knew how Yasushi seemed to know everyone. When Yasushi bent down to whisper in the governor's ear, Roger grew suspicious. The governor lost his politician's smile until another man spoke with Yasushi, and they both laughed.

Roger allowed his mind to wonder as he sipped his club soda and wove his way through the throng of hungry guests.

"What's with the rev?" Derek's voice filled Roger with dread. He had allowed Yasushi to leave his direct sight. "He's stopped talking."

Roger looked toward the patio. Yasushi stood at the edge of the patio looking onto the crowd. Even from this distance, Roger could tell something was happening. He followed Yasushi's gaze to the center of the crowd. A stunning woman stood next to a man with a large, black floppy hat. Three other men stood with them. A shortish, round man with a bright red bow tie, a handsome olive-skinned man in a custom tuxedo with a large diamond on the lapel, and a man with slicked-back gray hair and an expensive-looking gray suit all spoke to each other. Three of the men turned to walk away. The man in the floppy hat and the stunning woman turned toward the entrance.

Roger looked at Yasushi standing and staring into the crowd from the patio and pulled put his cell phoneto his ear. "Taking pictures now. Two possibles are leaving. Follow, find out what you can. Do not engage. I'll track the other three here."

*****

Three kinds of cheeses mixed with jalapeños and chipotles oozed out the sides of perfect Texas toast as golden drops of grease trickled down Kitten's chin despite her attempts to be neat. She took a second bite, letting the heat of the cheese and peppers dance along her tongue and throat. The coffee, rich, sweet, and creamy, cleansed her palate. "No way I would get anything as good as this at the gala," Kitten wiped the drippings from the corners of her mouth with her napkin.

"Glad you like it," said Harry. "I'm not in coffeehouses often. I wasn't sure they would have anything for you to eat."

As they walked from the gala to the coffeehouse, they chatted about nothing of importance and laughed at the people they had seen at the gala. He was comfortable to be with.

Harry, she decided, would be an affectionate relationship. As he sat across from her watching her enjoy her meal, he kept his eyes focused away from her cleavage and his hands folding and refolding paper napkins into animal shapes. Most men found it difficult not looking at her cleavage.

"Coffee shops usually have comfort food of some sort. This place is known for excellent grilled cheese sandwiches." She wiped her mouth with a new napkin. "But you're not a comfort food man, are you?"

"No, restricted diet."

"I will need to diet after this. I don't even want to think about how many calories are in this thing."

"If something makes you happy, you shouldn't worry about the consequences."

"You'll change your mind if you want me to model for you. Too many of these, and I'll be the classical Venus—all roundness and hips."

"I like roundness." Harry shifted his eyes, glancing at her breasts and back to the table, while he continued to fold different animals out of napkins.

"Curves are good, as long as they're proportional. Don't you think? As an artist, you study the human form."

"Yes, proportion is important, but so is realism. Thus Sleeping Beauty's robe isn't open. I've always painted nudes and am known for beautifying women's breasts, but I paint what is there. I don't embellish or delete."

"I've been known for my breasts since I was thirteen. Daddy just about went crazy with the boys constantly over at the house." Kitten tried to keep her face serious, but the direction of the conversation forced her to laugh.

Harry's face broke into something of a grin, as much of one as his face allowed. "I bet he had many sleepless nights if you had those breasts when you were thirteen. But, I've studied breasts. It's important that a woman's breasts are perfect when I paint them."

"Were you disappointed my robe didn't fall open?" Kitten pictured the small demon on the sleeper's chest deciding whether or not to pull open the robe. "You thought about pulling it off."

"Yes, but I wouldn't do that. You must invite me to paint your breasts."

Kitten found her heart pounding, a flush of heat moved through her. Her breath quickened. Harry's dark eyes stared out the window. He avoided looking at her. There was nothing handsome about him. He was old, pale, otherworldly-looking. Perhaps it was his intensity, his honesty, his unearthliness she found alluring.

She sought distraction by scanning the room and hid her face by drinking her coffee. A man and woman in formal dress walked in. The woman sat on one of the couches and pulled off her high-heeled shoes. Her companion walked to the bar and ordered coffee. Four young men dressed in baggy jeans and oversized T-shirts played a board game. A middle-aged woman sat in a corner chair, alone, reading a newspaper. Her distinctive visage struck Kitten as odd, even for Austin, with her steel-gray hair clinging to her nape and her eyebrows plucked thin and pointed like starlets from old movies. They made her look old, but something about her wasn't old. Her dress, a large bright floral print cut narrow at her waist but with a full skirt—any fuller and she would need a petticoat to keep it neat—disguised her age. A large wooden cross hanging from her neck looked out of place. Kitten saw no faith in her countenance. The woman noticed Kitten looking at her. She turned the page of the newspaper and placed it in front of her face.

A very gray man entered the shop from the side entrance. His haircut and stature screamed ex-military, while his silk suit shouted bored husband. He walked in, nodded to Kitten in recognition of her gaze, and sat at the bar to order.

"Will you let me paint you again?" Harry's voice broke Kitten's trance.

"Yes," she answered without thinking. Harry felt good to be around. "Who will I be this time?"

"I don't know, yet. Come to my studio Monday night. I'll do some sketches. We'll see where they lead." Harry grinned, and Kitten once again thought of the demon on the sleeper's chest. As comfortable as she felt around Harry, he could be dangerous. She just didn't know how or why.

"All right. Monday night." This time Harry looked into her eyes. Kitten could see a deepness, almost a timelessness inside his eyes. She was not in any danger from Harry.

*****

Lisa heard a gasp and the crunch of twigs from the clump of live oaks to her right. She turned as a shadow within the shadows passed from the trees and the glare of the lights along the path. In hindsight, the noise was most likely a rodent or small animal frightened by all the people in the gardens after dark. The shadow was nothing more than a loose hair floating in her peripheral vision. The rock sticking into her back caused her more than a little pain, but the pain in her leg, broken, caused the cold sweat running up her back and over her face. She tried to take a relaxing breath in, but it got caught in the back of her throat, and a coarse grunt hissed out of her lips. "Childbirth was worse than this," she whispered to herself. "I'll be okay. Just relax. Someone will be along soon to help. You didn't scream giving birth, you won't scream now. Control yourself, Lisa LeBrere. All will be well."

She waited. Soon, the urge to scream for help filled her lungs as the pain in her leg spread to her hip and into her back, but the shivers moving along her nerves tightened their grip around her larynx. The smell of the spilled Champagne seeping into the earth next to her sent her mind wheeling.

She willed herself to think and speak to herself in complete sentences. "Sickly sweet? Earthly sweet? Who knew Champagne and dirt smelled like death when mixed together?"

The surrounding lights faded. The smells of the garden washed away as another shiver ran along her spine.

"I've got you. Look at me." The male voice, commanding, quiet, and kind, came from above her. She felt a cool hand on her forehead.

"She's still with us. Aren't you, Lisa?" A woman's voice tinkled like a bell from far away.

Lisa opened her eyes. The whitest face she had ever seen looked back at her. Pink eyes twinkled with the lights from the path, and a smile like kindness incarnate radiated.

"Hold on to my hand." The woman's voice sang over the roaring in Lisa's ears. "This will hurt, but he's a medic and knows what he's doing."

Lisa opened her mouth to ask what the man was doing. He was out of sight, when she felt a rush of pain as her leg bones snapped into place. A momentary squeak faded before it began as she felt warmth returning to her leg, and the pain running along her body disappeared.

"I'll call for help," the male voice said.

Lisa wished she could see the face of the man, but she couldn't take her eyes off the incredibly white face above her.

"Feeling better already. Told you he knew what he was doing."

The smile on the very white face comforted Lisa. She allowed her body to ease into the ground beneath her. Even the stone in the middle of her back relaxed its piercing punch.

She remembered saying, "Mama."

The very white woman's cool hand brushed her forehead. "It's okay. David's going to her as soon as he's done calling for the ambulance.

No worries now. Close your eyes, and for once let someone take care of you."

Lisa opened her mouth to say more but found only weariness in the effort. She drank in a deep breath of cleansing air. As she allowed her eyes to close, her head turned to the side. Beneath some bushes and tall grasses, near a clump of trees, reflected in the overhead lights, she saw a face looking back at her. Gray-brown skin tight over high cheekbones and wide brown eyes dead with terror stared at her.

"No," she whispered, not intending to be heard. "Shock plays with the mind."

2

Esmeralda with Phoebus and Claude

Overlooking the river, admiring the starlight, the moonlight, the city lights, and the darkness that only comes at the hour of the jackal, he breathes in the life that ebbs and flows. Surrounded by the wealth and comfort, the purpose and honor, the responsibilities and dependents, the fear and loathing of it all going wrong, he waits. Only the stillness of the hour, one moment of respite, allows him a touch of fondness longed for. He feels the changes in the breeze; he smells them in the air; he hears them in the voice he loathes and loves. The joy of change and the pain of loss mingle in his heart and mind. "When?" he asks the voice flowing on the flutter of wings in the night.

No crisp breezes cool our heads.
October's days clear as we glide into Fall on the wings of new beginnings.
How the young play and the old laugh.
Even the heat of a Texas summer must give way to Fall's changes.
Let the old mingle in the shadows.
The young will dance under stars.
Only Winter's depths reveal who will spring eternal.

As though that's what you wanted.
You're listening to the newest online choice for nighttime rhythms.
I'm Mary Midnight. Let me guide you through the perils of Autumn's risk.
Soon, I will walk your streets alone.
Dance in the shadows if you dare.

"You're very quiet tonight," said Kitten, wiping the oyster juice off her chin. "What's up?" Stacy calling on a Sunday evening looking for a dinner partner didn't surprise Kitten. "You want something, or you would never have agreed to walk here so easily." Stacy hated walking anywhere, even though Abel's restaurant was less than half a mile's easy walk from the condo.

"I have to have a reason to agree to a pleasant walk on a beautiful day? You think too little of me, Kitten." Stacy's false sincerity oozed out as easily as if she were talking to one of her lobbyists.

"I think too well of you not to know you're up to something. We've been friends too long." Kitten grinned and winked. "Come on. Out with it."

"Ok! You got me." A school girl's enthusiasm melted Stacy's cool aloofness. "I've been dying to show you all day. You're going to love this." She reached into her large bag to pull out a rubber band-bound manuscript.

"No!" Kitten didn't want to see it.

"Yes!" Stacy glowed with excitement. "This is perfect for you. You're going to love it." She unbound the pages and set them in front of Kitten.

The Count's Broken Heart stared at her. Kitten felt her heart pump loathing throughout her chest and fill every artery in her body. Her brain worked overtime in search of excuses, but none landed in her head fast enough.

"Vampire romance? Seriously? You said you hated vampire romance, and you know how I feel about romance, yet you want me to edit a vampire romance you wrote? You know how this sounds?"

"You're my best friend, Kitten. That's why this is perfect for you. You've got to stop fighting it. You're a terrific editor being lost on those stupid textbooks. Besides, this one will give you plenty of leeway to make whatever changes you want to make. No problem with the author. I guarantee it."

Kitten turned to the first page. The cheesy title alone confirmed Stacy as the author. Stacy loved reading and loved romance novels but couldn't put two fictional sentences together to save her life. Seeing the mismatched margins, multiple fonts, and coffee smudges on the pages confirmed Kitten's hypothesis.

She forced a smile and looked at her friend. "I can't. I have no imagination for this kind of thing. You're the one with the heart of a romantic. You should do it."

"I tried, but I'm all sex. This needs romance. Not a quick fuck."

Kitten stopped turning pages to read:

The thunder clapped and the light end clapped as the dark night stormed around her. Angel knew she had to reach the Count's castle, he as calling her her crotch ached her breasts swelling. She felt moistur forming between her legs ...

"It's crap," she said before she caught herself. How many times had Stacy said she would one day write the world's greatest romance novel? This wasn't it. The fact that Stacy actually completed a novel proved to Kitten she would be stuck rewriting it. She tried to remain as business-like as possible. "Even if we forget about the lack of grammar, how would you list this? This reads like erotica, not romance. Think about it, how many times have you called me a prude? And you want me to make this good?"

"You've got it!" Instead of being insulted or dissuaded, Stacy's face brightened with Kitten's words. "It is crap. You can make it good. Don't give me that look. I've read your poetry. You've got a great ear for romance. You'll be brilliant at it. I'm so sure of it, I've put it in the project list."

"You didn't." Kitten's mouth fell open. The project list was sacrosanct at Hearts and Minds Publishing. Everybody followed who was doing what, how long it took, how much it cost, and how much money it made. Once a project was on the list, it wasn't taken off without everybody knowing the somebody who failed. A failure on her part to complete this task would hurt not only her career but Stacy's reputation. Kitten didn't know whether to cry or laugh.

"Yes, I did. It's all on you now, Kitten. The other board members have been on me for years to write a book, so I finally did it. Been wanting to forever, but you know how that goes. Well, I followed your example and did it. I said, if you can become a famous artist's model, I can be a writer. That scenario alone could make a romance novel. So, when I got home from the gala, I got to work. I've been at it nonstop. Sure, I had a few pages already written here and there, but something about Leonard inspired me. He's so romantic and mysterious at the same time. So forceful, yet beneficent. So old, yet so young. Times are weird. I hardly ever go out with anyone so much older than me."

Kitten tried to listen as Stacy droned on about Leonard. She barely remembered Leonard—handsome, distinguished, but surprisingly unremarkable in her memory. Stacy's infatuation with him surprised Kitten. Stacy courted young, handsome men in need of sponsorship. Her first divorce left her immune to talk of love and half of a failing publishing company. Within three years, she turned Hearts and Minds Publishing into a profitable company, convinced the board to kick her ex-husband out, and made a name for herself as a driving force in twenty-first century publishing. Ten years later, Stacy managed to contract two more aspiring model/actor/author ex-husbands out of existence and lead her company to the Forbes list of leading businesses. Now, Stacy would add author to her resume, but only if Kitten turned around ill-grammared smut into something people would actually want to read.

*****

The rest of Sunday evening blurred into one long muddy night. Kitten sat at her desk staring at Stacy's manuscript, drinking one glass of wine after another, and wondering what to do. No matter how many glasses of wine she drank, Stacy's book continued to remain horrid.

The crowd parted and there he stood, lonely, desirous, ready to pounce. She wanted him right then, she longed to feel him pressed against her. Longed to feel his tongue in her mouth his penis between her legs. He felt her staring. He wanted her as much as she wanted him.

The bottle of wine she had opened when she got home now stood on the desk deprived of contents, but the words on the page remained flat, ill-used, and without purpose. The clouds forming in her head drifted from ear to ear, causing the letters to soften and swim across the page. With a start, she realized the vibrations near her hand emanated from her phone. Gary's name lit up in front of her.

"Not now," she said aloud and tapped to answer her phone as she shook her head to stop the clouds. "Hi, sweetie. Where are you?" She did her best to not slur her speech.

"Hi, hon. You ok? I didn't wake you? Was sure you'd be awake."

Kitten could hear Gary's fingers tapping the screen on his phone to check time zones. "No, you didn't wake me. Stacy and I had a big dinner tonight, it was a long weekend, and I'm doing a bit of reading. Must have dozed off. No problem. I'll head to bed soon."

"Ooh, I'd like to head to bed with you." His fingers stopped tapping.

"And who wouldn't, with a body like mine. When do you get back?" She wanted to sound sexy, but too much wine, Stacy's novel, and her torpedoing career grated against her throat.

"Planned to be back next week, but this job is taking longer than I thought, and my guy in Singapore's having problems. I may need to take over to keep the client happy." His disappointment merged into silence.

"The price you pay for success."

"I'm scheduling plenty of time off for the holidays. A quiet Christmas, you know, for the two of us. What say we get a place in the mountains, someplace out of the way?"

"For you, me, my folks, and half of Dallas, right?" Kitten laughed. Both of them knew her parents expected them at the annual holiday shindig. It was the event of the year in Dallas. Everybody who was anybody showed up whether invited or not.

"I—I don't know," began Gary. He seldom stuttered, but tonight he fumbled over what he was saying. "I was thinking maybe we could do something ... different this year."

"We'll see when you get here." Kitten sat straight as sobriety descended on her. She recognized the much-too-serious tone in his voice. Droplets of sweat eased their way down her forehead, cooling her temples. "I'm sorry, Gary. Let me get to bed. Right as rain in the morning."

"Sure, hon. I understand. Take it easy. I'll call again in a couple of days." Gary sighed, but his voice lifted a little as though pleased to be released from the call.

Kitten stared across her desk, across the patio, and across the water seeing nothing. Gary was entirely too serious. They had always been the best of friends and often lovers. She envisioned their futures if they continued as they were: He'd buy a big house in Dallas, close enough to his in-laws for them to see how well he was doing. She'd host parties for charities. His business would grow as he took on more clients and more employees. Eventually, he would travel less. He wanted kids. Plans within plans snaked their way through Kitten's brain until her breathing increased and carbon dioxide replaced oxygen. And then, she looked across the water to the house with the eyebrow window where Harry lived. The golden glow from the windows beckoned adventure. Her breathing slowed back to normal. "Take your time, girl. All is good. Gary knows it will never happen."

She opened Stacy's novel once more. "Let's begin with the beginning."

"I'm so sorry, my dear." The Dukes voice faltered as tears rolled down his cheeks and his hung his head in shame.

"Then, it's true. We are ruined." Angel turned to face their faithful Stewart. She knew her father had extravagant taste, but she never thought the family fortune would be thrown away.

"I've done all I can, my lady."

That's when Angel noticed the shame hiding in the stewart's eyes. It was he that allowed my father to squander the family fortune. How much must Leonardo be paying him to enforce his proposal?

Kitten closed the manuscript. "How the hell am I going to fix this?"

*****

Kitten questioned her decision to walk to Harry's house, a short twenty minutes door to door. Humidity crawled along her skin, making her silk blouse cling to her back and chest. On recalling Harry's fascination with breasts, she tugged at her blouse. "Don't be such a prude," she whispered to herself as she walked along the lighted garden path to the front door. "Time to step out a little."

Before she could ring the doorbell, a large and gorgeous man opened the door. "Hey," boomed from exquisite pink lips. "Your friend's here." He reached out his hand, "I'm Eddie. Nice to meet you. Gotta go." And he left.

Kitten watched him walk away. His tight, curved, and lifted derriere nonchalantly glided toward the street and a burnt orange sports car glittering in the setting sun.

"Easy on the eyes, isn't he?" asked Harry before Kitten could turn back to the door.

"Indeed. A friend of yours?" Kitten cast a knowing smile.

"Model. Come in. He's one of my latest. Anthony found him. Wasn't sure he could sit still for any amount of time, but he's turned out to be a receptive model." Harry guided Kitten through a darkened hallway and into a large studio filled with soft light, pillows, curtains, canvases, chairs, and divans seemingly scattered about the room but all where they should be. Along the east wall, large French doors draped with billowy, white curtains stood open. Opposite, canvas panels of blue and gray swirls hung from the ceiling, concealing the wall, while an old-fashioned red divan centered in front of it, surrounded by more pillows and throws glimmered in the glow of spotlights. The scene reminded Kitten of Basil Hallward's studio with Dorian Gray standing behind the bar. Easels, some occupied with canvases and some not, stood in a semicircle around the red divan. On one, a large painting in progress gleamed light and dark. In it, Eddie sat on the floor leaning against a crumbling stone wall, his naked body glowing from a light source not yet determined. Despite the partial completion of the painting, Kitten found herself hypnotized by the details and symbols forming on the canvas.

"Phoebus de Chateaupers," stated Harry as he watched Kitten examine the painting.

"As he's seducing Esmeralda?" There was not enough of Eddie's face for Kitten to determine his expression.

"Never question the artist before the painting is complete." Harry smiled and covered the painting. "However, he must at least try to seduce her. Like his character, Eddie enjoys the pleasures of the flesh, and with his amiable smile, he usually finds opportunities for pleasure when he wishes it."

Kitten laughed. "I imagine he does. He's beautiful. My friend, Stacy, would enjoy his company. She may not be young, but she has enough money and power for all things pleasurable."

"The woman you were with at the gala? Would you like something to drink?" Harry motioned Kitten to the bar. "Plenty of bottled water and wine if you like. Stacy Ghoode is her name, isn't it?"

"Yes. She spent a lot of time with one of your friends. Wine would be nice. Stacy's my friend and my boss. But I don't want to talk work. You promised me a glimpse at your other works."

"Yes, she spent a good deal of time with Leonardo Bellini. Leonard." Harry poured chilled wine and led Kitten to a table covered with sketch pads, loose drawing papers, and old, rolled canvases. "You're at a distance in these. I've decided you're Esmeralda. I need a close-up of you."

"Me as Esmeralda? You have a dramatic imagination. I'm much too old. She's young and wild."

"You watch too many Disney cartoons."

"Esmeralda was fifteen, sixteen at most."

"Now you're being too literal. If I made her fifteen, the painting would verge on child pornography. Fifteen in the time of the story is more like twenty-five now. Look at yourself here." Harry handed her a sketch of her leaning on the railing of her patio. The hair of the woman in the sketch flew around her head hiding much of her face, but her hand held some of her hair away from the right side of her face, revealing an eye drifting into distant lands.

"The detail is amazing, especially considering how far away you were from me. And I'm hardly twenty-five."

"Don't be too literal. But come, you're here now, and we're wasting time. Sit over here." Harry placed Kitten on a stool under a bright light near the red divan. He picked up his sketch pad and took the stool opposite her.

"How do you express so many emotions with a simple pencil? I've never understood how artists work." Kitten found it amazing how easy it was to talk to Harry. Nothing seemed out of bounds with him. Nothing seemed out of place.

"You work with artists all day, don't you, editing books? It's the same thing." He looked at her, then back to his pad as his pencil continued to move over the page. "I work with lines, you work with words."

"No, it's different. Besides, I correct grammar and formatting. There's nothing artistic in it."

"Isn't there? You surprise me, Kitten. You're intelligent and insightful. A pity you should feel so little about your chosen profession."

Kitten said nothing. When she tried to look out the window, Harry cleared his throat, and she returned her gaze to the back of the sketch pad. She considered what he said and recalled her reasons for wanting to work in a publishing house. "I suppose I am an artist too, in a way. There is something beautifully simplistic about a diagramed sentence."

"Precisely. Words must flow and join if they are to convey beauty, just as my lines must flow and meet at the right places to produce a beautiful sketch. Don't we do the same thing but with different tools?"

"In the day-to-day world, it's easy to get lost in frivolous details. Once upon a time, I wanted to be a poet. I haven't thought of that in a long time."

"Is there no one to encourage you?"

"I rarely tell anyone I write poetry. Gary knows I dabble, but if it's not made of bits and bytes, he doesn't much understand it."

"Gary?" Harry's eyes darted toward her as one of his bushy eyebrows pointed up.

"Boyfriend, a very conventional word. Not sure I'd use it. Escort, friend, admirer might be better words. We've been together for some time, but things have changed."

"Marriage?" Harry stopped sketching.

"He might be thinking it, but it won't happen. Daddy and Mommy like him, and he's a good man. I couldn't ask for a better friend."

Harry returned to his sketching. "What about your friend, Stacy, with all the passion?"

"Oh yes, she's encouraging. She's read some of my old poems and likes them. Says I'm wasted editing textbooks. Afraid I'm now having to work on her great romance novel. It's crap, and I have to make it good enough to protect both our reputations."

"Enough for now." Harry stood. "You're fidgeting. Would you like another glass of wine? I find a good wine aids philosophical discussions."

"Excellent idea."

*****

Kitten relaxed as she leaned back on the red divan. "Have you lived here long?" she asked. "You've talked about the night of the storm, but I don't think I ever noticed your lights on till recently."

"I had business out of town over the summer," began Harry. "Once upon a time, I traveled a great deal but not so much anymore. This summer's travel was unavoidable."

"Was it anything exciting? Meeting some mysterious underworld figure, seducing a beautiful and wealthy patroness? I can see you doing either." Kitten laughed, causing Harry to look up from his sketch pad.

"If I need someone seduced, I send Anthony to do it. He's in a class unto himself when it comes to seduction. Afraid my looks work against me."

"Nonsense. Seduction has nothing to do with the way one looks and everything to do with the looks one gives." The blood vessels in Kitten's cheeks burst with heat. She sat up, draining the last of the wine from her glass. "I mean, anyone can seduce anyone if he or she has a mind to. You know, Mother always warned me about the lines men use to seduce a woman with money. Not that I have money, but Daddy does. Well, stepdaddy, but most people assume I'm his daughter, and he's the best daddy any girl could want. He has no children of his own, so it's assumed." She stopped, picked up a scarf lying on the divan, and patted off the small beads of sweat on her forehead. "Do you suppose I could have more wine? It's so cool and refreshing."

"Of course." Harry kept his eyes cast down, but the smile on his face grew. "Your mother sounds like a wise woman. I wish I could tell you of some entangled affair or mysterious meetings over the summer, but I don't want to spoil my mystery. And I do like to be a mystery." Harry put down his sketch pad to pour the wine.

Kitten realized she was giggling and sipped the new glass of wine with care. "I assure you, you are keeping your mystique. May I see the sketch?"

"It's done for now, but it's not the look I want. Tell me if this is you?"

Kitten gazed at the sketch, awed by the detail Harry drew with so little effort or concentration. She followed the line of her face as it moved down her neck and billowed on her blouse. Heat once again rose in her face. "Extraordinary. It's amazing how you can create my likeness and not at the same time."

Harry snatched the sketch pad. His thin lips scrunched together, and his eyes fixed on the sketch in deep concentration. "It's not like you?"

"Oh, the face is mine, but how can that be me? I'm hardly the romantic type, and this woman bleeds romance."

"But you are romantic, Kitten. Why do you think I like to draw you? You'll be the perfect Esmeralda."

"Well ..." She tried to remember the last time she'd held a conversation with anyone and felt so comfortable talking about her looks. "You're the artist. I'll leave you to decide. By the way, this wine is divine, perfect for a long, hot night."

"I'm glad you like it. Anthony brought back a case from Italy. It's been sitting for some time. Another glass?"

The empty glass in Kitten's hand surprised her. She giggled again for no reason. "You'll think I'm a lush. But I shouldn't. Some of us get up early in the morning to go to work."

"Of course." Harry set the bottle down and shuffled the sketch pad between his hands and the table with all the other sketches. "Will you come back tomorrow night?"

"Yes. I'd like to."

He took her hand and led her to the front door. "I can't let you walk home alone this time of night."

"Don't be silly. I'll be fine. You can watch me from your balcony if you're worried."

"And what would your wise mother say to a man who didn't escort you home at this late hour?"

His intentions clear, she accepted his company as they strolled toward her condo.

Halfway home, where the road bent around the inlet separating their homes, Kitten spotted the long-haired white cat she'd seen the night of the storm walking across the street toward them. As she stepped into the street to pick up the cat, a beam of light caught her attention. A large, dark car filled the void behind the bright lights rushing toward the cat. Neither car nor cat made a sound. The cat stood frozen by the coming lights. Kitten's heart pounded in her chest. Before she could react, she discovered herself standing on the median of the road with the cat in her arms and Harry caressing her shoulder. "Are you all right?"

"Yes," was all she could say until her heart slowed, once again beating the correct number of beats, and her head no longer tried to float away. "Thank you. I must be more tired than I realized not to have seen or heard the car. Luckily, you're fast on your feet."

Harry's gaze followed the car as its rear lights faded down the darkened street. "Electric cars are good for the environment but not for being on quiet roads so late at night. Now, let's get you home."

The cat curled into a ball and slept at the foot of her bed. Kitten lay back, staring at it. "Why am I making such a fool of myself?" She fluffed the pillow behind her head. "Either I'm saying things I shouldn't say, or I'm standing like an idiot as cars speed down the road to run us over." She closed her eyes, willing sleep to come as the cat rolled over onto its back. Its slow steady purr ran up Kitten's leg, into her torso, and filled her head. "You're no help, cat." But sleep snuck up on her. Sometime before consciousness left and sleep embraced her, she saw the car's lights reflected in the cat's eyes, Harry putting the cat in her arms, and the passenger in the car zoom past her. "A peculiar looking passenger," stumbled out of Kitten's lips, but the cat didn't reply.

*****

"These Diggers and Leitz characters. They ok?" Roger, as always, leaned back in the driver's seat. Yasushi often wondered if Roger could drive sitting up, but he couldn't fault Roger's driving skills. Even at high speed, Roger leaned back, resting his head against the seat and tilting his head toward the road.

"Fully vetted, I assure you, brother." Yasushi waited. He learned early in his career the best tactic when people wanted to talk to him but were afraid to speak was to wait. Roger was no different, except that Yasushi trusted Roger's opinion above all others.

"Leitz I can understand," began Roger.

"Anna," butted in Yasushi. "She likes first names, Anna."

Roger rolled his eyes. "Anna, then. She, I can understand. She's like a lot of 'em who come to the group. Devoted churcher, wants to fight evil, has already had some sort of run-in with demons, prepared to do whatever it takes, assuming she understands what it's going to take. This Diggers fellow—he just doesn't sit square with me."

"I bet he'd sit better with you if my big sister didn't grumble so much about him." Yasushi watched Roger shift his shoulders beneath his shirt. Madeline might not see the affection Roger had for her, but everyone else did.

Yasushi smiled and eased back in the seat. Surveillance was boring but an essential step in planning. Roger parked the car a block away from the artist's house, just beyond a large live oak tree reaching over the road and behind a new SUV. Surveillance provided him with one-on-one communication with the men and women of the group. All were loyal and dedicated to the cause, but it was a thankless job no one outside the group would ever know about, and if anyone outside the group learned about their work, they wouldn't understand it. There was no glory except that which God would bless on them. As the group's leader and spiritual advisor, Yasushi ensured all had the opportunity to vent their fears, frustrations, and doubts in confidence.

"Your faith in Madeline's judgment does you credit, Roger, but don't forget, for all her devotion to our cause, she has the greatest stake in our success. She, alone, saved me when the demons came upon us. She's more scared than the rest of us." Yasushi stopped as Roger considered his words. "Now her prize is in sight, she's anxious. We all are. Diggers is an army officer. You remember how she felt about you at first. But you know what it takes to make it in officer training, especially when you come from a family of officers expecting you to carry on the family tradition. He wanted to break tradition for seminary—become a priest. My sister hates priests almost as much as she hates officers. All I ask you to do is consider the facts before judging him. I love my sister more than I love my life, but she can be hardheaded. I believe you would second that."

Roger continued to stare out the windshield watching the artist's house. "He steered us right back in California. We wouldn't be here now if he hadn't gotten us the information about what happened in Galveston."

Yasushi didn't need to reply. He watched the house and waited for Roger to tell him he doubted Diggers's commitment. He pulled out the thermos of coffee and poured both of them a cup, careful to only fill it halfway in case they had to drive away in a hurry.

"Thank you," began Roger, taking the cup. "The thing is, Madeline's got as keen an eye for what makes people tick as I've ever seen. I trust her judgment on people as much as I trust you to lead us. I'd feel better if you held Diggers off for now. Let's see how he shapes up."

"Indeed." Yasushi thought for a while. In all the years he and Roger worked together, Roger had never questioned one of Yasushi's decisions. "If you believe he should be kept at a distance, I will. Trust is a highway we travel together, brother."

"Amen. And we have movement."

Yasushi sat up. The artist and the woman walked out of the house. Black covered the artist from the large floppy hat to the baggy pants. In the shadows of the night, he disappeared. Roger didn't move until the couple walked out of view. He pressed the button on the driveshaft and steered the car into the street. Yasushi listened to the tires move along the street. They were fifty yards behind the couple when Yasushi saw the woman step into the street toward a white cat walking under a streetlight.

"Madeline thinks there's something about her too." Roger nodded his head at Kitten.

"Everything we've got says she's no different from you or me, Roger. I'm worried he's going to do something to her."

Roger pressed a button on the dash. The high beams flared. He accelerated. Before Yasushi could object, the artist, the woman, and the cat stood on the median in his side-view mirror. "Were you aiming for the cat or the woman?"

"Does it matter? If he wanted her dead, she'd be dead now. Looks like he wants her alive."

"Indeed."

"Something to consider, just saying."

"Indeed." Yasushi closed his eyes and prayed the group he had formed would not become the cold killers he was afraid they were becoming.

*****

Yasushi's knees hurt, but he ignored the pain as he continued to pray. The smell of incense filled his nose as the ringing of the bells and the melodious voices of St. Mary's priests reciting the Mass flowed into his ears and into his soul. He sought peace but found only pain as he realized madness was slowly choking reason, logic, and faith out of his sister. Even his best friend, Roger, drifted close to disaster. His own faith was being tested as he sought solace in the ritualistic rhythms of the Mass. Long after the Mass ended, he remained kneeling. The priests knew him and didn't question his need to be near the altar.

The sounds of people moving in and out and the slow murmur of parishioners' prayers as they entered and left the confessional ebbed, but silence did not come. He wanted solace, but it eluded him. He didn't notice when a man knelt beside him, not until the man spoke.

"In the old days, they didn't lock the church doors. We came and went to pray when we needed it."

Yasushi jumped back to the seat of the pew, surprised to see Harry kneeling beside him.

"What are you doing here? This is the house of God." Yasushi kept his naturally booming voice to a coarse whisper.

"Are we not all children of God, *brother*?"

"But," Yasushi could not speak. He looked from altar to demon. His heartbeat filled his ears as it beat louder and louder. "Why are you here?" He returned to kneeling when Harry showed no sign of sitting on the pew.

"You're losing control. Your friend tried to run us down, cause harm to the woman. I've told you before, she must be left alone."

"I didn't know he was going to do it. I'm sorry. We were just going to follow—"

"If something happens to the woman, the deal is off. My control rests with her living." Harry's voice left no doubt of his authority.

Yasushi stared at the deep blues and golds of the ornate ceiling of the chapel. He breathed in, counting how long it took to fill his lungs, and then he breathed out, reversing the count. He did this several times until calm settled over him. Harry said nothing but continued to kneel with his head bowed toward his clasped hands.

It no longer unnerved Yasushi to see Harry in the church. *Are we not all the children of God?*

"I intend to honor our arrangement. My failings will not destroy the peace we seek. I've brought in someone to help me with the others. They will follow me."

"Diggers." Harry spoke the name as though it was poison. "He will not be your salvation, brother. Send him away. I've seen too many zealots. He has an agenda you know nothing about. His kind always do."

"What do they see in Diggers I don't?" muttered Yasushi. He tried to count his breaths in and out, but this time it did not calm him. "Our agreement protects all my people. Who is in my group is of no concern to you."

Harry shook his head. "Everything I do is to keep my people and your people safe. I only came to warn you to keep your people in line. It's the only way we'll both have justice."

Harry genuflected and stood to leave, but before leaving he leaned down to whisper in Yasushi's ear. "And keep your people away from the woman. Without her, we're all lost."

Yasushi remained kneeling, praying, contemplating. Behind him, silence loomed in the darkening church. The arrival of the priests for Compline stirred him to action. He took part in the prayers, before walking down the long, center aisle to the door. The old priest at the door blessed him before locking the doors. Yasushi looked around. The streets, while full of revelry, remained quiet near the cathedral. The shadow of a man near him didn't frighten him. He reached into his pocket for some cash to hand the man, but when he looked, the man was gone. Yasushi stared into the shadows, but the shadows were empty. He breathed in the night air and made his way back to the house.

* * * * *

Harry stood on the ledge of the Westin Hotel overlooking the city. The lights from the pool dappled shadows across the space, reflecting the light from the stars in the inky sky. He liked to survey the city at night as the city quieted. Life ebbed and flowed through the city filled with the youth of Texas and the old money of politics. He would miss this city.

"He felt my presence but wasn't afraid." Tomas spoke only when Harry turned to him. He had arrived minutes before, but whether fear or respect dictated his actions, he would not speak until one of the Eldest of the vampires allowed him to. "I waited in the shadows of the entryway, as you suggested. The old priest didn't know I was there, but the large man you spoke to did."

"As I expected," Harry examined Tomas from head to foot. His face had aged in the few months since he had seen him last, but his golden curls and heart-shaped mouth belied a man of youth and vigor. "You understand the need for discretion?"

"Yes, sir." Tomas kept his face straight, his eyes lowered, and his stance humbled. "Are the others like him?"

"I believe they are, but they'll fear you. Each has been touched by the brute you call a friend."

"A friend no more," Tomas said looking into Harry's eyes. "I understand now, not everything, but I'm trying to see it all. I will follow whatever commands you give."

The edge of Harry's lips quivered up for a moment. "Even unto the final death, Tomas?"

"Even unto the final death." Tomas returned his gaze to the street below them.

"You've grown, Tomas. Not long ago, you would have lied as easily as you stand there, but I see something new in you."

"The slaughter, it's not what I wanted. Such a waste, and it exposed us. And, the girl," Tomas's eyes hazed over as though a memory haunted him. He said no more.

"The girl is a grown woman now and more dangerous than you can imagine, and my time here draws to an end. I suspect your Duchess already told you."

"I wasted a lot of years calling him my friend. He called, wants to see me."

"So predictable!" Harry spat out his words. "But the woman complicates things. Do not underestimate the danger you'll be in as long as she lives, and she must live for a while longer. Remain his friend."

Tomas closed his eyes. "Yes, sir."

"Do this, and I will forgive your sins. The Duchess agrees, although her faith in you is more limited than mine."

Tomas rubbed his neck as though pain seared throughout his body. "I'll make it right. I promise."

"You will, or you will die. Let no one else know you're in town. Watch, learn, and contact your old friend when you see fit. Come to me when I call."

Tomas bowed his head to Harry and stepped off the building. Away from the presence of the Eldest, he walked along the street, taking in the aroma of the living. His shoulders did not relax. He watched all around him. Harry's words burned in him as they never had before.

*****

"What do you think?" Kitten twirled the large red scarf trimmed with strands of golden beads around her head. "Gypsy enough for you?"

"Perhaps too much." Harry placed the charcoal on the table and moved out from behind the canvas to sit on his stool in front of his models. "Eddie, you want to make love to her, not join her in a drunken orgy. Imagine she's one of those girls who dance next to the field when you're playing football."

Eddie lowered his long, lean body to the floor, resting on his right arm, and looked up at Kitten sitting on the tired, red divan. He stared at her, staring at him. "Cheerleaders? Really? My imagination only goes so far. It's the whole getup," he told her. "I can imagine doing all sorts of things with you, but you look like you're made up for a costume party at the old folks' home." He lowered himself onto both elbows to turn to Harry. "You said Esmeralda seduces as much as she is seduced?"

"He has a point, Kitten. You're trying too hard to be a gypsy. Be yourself."

Eddie placed his left hand on Kitten's bare ankle. "Seriously. Is there anyone else around here you can imagine seducing? I mean, if I can't tempt you, what chance does anyone else have?" By the time he finished asking his questions, his left hand rested on her bare knee under the large gypsy skirt she wore.

Before Kitten responded, Eddie reached his head under the skirt and blew a kiss behind her knee. Kitten roared with laughter as Eddie exaggerated his body being thrown as she kicked him away. He lay on the floor, roaring with mocked pain. "My heart! You've broken my heart with your rejection."

Even Harry seemed to laugh, although his face missed true humor and only managed his usual all-knowing smile. "If you two can't sit properly, I'll have to start all over."

"That would be a shame. I like what I see so far." Anthony stood behind Harry, looking from the painting to the models and back to the painting. "There's not much there now, but—"

Harry returned to his easel and placed the old oil cloth over the painting. "You're not supposed to look when I'm still setting the scene."

"Couldn't help myself. It sounded like you were having a party in here and hadn't invited me. Had to come in and see what was happening. Eddie," Anthony's dark eyes honed in on Eddie's lean, muscular torso stretched out in front of him. "Are you behaving yourself? I hope I wasn't wrong to offer you to Harry."

Eddie rolled onto his left side, sliding the red cover hiding his lower body closer to his groin, revealing well-developed and curved abs. It enhanced his growing erection. "It's a matter of seduction, Tony. We're discussing the proper way to seduce a man."

"Then it's a good thing I'm here. I know how I can be seduced." Anthony walked around Eddie and offered his hand to Kitten. "Very pleased to see you again, especially since you're the woman who seduced my old friend into painting again."

Kitten took Anthony's hand. Instead of shaking, as she expected him to do, he placed his lips on her fingers. "As you're a friend of Harry's, you're my friend as well." Kitten recalled how handsome Anthony looked at the gala in his finery. In the intimacy of Harry's studio, dressed as a casual man of fashion, he glowed sex appeal with his olive skin, thick, dark hair, and large brown eyes surrounded by lashes no mascara could ever hope to reproduce. Her heart fluttered uncontrolled for a moment. "But all things considered, I'm sure Harry will get exactly what he wants from us without much help from anyone else."

"Wine, Anthony?" Harry stood at the bar, pouring glasses of the white wine Kitten liked. He lost his smile as he handed Anthony his glass.

Anthony's eyes gleamed as he took the glass from Harry. He turned to face Eddie. "Eddie, I hope all this isn't taking away from your training. We expect great things from the team this year. I don't want Coach accusing me of diverting your passion for the game with art."

"I manage my passions well." Eddie took another glass of wine and leaned against the old, red divan. He placed his head on Kitten's lap. "I know my place in all of this."

"Of course you do, dear." Kitten patted his head as though he were a lapdog. "Now, if you will excuse me a moment, I need to think, to get into character." She went to the back of the room where a Japanese screen blocked a small corner of the room.

Anthony sat on the divan. "Are you spending time with the trainer I sent to the team, Eddie? He's amazing when it comes to flesh and muscle."

"Does this have anything to do with me, Anthony?" Harry concentrated on his canvas.

Kitten saw Harry in the small mirror on the wall behind the screen. Her jeans hung on a peg next to it. Harry set up the screen for her to change into the skirt he bought her. She wondered if he placed the mirror so he could see or for her to see him. The long edge of the divan stuck out from the corner just wishing for sight in the mirror. While she couldn't see Anthony or Eddie, she heard their flirtations. Neither seemed concerned with the surrounding company.

Half the buttons of her blouse were unbuttoned when she noticed Harry looking into the mirror. Whether the wine gave her courage or flirtations were contagious, she discovered him watching her undress excited her in a way she hadn't expected. Each beat of her heart echoed through in her ears a little louder. She felt the blood push and pull in her veins. Heat rose from her torso and caused a blush in her cheeks. She slowed the unbuttoning and allowed the blouse to fall off her shoulders before reaching behind her and loosening the strap to her bra. Harry's eyes remained focused on her. Her eyes remained focused on him.

Anthony and Eddie roared with laughter. "No. I don't think Harry would like it at all." Anthony stood, blocking Kitten's view of Harry.

"In the end, you'll be an expensive model if you carry on this way," said Harry. "There are rags under the bar. Please use those and not your wrap to clean up the wine."

Anthony turned toward the bar as Kitten wrapped the red scarf trimmed with long golden beads over her shoulders and crossed it over her breast. She saw Anthony looking at her in the mirror and smiled. Unlike most men, Anthony looked at her with the eye of an art lover. He neither leered nor gawked. She lowered the scarf, revealing bare shoulders. He lifted his glass to her, and she returned the compliment with a slight nod of the head.

"How's this, Harry?" She stood in front of the screen. Eddie sprawled on the floor cleaning spilled wine. His erection remained firm.

"Perfect." Eddie blew her a kiss.

"It will do well," said Harry. "Places, please. I'd like to get the sketching done tonight. Anthony, business will have to wait 'til I'm done. Stay if you wish, but out of the way."

Kitten returned to the old, red divan, sitting straight and staring down at Phoebus, who resumed his spot on the floor looking adoringly at Esmeralda. Anthony took a seat opposite Harry in an extra-large cushioned chair. He turned on his phone and began to read but looked up from time to time to gaze at Kitten. In return, she looked at him—from time to time. Each managed to pretend they did not notice each other's gazes.

*****

"Old fart's hit me up twice already," said Sonja. She took a long sip of her tequila and let a large piece of ice dance on her tongue. She let the ice cube fall into her hand and placed it on the nape of her neck as her other hand lifted her long red curls off her skin. "What does it take to get an old man uninterested?"

"Old? Maybe a little. He looks rich. Might be a good time."

Sonja dropped her hair and laughed at her aunt Danita. "You should go for it."

"No, chiquita. Men like him, in this place, he's looking for someone young and fresh—like you. Then again," Danita licked her lips as she watched the man with gray hair leaning against a pillar near the front of the bar, "you tell me all the time I look like a student."

"You know it." Sonja smiled as a tall, broad, dark-haired man danced up to her. She recognized him from one of her classes and giggled. Before she danced toward the center of the floor with him, she leaned over and kissed her aunt on the cheek. "Knock him dead, auntie."

Danita pulled the ruby lipstick from her pocket and ran it along her lips. Before dancing back onto the floor, she glimpsed her reflection in the mirrored column next to her. Her green eye shadow and blue liner remained perfect. She pulled her black, silky hair behind her ear. Rotating her hips to the beat, she eased her way through the crowd to the gray-haired man.

Dancing toward the old man, she took her time to rub against a handsome man with golden hair. He looked down at her, smiling, and rubbed his body against hers. She turned, looking at the gray-haired man as he looked at her niece. The golden boy next to her leaned down, asking if she wanted to party. "Let me see how you move, bebe. Buy me a tequila?"

The golden boy nodded and moved away from Danita. Danita saw the gray-haired man scanning the crowd. She took her chance and shimmied up to him. As she approached, his gaze fell to hers. She opened her mouth and spun around, making sure her short skirt hugged her hips. As she returned to his gaze, a shiver ran up her spine. She expected an answer from those gray eyes but got the obscenity of hate. Her hips stopped shimmying as her heart missed a beat. At that moment, the golden boy swayed next to her with a glass of tequila. She downed the offered shot in one swallow and put her arms around the golden boy, allowing the heat of his body to flow over her.

The golden boy led them toward a spot near the gray-haired man. Danita tried to lead them away, but he pressed her against the far side of the column the gray-haired man leaned against. For a moment, she forgot the hate she had seen and enjoyed young, inexperienced hands feeling their way up her back.

"Anthony won't be here for a while, Leonard," a man's voice said. Danita recognized Stanly, head of security for the Phantom's Menace. She liked to flirt with him. He always said the right things even if the flirtations never went further than talk. "Afraid business is taking longer than planned."

"Of course it is. I'm going back to my hotel." Leonard's voice made both Danita and the golden boy look toward him. Danita felt the same shiver run up the golden boy's back.

"You two," Stanly pointed to Danita and the golden boy, "back on the dance floor or take it to a hotel." Stanly winked at Danita and walked away.

She smiled as the golden boy excused himself, his erection obvious in his tight-fitting jeans. Danita kissed his cheek and shimmied back to the dance floor. She lost her breath for a moment as she saw Leonard stop in the middle of the dance floor and whisper into Sonja's ear, but he left without waiting for an answer, and Sonja didn't stop dancing.

"Chiquita," Danita said as she danced next to Sonja. "What did the old man tell you?"

"What old man?" Sonja laughed as Danita's eyebrows drew close together. "Nothing, auntie. I didn't hear, and he didn't wait around to repeat. I think my boyfriend intimidated him."

Danita danced the rest of the night with Sonja, other young men intrigued with her moves and an older woman, and even with the golden boy until the bar closed. Stanly winked at her again as she left the bar with the golden boy.

*****

"Did it occur to you to say no?" Margo's fist clenched into a ball around her beer glass. Her chest puffed out, and her eyes bore into David's as though they were knives cutting the steak on the plate in front of her.

"You want to leave Austin?" David leaned forward biting into his burger. They sat on the rooftop restaurant overlooking Sixth Street. The music from the surrounding bars blared at a deafening volume.

Margo's shoulders rolled back and her dark eyes became black orbs of anger.

David winked at her. "We're in public. No biting or growling."

Margo leaned forward scowling. "You don't know who'll win this war. I've been through this too many times, David. When Daddy died—"

"That was different." David put down his burger and placed his hand over hers. "He was out of control. Anthony's been good to you and us. He won't lead us down a blind alley."

"I like you, David. Your wife's a little flakey, but she has a good heart. I know you both mean well, but if the vamps are getting ready for a fight ..." Margo gazed through David, her eyes focused on the past. Then she blinked, and she shook her head. "You've never seen them going at each other. You don't know how bad it can be."

David sipped his beer. One of the doorman at the Phantom's Menace stepped to the edge of the street and looked up at David, nodding his head.

"You don't have to be part of it, Margo. I'll do the work Anthony needs done to keep the city safe. All I'm asking you to do is to keep an eye out, like you always do. When we know who the traitor is and things heat up, leave town. Go visit your daughter in San Antonio, take Ezra with you."

Margo slammed her beer glass on the table. "You'd like that, wouldn't you? Get us out of the way—"

"Enough!" David growled. Three college students at the table closest to him reached hands up to their throats as though protecting themselves, but only one turned in David's direction looking for the source of the threat.

Margo wiped a tear away from her eye. "I'm sorry, David. You deserve better from me. You never once said told-you-so or held my past against me. It's just -. I thought we'd be safe here."

David saw Leonard walking out of the Phantom Menace. He gulped down the last of his beer and stood. "That's all any of us want. Margo, I have to go." He bent over and kissed her cheek. "I won't do anything that puts you or Ezra in danger. I promise."

Margo looked over the edge of the half wall surrounding the restaurant. "You can count on me, David. It took a long time to make this town safe. I'll be damned if I let a rogue vamp drive me away."

"Thanks for dinner." David nodded to Margo and left.

*****

Cesar walked around the house once more. In over thirty years of working for Anthony, he never shirked his duties. Too many times, enemies came close to attacking, but Cesar made sure they never tried again. Something in the air irked him tonight. Once again, there was no one or nothing in the vicinity threatening security. Even the black Tesla Harry said to look for had not turned up. And yet, something felt wrong.

"Three bodies," he whispered to himself. That's what bothered him. Three bodies had been discovered by police in as many weeks. Each body laid out and drained of blood. "At least they didn't leave any bite marks. So whoever's leaving the bodies isn't stupid."

He skipped a stone across the water, watching it hit the surface five times before sinking. The young moon peeked in and out of rain clouds in the early October sky. A few of the houses across the water had orange or purple lights twinkling across patios and in trees in anticipation of Halloween. The world looked as it should. A soft rain fell. He walked toward the patio stretching his neck to look into the windows. He didn't want to walk into Harry's house without an invitation. Harry still frightened him.

Anthony stood on the patio with the woman Cesar had seen talking to Harry at the gala. He smirked but stopped and studied her face. She exuded a certain allurement. Cesar had to admit there was something about her, but seeing Harry with a woman was difficult, and seeing him with this woman concerned him, and he couldn't understand what it was.

"It's raining, Kitten. Let me drive you home." Cesar bit his lip as he heard Anthony offer his car to the woman. He wanted answers and wouldn't get them playing chauffeur.

She stepped through the French doors. "It's only a mist. I'll barely get wet, but thanks." Cesar was glad. Anthony motioned for him to come inside. He leapt the ten feet over the railing and onto the patio. Anthony shook his head in disapproval, but the woman was inside and saw nothing.

"Let his driver take you home. You're tired. Sorry I kept you so long." Harry took Kitten's hand.

"When do I get to see the painting?" she asked.

"When I'm done. Cesar, drive Kitten and Eddie home. She lives in the condos down the road. You know where Eddie lives. Anthony and I have business." Neither Harry nor Cesar looked to Anthony for approval.

"Seriously," she sighed. "You're all a bunch of old fuddy-duddies. Come on, Eddie. We're no longer needed."

"I obey my mistress's call." They laughed and took each other by the hand as they walked out.

Cesar beat them to the car and opened the back door for them.

"Bar stocked, Cesar?" Eddie smiled at Cesar, who didn't smile back.

"Yes, sir." Cesar kept his face indifferent. "Toys," he muttered as he closed the door.

"Awesome! What'll you have, darling?"

"Nothing. Thanks. I won't be in the car long enough to enjoy anything. Besides, I'm getting a headache from all the wine I've already had."

"Lightweight."

"You have practice tomorrow." Kitten sighed and wrinkled her nose. "I sound like my mother."

"Whatever turns you on, honey."

Eddie talked about his feats as lineman for the Longhorns. Cesar tuned him out. He noticed the woman did too. A point in her favor.

*****

When Cesar opened the car door for her to exit the car, his cold stare neither threatened nor offended her. His eyes were too deep. His stare searched her soul. She might have been curious about what he found, but her head wanted only to lie down and sleep. So she did. Yet, sleep once again eluded her. The vice grip turned tighter in her head until she gave up on sleep. Had it not been so late, she would have taken a pain pill, but with only a few hours before the workday began, she decided to tough it out.

Across the inlet, Harry's house darkened as the first rays of sun mingled with stars and clouds. A few kayakers made their way up the river. Their silent, early morning vigil reminded Kitten of the awakening city. A couple in a rowboat meandered in the inlet, letting the current guide them toward town. Their silhouette reminded her of the pair she had seen when she was standing on Harry's patio with Anthony.

The white cat with the long hair jumped onto the patio and strolled along the banister to Kitten. Kitten reached over and scratched its ears. "That couple must really love to fish if it's the same couple I saw earlier."

Kitten closed her eyes and sipped hot tea, allowing the steam to fill her nose, move to her sinuses, and ease the aching in her head. She hoped the headache would fade away, but it wouldn't.

Logging into her work mail on her tablet, she shifted meetings to next week. Meetings were the last thing she wanted to do with the pain growing in her head. Only the meeting with Stacy and the management team to review the project list had to happen today. The more she thought about what she would say when asked to update the status of her project with Stacy, the more her head hurt.

The glare of the screen burned the backs of her eyes. She turned off the tablet and picked up a pen, paper, and Stacy's novel. Across the water, the large eyebrow window of Harry's house reflected the morning. She closed her eyes to remember all the strange feelings she had had during her visit. Kitten set her pen on the paper.

*****

Danita felt her last tequila buzzing in her head. She searched through her purse but couldn't find her car keys.

"Come on," begged the golden boy. "I only live a few blocks over. Come home with me." He stood behind her, rubbing his hands up and down her bare arms and kissing her neck.

"Oh, bebe," Danita turned, giving her golden boy a long, wet kiss on his lips. "You're such a pretty boy. You get a Lyft or something, yes. And we go home. We're both too drunk to enjoy ourselves."

The golden boy giggled and would have fallen if Danita hadn't steered him to a bench. "Okay. Sit there for a while. I'll find us a way home." She slipped and fell onto the bench next to him. She took off her high heels. "But maybe I'll just sit here a while. Give me your phone."

She took the golden boy's phone from his pocket, put it in front of his face, and turned it on. When it opened, she swiped until she found a ride app. The lettering was out of focus, but she hadn't brought her reading glasses, so she squinted until she found the right buttons to call for a ride.

With the ride ordered, she leaned into the golden boy and might have fallen asleep until she heard, "Keeping me waiting!" It was Leonard's voice. Danita sat up straight, looking around. Across the street, the gray-haired man walked onto the street from around the corner and almost tripped over a bum sitting on the ground with his feet extended onto the sidewalk.

"Dollar, mister?" said the bum as he looked up and coughed.

Even from across the street, Danita heard the lonely apathy of the bum. Her heart skipped, waiting to see what Leonard would do.

She heard a hiss, and the bum pulled his legs into his body, wrapping his arms round his knees.

"Jesus, save me," she heard as his whisper echoed across the street.

Leonard leaned over the displaced man. "Yes. You need someone to save you." The words spat out of his mouth.

At that moment a group of banker types walked out of the building. Four men and two women with navy suits and starched white shirts marched out with briefcases in hand. They stood backlit by the overhead door light, waiting. Two turned up arms to look at watches. Others pulled out phones, the blue lights highlighting the gray, tan, and balding heads.

Danita no longer saw Leonard. A loud coughing—or perhaps it was a gasping—broke the silence, but none of the banker types noticed. Danita slid to the edge of her seat. Another man with a navy suit and white shirt, younger than the others, stepped out the door. "All locked up, sir."

"Good," replied the tallest and grayest of the men. "Let's get to the hotel. I want to review our reports before the presentation in the morning."

The banker types walked off. Danita wanted to yell for them to stay. She didn't know where the bum or Leonard was. She shivered although the night was warm, and her golden boy snored.

The young banker who had locked up stopped and bent over. Danita saw the bum now in the light of the banker's phone. The young banker reached into his pocket, pulling out cash. He put the cash into the hand of the old man. "Here you go, granddad. Maybe get a hot meal instead of a bottle."

"Simon," shouted the leading banker.

"Coming, sir," Simon replied and increased his speed to catch up to the other bankers.

Leonard stepped out of the shadows. He followed the bankers. His face relaxed into a smile, or was he laughing? Danita shivered at the sound of his laughter.

And then her ride arrived.

*****

"Now?" CC rolled her eyes and stretched her back. "Seriously? We spent most of the last two nights in that damn rowboat. I need sleep."

"It's cool, rev," James Earl stretched his bare arms, allowing his muscles to ripple. He pulled his sweatshirt over his head, concealing his well-built torso. "The group needs answers, CC."

CC sighed in recognition. "I'm just so tired."

"If you have something else to do ..."

Madeline's sharp retort was cut short by Yasushi's voice. "We'll keep it short. It's been a trying few days and nights for everybody."

"I'm sorry. Let me stand a while. Rowboats are NOT comfortable." CC moved to the table where the coffee maker sang the happy tune announcing coffee was ready to pour. This assignment bothered her more than the other assignments. James Earl understood her fears, and despite never taking the lead in any of the group's work, he did so this morning.

"We took the boat out when Torres called us about Mugello arriving at the artist's house. The driver kept a good watch on the house and grounds. We stayed far enough away to not draw attention to ourselves. The driver didn't seem to notice us at all. After he'd walk by the river toward the front, we'd row nearby to see if we could catch any of the conversations from inside the house, but we couldn't get close enough."

CC looked out the window over the table. The house the group rented overlooked the river and crags of limestone Austin was famous for. She couldn't see the city from here, but across the river a freeway sat lined with cars bumper to bumper, heading for offices in and around the city. She tried, but she found her mind wandering between floating on the river in the boat, the traffic across the river, and her warm, waiting bed at the house she shared with James Earl.

"How can you be sure they were all there? They move like shadows when they want to. What do we know about the driver? He could be one of them. He must have seen you watching him." Madeline's abrasiveness floated over CC this morning. She was too tired to care.

"Doubt it." Nothing bothered James Earl. It's one of the reasons CC liked him so much.

"You don't know," Madeline's voice was rising in volume.

"Let's slow down and hear all they have to report." Yasushi's voice always calmed Madeline, but CC decided there was more bitterness in Madeline's voice this morning, or did she hear it in Yasushi's voice?

"I wish we had more to tell you." James Earl continued in the same plain but purposeful way he always spoke. "The doors on the patio were wide open. With the lights inside, we saw everything they were doing. The woman and the young guy looked like they were modeling. The artist mostly stayed near his canvas. Mugello arrived after eleven. He sat and watched while the artist painted. Eventually, the woman and the young guy left. Mugello and the artist talked for a long while. I think Mugello's driver must have taken the other two home, because he returned about an hour after they left. He and Mugello left a little later. The artist kept painting till nearly sunrise, turned out the lights, and closed the doors. That's it."

Madeline was quick to add to the conversation. "That's all they wanted you to see."

"Geez! Madeline. What do you want? If they're really demons, do you expect them to start killing people and tossing the bodies into the river right in front of us?" CC didn't care if she offended Yasushi this morning. Madeline's continued hints at her and James Earl's incompetence was too much. "Even the rev says there's nothing connecting the artist ..."

"You haven't had to look at any of them square in the face ..." shouted

Madeline. Anger swelled in her voice, but she kept her face even and remained in her chair.

"Enough," Roger rose from the couch and stood behind Madeline with his hand on her shoulder. "We have questions and few answers. This will take a while."

"You're right." Madeline took a long breath. "I'm sorry, CC, James Earl, all of you. We're just so close. I can feel it." Madeline closed her eyes and rubbed her hands along her lap, but not before CC noticed the fire in her eyes still burning.

"Indeed," Yasushi looked at his sister and CC. "Assuming there is a connection, let's find out what it is and get our proof. Our prey is close. We must make certain before we act or innocent lives could be lost."

"Innocent?" Madeline sighed. "There's no such thing as innocents when it comes to cooperating with these demons."

"Torres," Yasushi did not answer his sister. "What can you tell us about Mugello after spending the day watching him?"

"Not much. He's a rich man doing rich man things. People come in and out of his house all day—more like his compound. The place is huge. He's got elaborate security, including armed guards at the gates and a whole kennel full of dogs walking the edges of the property." Torres's eyes darted between Madeline, Roger, and Yasushi. They finally rested on Madeline. "I'm sorry, Madeline. He left the house about midday. He walked around downtown with a group of businessmen—including the gray-haired guy at the gala with him. I mean, sure they wore hats, dark glasses, that kind of stuff, but who isn't in this town. The sun is bright and it's hot. There was nothing suspicious about either of them. I only handed him over to James Earl and CC when he got to the artist's house. Not too much activity on the road, and the driver was looking. Had I stayed, he'd have spotted me for sure. White rentals sort of advertise their presence, you know."

"Thanks, Torres. We'll find the connections." Roger remained standing behind Madeline. "There was an incident the night before we haven't told you about."

"Hardly an incident." Yasushi sounded annoyed.

"Everyone needs to know all the facts, brother." Madeline forced her voice while tightening neck muscles.

"Indeed." Yasushi said nothing else.

Roger began, "The artist was walking the woman home. It was late. There was no one else on the road, and the lights in most of the homes were dark. The woman stepped into the road to pick up a cat. You know I can speed up very quickly. I aimed for the woman and cat."

CC stared hard at Roger, wondering when he decided to put lives at risk.

"By the time we passed them, all three were standing safely on the median. They had been walking on the sidewalk."

"Only proves they saw you coming." CC would not hide her displeasure at risking lives.

"Or at least one of them is unworldly fast," Roger said. "I was fast. Even the cat should have been run over."

"So, killing cats is okay now?" James Earl asked. CC saw his eyes boring into Yasushi, who looked at him before speaking.

"It could mean many things. And we're not risking innocent lives to find our demons. It's what they would do." Yasushi stood. "Let's not rush to any conclusions or do anything rash. Roger, let's continue with the surveillance, but keep it at a distance. Should they discover us now ..." He paused as his breath skipped an intake. "Well, we're all aware of what our prey can do when cornered."

CC turned back to the window. She remembered the smell of burning flesh, the screams, the pain, the hopelessness.

The familiar touch of James Earl's hand rubbing her back between her shoulder blades brought her back to the present. "Let's go," he said. "The morning's running away, and I'm beat."

CC heard the others leaving and speaking to each other in forced tones of casualness.

"Get some sleep, you two," came from Roger as James Earl opened the front door. "Afraid you'll have the night watch again. I'm keeping you on the Carlisle woman."

"Got it," said James Earl.

CC wrapped her arms around James Earl's waist as he started the motorcycle. She leaned her head into him, breathing in his earthy scent. He turned his head to look at her.

"Said it before, bitch has lost it. Rev knows it, he just don't want to see it. Put your helmet on."

"I'm seeing it now too." CC put on the bright red helmet, which matched James Earl's pearl blue helmet, and they rode away from the house. CC held tighter than usual to James Earl. She wondered whether she was afraid of falling because she was so tired or if she was afraid of what was becoming of the group.

*****

Frank Jarvis sighed when he noticed Special Agent Williams standing next to the coroner's van.

"What are the Feds doing here?" asked Renaldo standing up after leaning over a body.

"Relax, Renaldo. Hank's okay. Had to figure these many bodies in one spot would bring out the works. Let's see what he knows."

Frank walked up the hill, around the evidence tags, pulling himself along with limbs from trees. Sanchez passed him and stood in front of Agent Williams.

"Frank. How you doin'?" Agent Williams shook hands with Frank while helping steady him as he stepped over a large branch.

Frank coughed and pulled out a handkerchief to wipe his brow. "Hank. Wish I could say it was good to see you, but I'm betting this is a business call, and it won't be pleasant."

Agent Williams nodded toward Sanchez.

"You haven't met my new partner. Renaldo Sanchez just moved here from El Paso. This is Special Agent Hank Williams."

"Sanchez. Good to meet you. Look like cartels to you?"

"I think it looks like someone wants us to think it's cartels."

Hank removed his Stetson and scratched his head. "Interesting. I think we should talk. Your place or mine?"

Frank stroked his beard and shook his head at Sanchez. "Better make it our place, Hank. I suppose you're wanting to have a look-see before we pack up here."

"If you don't mind." Hank didn't wait for an answer but headed down the hill through the maze of trees, bushes, and evidence tags to the river and the shrouded bodies.

"With a gut like that, I'm surprised he can move at all," Sanchez said to Jarvis. "What do you think is going on?"

Frank said nothing but watched as Hank walked around each of the covered bodies spread out in the brush on the bank of the river. He didn't look at the reporters' cameras lining the edges of the barricade tape and the balcony of the hotel hovering overhead.

Frank pulled off his gloves and took out his notebook. Five bodies dumped in the middle of downtown Austin invited all the news agencies and citizen reporters in the state. Since the bodies were all dressed in expensive-looking suits, every agency in Texas would make this a priority.

"Let's let forensics finish up here." Frank patted Sanchez's shoulder. "Hank will be along when he's ready, and we'll know how this ties in with the Feds."

"You sure there's a tie-in?"

"Get your head together, Renaldo." Frank turned to his car. "Of course there is. We're in the capital city of Texas. Those folks down there are professionals. There's money involved. Call your mama and let her know you won't be home for the weekend. This will be our only case for a while."

*****

The Count's Broken Heart," said Kitten, sipping her mocha.

"Seriously?" asked Leigh Brown. "This from the woman who practically made Romance a respectable household genre."

"Frightening, isn't it?" Kitten placed her mug on the table and looked at her old friend. "So, what do you think of my proposal?"

"I don't know, Kitten." Leigh looked out over the water. She stretched her long brown legs in front of her and leaned back in the chair. Her mouth contorted as though holding back an immediate negative. "I know the two of you are friends, and I know you can write well, but attaching *my name* to *her* book?"

"Big picture, Leigh. Think about it. She knows what she gave me is shit. She knows I'll rewrite it—changing that ridiculous title to start with. What we've got here is a chance to write a romance novel the way we've always said they should be written. Everyone in the business will know we did it, even if Stacy's name is on the byline."

"It's tempting." Leigh continued to speak as though considering each word.

"And if it bombs, it's all on her." Kitten produced a satisfied smile but saw the doubt still on Leigh's face. "But it's not going to bomb."

Leigh lingered her lips on the edge of her cup. Emotions ran across her face. Leigh was talking herself into accepting the project. "You make a good argument. Back in the day, when we shared an office editing textbooks, playing word games, and making espresso, we had a great time. It'd be cool working with you again. We know each other's style. When Hearts and Minds Publishing took us over, you persuaded me to stay on by talking about all the opportunities to expand into something new. Heck! We dove in headfirst and had a blast. I love my romance writers! They're some of the most prolific and imaginative people I know, and just a lot of fun to work with, but writing a romance novel like this—"

"No buts, Leigh. Just say yes. Remember all those going-away parties we had for those who refused to stay on when Stacy took over? Remember talking over drinks about what the perfect romance novel should be? This is our chance to do exactly what we talked about doing."

"Back then I didn't have a family to think about. This is going to take all our free time for the better part of a year at the very least. I've got school plays, parent-teacher meetings, and a husband who likes to see me from time to time."

"When the project works, Stacy will gift you advances for further books. This will set you up to be the author you want to be. Admit it. It's what you've always wanted to do."

Leigh sat up straight, looking her friend in the eye. She took a long, deep breath before issuing, "Title changes. Something about tides, I think."

"Cheers!" Kitten held up her mug and toasted Leigh. "We're going to write a great book. It's vampires. What about Blood Tide, Blood Stream?"

The two friends sat quietly, the way good friends can. Each watched the sun's light fade and the shadows of the hills across the water loom longer and longer until night settled over them. Mozart's Coffee had a duo singing and playing guitar on the far side patio. They listened as the soft tunes wafted on the breezes. Lights sparkled from the great tree overhead. For the first time in months, they felt a cool comfort in the breeze brushing the skin of their arms and tickling their ears with loose hair.

"What will be your niche?" Kitten asked after a while.

"Romance for women of color, underrepresented and greatly in need of a good voice."

"I can see you leading the charge. You've always been a passionate person. I bet the guy back there with all the dreadlocks will be your romantic hero." Kitten winked at Leigh.

Leigh turned and looked at the dreadlocked man leaning against the wall separating the large patio between Mozart's and the yoga studio. "Agreed. He's a secret agent for an organization sworn to protect those in need from unscrupulous corporations planning on wiping out neighborhoods of the under-served and booting out the residents."

"But the twist?" asked Kitten.

"His family is the sole owner of one of the largest evil corporations. His father thinks he's working for him. Oh, and he just spied the beautiful heroine who's rallying the neighborhood to fight the takeover. It's love at first sight."

"Too easy. He thinks she's a do-gooder bitch who doesn't know what she's doing."

"No swearing in my books, please. He believes she comes from one of the evil corporate families." The grin breaking across Leigh's face almost burst.

"You are so going to take over the Romance world. I always knew your cool façade was only a bluff," laughed Kitten.

"Talk about a cool façade, Miss I'm-not-interested-in-romance," Leigh laughed. "Now that you're hanging out with a world-famous artist, I expect you'll be writing your own literary masterpiece soon. It will be an incredibly thick book and absolutely everyone who wants to say they're literary will have to read it and praise it, although only a chosen few will understand it."

Kitten laughed out loud as she had not done for months. "Of course, I will. And you'll be my editor and do all the talk shows about what a demon I was to work with."

Leigh raised an eyebrow, "Was?" she asked. "Are you planning on writing only one book?"

"And risk spoiling my reputation as a brilliant writer with a second book?" Kitten kept her gaze on the water. "No, I'll become more reclusive than Harper Lee."

They sat in silence again until Leigh's phone beeped. She grabbed her phone. "Dinner's ready. I gotta go. Hubby and kiddos will be hungry. Picking up Indian tonight."

"Goodnight, and thanks for agreeing to help. I'll work on Stacy to make sure you get your due." Kitten glanced up as Leigh picked up her handbag. She noticed concern in her friend's eyes and quickly turned away.

"Goodnight, Kitten."

Kitten sipped the last of her mocha before leaving. As she walked up the steps and into the parking lot, she turned for a final view of the large oak tree twinkling with white lights and imagined what it would look like in a few weeks with the holiday lights. She smiled at the thought of hot cocoa and carols under the tree. She noticed the dreadlocked man sitting under the tree. He turned, looking for someone. A large gold earring glimmered from beneath his dreadlocks. He didn't look at her.

*****

Derek took his refill from the barista and went back to the patio. The light crowd as rush hour ended in Austin made remaining invisible difficult, even if it made watching the Carlisle woman easy.

Derek walked up the steps toward the yoga studio, placing the large tree between him and the two women. He leaned against the wall separating the coffeehouse patio from the yoga studio's entrance. He could watch almost everyone on the patio from this vantage point. He liked neither the surveillance work nor this hangout for Austinites to soak in the sun, moon, and coffee. In truth, he didn't like Austin anymore. Kitten and her friend had arrived almost an hour ago and still sipped on the same drinks. They just sat there, talking, not moving.

Small white lights in the giant tree in the center of the patio sparkled to life, causing Derek to stir. He moved to an empty table to sit and remember how the tree sparkled like magic at Christmas time when his mom and dad brought the family here to see the annual light show. He and his sister would sit on one of the railings in the standing-room-only patio, sipping hot cocoa as the lights danced to familiar carols. On the way home, they would sing carols in the car. Derek liked singing when he was a kid and always sang louder than everyone else.

Derek shuddered as a chill ran down his back. He looked around him. The breeze blowing in over the water seeped under his long dreads and cooled the sweat on his neck. The Carlisle woman and the woman she was with looked around the patio. He turned his head away, noticing a blond kid sitting behind him. He hadn't been there when Derek first sat at the table.

"Pay attention, Derek. This may be a shit assignment, but the rev is counting on you," Derek mumbled to himself.

The Carlisle woman and her friend laughed, but still they sat.

"Sorry?" The blond kid sitting behind him turned his face to look at Derek.

"Nothing," Derek answered, noticing how blue the kid's eyes were and realizing the kid wasn't actually a kid. He had one of those faces, always looked young and perhaps a bit feminine. Derek could think of no word other than beautiful to describe the face. At the same time, Derek didn't like the young man. He felt the hairs on the back of his neck standing up the longer he looked at him.

Before Derek could say anything to him, the young man stood and waved to three young men walking out of the coffeehouse with steaming cups in their hands. The beautiful young man followed them to a table on the far side of the patio. The men laughed loudly with abandon.

The Carlisle woman's friend stood to leave. He jumped to turn his back and sit in the chair the beautiful young man had sat in. The wooden bench felt cool as he sat into it. The Carlisle woman left soon after her friend. She looked at him once before turning to walk home.

*****

"I don't like it." Derek sat across from Yasushi, drinking his mocha too fast.

"Derek, it was so long ago. Madeline and I were kids. Our memories are bound to be a little fuddled." Yasushi slowed his voice as he watched Derek's leg bouncing without acknowledgment. Derek's eyes continually darted around him, unable to look at Yasushi.

"You don't forget the face of the thing that killed your family."

Yasushi took in a deep breath. "Do you think the demon that killed your family was at the gala?"

"I know he was. I saw the pictures Roger took. It was him. It's the same demon you pointed out as killing your family. What the hell is Madeline doing saying it's not him?"

Yasushi turned his gaze to the water. Darkness flooded around them where the lights of the coffee shop stopped. "She was forced to be with him for so long. You know what he did to her. I don't know. Maybe we're wrong about—"

"I'm not wrong," interrupted Derek. "I will never forget that face. He stood in front of me with my wife's body dangling from his arms. I heard my baby's cries. There was fire everywhere, but he wanted me to see him. He wanted me to know he killed my family because I asked too many questions."

Sweat slid down Derek's forehead, dripping on the table. His hands shook the mocha in his cup. Yasushi took the cup from Derek's hands. "Breathe, brother. Remember how to breathe when the terrors come. Close your eyes. Find your spot. Breathe."

Yasushi clasped Derek's hands in his, focusing his own breathing to mirror Derek's. "We can do this, Derek. We're leaving the place of terror. Walk away with me. One step at a time. Walk away, toward the spot where we hope."

Derek's breathing slowed. His hands stopped shaking. His leg stopped bouncing. "But I can't hope. As long as the demon lives, I will never hope."

"I can, brother. I can. And you will too. We're going to destroy the demon together. But we've got to do it right."

"And how can we with your own sister contradicting you? Why does she keep pointing to the artist and woman? What's going on with her?" Derek's breath started to quicken, but he slowed it down. "I'm sorry." He paused before looking back into Yasushi's eyes. "I know she's also in a lot of pain, but she is wrong about this."

"Do you trust me, Derek?" Yasushi stared into Derek's eyes. "I need to know you trust me completely."

"Yes," Derek did not hesitate to answer. "You brought me back from the edge. If it weren't for you, I'd be dead."

"Then please, trust me a while longer. Let me take care of Madeline and you. I want the demon returned to Hell as much as you do. I won't rest till he is."

3

Venus Conquers Mars

Beating wings flutter past and disperse above the lights of the city. Crowds flow up and down the streets roaring with the scent of lust and life. Drums beat rhythms keeping time for heartbeats and slow, melodious songs of love. The only man alone, surrounded by the youth of plenty, rests his head against the cool bricks. Shimmers into the shadows escaping blows and catching coins. A nap, he thinks, and then he'll have enough for a bottle of dreams. And then the cold man comes.

In the halls of our minds dwell the truths, the beliefs, and the absolutes of our souls.
Which will you follow?
As Autumn knells away long summer days, we grieve and rejoice.
New beginnings for the young, long nights for the old.
Spirits summoned turn tears to laughter and laughter to fear.
Let the young dance and explore the nights,
while the old drink to life and lost days.
I'm Mary Midnight and I speak of beliefs and truths.
How are your absolutes?
You're listening to the newest online choice for nighttime serenades.
Walk these paths alone, and you remain alone.

Walk with me where shadows dance beside you,
And be the essence of what is.

"What about Halloween? Hadn't planned to do a party this year, but I could start lining up acts now. And I'm sure I could get a good venue. We could announce its completion then." Stacy walked too fast for Kitten. The weekly project list meeting had gone well. When Kitten announced she had a good start on the book, Stacy squealed with excitement, and she broke off her speech to squeal again as they walked down the street to the Grove for a late lunch.

"Seriously? Did you listen to anything today? I just started on the book. There's no way, even working full-time, anything will be done the next couple of weeks. Notice I'm not saying anything about the load I'm already carrying." Kitten's tone did not hide the pain she felt in her head.

"Oh, poor K." Stacy stopped walking and turned to look into Kitten's face. "You've got one of your headaches again, haven't you? You should have said something. I'd have ordered delivery instead of making you walk out here."

"I can walk, but I'd appreciate it if you'd stop volunteering me for more projects. Your book will take all my free time. I'm sorry to say it, but—"

"Of course it is." Stacy continued walking. "That's why you've got it. Just because I could write it in one weekend doesn't mean you can rewrite and edit it in a weekend. I know that. I'm just so damn excited! It's really happening. You know how I get when I'm excited about something. I'm hiring a couple of new textbook editors for you. Give you more time for me."

"Stacy! I hire my editors. I need people who—"

"Of course you do. And since when do I interfere in your precious textbooks? I've got HR doing the initial screenings. They'll start sending you resumes later this week. But I'll put them off till next week. If your head is bad now, you're going to be a bear the rest of the week.

Finally," Stacy opened the cafe door. "Smell that? Tortilla soup. Most excellent."

Kitten admitted the aroma of comfort foods teased her out of her headache doldrums. As they ordered their lunch and sipped on the Prosecco, Stacy insisted on drinking to celebrate her book being edited, Kitten relaxed.

"To be honest, I need help with textbooks. We're overloaded. And as long as I'm being honest, your book is a challenge, but it's a challenge I'm up to." Kitten's eyes watered as she spoke. It was one of the things she hated about her headaches: they made her too damn emotional.

Stacy pushed her plate aside and waded through her large handbag. Without looking at Kitten, she pulled out a carry pouch of tissues and handed them to her. "I told you. If anyone can make my somewhat pornographic shit into something romantic and literary, it's you. Here, drink more wine. You won't get fired if you show up to work a little sauced. I'm good friends with the boss."

Kitten laughed at herself for wanting to cry and at Stacy for being a good friend. "Liquor me up all you want, but there's no way I'll have enough by Halloween to announce it."

"I know. I know. I can dream, can't I? You'll have it done before the Romance Writers' Conference next summer. All I had to do to get it moved to Austin! It was exhausting. And now I can wow them with my book. So, Halloween. Gary in town, or will you step out with your new artist *friend*?"

"Not sure about Gary, and Harry isn't a party person. I assume you have plans to attend parties with a multitude of handsome young cover models."

"Who else would I be seen with? Although I would like to get to know Leonard better. He's taking me to dinner later this week."

Stacy continued talking as fast as she could about which books were hitting the shelf for the Halloween reading lists and which models and authors she'd be attending parties with. Kitten caught a few words but concentrated on her head not hurting. Her eyes roamed the room. Outside the window, on the patio, sat a familiar woman. Her tightly bound hair and floral dress fit well in downtown Austin, but the large wooden cross around her neck reminded her of someone. *Where do I know her from?* She heard Stacy mention a conference in Vegas and seeing if Leonard would go with her. Kitten sat up and returned her attention to Stacy as she felt a shiver run down her back.

*****

"This is the best part of being in Austin." CC crunched through the taco shell, enjoying the squish of sauce filling her mouth. She slurped it up between chews. "It's such a cool, vegan friendly city. I can't remember the last time we ate so well."

James Earl laughed and handed her another paper towel. "Maybe we should stay for a while."

CC stopped laughing and set her plate of tacos on the picnic table. She searched around at the few people sitting, standing, laughing, talking, eating. It was an ordinary food truck court, where ordinary people stopped to eat on their way home from ordinary jobs or before going out for an ordinary night with their ordinary friends. "Staying in one place for a while." She repeated his words, clarifying their meaning.

"I mean," began James Earl with a stutter. "It's like the rev says, our prey is here. Once we get him, we're done. Right? We don't have to keep going, do we?"

CC continued to stare without speaking. When she spoke again, her words came with deliberateness as the idea of not being with the group sank in. "I'd be dead if the rev and Roger hadn't been looking for me, if they hadn't been in the parking lot when that vamp attacked me. I owe them not only for saving my life but for proving to me I wasn't crazy— that I had a reason to keep living. All the same, I never believed the day would come when I would want to leave the group."

James Earl placed his arm over her shoulders. "It's time to think about it, that's all. I'm not saying we just up and leave. They need us now, but neither of us actually owe them anything more than what we've already given."

"What do you owe the rev?" Her story was like the others. She crossed paths with the demons, they stalked her, she lost everything but her life. The rev showed up, and she survived. The rev knew everyone's story, and maybe Roger did too. She had never asked James Earl his story.

James Earl finished eating his taco before answering. "I got nailed for hacking a while back. I was still at MIT working on my master's. Feds could only prove I broke into that one bank. Couldn't prove I took anything. I didn't, by the way. Anyway, when I got out of jail, my family wouldn't touch me. Probation rules said no job with computers. Good luck getting a job these days that don't use computers. I was cutting lawns and bussing tables when one day I had it. I tried to follow the rules, but I was in debt and bored out of my mind. Didn't take long to realize my probation officer didn't know shit about computers, so I started hacking again. PIs pay me cash to gather emails for divorces and chase deadbeat dads. It paid the bills, but it was boring, so one day I'm messing around with some military emails. I come across this weird email from a Colonel Deitrick to a Colonel Espinoza. He's the one Roger and the rev were talking about the other day at the church. Anyway, the text was so weird, I figured it had to be a hoax. So, I searched around. Found files about a project in Los Angeles, catching a vampire. I don't have to tell you how crazy it sounded. But I found this report made by that Colonel Espinoza about the vampire dying in Galveston. Anyway, stayed too long reading classified documents and let down my defenses. Before long, I had the army gunning for me. Hit the road but kept researching. I found out about the rev, Roger, the others. Searched them out, and here I am."

CC said nothing as James Earl told his story. She now sat upright as pieces of the puzzle over who he was fell into place. "You've never actually seen one of them, have you?"

"From what I've read, I don't want to. The ones Diggers brought the rev are nothing. Roger's been chasing them almost as long as the rev, first when he was a marine and now with the rev. I've seen the pictures of what they can do. But the one thing that gets me is why they don't do more killing. Where are all the bodies going? Why don't people know about them?"

CC stood. She looked around at all the people sitting and standing near them who might hear their conversation. "I feel like moving." They mounted the bicycles James Earl had bought them and rode toward the park on the lake. The ride allowed her mind to clear. She had always known that James Earl hacked networks for the group, but now it made sense how the group paid the rent for the house on the river and how James Earl afforded the small house he shared with CC, the new car for Roger, and even the bicycles they were riding.

She laughed out loud as they slowed their bikes at a grassy knoll next to the water.

James Earl squinted at her. "What's so funny?"

"There was a time when I would have arrested you for telling me about what you did. Now, I'm just impressed."

"Would you have been impressed if you arrested me?" James Earl laughed too, but in his own quiet way.

CC took off her shoes and stood in the water. The end of warm summer weather tickled her toes. She smiled at James Earl. "Yes, but I would still have arrested you. Now, let's think. The group's going about this all wrong. Why aren't we following the money?"

James Earl skipped a stone across the tranquil water. "I'm working on that, but Mugello—"

"You find the funds, and I'm using the term *find* loosely here, that keep the group going. Right?"

"Yeah, but I'm not stealing. The rev—"

"So, where does the money come from?"

"Lots of small accounts. The rev gave me the numbers to use. And sometimes, I find money in other places." James Earl stared upriver.

CC wanted to laugh but held it back. "We're stuck watching the artist's house on the river again tonight, so tomorrow, I want you to show me how you move around our funds. Then I want to find out where it comes from."

"Okay, babe." James Earl sighed and sniffed the breeze blowing across the water. "It's going to be a long night."

*****

Stacy insisted on driving Kitten home that evening and ordered dinner for the both of them, but she stayed only long enough to see Kitten eat a few bites. Sleep crept in on Kitten almost as soon as Stacy left, and Kitten lay on the couch with an ice pack on her head. At midnight, she woke. Her head still hurt, but at least sleep didn't hamper her thoughts anymore. The cat had left in the morning, but now meowed and rubbed against the French doors of the patio to be let in.

"Hey there, cat." Kitten opened the doors and looked across the lake. Harry's house was well lit. She wasn't expected tonight, and while part of her longed to sit and listen to Harry talk about art, she relaxed knowing all she had to do tonight was pet the cat. She made a cup of tea and sat on the couch, but she wasn't allowed to relax. Her phone rang loudly, causing the cat to jump from her lap and race under the couch.

Gary's name and picture lit the screen. She tapped the answer button. "Hi, Gary. How's it going?"

"Terrific. I don't have to go to Singapore. I'll be in Austin next Friday. We've got at least a week together before my next job. If I can manage it, maybe longer."

"Perfect. We haven't had much time together for a while. Want to do anything special?"

"Other than make love to the most beautiful woman in the world, can't think of anything."

"I'll see what I can do to help you out." Kitten sighed.

"You ok, Kitty Kat? You don't sound good."

"Got one of my headaches. Afraid, I'm not much fun tonight."

"You go to bed and rest. Take care of yourself. I worry about you being on your own these days."

"I know you do. I'm fine."

Gary hesitated before saying, "OK. I'll see you next Friday. I've got a car arranged, so don't worry about picking me up."

"Safe flight." Kitten hit the call cancel button, tossing the phone onto the couch next to her. She was more awake now than when she let the cat in. It stretched itself out from under the couch and jumped to the soft cushions where it curled into a ball and purred steadily as sleep closed its eyes. Kitten went to her desk and pulled out Stacy's novel. Perhaps a little work would keep her mind off her headache.

He laughed. He thought he new my mind better than i did. But I would show him. I would go to my prince, I would be happy. I didnt need his money. I was an heiress. My prince would give me the happiness he never could. Even in darkness there would be light.

Kitten decided to take a pain pill instead.

✳✳✳✳✳

Harry sent a few texts through the weekend, explaining that the painting was going well. Kitten's head stopped hurting by Monday morning. She felt another coming and hoped more than expected it to hold off. Stacy's book required her full attention after work. At the office, she interviewed and set up training for the new editors and pushed authors to get their final proofs for the next fall textbook offerings. She didn't have time to think of Harry, Gary, or headaches.

Thursday evening, Kitten drove home early. The twinges of a headache came steadily now. Soon, it would be a full headache. She hoped to have a good night's rest.

The differences, while subtle, spoke loudly as she opened the front door. At first glance, things appeared as they ought; however, the books sitting on the coffee table listed slightly askew from the way she liked her books stacked. The checkbook remained in the cubby of the table next to the front door, but the organizing tray in the drawer sat too centered. Her coffee cup from the morning rested in the sink instead of on the counter.

Kitten might have blamed her suspicions on the headache, but then she saw the miniature red roses in a decorative box on her desk. On top of the flowers sat an envelope with her name on it. The writing wasn't Gary's. The envelope and note card gave off a faint lavender scent. The silkiness and weight of the paper felt good in her hands. The handwriting glided across the page both classically and artistically.

It's done, Esmeralda Conquers Phoebus and Claude. Anthony is holding a soirée at the house tonight to celebrate. Please come. Bring your friend if you like.

Had anyone other than Harry left the note and roses in her home, she would feel uneasy, scold the intruders, and change all her locks. But Harry's presence was not an intrusion. He would not be scolded, and changing her locks would do no good. His presence provoked comfort and security.

Stacy squealed when Kitten called to invite her to the soirée. "If Anthony is holding this shindig, Leonard will be there for sure. I might just have to leave you alone once we get there."

As predicted, Stacy left Kitten almost as soon as they walked into the studio. Leonard swooped in to talk to Stacy, diverting her to a corner where he had been talking to two young, professional-looking women. Kitten found Harry in a corner on the balcony as far away from the guests as he could get without leaving.

"Should the host of a party be hiding on the balcony?" she asked, sitting on the lounge chair next to him.

"Anthony is the host. It's at my house under protest. I couldn't refuse him. He's too good at what he does. He wanted to show the painting, and the oils need time to dry before moving."

"Show me."

"You didn't see it?" Harry stood, offering his arm to Kitten to lead her into the main room.

The painting hung high on the wall to avoid accidental knocking and bumping. The canvases usually lining the walls, floors, and corners of the room hid in other rooms. Around the studio, the beautiful elite of Austin's young, hip art lovers mingled and drank Champagne. A few took the time to look at the painting.

Harry's ability to walk through a room unnoticed no longer surprised Kitten. His casual conversation in the middle of a room full of people did. "Anthony wanted an excuse to play tonight. I provided it. These people want to do business with him or go to bed with him."

"I imagine he would like to do both with most of them."

"He would." The side of Harry's mouth turned up as he watched Anthony flirting with an attractive woman with purple hair and dark eyes as an even more attractive young man with dark skin and green eyes stood next to him, watching Anthony flirt with the woman. "I think the woman talking to Anthony owns that new restaurant everyone is talking about, the one with all the soups."

"Haven't been there yet. Hard to get reservations. The invitation for tonight was surprising. I like the painting." Kitten's eyes had not left the painting since she walked in with Harry. She tried to follow Esmeralda's hand to the beautiful and pained Phoebus, but her gaze—like Esmeralda's—kept staring into the shadows concealing Claude. "Who's Claude? I thought it was you, but it could be Anthony. Then again, it could be someone else. You have him so well hidden in the shadows."

"Just because I'm a realist doesn't mean I don't take liberties."

"So, my love kills?"

"I haven't decided yet," said a young, pretty woman, with long brown hair and freckles. "When I first looked at it, I thought for sure Esmeralda had killed Phoebus, but that's not her story, and now I'm thinking Phoebus is dying for love."

"And Claude?" asked Kitten.

"I don't know. He's covered in so much shadow, it's hard to tell. I need better light and time to think about it. Any hints, Harry?"

"I leave it for the viewer to decide. Kitten, have you met Maria Toledo? She's the newest artist in residence at Laguna Gloria." Harry neither smiled nor grumbled over the interruption.

"I heard Anthony mention your name. Your work impressed him."

"I hope so. I'm broke except what I'm getting as the artist in residence, and I have some plans—"

"Have you ever seen such use of color," the familiar voice of Kevin Vasquez rose over the crowd.

"Shit," began Maria, "I'm so not in the mood for him."

"Come, let me take you to Anthony. He'll want to talk to you. Kitten, shall I meet you outside?" Harry took Maria by the hand, and they merged into the crowd.

Kitten took one more longing look at the painting and made her way back to the patio and into the dark corner where she'd first found Harry. She leaned back on the lounge chair and stared across the lake at her condo building. Stars twinkled on the glassy water of the river. She felt Harry sitting in the chair next to her before she saw him. "From here, I can hear the restaurants and bars. I don't hear so much noise from my balcony."

"A more direct route for the sound waves. I like to listen to the sounds of life."

"And a clear view of my condo."

"Yes. You don't mind that I entered your home to leave the invitation?"

Kitten sipped Champagne, hoping it would ease the pain growing in her head. "No. Once I realized it was you walking around my living room, it seemed somehow natural. I don't suppose you've asked anyone for permission for anything for a long time."

Harry stared across the water at the condo building. "No," he finally answered. "You don't look like yourself tonight. Is something the matter?"

"Gary will be in town tomorrow. I won't be able to see you for a little while. Maybe a week longer. If I didn't have a headache, I could enjoy a long evening, but I don't know about tonight."

"Let me take care of that headache. Go home. I'll be there shortly."

"But your soirée? You shouldn't leave."

"It's Anthony's soirée. Not even Vasquez will notice I'm gone. I'll get Cesar to drive you home."

Kitten didn't argue about a ride home. A quiet evening at home with Harry appealed to her.

*****

"You never even lose your house keys?" Cesar paced in and out of the shadows of the trees near Anthony's house. The chatter from the party wove over the silence of the river as it flowed. "How did you lose a vamp in the middle of the city?"

"Even I have bad days now and then, and he didn't want anyone following him." David leaned against the trunk of a tree and stared at the couple in the rowboat pretending to fish in front of Harry's house.

Cesar shook his head, then looked across the water at the same couple David was looking at. "And why the hell are they here?"

"Chill," David said. "They're watching the house, it's full of the who's who of Austin. We don't know who they're watching."

"You don't believe that." Cesar turned his head to see Harry and Kitten Carlisle talking. Their heads were too close.

"You don't give a shit about them." David smiled following Cesar's gaze to the patio. "What's got you so wound up? Harry's had girlfriends and boyfriends before. Why does she bother you?"

"Don't know." Cesar put his hand to his chin. "Something's odd about her, that's all. It's the killings. It's not just sloppy. Something's going on."

David nodded. "It's been a long time since I've had to clean up somebody else's mess. If I hadn't found her, who knows how messy it could have been for Anthony."

"Exactly!" Cesar continued to pace. "Something's in the wind, David. It's not just the killings that's got Harry wound up. Thanks for taking care of the girl, by the way. I know Anthony appreciated it." Cesar stopped and nodded his head to the patio where Harry and Kitten lounged. "That woman's connected to it. I'm sure of it."

David nodded, wondering about his own fears he heard echoed in Cesar's voice. He dropped his voice to a whisper. "Mary's in town."

"I know." Cesar pushed his hands into his pockets. "I wish I knew why. I don't like it. Two Eldest in one town can only be trouble for the rest of us."

David waited, expecting more from Cesar. When it didn't come, he added, "She hasn't been in touch?"

"Harry wants me," Cesar said and turned to the house. "Probably wants me to take his little girlfriend home. Keep an eye on those two." He signaled the couple in the rowboat and disappeared around the house.

*****

She's dying. It surprised Cesar he hadn't sensed it before. Maybe he ignored the faint tinge of death about her because he didn't want to pay attention to her. Maybe the faint shadow about her was too faint for him to notice before, but now Harry wanted her place checked out. He didn't say why, and Cesar didn't ask. Kitten started to sway as she got out of the car. He took her hand to steady her. That's when he was certain death was leaching its way into her.

"Too much wine and not enough to eat?" Cesar smiled as much as he could, but it had been so long since he smiled, it turned into a smirk.

"Just tired. Thanks for the lift." Her pale complexion made sense to him now.

"Better walk you to the door. You stub your toe or trip into a wall, and Harry will skin me alive."

"Probably." Cesar hid his surprise with Kitten's flat tone. *Does she know what Harry could do?*

He walked an even two paces behind her. In the elevator, his eyes remained fixed on the door. Kitten neither swayed nor swooned. At the front door, he stepped inside before she could. He had only a moment, but the essence of someone other than Harry's lady friend stood out to Cesar. He needed time alone to make sure but didn't have it.

"Nice place," he said and left. He stood at the door long enough to hear the dead bolt bang into place. Along the edge of the keyhole, small scratches, perceptible only to skilled eyes, hinted at an unwelcome entrance to the flat. He looked at both ends of the open-air hall. *No cameras.* After one more check to ensure no one would see him, he jumped twenty plus feet to the ground. He didn't like stairs. He walked around the building. The gate leading to Kitten's patio remained locked. No one had forced it open, but someone large and male had stepped in the gravel below her patio.

"Someone was here." Cesar said, realizing Harry stood behind him. "A man stood under the patio for a while. A woman walked around the flat. That's all I know without more time inside, and I don't think your friend wants my company."

Harry carried a small basket with a large white napkin covering the opening. "Put out feelers. Look for Hunters."

Cesar gasped. The last time he fought Hunters, he was a nobody fighting the Francos in the mountains of his homeland. Hunters hid themselves among the Loyalists back then. Such a different time, before the age of community, back when the strong ruled without mercy and the weak perished by their own hands. When Anthony confirmed another Eldest was moving into Austin and Harry had made no objections, Cesar wondered why. It made sense now. War was coming.

"You know where to look," Harry continued. "Keep it quiet."

"Yes, sir." Cesar returned to the car. As he drove the short distance back to Harry's house, he noted the vehicles along the road. He walked around Harry's house, making sure no one other than him watched the house. The couple in the rowboat were back, but Harry had said not to worry about them. They stayed far enough away for comfort. He made phone calls. Two local police officers owed him a few favors. They would patrol this street with regularity. His real estate contacts would rent a house across the river where he could set a watch of the river. He made one more call for reinforcements, someone he could trust but who wouldn't draw attention.

As he retreated to the shadows to watch the road and the river, his mind wandered to the old days, the bad days, where he would be if Harry hadn't found him all those years ago, living in a cave and killing Spanish Loyalists to survive.

"The accountants," he said to himself. "The war's already started. But why would the Hunters kill humans?"

*****

"You don't look well." Harry stood over Kitten as she lay on the couch with an ice pack on her head.

"It's just a headache. Geez! I wish people would stop fussing over allergies." Kitten's lethargy obscured annoyance. As a rule, she didn't like a fuss over her headaches, but she lifted part of the ice pack away from one of her eyes.

He bent over, lifting the cold pack the rest of the way. "I have a much better cure than this."

Kitten pushed herself up. "I have pain pills if I need them, but thanks. I've tried everything else legal and otherwise."

"Not this cure." Harry walked into the kitchen. He pulled a dark green wine bottle from his basket. "Pots?"

"Clean one on the stovetop. Too much wine and I'll have a different kind of headache in the morning. I've tried the too much wine cure."

"But you have not tried one of my hot toddies. Starts with a decent port. Learned the recipe ages ago from an old woman in Portugal. Used it many times on friends, and there are no nasty side effects to pollute the blood. Just sit back and relax. I won't make a mess."

Kitten leaned back on the couch, listening to Harry as he turned on the stove, shifted pots, ran water, and found a spoon. The smell of the port simmering on the stove grew as herbs or spices or something was blended with it. The fragrance filled her head with memories of simplicity, earth, life, and blood. She remembered Mommy picking up a snake that had slithered onto their small concrete patio in Vegas. "See, sweetie? Nothing to be afraid of. Respect the wild things, and they'll respect you. Hold the bag open a little wider. We'll take him out someplace where nobody will bother him."

Kitten jolted herself out of her memories when she heard Harry mention Leonard and Stacy sitting in a dark corner talking to each other as he left. Stacy liked Leonard, but Kitten didn't think it would be more than a fling as Leonard seemed as comfortable being in command as Stacy did.

When Harry stopped talking, Kitten turned around to see him standing between the kitchen and living room, swirling a large mug in his left hand. He sucked on the index finger of his right hand as he stared at her.

"Is part of the cure praying over the drink?" Kitten broke Harry's reverie.

He looked at her. "Thinking good thoughts never hurt anyone. But I was wondering whether you really wanted this or not."

Kitten studied Harry's expression. He wanted to say something else but wouldn't. "I trust you, Harry."

Harry's face opened for just a moment into one of inexplicable happiness. "Drink it while it's warm. All of it." He sat next to her on the couch as she drank the toddy.

Kitten fell into Harry's outstretched arm, relieved that the toddy tasted good. The port glided over her tongue while the herbs tickled her nose. Another flavor excited her tongue, but she couldn't place the origin. "Delicious." As the warm drink made its way down her throat, she felt weariness overcome her.

"When your friend leaves, you'll pose for me again. I've already arranged for Eddie to pose with you. He's perfect for Mars." He spoke as though to himself. She relaxed deeper into his arms as his cool fingers glided along her forehead. With each stroke of his hand and each sip of the toddy, the pain receded a little more. "Of course, with you as Venus, this will be nothing like Botticelli's piece. I see it all, complete. It will shine."

She tried to follow his conversation. The thought of her as Venus laughed its way through her brain, but she could do no more than lift the corners of her lips in an attempted smile as she drifted away to blissful sleep.

*****

Harry lay Kitten on her bed and pulled the coverlet over her. She would sleep and dream until morning. There would be no headache in the morning, but there would be other headaches. He sat beside her for a while, looking out the bedroom window across the inlet to his house. The small boat with two fishermen/Hunters sat lonely in the middle of the inlet. Cesar walked around the house, staying in the shadows to remain unnoticed by anyone other than Harry. David stood near Cesar. They spoke to each other in hushed tones. So much was happening and much too quickly. Harry wondered that he hadn't noticed the signs before tonight, but his mind was so occupied by art and Kitten and death.

"I should have listened when Mary offered to take over for me." He stroked Kitten's forehead. "But it's all on me now—and you. Let's hope all goes as planned. We don't need more killings than there has to be."

He straightened and walked out of the bedroom. "You're too old for war, Harry." Before leaving the condo, he walked around the living room and kitchen. He felt the essence of the woman he feared. It lingered in the air like a windless day. He would have Cesar watch Kitten.

*****

Sadie sat under a tree close enough to the house to hear the murmur of the partygoers but far enough away no one would complain about her cigarette smoke. The autumn night chilled her, but she ignored the cool breezes and imaged what it would be like to live this close to the river. Michael promised her a good time, but the party was hardly her scene. Despite her new sequined shirt and skinny jeans, the partygoers looked down their noses on her. Michael didn't help matters. He refused to change from the paint-spattered jeans and T-shirt he'd been wearing for the last two days. He kept lighting cigarettes, and a man she assumed was the host kept telling him to put them out. She didn't like the man. He wasn't Harry Reign, not with that gut and blazing bow tie.

Altogether, the night was a bust. Michael, pissed off at the meager beer and food spread, decided they needed a couple of rocks to lift their moods. Her mistake was letting him leave the party to get them.

"How the fuck am I going to get home?" She stood and pulled out her phone to text him, again.

He still did not reply. She could ask someone inside, but it would be obvious she wasn't yet sixteen. "The rich bitches at this place don't want nothin' to do with me," she sighed. She would have to walk downtown to find a way home.

At Mozart's, she hoped to find someone still around who could take care of her, but only the workers remained clearing up other people's messes, and even most of them were gone. Sighing, she trudged on. A limo drove past her a half mile away from Mozart's. Two expensive-looking sports cars followed. She even saw one of those fancy electric cars that were becoming so popular. It nearly passed her before she noticed it. "Cool," she mumbled, impressed by the sleek silence.

She passed the golf club when she sat on the ground and lit another cigarette. "Fuck you, Michael. I hate walking." She looked up realizing the house in front of her was dark. Not dark as in everyone's asleep, but dark as in no one is home. A smile flicked across her face. "If nobody's home, nobody will mind me crashing here, will they?"

Sadie rang the doorbell to make sure no one was home. Before she could walk to the back to find an open window, a dark BMW pulled to a halt in front of the house. Sadie froze until she recognized the grin on the old man's face as the passenger side window lowered. Even the line he used rang opportunity to Sadie.

"You look like a lady in need of help."

It took less than a minute for Sadie to size up this customer: rich, old, horny, and in a hurry. Her best sweet grin spread across her face.

"Sure am." Her sweetest voice and Texas twang made her sound like she was twelve instead of an adult like she thought it did. "I was out with friends. I just got home to find I've lost my keys. And nobody's home to let me in."

"I can't let a young lady stay out here all alone. Come with me. I know someplace where we can wait and have a cup of coffee."

Sadie giggled on cue and batted her eyes. "I don't know how I can ever thank you enough. It's very scary out here alone."

This old man knew the game. A quick blow job, maybe a dance or two naked for him, and she'd have enough cash for a full bag of crack and maybe even a hot meal. *Up yours, Michael.*

The door opened, and she slid into the seat. A shiver ran up her spine, sending goose pimples down her arms. Sadie shook her head to chase away a sudden fear.

*****

"You shouldn't take chances you don't have to." Yasushi paced around the small living room.

Madeline sat with back straight in the dining chair brought into the room for the meeting earlier in the evening. She hadn't moved since the others left.

"You know better. You both do." Yasushi tried to sit on the couch but only fidgeted until he stood to pace once more.

"There's no trace of us." Roger looked at Madeline as he spoke. Yasushi seldom complained about anything either of them did, but he was right to complain today. He looked at the carpet, and his shoulders drooped before he spoke again. "There is no such thing as *no trace* when we break into a home. I know. I deemed it appropriate."

"We act as a whole or we die alone. How many times have we seen others fall because one or two people acted on their own? You're a marine, Roger. You know that. The group voted to leave the Carlisle woman alone. We are not fighting an ordinary evil. We're fighting—"

"I know what I'm fighting, brother." Madeline spit out the last word. "You seem to forget—"

"Do not tell me I forget anything." Yasushi's body shook as he knelt in front of his sister and placed his hands on her shoulders. His voice boomed and echoed throughout the house. "Do you think it's possible I could forget the night those demons came on us? Do you think I could forget the blood, the screams, the pain? Do you think I can ever forget how my big sister pulled me to the safety of that little shithole? Do you think I can ever forget the tears we shed when no one would believe us, when they tried to separate us, send us to foster homes? I remember every moment. And I remember how we worked together to escape the horror and make our way here. You are my sister, Madeline, and I love you like I could love no one else, not even God, but you must let go of the pain. It's the only way we will defeat them."

Madeline did not move but continued to stare forward into nothing. Yasushi returned the stare.

Madeline broke the silence. "She's working with them. That makes her one of them. You will never convince me otherwise."

"I know, sister mine." Yasushi continued to stare into his sister's eyes. His bellowing voice quieted with anguish and disappointment. "You are right, but so many work for them, and they don't know what they are. Once we destroy the demons, people like the Carlisle woman will be free to see them for what they are. If we kill all the ones like her, we'll be just as guilty as they are and our friends who help us will turn their backs on us and lock us away. We've discussed this many times."

"Blame me, Yasushi." Roger leapt from the chair. "It was my call to break into the Carlisle woman's home. Madeline's instincts are usually very good."

Yasushi stood, his shoulders slouching and as he slowed his breathing. He stared at the door leading to the kitchen. Anna stood silently in the kitchen not making more coffee. "We stand or fall together, but if you work outside the group again, you're out." He looked at his sister. "That goes for both of you." He walked into the kitchen, closing the door behind him.

"I'm sorry I got you into trouble with my brother." Madeline's calm exterior conflicted with the croak in her voice.

"I agreed with you that we should check out the woman. James Earl can hack all the data he wants, but only physical study can show us what people really are."

"You're kind to say so, but don't take the blame. The group needs you too much. I'll back off the woman for now. But know I haven't changed my mind." Madeline got up from the chair and walked toward the bedrooms. "I'm going to bed." She halted for a moment before closing the door behind her. "It might be time to call the others."

Roger sat on the couch, putting his face in his hands, unsure whether to cry or pray. Confusion filled his head until he practiced the meditative breathing exercises Yasushi had taught him. In the silence of his mind, he realized he could hear Yasushi talking to Anna.

"It won't happen again," Yasushi said.

"Is she out of control? What about Morgan?"

"I can control her. And Roger is a good soldier. If you knew what she did to help us survive even before the demons came, you would not question her."

"I've heard the story—"

Yasushi's voice rose as he interrupted Anna. "It's no story. Our mother was a whore. Twelve of us brothers, sisters, and cousins lived in a one-room shack full of our own shit. Madeline was the oldest to survive. The whore brought the demon to us. We'll never know if she knew what he was, but he came to rape Madeline. And he did. I had to watch as she screamed and begged him to stop. She went to the local priest, and he sent her back to our mother, calling her hysterical. Our own mother pimped her out, and Madeline was labeled a hysterical harlot."

"I'm sorry," Roger heard Anna say. "Is she the right one to have so much control of the group?"

"All the times she was forced to be with the demon taught her a great deal about how they live and think. That knowledge allowed her to save me when the other demons came to take us. They turned on our mother and wanted to kill us all. Madeline and I only survived because she pushed us into the shithole in the back of the house."

"Yasushi—"

"If you want the synod to remove their support, make your report. I won't send my sister to an institution where she'll spend the rest of her days drugged with no one believing her."

Roger walked out of the house careful to make no sound. He had heard enough. Outside, he looked at the sky, praying to any god that might listen. "All the demons will die."

He made up his mind. He needed the support of those who felt as he did. Yasushi's way of doing things no longer worked.

*****

"No. Really, I'm fine." Kitten stretched her legs out from under the cushioned chair in Stacy's office. The editors and managers had been sitting for over an hour, reviewing project updates. Everyone twisted in their chairs. The meeting needed to be over.

"Sure?" Stacy asked. "You left the party early. Was sure you'd be out today with one of your headaches."

Leigh Brown smirked and caught Kitten's eye. Kitten rolled her eyes back at her. "Are we done? It's time for lunch."

Stacy turned back to face the long table. "Any other business?" She didn't wait for an answer. "Good. Go. Get out of here. I need lunch."

Everyone except Kitten left. "So, how did it go with Leonard last night? You two seemed very chummy."

"Chummy?" Stacy pondered the word for a moment before answering. "A good word for it. Very disappointing. You know, he's not normally my type, being on the mature side, but there's something about him. I got the impression he wanted me around to keep the younger women at arm's length."

"No." Kitten smiled, wanting to laugh but thinking better of it. "Imagine putting someone on your arm just for show."

"Don't be smart. You didn't hang around long. What were you and your artist up to?" Stacy moved to her desk and banged on her keyboard. "Piece of shit. I hate the new mail system. Carol!" She yelled. "What time is my next meeting?" She pulled her purse out from under her desk. "So, what do you want for lunch? How does chicken tortilla soup at the Grove sound to you?"

"Works for me, but I only have a few minutes. Got a couple of on-line consults this afternoon." Gary stood at the door to Stacy's office with pink and red roses in one arm and a large box of chocolates in the other.

"Gary." Kitten moved to him, smiling, and kissed him. "You weren't due in till this afternoon."

"Change of plans, I'm afraid. Possible new client wants to meet this afternoon. Had to get here early enough to boot up at home and get the conference set up. Looks like you're set for this afternoon, anyway. I'll order us dinner and meet you at your place later."

"Sounds good. For me?" Kitten winked at Gary as he pressed the roses into her hand.

"But these," said Gary as he moved toward Stacy, "are for you. Your favorite."

"Oooooooo." Stacy cooed as she took the box of her favorite Swiss chocolates from Gary. "You know how to win my heart."

"If I'm lucky one day you and I might have a wild affair." Gary hugged Stacy.

"The possibilities!" exclaimed Stacy. "Give me those flowers, Kitten. I'll put these in water while you two kiss."

"See you tonight." Kitten kissed Gary as he left.

"He's a keeper, Kitten." Stacy took Kitten's flowers to the wet bar.

"Yes, he is."

Stacy turned to face Kitten. "You're not thinking of dumping him? But you are." Stacy dropped into the nearest chair as her jaw dropped open. "You sly dog, you. I bought the whole story about you and your headache last night, but you and your artist were making more than headaches, weren't you?"

"Stacy! Gary is a good man. We've always had an understanding, but lately I'm getting a different vibe from him."

"Marriage?"

"Afraid so."

"Come on." Stacy tossed the flowers on the conference table. "We definitely need a long lunch to figure this one out."

*****

"What's to figure out?" Kitten said for the umpteenth time. "I've been seeing Gary for seven years, but he's always wanted a family, and I don't. And as much as I love him, I don't love him that way. Just as importantly, he feels the same. We're more than friends, but not that much more. And as for me and Harry, there's nothing there. Yes, he fascinates me. He's a great artist. It's very flattering that he wants to paint me. He's interesting to talk to."

"Don't shit a shitter, girl." Stacy poured them each another glass of wine. Stacy's phone beeped with another reminder about a meeting, but Stacy ignored the text, again. Carol would fix it. "When we met five years ago, there were no males in your life but Daddy and Gary. You meet Harry Reign, world-renowned, hottest motherfucking artist in the world, and you're suddenly doubting what you're doing. You're falling for him."

Kitten wanted to argue, but Stacy stopped her. "Don't get me wrong. I'm not saying not to have a fling with the guy, but he's not for you. So, he's famous and rich. He's also ugly as sin and spying on you. You said yourself you had no idea he'd been painting you when you first met. Rings stalker to me. Does to you too or you wouldn't have reservations about him now. Fess up. You want him. It's okay. Have a good long fuck, then hop back into Gary's bed. It'll be good for. You'll experience something new, and you'll get him out of your system."

"I have no intention of having sex with Harry. It's just not ... not that way with him." Kitten didn't realize she was stuttering, but Stacy did and pointed it out to her.

"You can't even talk about Harry and sex in the same sentence. You want it girl. Go for it. Better yet, read a couple of romance novels. They'll show you how to do it right. If you don't, you'll marry Gary, he'll travel all the time like he does now, you'll work here, but you'll always find your eye wandering. You'll both be miserable. Look for something new and exciting while you're free. I like Gary. Like you say, he's a good man, but he's boring. Harry's not boring."

"You're making waaaay too much out of this. I had a headache last night. Harry took me home and fixed me a hot toddy. It got rid of the headache, and I slept like a lamb. Gary and I will be okay, although I might have to find the right woman for him. And I'm not having sex with Harry. I'm not even sure we could."

"Why not? What's wrong with him?"

Kitten pursed her lips letting her thoughts run where they wanted. "We just wouldn't." Images of *The Lovers*, the first art piece she had seen by Harry, filled her head. She wanted to feel that passion, to match it with a passion of her own, but tonight she'd be with Gary; stable, secure, confident Gary, whose greatest fault was not being Harry.

*****

Gary could not have executed a more romantic night without a direct connection with the goddess of autumn. The waxing moon glistened among brilliant stars. Wispy clouds flew across the sky, following various winds high in the stratosphere. The lake mirrored the sky. Nighttime boaters floated down the river toward the restaurants and bars filled with Friday night revelry. Kitten sat watching the tiny flames from the candles on the table twinkle and sputter in the gentle evening breeze. Gary sat across from her, staring at the sky.

"Good choice for dinner." Kitten sipped rich, black coffee and smiled at Gary. When she'd arrived home from work, he'd already had the table set for dinner, which arrived shortly after she did. They sat on the patio, talking and laughing as the sun set.

"I've missed good Italian food. Plenty of good restaurants in Hong Kong but no great American-style Italian ravioli to fill a man."

"Not too full, I hope. There's dessert."

"Maybe after we work out a little." Gary grinned eagerly.

"We've got all week for that. Once I get you on your back, you'll be out for the night. I can see the jet lag rimming your eyes even in the candlelight."

"I intend to hold you to it." Gary leaned over the table to kiss Kitten. Kitten kissed back, but as she straightened, her eye caught a movement near the water in front of Harry's house. It wasn't Harry, not tall enough, perhaps Cesar. He always wandered around the outside of Harry's house when Anthony was there. She wondered what business they were doing tonight.

Gary looked over his shoulder to the house. "That where the artist lives?"

"Yes. The lights are on, so he's home painting tonight."

"Your daddy couldn't decide if he was pleased or pissed that an artist was painting his little princess."

"When did you see Daddy? And how does he know about the painting? I only just told you."

"A world-famous artist like Harry Reign has a grand viewing in Austin hosted by the infamous Anthony Mugello, and all of Texas knows about it. When the model is at the opening standing next to him, well, your parent's gossipy friends couldn't wait to congratulate or scold your folks." Gary laughed at Kitten's face and opened the second bottle of Champagne. "Come on, Kitten. You like the attention it got you. Once they see you're not naked, they'll be fine with it."

"You think?"

Gary took her hand as she reached for the Champagne. "They love you. You can do no wrong." He kissed her fingers.

Kitten blew him a kiss before taking a large sip of Champagne. "Silly. I just don't want them thinking I'd do anything, well, you know, that might embarrass either of them. And you still haven't told me when you talked to Daddy."

"Flight from Portland. Told you I had a quick change in my schedule. Luckily, I have plenty of points and got on the plane I needed right away. Turns out he was returning home from a meeting. We got our seats moved so we could talk. And you're worried now about doing something you don't want your parents to know about? I have a feeling they know what we do when they're not looking."

"Hardly the same thing, silly." Kitten's gaze kept turning toward the house across the inlet. Knowing Harry was in the house and she wasn't bothered her.

"So, tell me about this romance you're doing with Stacy. She seems to think it's hotter than *Fifty Shades*." He glanced at the house again.

"It's the biggest load of shit I've ever had to work with. Stacy thinks she wrote the end-all romance book and I'm somehow or another going to make it a literary masterpiece. It'll be the death of me."

"That bad? Kind of figured when Stacy told me she wrote it in a weekend. But she says you're turning it into something wonderful."

"I've only shown her a page or two. It's just too painful to work on. Now she wants it out by the conference next summer. Afraid it's going to take most of my free time. We won't have the time together you hoped we would."

"Clearly, I'll have to do her in to have time with you. Between her and your artist friend, there won't be much of you left for me."

"We've got all week, remember."

Gary got up to stand behind Kitten. He leaned over to kiss her neck and rub her shoulders with his hands. "Laisse ça jusqu'au matin. Allons au lit."

Kitten looked up. She imagined, or did she see, Harry looking across the water at them. "I don't remember much of my high school French, but I get enough to agree," she said. Kitten felt eyes watching. A party barge full of wine, hard liquor, and loud music made its way down the river toward them.

In the bedroom, Kitten slowly undressed, conscious of Gary watching her. She turned her back to him and looked out the window. Across the water, Harry watched. She felt his eyes on her. She imagined him transfiguring *The Lovers* from clean, smooth marble, consummating the feeling into art.

She let her bra fall off her shoulders. "You have a beautiful back, Kitten." Her slow undressing excited Gary. She allowed her panties to glide down her legs and stood for a moment in full view of the window before turning and crawling up Gary's body as he lay on the bed. She covered his mouth with hers, caressing his tongue. Then she mounted him and moved in a slow and deliberate rhythm. His eyes closed as his body tensed and tightened. She turned to look out the window and stared at the Harry's house.

She lay on her back, letting the sweat cool her body. Gary slumbered on his stomach with his head resting on the pillow next to her. She placed her arm behind her head, satisfied in her ability to please her man even as she dreamed of another.

*****

"We'll be at this all night if you don't keep still," snapped Harry. He put the paintbrush down and massaged his neck while looking out the window. Kitten and Gary sat on her patio. She smiled and sipped Champagne. Gary grinned like a schoolboy.

"Sorry. The new trainer worked me hard this morning. I'm stiff as a board. I need a quick break to stretch and take a piss." Eddie stood without waiting for Harry to answer. The front of his naked body glistened with sweat. "Tonight, you'll have to let me move from time to time. No choice. What's wrong with you tonight?"

"Everyone has off days, Eddie." Anthony sat in his usual chair at Harry's side, sipping bourbon and admiring Eddie's bulging muscles. "Give Harry a little slack. He's got a lot on his mind these days."

"Some days it doesn't pay to get out of bed, but the trainer only worked me so hard because I've been here so late I've missed curfew three times this week. I'm not a fucking mannequin." Eddie continued to ramble on as he walked out of the room toward the restroom.

Anthony laughed, "Not like once upon a time, is it, Harry? I remember when young men boasted about posing for renowned artists. Haven't figured out what's got these young American men so aggressive."

"Too much television." Harry stood and watched Kitten dining with Gary. He avoided listening to their conversation.

Anthony stood behind Harry. "Would you like her friend to disappear?"

Harry thought before answering. "No. She's a good model. I don't want her distracted."

Eddie walked back into the room, yawning and stretching his enormous limbs. "Trainer promised another grueling workout if I'm late again. We going to be much longer? I need sleep."

"Let's try one more sitting before calling it a night." Harry sat back on his stool and picked up his brush while Eddie resumed his pose, lying on his stomach amongst the many pillows and blankets next to the divan.

"Then I'll have my car drive you home while Harry and I talk business." Anthony resumed his place, watching Eddie.

"Thanks," laughed Eddie. "Wake me when it's time to go."

Harry focused his attention on his painting, allowing his brush to stroke Eddie's thigh, licking color and texture to his skin as it glistened pink, hazel, amber, and fawn against what would be rubies, cardinals, fuchsias, and blood. Kitten's delicate laughter tinkled over the water into Harry's ears. He couldn't help but look. She looked toward his house. Harry returned his gaze to the painting. Eddie's lean muscles tensed as he struggled to maintain position.

Kitten's voice no longer drifted into Harry's ears. He turned to look, again. Gary bent over her, kissing her neck. She looked at Harry as they stood and walked into the condo.

"That's enough for tonight, Eddie. I'm sorry for keeping you so late." Harry opened the French doors and stared across the water.

Eddie relaxed, sighing out loud. "Call me when you want me again."

Cesar stood beyond the patio. He signaled Oscar to get the car ready. He'd added people to Anthony's security. A new driver made himself conspicuous as Eddie pulled his shirt over his head and headed for the car. Anthony handed him cash. Around the building were four other security guards hidden and watching.

Anthony watched Eddie get into the car. When he returned, Harry gripped the doorframe. "Get him out of town, just don't kill him. He could be useful."

Anthony saw Kitten lying back in her bed, her body breathing deeply and slowly as she relaxed, allowing her body to cool. The red-headed man next to her slumbered with sweat dripping off his back. "Of course," he answered. He said nothing else, knowing Harry had claimed the woman, but his eyes lingered over the curvaceous, glistening body. "I'll make some calls on the way home, but first I need to know what you know about the Hunters."

Cesar walked into the room but remained standing near the door. Anthony approved of his interest. Harry stared for a while across the water before answering. "It's a small group but dedicated and sophisticated."

"How do they know we're here?" Anthony kept his eyes on Harry studying his movements.

"Someone is helping them."

Cesar blurted out under his breath, "What?"

"Impossible! No one would help Hunters." Storm clouds blew across Anthony's face. "Everything we've built, and someone is betraying us? It's all been going as planned. Who?"

"I have my suspicions." Harry sat, allowing his paintbrush to touch his paints and canvas with control and purpose. Mastery of his thoughts returned to him. "Someone has been helping them gather and kill our kind for almost five years now."

Harry allowed his words to take hold of his best apprentices.

"What happened in Galveston over the summer was merely a prelude to the changing times. I made a crucial error, and I don't intend to make another one, but I need to know you are true to me."

"Of course," Cesar's deep voice echoed through the room. "What do you need me to do?"

Harry turned to Anthony, who stared out across the water. He said nothing until he realized Harry waited for him to answer. "You know I trust you, but I need to understand. I thought you and the Duchess took care of the problem in Galveston."

Harry grinned the annoying grin that told Anthony and Cesar they would get only a few answers tonight. "When she was a Duchess, you were only a babe, Anthony. Funny how names have a way of lingering."

But Harry spent no time reminiscing tonight. "Yes, in the end, she took care of it, but it was my fault she had to, so she's in town now, respecting my authority here and not interfering unless she must."

"These Hunters are military too? Did they kill my accountants?" Anthony sat back in his chair, his eyes closed, but thoughts and decisions raced across his face.

"Some of them were military, and they did not kill your accountants. Getting the army contract is now crucial. The government knows too much about us to ignore us anymore. Once we're inside their management team, we will stay ahead of them. But this group is different. They've all been touched by our kind. They know when we're near. It's their potential for danger that worries me."

Cesar spoke, moving close to Harry and Anthony. "I know everyone here. There's never been any talk of dissatisfaction with how things are run. No one's ever said a word of betrayal."

"I didn't say anyone here was betraying us, Cesar. The Duchess, as you call her, and I have our suspicions. We'll deal with the traitor. You and Anthony keep our people safe."

"Plans are in place to keep everyone safe," Anthony's voice betrayed his growing anger. "But you have to give us some idea—"

"Too dangerous." Harry continued to paint. "I trust the two of you completely. There is more at stake than our safe little enclave. If I don't force the traitor to reveal himself and all working with him, none of our kind are safe."

Anthony laughed out loud. "I knew shit was up when I first heard the Duchess on the radio; Mary Midnight is a fitting name. Harry, this is what you've been training us for."

*****

"Not a passion, but a calling." Roger sat back in the worn leather chair of the downtown coffeehouse. He chose the place so if anyone in the group saw them, they would not appear to be plotting: simply two associates talking over coffee. Outside the windows, people walked up and down Congress Avenue as the evening rush hour gave way to the early weekend party crowd. "I spent too long seeking justice to allow these demons to continue killing."

"When my brother died, the army called it an accident. I didn't believe it even if his wife did." Anna smirked. "After all, what would her husband be doing with black ops? He was an accountant. Even secret operations have accountants, and they know what's going on around them. It didn't take long for me to find someone to tell me the truth." Anna sat opposite Roger. Unlike Roger, she remained sitting upright with her hands in her lap and a bottle of water resting unsipped before her. "I made it my mission to find justice. Luckily, I've found those who not only believe but are willing to do something about it."

Roger sipped his coffee, realizing Anna did not mean Yasushi.

"I appreciate your candor, Anna." Roger breathed in the roasted coffee and milk from his cup. "But it's easy to see you're doing this for vengeance. It's obvious even to Yasushi."

Roger let his words sink in. He watched as Anna's face flashed emotions ranging from rage to understanding. "And yet, Yasushi understands the value in all purposes. You and I seek the same end, the destruction of all these demons."

"*All* of them." Anna answered too fast, but she sat back in her chair.

"Yasushi is right, we need proof who is in league with the demons and who are pawns. I have an idea how we might nudge things into happening."

Anna sat up again, leaning close to Roger as she lifted the water bottle and placed it to her lips. Roger smiled to himself as he saw interest.

"I agree with Yasushi, we mustn't harm the pawns, but we can use them. After all, they are already being used." He drank more coffee to gauge Anna's reactions. "But we need to remain hidden."

"Go on." Anna's eyes twinkled with excitement.

"I've been talking with Woods—Derek. He knows some people here in town willing to work for us. I also have surveillance gear. I'm putting together an operation to prove what kind of monsters we're dealing with."

"Bringing in outsiders? Is that wise? We have good people arriving soon." Anna spoke in a hushed voice as she turned her head to look around her.

Roger emptied his cup to hide the satisfaction on his face. He stood and turned to the barista, signaling for another coffee.

"If I'm right about Mugello, these men won't survive. We'll need all our people for the next phase."

Anna pursed her lips. She bit her lower lip to keep her face straight. "Let's hear the plan."

"You know about the dinner party Saturday night?"

"Yes. Diggers told me."

Roger smiled. Once again, his instincts regarding Diggers proved correct.

"Yasushi talked to you about getting someone into the party?" He wanted to make sure Anna realized he already knew the answer.

"It's in the works. I'll have a pass for CC."

"Good. I have the details for the concert Mugello is going to first. We'll strike there."

"In public?"

"Let me take care of this my way." He stopped talking as the barista arrived with his coffee. He smiled, "Thanks."

"If you're not going to trust me—" began Anna.

"It isn't a matter of not trusting. It's a matter of practicality." Roger took care to look into Anna's eyes. "I'm a marine. I do what needs to be done. Count on me for this, and you can count on me for the rest. If all goes well, we'll have the demons on video. They won't be able to hide anymore."

Anna's eyes still flashed doubts as the right side of her mouth clenched, but he could see her coming to the conclusion he wanted.

"I'll trust you, this time." She returned Roger's stare. "I want them dead, and I'll make it happen with or without your help."

Anna stood, grabbing her purse from the table. "Call me when you have it."

Roger stood to shake her hand. "I will. We'll both have what we need tomorrow night."

Anna left.

Roger sat back down, stirring cream into his coffee. The certainty of his plan depended on Anna getting him the information he needed and his ability to hide what he was doing from Yasushi. He disliked working without Yasushi, but when the killing started, Yasushi would not approve. And the time for killing was approaching.

*****

"Come on, Hank. Spit it out. You've been holding back, telling me nothing since the start." Frank Jarvis blew steam away from his coffee as he watched the neat and plump, middle-aged woman sitting with her back like a stick on the other side of the coffee shop behind Hank. He'd told Renaldo to return a phone call outside. Renaldo scoffed but did as he was told. Hank was a good agent, as far as Feds went, but he was holding something back. Frank hoped the two of them having coffee alone would convince Hank to talk.

"I'm telling you nothing, Frank, 'cause there ain't nothing for me to tell you." Hank kept his arms wrapped around his wide chest and continued to stare at his coffee mug. "That's what's eating me."

Frank focused on his old friend. Worry lines inched further into the corners of his eyes than they had last time he was in Austin. The hair in his beard, usually trimmed to perfection, bushed in odd spots across his chin. Even his neat, short, black hair sprouted a few curls near the nape of his neck.

Frank scratched his chin, deciding it was time for him to trim his own beard. "Nothing?" he asked.

"Nothing!" Hank picked up his coffee mug and held it to his lips without drinking. "Every time we think we know something, it evaporates away. No way the cartels did this killing, but somebody's sure trying to make it look like they did. I just don't get it."

Frank watched the middle-aged woman sit back into her chair. The man she was with looked pleased with himself. *Who's the boss there?*

Renaldo walked past the window, his phone still held to his ear. Frank kept his voice low. "Renaldo said the same thing the day we found the bodies—about it not being cartels."

"You like the kid, don't you? You don't usually partner with newbies."

Frank grinned. "He's good. Still hotheaded, but he'll grow out of it. So, we're back to something going on at the bank?"

"Yeah," Hank sighed and leaned forward, cradling his coffee mug with both hands. "The bank president is all hush-hush, saying the auditors had barely gotten started. Seems someone is buying the bank. The president and board want it done quickly, but the buyer won't move forward without an audit."

"But I bet the bank's not letting you see the books." Frank leaned back in his chair.

"I got a team of accountants coming in tomorrow with the warrant. If there's anything in there, we'll know about it in a few days or maybe a few weeks. Hell, I don't know. You know how long these things can take."

Frank noticed Hank remained sitting forward continuing to stare out the window. Frank relaxed his neck muscles, waiting. He watched Hank's eyes focusing on the lettering in the window. Soon, he'd tell Frank what he wanted to say.

Frank sighed, sipping his coffee and turning his attention back to the couple behind Hank. The woman stood, then the man stood and shook the woman's hand. She looked pleased with herself, but the Cheshire grin on the man told Frank the man got the better of whatever deal they had just made.

"Anthony Mugello," Hank's hushed voice raced into Frank's head, jerking him back to their discussion. "He's the one buying the bank."

"Shit!" explained Frank. "That's all we need. You going to question him?"

"I got a call into his lawyers. Thought I'd take you with me, keep it local, simple. Don't want him stalling."

Renaldo burst into the coffeehouse before Frank could answer. He leaned down to Frank's ear, "We got another one. Just like the accountants but a kid this time."

Hank raised his eyebrows and opened his mouth to speak but stopped as Frank replied. "Anybody we know?"

"Not yet. Face battered, but female. Signs of rape."

"So not like all of them," said Hank.

"Execution style killing. Little blood on scene." Renaldo pulled the car keys out of his pocket.

Frank stood gulping the last of his coffee. "Hank, I'll let you know as soon as I know something more. And when you get that other thing arranged, let me know."

"Will do," Hank leaned back in his chair to stare out the window again.

"You drive, Renaldo."

Frank and Renaldo got into the car to drive away.

Renaldo asked, "So what did you want me out of there for?"

Frank grinned. "You're a good cop, Renaldo, but sometimes you gotta know how to talk about things so nobody knows you're cooperating with each other."

"Whatever," Renaldo said, rolling his eyes and pulling out of the parking spot.

*****

"You have all those numbers memorized?" CC asked as she sat next to James Earl in front of three large computer monitors.

"Yes," replied James Earl.

"You never cease to amaze me, babe." CC leaned over and kissed him on the cheek. "Now, where does the money in the rev's accounts come from?"

"I dunno." James Earl raised his eyebrows. "Rev said not to bother with it. I just move the funds out of these accounts to those belonging to the group."

"Seriously, you never looked?"

"Rev said not to." James Earl turned to CC his eyes wide. "Don't you trust him?"

"Oh, babe, I trust you to not be so naïve. Of course I trust him. That doesn't mean I trust everyone in the group. By the way, who all has access to the group accounts?"

James Earl's fingers tapped away on the keyboard, but his eyes wandered in thought. "Here," he pointed to the screen on the left. "I broke it down. Rev can access all of them. Roger has access to this one. Mostly, he has me access it to pay for weapons and surveillance gear. Madeline has this one. She keeps tabs on it but doesn't take much out of it. I think rev set it up so she could have some cash. Never more than five or six hundred in it at any time."

"When was the last time Roger or the rev asked you to pay for anything?" CC wrote the numbers on a pad of paper in front of her.

"Last week, to pay the deposit and rent on the house, purchase the car, and to buy Roger a new suit. And of course, I pulled out cash for Madeline to purchase groceries and such."

"And this house, the bikes, and what we spend to live here?"

CC watched as James Earl looked away from her as his fingers once again typed in information.

"Well," he began, "here is an account I set up when we moved to Austin."

CC whistled as the account opened on the screen in front of her. "You value your work, don't you?"

"I didn't steal it," he said. "I hack, but this is all legit. I promise! Security companies offer good money for anyone who can test out their systems, and they don't ask questions about identity. You think I'm only playing games all night?"

"Oh, babe," CC put her arms around him and kissed him again. "You are so much better at this than I dreamed you were. So, let's put those skills of yours to work. I need to know where the money the rev is using comes from. Pick one of these small accounts first. Might be easier than the big ones."

"What if the rev finds out?" James Earl smiled at CC's kiss but shook his head at doing what Yasushi asked him not to do.

"Are you going to tell him?"

"No, but—"

"And how much are people paying you to hack because you're not getting caught?"

"A lot."

"We need to know, babe." CC placed her hands on either side of James Earl's face looking at him in the eye. "Sooner or later, the rev or Roger will find out how special you are. We need to protect ourselves. The rev is a good man, but do you really trust everyone else to keep you around if your secret gets out? I love you, babe. I'll do what I need to do to keep you safe."

*****

Neither minded the silence, but words unspoken hid behind their lips as Kitten drove Gary to the airport. They arrived at the airport early, as they usually did, for a final cup of coffee together.

"I can probably get away in a couple of weeks. I'll have Li take over for me once I get the work started." Gary watched a family walk past their table. The children wore their Mouse Ears and Disney backpacks. The parents looked exhausted.

"You don't have to, Gary," Kitten said, also watching the family returning to Austin. "I'm fine. Really." She placed her hand on his.

"You're always fine." Gary finally looked at her. His eyes were wet, but they did not cry.

"If you hadn't gone to Houston to see the specialist with me, I don't think I would be here now. I owe you." Kitten feigned a smile but had to lower her head as she felt her own eyes watering.

"I want to stay and help." Gary squeezed her hand.

For the first time, the silence felt awkward but necessary. "No. You've already done too much for me. I love you more than I can say, but even if I didn't have this thing in my head, you know we'd never stay together. We don't love each other that way."

Gary sniffed as a little laugh escaped his lips. "I love you too. I can't bear to think of you alone, not now."

"I want you to remember me as I am right now. You're an amazing person. I've been lucky to be with you. I want you to find someone who will love you and give you the family you want. You know I never will, nor would I if things were different."

"I know, but I'm going to miss you more than you can know. I don't think anyone will ever be as close to me as you are."

Kitten took a deep breath, allowing a single tear from each eye. She wiped them away as she leaned over to kiss Gary. "You'll find someone who loves you and wants to make a family with you. I know you will, even if I have to find her for you."

Kitten laughed, which made Gary laugh. The words, once spoken, released both to feel good about their time together. When it was time for Gary to move through security, they hugged each other a final time.

*****

Isabella Iandanza examined the bench with the day and night sky on it in the airport. Since walking out the gate from her plane, she stopped at all the art pieces spaced throughout the terminal. An artist herself, she wondered at the colors, the simplicity, and the boldness of the artist to place this bench with its colored porcelain attached to the wood of the bench and juxtaposed with the steel of the feet. She sat feeling the delicate hardness beneath her. She found a smile forming on her face as she considered the act of sitting on art.

La Musica Sigue stalled her from exiting the secure area of the airport by its sheer size, but the story it told of Austin's musical history captured her imagination. She pondered the journey from lone folk singers to world-class musicians, shaking her head as she returned to the present. Arriving on the last flight into Austin meant few people blocked her views of the rotating art exhibits, but it also meant security cameras could easily capture her image. She didn't worry. No software would match her image with anyone of interest to security. Still, she had been warned about dawdling in public places. That and the smells of so many people, so many children, so many animals, so much food and drink clouded what might have been a pleasant evening of viewing public art.

Determined to meet her driver, she pushed herself out of the secure area toward the stairs leading down. She still didn't trust escalators. *The Austin Downtown Cruiser Night* caught her eye, and she stopped again to take in the images of Austin forming the steampunk airship. She might have studied the piece all night and even gone to look for its counterpart, *The Austin Downtown Cruiser Day*, if the old man in the chauffeur's uniform had not sighed as loudly as he had.

The old man was taller than Isabella, but most people were. Under a thick gray mustache, pale cherry lips grinned at her like a proud grandfather. He stood with his hands behind his back, relaxed in his plumpness. As she approached, he took off his cap, revealing a full head of thick, curly gray hair.

"Good evening, Ms. Iandanza. Welcome to Austin," he spoke with the confidence of his age.

"Isabella. My mother was Ms. Iandanza. Good to meet you." Isabella returned the man's smile and shook his hand with the force of kindness.

"I'm Mike, most of the staff call me Ol' Mike, to distinguish me from Young Mike. Mr. De La Rosa sent me to pick you up. Luggage?" Mike asked and reached for Isabella's carry-on.

"This is it. I got it," Isabella said and followed Mike to the waiting town car parked where cars weren't supposed to be parked. Mike opened the back door for her.

"Gosh!" exclaimed Isabella with wide eyes. "I haven't been treated so well in ages. I can tell we're going to be friends."

Mike smiled at her, "If you're going to do a job, do it well, I always say. May I put your bag in the trunk?"

"Sure," said Isabella and sat in the back seat of the car, leaning back and stretching her legs.

"Straight to the house?" asked Ol' Mike as he started the car.

"Do we have to?" Isabella asked. "Don't think I start working right away. Would love to see the city."

"Mr. De La Rosa didn't say get you there at any particular time, so I'm game for a tour if you are."

With only the slightest of movement, Isabella dove over the seat to sit next to Ol' Mike as he pulled away from the terminal. "This is sure swell of you, Ol' Mike. I can already tell we're going to be friends. What are you going to show me first?"

"Fasten your seat belt, and we'll start downtown." Ol' Mike did not cringe, jump, or otherwise act surprised at Isabella's sudden position in the front seat. "I know you vamps like to see where all the life is."

*****

Thursday night, Kitten reclined on a stack of silk pillows draped in a silken red sheet with gold brocade. Eddie lounged at her feet, confident in his nudity and exhausted from a full day of workouts. His beautiful body glistened under the hot lights, but Kitten's eyes remained on Harry. She tried to look at Eddie, but when she did, Harry would move or speak, drawing her attention back to him.

"So, he's gone." Harry didn't ask. They both knew the answer.

"He's pleased with his new client. He'll be gone for some time."

An almost silent growl grumbled from Eddie's throat, and he shook his head, opening his eyes.

Kitten reached over and tickled his left foot. "Someone's in need of a nap."

Eddie lightly lifted his foot. He would have laughed if sleep didn't mix his thoughts. "Coach is working us hard, and I had to go to class today. My art teacher said I would fail if I didn't start showing up. I don't get it. We're not even at midterm yet." He reached over to the goblet of wine Harry had given him. "This is good wine, Harry, but it's putting me to sleep."

Harry continued painting as though the conversation didn't concern him.

"It's all right, Eddie." Kitten continued to massage his toes. "Mars is worn out from his encounter with Venus. Sleeping is your perfect pose right now."

Eddie's mild laughter rippled through his body. "Perfect. I'm sleeping. Wake me when we're done." And he tumbled into the deep, innocent sleep of the man with a conscience of gold.

Kitten watched Eddie as multiple layers of sleep danced over his face. "You spiked his wine."

"Just a little." Harry continued to paint. "His conversation does not inspire me."

"Mine does?" Kitten imagined herself once again in the sculpture of *The Lovers*.

"You're very stimulating, but you know that." Harry still did not look directly at Kitten.

She raised her arm behind her head, closing her eyes, relaxing in his platitudes. The silk sheet slid along her chest. Had she planned it, she would have revealed an entire breast for him, but it clung to her sweat, stopping short of full exposure.

She opened her eyes to the feel of his icy finger running along the side of her face, down her neck, and along her exposed chest. Her heart pounded in her ears as tingles of excitement and dread filled her. She stared into eyes of unending darkness. Their faces had never been so close. She wanted to kiss him, but she couldn't.

"There is no petite mort with me." Harry placed his lips on her forehead. "If we come together, I will kill."

"I know." Kitten breathed deeply, trying to quiet the drumming in her ears. She closed her eyes, wanting to kiss him but afraid to. "But I don't know why."

"Instinct," he whispered, placing his hands on either side of her face. "Or perhaps we're together already." He moved closer to her, their lips separated by only air. Tremors slid down her back as his cold grip surrounded her. She opened her eyes when she recognized the heat beating through her.

Harry knelt beside Eddie. He placed his right hand on Eddie's forehead and his left hand on his chest. The image of the two blurred. Eddie gasped, and when Harry raised himself back to his knees, blood dripped from his mouth. He lay down and closed his eyes. Kitten stopped breathing.

A warm hand grabbed her ankle and slowly slid its way up her leg. Eddie moved in slow motion as he followed her curves, allowing his lips to feather over her skin. He pushed away the red silk, rubbing his hands along Kitten's body. She lay frozen until he moved his face in front of hers. The face, the body, the breath, the taste was Eddie, but the eyes and touch were Harry. She leaned forward, pressing her lips to his. They moved together, they connected, they loved. His powered thrusts beguiled her and coaxed her to overcome all obstacles. She abandoned everything for the release shared by *The Lovers*. She and Harry became *The Lovers* but something more than a statue.

The vision of *The Lovers* faded as she gripped the sides of her head. Pain scoured out the fire of the passion. She felt nothing but pain. Her head wanted to burst until cold arms encased her in ice, and spidery fingers cooled her forehead. Harry held a cup in front of her. "Drink." She recognized the warm, herbal toddy he had made for her before. She leaned back in his arms, allowing sleep to ease her body as the pain abated and her heart slowed to normal.

"Sleep," he said and turned her head toward him. "Don't think of anything. See nothing."

The moment before sleep cradled her in forgetfulness, she saw what he did not want her to see: Eddie, motionless and drained at her feet. A trickle of blood running down his throat. She knew he was dead.

*****

Kitten mixed reds, pinks, and a delicate touch of black on the palette and lifted the brush, maneuvering it into that delicate balance of control and freedom necessary for the stroke. Mars lay bleeding on the floor. Venus, that is to say she, stared back at herself on an opulent canvas. She lifted her hand to touch the face before her, but it was Harry's hand. And then she woke.

She stretched and yawned, relishing the sunshine radiating in from the windows, feeling refreshed and comfortable in her own bed. Warm blankets and pillows hugged her as maddening passion mixed with terror and anticipation raced through her head. She closed her eyes as her skin reacted to his hands caressing her arms, her breast, her thighs. She smelled the blood pooling on the floor beneath Eddie. Her mouth watered for a taste. Her breath quickened almost stopping, "What did I do?" she whispered. The cat woke and jumped from the bed at the annoying question so early in the morning.

In stillness, she waited for answers, for the consciousness of shame, regret, and disgust, but none of these feelings came. Only the thrill of awakened passion made her heart beat. Sunshine dancing along the gentle ripples of water answered her. The aroma of hot bread and bacon filled her senses, making her stomach grumble. She rose, covering herself with her reliable and comfortable white robe, and left the safe enclosure of her bedroom. Her living room was as it should be. Outside the French doors, the river flowed. People rowed their kayaks and laughed. Trees billowed in breezes unseen, and a note sat on a plate on her table. "Eat" sprawled across the note card in Harry's distinctive hand. A lush breakfast, still hot, spread across her table. Hunger took over the search for guilt or shame. She ate. Vitality filled her core. The sun filled her with the joy of passion's embrace. Eddie slid from memory.

Whether it was the breakfast, the deep sleep, the wild night, or some deep-seated defense mechanism, massive amounts of energy ran across her limbs and into her fingertips. She dressed and cleaned the house. She paid bills. She did whatever she could to keep her mind and body occupied. Finally, she opened Stacy's manuscript and wrote.

4

Red Riding Hood

The solace of prayer floats above the cacophony of youth living, dancing, experiencing only that which young can experience. The city rejoices as the harmony of life flowing like the river that runs through its heart. The tower burns orange and victory lifts the spirits. In this hub of life, death walks between rivulets and torrents. No one notices the single soul, flowing alone against the tide.

Eidolons gather in the mist.
Phantoms lurk in the corner of the mind.
Apparitions wander between this world and theirs.
All Hallows Eve rests before us—a day just like any other.
Don't fall victim to illusions or let the allusions guide your sight.
Hold your lover close if you fear the new day.
Let your lover go if love is too dear.
I'm Mary Midnight. You're listening to fragments of what is—online and in your mind.
We meet in purlieu where night and shadows mingle.
Walk with me if you dare.
Dance with me and live.
Does Sleep tickle your mind, or is that Death calling your name?

Dawn long ago crested. Cesar tried to sleep but couldn't. By eleven o'clock, he gave up. The guardhouse where he lived was quiet. His security guards patrolled the large Mugello compound without making a sound and often out of sight. They were his chosen security personnel, but their presence could not shake the unease troubling him. He walked to the control room where Brian and Young Mike sat monitoring the electronic security system. Although surprised to see him, they didn't react as Cesar scanned the wall of monitors surveying the estate. They didn't see him often, but when he did show himself during the day, he never spoke but to give orders, unless someone was doing what he shouldn't be doing. Having witnessed Cesar's wrath on more than one occasion, they made sure they always followed instructions. They clicked through multiple camera views, monitored on/off switches at various checkpoints, and watched the perimeter guards patrol their areas. Everyone and everything was in place. The Mugello compound remained the most secure facility in the city, if not the state.

Satisfied with the electronic side of security, Cesar took the underground corridor to the kennels set back in the trees near the river. Like everything Anthony did, the underground corridors were clean and well maintained. Most, like this one, contained benches and shelves holding sleeping bags and weapons. It made Cesar relax knowing the underground corridors existed, but the nagging feeling that something was wrong refused to leave him. He decided to place guards in the corridors.

The smell from the kennels hit him before he opened the doors. While always pungent, he didn't find the mix of canine and bleach distasteful. Since David and his wife, Jenny, arrived, the kennels had become an immaculate, picture-perfect example of what a kennel should be. The whiteness of the walls and floors sparkled in the sunshine beaming through the trees and the windows near the ceiling. Even the dogs seemed to fold their bedding and put their toys away. Cesar approved of the neatness and efficiency with which David cared for the dogs. He even liked the framed black-and-white photographs of the dogs that

Jenny took and placed on the walls. The couple lived above the kennels, and while Cesar had not been inside their private space, he imagined it similarly clean and organized.

The open windows allowed fresh air to drift into the kennels, mixing the scents of the river, live oaks, and moss with the canine and bleach. The kennels were now home to Jenny and David. Jenny sat on the floor laughing and playing with a new litter of puppies. Their dam sat approvingly next to her. Jenny's white dress, white skin, and white hair blended into the walls and floor, making the puppies' colors stand out. Like Cesar, she wore dark glasses in the bright room.

"Are you out late or up early?" David asked, looking up from the tablet he was reading. He balanced his chair on its back two legs, but let the front two ease to the floor.

"Can't sleep."

Cesar watched Jenny playing with the puppies. He supposed she was pretty, a peculiar sort of pretty. If she wasn't his friend's wife …

"It's all right, Cesar," began Jenny. "They only bite a little." She held up the smallest of the puppies, its eyes only just opening to the sunshine of its first sunny day.

Cesar picked up the largest of the puppies. His dark face and ears made his tiny white teeth look fierce. "This one's going to at least look the part of the big, bad wolf." As if on cue, the puppy snapped at Cesar's fingers, nearly biting him.

"She's got the right temperament for it." David almost laughed. Jenny giggled without reservation. Anyone who didn't know David would think him indifferent or even rude with his stern expressions and lack of familiarity, but Cesar appreciated David for who and what he was. He was a strong and loyal ally. The only time he openly smiled was at Jenny and his dogs.

David turned off the tablet and set it on the table next to him. "You need me?"

When David and Jenny arrived from Galveston in the spring, Cesar didn't trust them, even though Harry spoke for them. Only when Cesar saw David in the full light of the moon did he appreciate David's fortitude and power. Anthony gave David the run of the kennels and discovered Jenny's flair with a camera. Apparently, she made a living as paparazzi and for-hire journalist, and now with Anthony's help, she created art. Cesar had to admit she took nice pictures.

Before David, the dogs were just watchdogs. They roamed the grounds at night, barking at every squirrel, possum, and passerby. Now, they took turns guarding the perimeter of the grounds, night and day, only barking at squirrels when allowed to play. When Cesar heard them barking now, he paid attention. They recognized the difference between the curious and a threat.

"I'd like to walk the perimeter."

"Okay." David stood and opened the door to the dog run where the day watchdogs played ball or slept in the spotted sunshine under trees until needed. "You coming like that?" David pointed his head toward the hooks near the door containing overcoats and hats.

Cesar covered himself.

"Ever think tan or brown might make you a little less conspicuous?" asked Jenny, smiling. "Or is it your intention to be a Matrix wannabe or the villain in a bad vampire movie?"

"I'll take your information into consideration." Cesar put on the hat, catching a glimpse of his reflection in one of the framed portraits. He shook his head.

David whistled, and the dogs ran to him, wagging tails and barking in anticipation. "Patrol," and the dogs formed a small pack and headed out the gate, spreading out in practiced perfection to cover the greatest ground possible. The largest dog remained close to David, watching the others.

They walked in silence until under the trees and near the river. David asked, "Hunters under your skin?"

"What do you know?"

"Mary warned us to keep an eye out when we left Galveston, and with you being so itchy, I figured they were finally making their move."

Cesar walked in silence in the shade of the trees. David and Jenny didn't talk to the others much, yet they were aware of everything happening in the city.

As the water lapped along the shoreline, David began telling Cesar what he knew about the events in Galveston the previous summer. "They weren't Hunters in Galveston, not in the traditional sense, but the government knows you exist. It's only natural to assume Hunters would come here. We didn't bring them. We're not eidolons dancing in the twilight, making spectacles of ourselves like some do. The way you've increased security, walking about in the day, even Harry and Anthony moving about more than usual says the Hunters are here."

"Everyone needs to know to keep their eyes open, but I don't want to start a panic. Anthony set up a good thing here. It's easy living for everybody." Cesar picked up a rock and tossed it across the water. It skipped six times before sinking. The dogs watched the rock but didn't stop their patterned patrol. "I can't find them, David. These guys are good. I should have found the sons of bitches by now. Why aren't they making a move?"

"Waiting has its advantages." David stopped walking and stared into a brush about twenty feet away. He bent over and whispered in the ear of the large dog at his side. It barked once, and the others stopped what they were doing and circled the brush.

"Watch." He signaled Cesar to stand quietly.

Cesar felt the sun's rays beating down on his neck through the leaves. He wanted to move but David's gaze remained firm. The brush shook as something moved inside it. Stillness followed but only for a moment, and then a rabbit dashed out of the brush with the speed of the wind. The dogs pounced, the largest grabbing the rabbit's neck. It looked to David. David nodded, the dog broke the rabbit's neck with a clean snap. The other dogs barked with delight. David signaled, and they devoured the creature.

"A good hunter knows how to wait for his prey to make a mistake. Give them something to pounce on and watch them."

*****

"Porn. Too Disney. Porn. Just, yuck. Porn. Too literal. Maybe." Stacy buzzed through the proposed cover art for a best-selling author at another publishing house who she intended to steal away and sign with Hearts and Minds. Even though the Romance Writers' Conference wasn't until summer, she was already planning his next book. An occasional tinge of pain shot across Kitten's forehead and to the back of her head, but so far it had yet to stick into a full headache. It felt good sitting still and listening to Stacy ramble about the ineptitudes of artists one minute and their uncanny ability to convey meaning the next.

"How about this one?" The artist posed Red Riding Hood clutching her basket under abundant cleavage while the big, bad wolf (one of Stacy's most recent, favorite models) leaned against an ancient dark oak, agonizing at the full moon gleaming between wispy clouds. He reached his muscular arm for Red. Long, hairy fingers with claw-like nails almost touched Red's breasts.

"Is it really another telling of 'Red Riding Hood?'"

"What isn't?" Stacy gasped. "Longing, lust, uncontrolled passions, contempt for authority. It's every story ever written."

"Red Riding Hood is a warning about rape."

"And being rescued by men, because only men can rescue women. Blah, blah, blah. You've said this before," interrupted Stacy. "Romance is about women taking control and screwing all the men along the way until she gets what she wants, literally and figuratively. The woodsman might rescue her, but she gets her own in the end."

"How about this one?" Kitten pulled the next cover from the pile created by the same artist. In this picture, Red's hand lifted a large revolver from under the checked cloth covering the basket.

"Perfect! Carol, we're going with this one." Stacy's voice filled the office.

Carol, sitting at the table next to Kitten, sighed. "I'll get right on it." She gathered the rest of the artwork, ignoring Stacy's rattling of instructions on how to get the contracts for the artist ready and directions for putting together a killer portfolio for the expected author.

Kitten laughed to herself and winked as Carol continued with. "I've got it. Yes. Aha. Right away."

"And you, where the hell were you all morning?" Stacy switched her tone from commanding to accusing. "You missed our regular meeting. Leigh said you had one of your headaches, but you don't look very headachy to me. In fact, I'd say you were feeling pretty good today."

Kitten pushed a folder across the table to Stacy. "First two chapters. Let me know if it's what you want. If not, now is the time to change editors."

Stacy squealed with excitement as she opened the folder to see the first two chapters of her novel neatly printed on white paper. "Oh my god! Kitten, you did it! I didn't expect to see anything for weeks."

"I've been poking at it for a few days, and early this morning I got on a roll. It might actually work. Go through it and give me your critique when you're done." Kitten walked out the door as Stacy settled into her chair and glued her eyes to the pages in front of her.

"You just scored big with me," said Carol, walking out of the office behind Kitten. "If I had to hear her go on about how long it was taking you to edit that—f'ing book, I was going to scream. Knew you'd come through." Carol patted Kitten's shoulder. "And turn your cell on. I called you four times this morning, trying to find out where you were. I can only come up with so many excuses before she figures out I'm covering for you."

"Yes, ma'am." Kitten laughed with Carol.

*****

The rich, earthy smell of espresso relaxed Kitten. She had written all morning, dressed and made it to work just as most of her colleagues were leaving for lunch. Now, everyone was back. Some conceded a fine Friday afternoon in Austin was meant to be enjoyed out of doors. The usual bits of conversations, phones ringing, scraps of music from different rooms, elevators dinging, and footsteps clicking in the hall all aided the espresso in creating a sense of calming familiarity. It was a good Friday afternoon. Any minute, Stacy would enter her office to tell her about all the changes she wanted to her book. The thought comforted Kitten with its surety and purposefulness. Kitten expected to feel rotten, disgusted, overwhelmed, decimated by the death of someone she knew and liked, yet none of those emotions troubled her in the light of the day, in her office, surrounded by her plants and colleagues. When she tried to focus on the events at Harry's house, all she recalled was the passion and the joy of being with Harry.

She jumped in her seat when her cell phone sang its invading tune, pulling Kitten out of her reverie.

"Hello, Kitten. It's Anthony." His voice was as rich as his eyes were dark. "I apologize for calling you at work, but Harry said you might be willing to help me out. Afraid I'm in a bit of a jam."

"Anthony." She hesitated only a moment before continuing. "I can't imagine how I can help you, but if I can, I will."

"Let me ask you the favor first. The symphony, of which I am a principal donor, has a benefit tomorrow night. Unfortunately, it's the Halloween children's concert, and my usual escort for these types of events is unavailable." He paused as though to clear his throat. "I'm comfortable going alone to these things, but I'm not very good with children. When I have a beautiful woman on my arm, parents keep their rug rats in control and away from the woman's pretty dress, thus away from me."

"You're assuming I'm good with kids."

"Not at all. You handled the crowds expertly at the gala the other night. No doubt you know how to turn the right phrase, shake a hand well, and take checks for charity."

Kitten bit the side of her cheek to not laugh as the smile in Anthony's voice beamed at her through the phone.

"I can promise the orchestra will play more than *Peter and the Wolf.* And the event benefits the Young People's Orchestra. It's all for art."

"All for art?" Kitten heard his words and heard him hiding something. Her curiosity won over her sense of warning. "I'll be glad to help you out, but I don't know if Harry will need ..."

Anthony interrupted, "He said he wouldn't need you this weekend. Something about finishing Mars."

She forgot to breathe for a moment. The image of Eddie lying naked and pale at her feet flashed into Kitten's mind.

Anthony's voice brought her back to the moment. "I stole a brief look early this morning. The painting is brilliant."

"Well, if Harry doesn't need me this weekend." She pushed the image of Eddie out of her mind and replaced it with thoughts of polite smiles and coquettish conversations and Anthony's beautiful eyes. "Of course, I'll help you out."

"Good. And there is a late dinner afterwards at my place. Some business associates are in town. The dinner is to finalize plans and sign contracts. We'll meet them at the concert before the show. Plan on staying the night. I have more than enough room. I'll send someone to pick you up at six so you can dress at the house and check on the dinner preparations. It'll be fun." Anthony ended the call.

"Son of a bitch." She said aloud, realizing Anthony had just hoodwinked her into a long night of hostess duties.

"Who's a son of a bitch? Not me, I hope." Stacy entered the office, waving the folder with the first two chapters of her novel and grinning wide enough to almost not fit through the door. "Actually, I don't care if you call me a son of a bitch. Call me what you want. You're brilliant! I love this. Everything about it. It's exactly right. I told you this project was for you."

"Sit. Tell me how you really feel." Kitten couldn't help but be sarcastic. When Stacy loved something, she loved it without question. It's one of the things Kitten admired in Stacy, her ability to focus her energy on a project she enjoyed and run with it. Kitten hadn't wanted to edit the book, but the project gave her focus when she needed focus most. Without focus, images of blood, Eddie, and lust filled her head.

"Get me one of those espressos first. Just a few tweaks, then you get out of here and come back with more on Monday. And you can't tell me you're not screwing your artist friend. No way you wrote this with Gary in your bed."

*****

Leonard leaned back to watch Stacy sway away from the table. He continued to pay attention to her, even though he didn't like women her age. Too pushy, too talkative, too independent, too old. The waitress arrived, a young Hispanic woman with deep brown eyes, a tight ass, and a bulging button-down blouse bringing another bottle of Champagne to the table.

"Shall I open for you?" the waitress asked with the sweetest of accents of a woman from the Valley between Texas and Mexico.

"Please," he replied, enjoying the pull of her breasts against the too-tight shirt.

The waitress placed the opened bottle in the ice bucket and walked away whispering "muy muy" under her breath.

Leonard laughed, hearing her and seeing her tug at her shirt.

"Old for you, isn't she?"

Leonard recognizing the voice of his old friend. He smiled. "Tomas, you made it." Leonard stood, embracing the young man with golden curls and a cherub face, to kiss each cheek. When done, Leonard motioned Tomas to sit next to him. "After the incident in Galveston, I wasn't sure you'd come to Austin."

"Seriously?" Tomas eased into the booth, sliding the dishes away from him so he could lean close to Leonard. "I thought you knew me better?"

Leonard toasted Tomas with his Champagne flute. "I like the new look. I knew you'd eventually tire of being the golden boy in the room."

Tomas sighed, staring at Leonard for a minute. "You know the Duchess wanted me flayed, but Harry put in a good word for me, though I can't figure out why. Anyway, as you can see, she shaved off a few years. Decided it was time I grew up. Going to follow the example of my mentor more closely now. It seems it will keep me alive longer."

"Good man. I always said you could charm your way through anything if you applied yourself. I see you kept the dimples."

Tomas laughed, allowing his heart-shaped lips to glow pink and his dimpled cheeks to blush. "They still work."

Leonard leaned forward to speak softly to Tomas. "Not the best timing, right now. I'm with a friend."

"I saw, way too old for you. Changing your moral outlook?" Tomas's sarcasm didn't escape Leonard's ears.

"Business," Leonard replied. "She has a friend I need to stay close to. When did you arrive? Have you found out anything yet?"

"Checked out those Hunters you talked about. They're watching the woman too. What is she, anyway?"

"I'll explain later. What did you find out about the Hunters?"

"Got close to one. He's got the touch. Would have made me if I hadn't moved away. Worked the dimples to joke around with some young business types."

"Interesting. Didn't think they were very bright. Check out the others when you can." A smile broke across Leonard's face as he noticed Stacy walking toward the table. "We shouldn't be seen together too often. Where are you staying?"

"I'm booked in here." Tomas stood to leave as Stacy returned to the table. "Harry wants to see me tonight. Call me tomorrow."

Leonard remained seated, "Darling, I want you to meet a young business associate who's just arrived from California. Tomas, this is my friend Stacy Ghoode. She owns one of the biggest publishing houses in the country."

"The *top* Romance publishing house," Stacy corrected him and held her hand out to shake Tomas's hand.

"Enchanté, madam." Tomas took her hand and bowed low to kiss her hand.

"The pleasure is all mine," Stacy replied, looking over Tomas from top to bottom.

"I hope we can meet again." Tomas gave Stacy a smile to melt her heart. He nodded to Leonard as he walked away. "I can see you have better company than me, Leonard."

"He's beautiful. Where did you dig him up? And do you think he'd like to be a cover model?" Stacy asked as she took her seat and moved close to Leonard.

"Known him since he was a kid in Paris. Lots of ambition. He may yet go far. Now," Leonard poured a glass of Champagne for Stacy, "you were telling me of your plans for your own book."

*****

The summer heat ebbed its way out as short autumn days took over the city of Austin. This morning she had picked black tights to wear with her favorite black flats that went so well with her favorite black pencil skirt and her favorite black turtleneck. She shed her purple vest and belt for comfort after work. Now, she looked at her reflection in the coy pond in front of Harry's house and wondered when she decided to go Goth. Her reflection seemed so different and yet it was her own, familiar face. The image faded as one of Haydn's Adagios floated out the open windows and door. A familiar man's voice spoke too fast but too soft for Kitten to hear distinct words. A woman's voice answered, annoyance braising her words.

Kitten stood for a moment outside the door, listening to the voices and wondering why she assumed Harry would be alone and why it annoyed her he wasn't. She turned to look at the street as a large dark car drove past the house. She watched as it slowed in front of Harry's house. For a moment, she imagined Cesar in the headlights, standing under a live oak tree across the street, but realized the man was taller, younger, and too dark-skinned. She turned her attention back to Harry's house and walked in. She needed to talk to Harry.

She walked toward the voices without making a sound and found Kevin Vasquez slumped in the oversized armchair with a glass of wine in his hand. With his other hand, he wiped sweat off his lengthening forehead with a bright red handkerchief.

"I still can't believe it. I mean, no offense Jermain, but he's of your generation. What does it say when he gets up and leaves without finishing his job? But what can we expect of the youth today, Winifred?

They're here one moment and flying off the next. The young have no appreciation for art! Poor Harry. What must this be doing to your schedule? And the painting! This is disastrous."

Kitten recognized Winifred Kane from her picture on the website for Laguna Gloria, listing her as artistic director. "I haven't heard Harry complaining. All it took was one phone call, and I had a replacement for him." Winifred's dyed brown hair fell where an expert stylist had cut it. Her gray jacket with a large red silk rose pinned to it lay folded across the back of the side chair where she stood, admiring Harry's newest model.

Kitten admired Jermain's ease as he stretched naked on the pillows and throws next to the old red divan. His beautiful body glistened in the heat of the lights and the humid Austin evening. He appeared a little taller than Eddie, and his rich almond skin shimmered, while Eddie's delicate, tanned skin glowed in the heat of the lights. Both men had large, well-formed muscles rippling and rolling in correct proportions for the professional soldier, Mars. "I told you, I only know Eddie from the gym. And I like art. I'm here, aren't I?"

"Youth!" exclaimed Kevin. "Wasted on—Ms. Carlisle! So wonderful to see you again. I missed you at the party the other day. Come, you must tell me all of Harry's deepest secrets. One knows how these artists are with their favorite models."

"I doubt Harry would want his secrets shared." Kitten perked the edges of her mouth to reveal the smile Mother taught her long ago when she needed to be polite but didn't want to be. Harry's attention remained on his canvas.

"You're not going to break my heart, are you?" Kevin took Kitten by the hand and led her to the front of the room to take in the scene of Jermain posing as Mars. "I promise the information will be just between us, my dear. You know, I'm writing a book all about our illustrious and secretive artist friend."

"Then she decidedly won't tell you anything, Kevin." Winifred rummaged through her oversized purse. "Besides, I'm sure it's time we were going. It wasn't necessary for us both to bring Jermain here. I'm sure Mr. Reign has a lot of work to do."

"Who's paying me for tonight? And you're giving me credit for this, right Dr. Kane?"

"Yes, Jermain. I've already put a mark in my grade book. And Mr. Reign will pay you. Come on, Kevin. We need to get going." Winifred turned to Kitten as she prepared to leave. "Don't let the bodybuilding fool you. He's got talent when he applies himself. One of my best pupils."

"Harry, surely you can spare a little time for us," begged Kevin one last time.

Harry stopped painting and looked up for the first time since Kitten arrived. "Afraid not, Kevin. I have a great deal to do. I want this done by the weekend."

"This weekend?" exclaimed Kevin. "Remarkable. Oh, can't I have just a wee peek?"

"No one sees the painting 'til it's done. But I assure you you'll be one of the first to see it when it's ready."

"Kevin, come." Winifred stood in the entrance to the hall leading out, rattling her key ring.

"I'm holding you to your word, Harry. Jermain, you make an excellent Mars." Kevin took Kitten's hands into his and kissed her fingers. "And my dear Miss Carlisle. You will, undoubtedly make a perfect Venus. Toodles, everyone." He trotted down the hall behind Winifred.

"Maybe it will be quiet now." Jermain sighed and shifted the weight on his arm. "Still OK, Harry?"

"Fine, Jermain. I should only need you for another hour or two. Would you like to take a break?"

Jermain stood and stretched his long body. "Perfect timing. I'll be back in a minute."

The natural grace and beauty of Harry's latest model impressed Kitten, even as a sharp pain rippled through her head as she recalled Eddie's physical beauty.

Harry took her hand and helped her to sit. Bending close to her ear, he whispered, "I'm sorry. I should have prepared you."

"I should feel something." Kitten looked into his fathomless eyes. Inside the dark inkinesss, her reflection looked back at her. "But I can't regret what happened. I know I should ..."

"Enough." He put his finger to her lips and returned to his easel as Jermain returned to the room.

"I'm good to go, Harry. Let's wrap this up."

"Yes. Do you mind if Ms. Carlisle remains? She's Venus to your Mars, but her part in the portrait is complete."

"Doesn't bother me." Jermain settled into position with the skill of a professional. "You sure I'm the right model for you? I mean, Eddie and I are about the same size, but my chest and abs are better formed. I'm a pro and he just did weights to run around a field all day. And I don't even have to remind you how white he was and how black I am."

"Jermain just won Classic Physique in San Antonio—no doubt on his way to greater titles."

"Congratulations. It's well deserved." Kitten's headache moved its way around her head, but she smiled at Jermain, appreciating his simple beauty.

"Thanks. My trainer says I need to bulk up if I'm moving to the Mr. Universe league."

"Not too much, I hope. I don't like men who are too big."

"All women say that, but I've seen them looking at the gym. The bigger the bulk, the bigger the smiles." Jermain remained still as he spoke, a trait Eddie had not mastered.

"I suppose it depends on which bulges the women are looking at." Kitten remained as straight-faced as Jermain, though the edges of his mouth curled into an almost imperceptible grin.

"I suppose it does."

"Headache, Kitten? You look tired." Harry continued to paint, but Kitten noticed his glance darting between her and Jermain.

"A bit of a headache coming on. I think I'll pour myself a glass of wine. Do either of you want one?"

Kitten opened the small refrigerator in the corner of the room and took out a bottle of her new favorite white wine from Italy. A glass stood ready for her on the table. The smooth, sweet, bubbled wine eased its way across her tongue and throat, sending a little tickle into her nose, but it did not relieve her headache.

"I'll make you a toddy when I'm done." Harry's eyes remained intent on his brushwork.

"Alcohol will ruin your figure," Jermain said. "Simple carbs are the worst. Neither passes these lips. How do you think I'm able to keep my waistline slim and stomach flat."

Kitten returned to the chair and closed her eyes, feeling a sudden fatigue as the events of the last twenty-four hours slammed into her. She drifted close to sleep as images or dreams flittered across her eyelids. Harry's eyes stared through her while Jermain's body pressed against hers. Her body shivered, and she woke to find Jermain lying where he should be and Harry at his easel.

"It can be a problem dealing with so many figures." Harry's voice remained calm and deep, but his eyes returned to moving from Jermain to Kitten to canvas. "Sometimes they merge into a new and unexpected image. You either need to accept the new person as the true one of your desire, or you must pull it apart, keeping each individual separate. Alas, we return to the problem of too many people in one place."

"I get it." Jermain pursed his lips as he considered his words. "Take this one you're doing now. You've got one model for Venus, but you've got two of us for Mars. How do you decide what to keep and what to take out?"

"There are many things to consider." Harry stood, studying his painting and Kitten. He moved to her and began to massage her neck. "You imagine I have only one model for Venus, but you see only a professional woman, tired from a long day at work, nursing a headache with wine. When she is Venus, she is both seductive and loving, but she must also be cunning. She wants Mars, she lusts for him, and she despises what he is. We equate Venus with love, romance, and joy, but she is also pain, despair, and danger. How can this woman be Venus?

I must see not only her true nature but recognize my expectations for what she is."

Harry walked over to Jermain and sat next to him on the floor. "Venus is all these things and still she understands what Mars is: loathing, hate, murder, honor, hope, life. No one can be all of these at once. I take the best and worst of you and Eddie and combine all the traits into one ideal. All images in the painting must work together."

"At the same time," began Kitten, "Harry paints himself. It's his version of Venus he sees when he looks at me, and it's also a version of himself. He does the same with Mars."

"This is wild." Jermain sat up and leaned against the old red divan. "This is why Dr. Kane told me I'd learn a lot posing for you. I've never given a lot of thought to the philosophical side of painting before. Gotta go back and rethink some of my work."

"Be true to yourself, and you can't go wrong." Harry walked over to Kitten and ran a cold finger down the side of her face. "What are we to be, Kitten? A great work of art, like Titian's poesie—classical and complex."

"Perhaps we'll become something altogether new." The pain in Kitten's head grew, causing her to close her eyes again. The heat of the lamps irritated her. Her lungs heaved, trying to take in more oxygen.

"Jermain, take another break. I think we'll finish tonight, but I need to make a toddy for my friend here and put her to bed."

"Sounds good to me. I have more questions for you, as long as you don't mind talking and working."

"I enjoy talking about art with a young artist. Kitten usually has interesting views, but she's not much for conversation tonight. Come, Kitten, you'll sleep here tonight."

*****

Black velvet drapes closed the smallish loft looking over the studio into a tidy guest room. A large bed overrun with pillows filled the room. A rocking chair and a small table with a dim lamp filled the remaining floor space. In every way she could imagine, the room wrapped her in warmth and comfort. She removed her clothes and slid between clean, fresh sheets. Without intending, she sank into the softness of the bed as though she might drown in the downy pillows. Total relaxation overwhelmed her. Her eyes closed without her willing them to until she felt Harry standing near.

"Drink it while it's warm. You'll feel better soon." Harry sat beside her, lifting her to lean against him as she drank. The drink's familiar warmth filled her with ease, and she sank into Harry's cold caresses.

"Sleep. You have a busy day tomorrow."

Harry's voice drifted in and out of her consciousness as the toddy took hold of her. She wanted to sleep, but she still needed answers. "Did you ask Anthony to make me his hostess at his dinner party?"

"Yes. He needs someone he can depend on. You like him, don't you? He likes you."

She thought how much her mother would like Anthony. Rich, good-looking, independent, and unattached. Until this moment, she had not realized she too valued those traits.

The heaviness in her body spread to her face. She murmured. "I suppose."

"Good. I want you to like him. Harry speech slowed and the volume of his voice lowered to a whisper. "You must be brave. Things are happening I can't explain right now."

Though sleep forced her eyes closed, Kitten asked, "Will you be at the concert?"

"Yes, but you won't see me."

Kitten's eyes fluttered as a long, heavy sigh drifted from her lips. She was going to a concert with the oh-so handsome Anthony—tomorrow night, but she also wanted to be with Harry, but she didn't want to kill again. Her head swam with questions until Harry asked the one question she dreaded.

"How long do you have?"

"Perhaps a year before it becomes too much to bear." Only Gary knew about the tumor growing in her head. Even as the toddy sent her deeper into oblivion, a part of her celebrated saying what she had refused to say to anyone. "And then, well, I thought I might go to Seattle or Portland. It's beautiful up there."

Cold lips kissed her forehead.

She did not remember him saying, "I won't let that happen."

*****

"You sure about this, rev?" CC asked. "We hardly know Leitz or the contact who got us the pass."

Yasushi could only grin. CC meant well, but he wasn't changing his mind about Mugello and the Carlisle woman.

"Anna is on our side, CC. I trust her. We know Mugello and Carlisle are involved somehow with the demons. We need to know how they're involved and if this meeting with the generals has anything to do with them." Yasushi took a deep breath, trying not to sound anxious about CC working the Mugello party.

He turned to James Earl who sat with his fingers typing away on his laptop. "Have you been able to find any more information about tonight, James Earl?"

"The generals flew in last night. They'll attend the charity concert before heading to Mugello's. Looks like it's been in the works for a while. The emails I've seen imply the meeting tonight is only a formality to sign contracts. Mugello's banks will take over funneling funds for covert projects. Diggers knew what he was talking about."

CC stared out the window, squinting more from thought than from the light. "Mugello's getting access to a whole lot of sensitive information."

Yasushi sat up and nodded his head. "Indeed. We need to know if the demons are using Mugello or if he's willingly working with them. It could turn out he's just nesting his own bank with government funds."

No one spoke as the possibilities of a government connection with the demons sank in. Yasushi voiced their fears.

"If Madeline is right about Mugello and the Carlisle woman, the demons are playing a whole new game, too big for us to deal with. With our primary target so close, we need to remain focused. We'll find out what we can tonight, regroup and decide our next move."

"We go making accusations without proof, we'll only make a lot of enemies." James Earl had a habit of adding the obvious to conversations.

CC visibly winced. "You don't have to remind me. I'd still have a badge if I'd taken the time to gather the evidence and not blabbed on and on about what I suspected. People like Mugello have important friends. This meeting tonight goes well for him, he'll have more."

Yasushi couldn't help but smile at CC. Like most people in the group, she rarely spoke about her connection to the demons or how she ended up with the group. Unlike the others, she had lost much of the bitterness and fear from her early misadventures with the demons. The redheaded woman with freckles and roses in her cheeks looked little like the hungry, nervous, and disheveled woman he had met five years before. Her purpose in life fueled her conviction for the truth in all things. Even the demon who she still feared, but no longer haunted her dreams, gave her strength. Yasushi wished he understood her better, but he appreciated her faith in him to lead them down the path to justice.

"Our hope is to find enough information to stop him from getting more power, if he's being used by the demons. I'm sure the woman's nothing more than arm candy for him," said Yasushi. "Now, let's concentrate on what we can do. James Earl, what kind of security will CC face entering the grounds?"

"Top of the line security in manpower and electronics." James Earl leaned back in his chair, lifting the edges of his mouth to CC. It was the closest thing to a smile he'd had for anyone in a long time. "No cell phones, no electronic trackers, no bugs will operate inside the house. You'll have to move outside to call if anything goes wrong."

CC returned his smile. "Nothing will go wrong. I've done this too many times. I'll pick up dirty plates, stay in the corners, and listen. They won't even notice me."

"You sure about this cover name, rev?" James Earl turned his eyes to his laptop. "You checked Anna's source?"

Yasushi was happy to see James Earl's growing affection for CC replace the fear and anger he had carried with him for so long.

"Very sure. Anna has worked with the planner, Jasmine LeBrere, before. Good woman, works hard. Had some family trouble a while back. Seems Anna helped her get extra work, so she owes Anna a favor or two. Got us the list of everybody working the dinner. The name you'll use is Lisa LeBrere, Jasmine's daughter and business partner. Lisa is overseeing a different party tonight and won't be there. Jasmine says most of the cleanup crew you'll arrive with are outsiders and won't know who Lisa LeBrere is."

"Sounds good to me." CC stood to leave but changed her mind. "What did you tell the others? Madeline would want to know I'm going to be there. There are no secrets, right?"

"Derek has family in town. He's with them tonight. Roger's taking Madeline to dinner, and Anna has business with her own church tonight. I'll tell them when they get back."

CC wrinkled her nose. "OK. Don't like going in without everyone being on the same page, but we can't let this opportunity slip past us."

"I'll be waiting for your call." James Earl handed her a cell phone. "Programmed the necessary numbers for you. Don't let me forget to wipe it clean when I pick you up."

"And I'll be waiting for you here. The others should be here by then." Yasushi stood and took her hands in his. Compared to his hands, everyone had small hands, but this afternoon CC's looked especially small and frail. "God bless and protect you." He felt a tear forming in his right eye and let it fall. It was hard not to care about his people.

"Amen," said James Earl.

Yasushi smiled, recognizing it as the first time he had ever heard James Earl pray.

*****

She might have enjoyed a lazy Saturday afternoon in the salon getting her hair and nails done, but at two o'clock Chef Gustav, the caterer for the dinner party, called. He needed the final number for the dinner party. It took a few calls to Anthony's cell and office, much to the annoyance of Markie, her hairstylist, before the guest list arrived in her email. The event planner, a woman Kitten had heard of but didn't know, was nowhere to be found even though the decorators had already arrived at the house. According to Chef, they, too, were in his way.

The guest list did little to improve her mood. She was hosting no intimate dinner party for a few business associates. Three of the eight guests, with their plus-ones, had fewer than three stars on their epaulets. Last on the list, without a plus-one, a lone lieutenant.

Kitten's mood brewed as red as the polish on her nails every time the phone rang. Chef Gustav called continually with questions about menu items, menu orders, and special plates. Decorators called with questions about seating charts, lighting options, and sundry items someone needed to deal with but she didn't want to deal with.

At four o'clock, Lisa LeBrere called apologizing for the confusion. She would oversee the preparations for the dinner as her mother, Jasmine LeBrere, had been called away on a family emergency. Lisa was on site now and had all under control until her mother arrived.

"If I'm still here, I'll be waiting for you at the front door. If not, please look for me in the entertainment space. I'm easy to spot these days; I'm limping around on crutches with an ugly cast on my leg."

Instead of Cesar picking her up, a smallish woman with long brown hair pulled into a ponytail arrived with a limo so shiny, Kitten had no problem checking her hair in her reflection.

"Isabella Iandanza, here to deliver you to Mr. Mugello's." The woman's contagious grin was all Kitten could see of Isabella.

"Thank you," said Kitten as Isabella took her bag to place in the trunk.

Isabella wore the same type of dark suit Cesar wore when driving, but a brilliant pink buttoned blouse, open from the collar to just above cleavage, framed a charming face half hidden behind large, pink framed wayfarer shades and equally hot pink wide-brimmed baseball cap. As she pulled away from the condo, Kitten watched as Isabella relaxed her shoulders and seemed to settle in for an enjoyable ride.

"I expected Cesar," Kitten said. "He hasn't trapped you into being my chaperone, has he?"

"Driving is sort of my thing," began Isabella. "An old boyfriend of mine taught me years ago. He was a bit of a crook, so knew how to handle a car in a crisis, if you get my meaning, Ms. Carlisle." Kitten could almost see Isabella wink behind her dark glasses in the rearview mirror.

"The best person to train a chauffeur," Kitten laughed. "But please call me Kitten. I hate to be formal."

"Kitty Carlisle! I knew I remembered the name from somewhere. Cool! Any relation to the actress?"

"Not likely. From your accent, you're not from around here."

"Chicago," Isabella sighed. "But business is business. So, I'm here. How about you? Been in Austin long?"

Kitten liked the banter with Isabella. She relaxed. All too soon, Isabella pulled through the guarded gate to Anthony Mugello's home.

*****

Isabella deposited Kitten in the grand entry of Anthony's house at five thirty. While Kitten had been in large houses overlooking Lady Bird Lake, none had guards working the gate or walking the fence with bulges beneath their jackets. Even Daddy relied on the latest electronic equipment, also evident at Anthony's house, to monitor his homes. She could only remember a few times in her life when he hired guards to be on the property. She didn't learn until much later in life those gun-wearing guards showed up following threats, real and perceived, made to kidnap her.

Chef Gustav waited for her in the grand entry with his white coat splattered with stains and panic eking out of his mouth. "Ms. Carlisle. I can't possibly proceed in these conditions. How can I create a meal you will always remember if I'm setting tables, only to have it moved around by people with no authority to do so?"

Jasmine LeBrere stood beside him. Her stout frame and khaki suit with bright red silk flower scarf screamed "woman in charge." Kitten was glad to see her, even if she was still miffed at her for being late.

"Very true, chef. I'm here now, and I'll take care of it. By the way, you are the Chef Gustav of Gustav's on the Bend, aren't you?" Kitten's grin spread from ear to ear.

"Yes. You've dined there?"

"Had the best Thanksgiving meal my family and I ever had there, two years ago. You must have some magical powers to prepare such excellent meals. How do you do it? Walk with me to the dining room, will you? Ms. LeBrere, I assume all is under control now."

Jasmine LeBrere smiled but said nothing.

Chef Gustav rambled about his training in Paris, New York, Chicago, Los Angeles, and his decision to settle in Austin. Jasmine LeBrere walked next to Kitten with the smile of a woman who knows when the boss isn't happy but is still willing to be impressed. Kitten listened attentively as they swooped into the dining room and found staff laying the tables and buffets, placing decorations while boxes of wines and liqueurs were unloaded and placed with care behind the bar. Within thirty minutes, Chef Gustav returned to commanding the kitchen, the waitstaff buffed silverware to perfect reflection, and barmen polished glasses and bottles till they glittered. A woman in white strode in from the open patio doors, where decorators continued to place flowers, pumpkins, ribbons, and candles. It was the same woman in white with long white hair and white skin she had seen at the gala.

Her dark shades covered her eyes, providing a mask linked to the black streak of hair. The lenses reflected the bright overhead lights with deep reds and burgundies. She laughed when she looked toward Kitten. "You must be Kitten? Poor dear, you look like you've been in battle. But you have things under control now. Come with me, we'll have a cup of tea in your room, and you can relax before getting dressed."

The woman in white led Kitten into a hall with coffered ceilings and decorative paintings. "I'm Jenny." She turned her head and removed her glasses as daylight ceased to penetrate the hall. "Anthony asked me to keep an eye out for you in case you needed any help. I would have been here sooner, but we've got a new litter of puppies, and try as I might, I just can't get enough of them. Of course, Cesar didn't bother to tell me he'd already picked you up. Here's your room."

"Thanks." Kitten followed Jenny into a room with dark paneling and green velvet curtains framing a wall of windows opening to a lush garden and vast green lawn. The room faced east, so Kitten admired the garden in deepening twilight. "Lovely."

"Aren't they just," replied Jenny. "I could spend all my time studying each rose and fern, getting just the right light to photograph each one. But between obligations at the gallery and Anthony, I hardly get a chance."

"You're the Jenny Bryte whose exhibit I saw at the gala. Loved your work, what I got to see. Afraid the rush around Harry made it hard to study like I wanted to. I want to get back out there to see the rest."

"Let me know when you want to go. Love showing my stuff off." Jenny might have blushed if she had any sort of color. "For now, you have a long night ahead of you. I had tea brought in. I take you for a green tea girl. Did I get it right?"

"Excellent. Mother always said a good cup of tea before the storm does more to brace the nerves than any whiskey, even if I do feel like taking a shot right now." They both laughed.

"Easily arranged. Nothing but the best for Anthony Mugello and his guests. But you look ragged. Sit, relax, have a sandwich. Thought you might want something before the concert."

"You're an angel." Kitten melted into an overstuffed chair as she ate a hot roast beef sandwich and Jenny poured tea. "If you're already here, why didn't Anthony ask you to take care of the dinner party?"

"Ick! Me? Please. The last thing he wants for a group like this is a freak at the head of the table."

Kitten felt the heat move to her face. She peeked into her teacup.

"Don't sweat it, Kitten. Albinos are rare enough, but a photographer albino is even rarer. I used to hide it, but I met David, my husband. Now, I flaunt it. I like being different. Keep people staring. It's good for them. Besides, it's not like a disease I'm going to give anybody."

Kitten laughed at herself for being embarrassed. "Yes, you may be too forward for a group of conservative military careerists."

"Besides, I'm only the kennel master's wife. Not at all appropriate for the most eligible bachelor in Austin."

"And I am appropriate?"

"You're one of the most eligible heiresses living in Austin. What says more about banking security than Anthony Mugello and Beau Parker's beloved stepdaughter?"

"Hmm." Kitten contemplated how well Harry and Anthony were playing her for this dinner party. "Mother and Daddy will hear about this. They are so ready for grandchildren. They will shit, wondering what I'm up to. Better plan the explanation now."

"Come on, relax, Kitten. Let them wonder. Besides, it's much more fun living with a bit of mystery surrounding you."

They both laughed and sipped their tea as Jenny helped Kitten get into her dress. The deep red satin fit as Kitten expected it to. Harry's attention to detail remained perfect. The tea length skirt was full, requiring a stiff petticoat to keep it in place, while the top hugged her waist in and pushed up her breasts to reveal an enticing amount of cleavage. The back draped to her waist, reminding them both of a hood. With a red beaded hairnet holding in her thick, dark locks, her red shoes, and her long red nails, Jenny declared Kitten ready to go to grandmother's house.

"Now," began Kitten, "tea is good, but a glass of wine will be a good way to start the evening, and it's a good excuse to check on the arrangements and make sure everything is under control."

"I'll walk you back to the dining room, but I need to get back to the kennel. Those puppies need feeding every couple of hours. Their mama is good but also gets testy if they're too demanding. Don't stray from the path or talk to strangers, Red." Jenny joked adjusting the back drape of

Kitten's dress as they entered the patio area. "And yes, you can come to the kennels later to see the puppies if business talk gets in the way."

"Thanks. I'll make sure no big, bad wolves spoil the evening for me. I only talk to wolves with good manners."

"And which kind of wolf am I?"

Kitten wasn't sure if Anthony had been on the patio when they arrived or if he only just entered. "You," she began, "are a shit wolf."

"Time for me to go. Enjoy your evening, you two. Anthony, I'll check back here once the puppies are back to sleep."

"Thanks, Jenny." Anthony turned to Kitten, smiling his most seductive smile. "You, my dear, are ravishing." He took her hand and kissed her palm.

"Not anywhere near good enough to make up for all the work you're making me do."

"I know. Will this make up for it, at least a little?" He produced a jewelry box with a necklace of blood opals and onyx. It matched her dress. Had Gary bought the necklace for her, she would have refused, knowing the price beyond his means. From Anthony, she expected nothing less.

"Lovely. Help me with it, but you're still on my shit list." Kitten smiled and turned, allowing Anthony to attach the necklace.

"I promise to be your slave if all goes well tonight." Anthony kissed her neck. She didn't move away.

*****

Isabella drove the car to the garage. Ol' Mike waited for her, sitting on a lawn chair in the shade of one of the live oak trees.

"Well?" he said as Isabella got out of the car.

"It's the snake's hips for sure." Isabella pulled out a handkerchief to wipe the door handle and frame. "You sure know how to keep 'em."

Ol' Mike grinned so hard, Isabella worried his face would fall off.

"Take care of 'em before they need help, and they'll take care of you," he said. "That's my philosophy. So, you like driving, do you?"

"For sure," Isabella lifted the hood of the car. "Look at that engine! Ol' Mike, I can see you take care of each part. I mean, there's not so much as a hair in here to clog the engine."

"I keep 'em clean to keep trouble away. Where'd a little girl like you learn about engines, anyway?"

"Chucky," Isabella said, allowing the memory to race across her face. "He was dreamy. He used to drive for Big Al and the boys until the day he forgot to fill the tank."

"I see. Got himself fired." Ol' Mike nodding his head.

"Got dead." Isabella pulled the hood down in time to see Cesar walking toward them. "Hi, Cesar. Picked up Kitten and deposited her at the front door as requested."

Cesar waved his hand for Isabella to come to him.

"Would it kill you to talk? Geez!" she muttered and rolled her eyes. "Later, Mike. Don't forget, you promised me another drive around town this week."

"You got it, Issy," Ol' Mike laughed as Isabella straightened her face before approaching Cesar. "She'll have him wrapped around her little finger in no time," he said to no one. Few people bothered to listen to Ol' Mike anymore.

Cesar stood with his hands in his pockets, but Isabella could see his foot tapping away.

"What's up, boss man?" She grinned and winked at Cesar.

"Expecting some hooey tonight. I want you on the Carlisle woman like glue."

"Nothing to sweat over. I'm no bunny, you know."

"See you're not." Cesar turned to walk toward the house.

Isabella screwed her face and rushed to keep up with him. "Hey, level with me. What's up?"

"You know what you need to know." Cesar did not stop his long strides toward the house.

"You called me, you know. Would it hurt to show a little trust?" Isabella stopped, stomping her foot. She put her hands on her hips and turned to walk back to the garage when she saw Ol' Mike looking at her and laughing. She had to laugh too. "I'm getting under his skin," she said to herself.

*****

Cesar walked without seeing where he was going. The path, smooth with fresh gravel, carried him along the familiar route from garage to house, allowing him time and space to organize his thoughts. Plans within plans evolved from simple ideas, and he didn't know all the plans.

"Leaving soon?" Cesar looked up to see Harry standing before him. Cesar hadn't felt Harry's arrival. After all these years together, he thought he'd be used to it, but it still bothered him.

"Yes."

Cesar said nothing more. Harry's surprise visits brought changes in plans, information, and revelations. Sometimes they brought danger.

"You expect trouble?" Harry turned so they could walk and talk.

"Yes. The Hunters have been watching long enough. It's time they gauge what they're up against. Something quick, something small just to test our strength. I'm giving them ample opportunity tonight. My people found cameras scattered around the entrance we'll use."

"You've engaged David. Is that wise?" Harry's voice remained level, revealing neither approval nor disapproval with Cesar's choice of weapons.

"He's the best tracker I know. These Hunters are smart enough to set up cameras. We found most of them, but there's always a chance we missed some. We'll try to stay out of sight, but the Hunters could force us into the open."

Harry remained silent and stopped as they crested a small hill separating the service buildings and the main house. It offered Harry and Cesar an overview of the grounds, the river, and the back side of the house and its impressive veranda overlooking the river. "I trust you to keep them safe, Cesar. They both mean a great deal to me and will one day to you."

"I won't let you down." Cesar pulled his shoulders back to look square into Harry's eyes. "We'll find these bastards and put an end to them. I give you my word."

The corners of Harry's mouth tweaked into a semblance of a smile. "Promises break as easily as necks, Cesar." Harry gazed absently around him. Cesar turned to listen to the sounds of pots clanking in the kitchen, decorators hanging lanterns, and hushed conversations of everyone mingled with the boats gliding across the water and the breezes in the trees.

Cesar waited for Harry to tell him something important or dismiss him. He recognized the importance of dealing with the Hunters. There must be some reason for the impromptu meeting. He noticed Harry's gaze fixed on the patio where Anthony and Kitten leaned against the railing talking quietly. Anthony leaned too close to Kitten as he draped her neck with a necklace.

"Do you remember when we met?" asked Harry. "You scurried from shadow to shadow in that filthy little village still burning from the Loyalist attack. Your instincts guided you well in those days, but you didn't see me coming."

"I remember always being afraid. When you pulled me out of that hole, I thought you were going to kill me."

"I almost did. You stank, you screamed like a banshee, and you scratched like a mountain lion. But when you spoke such lovely Spanish, I knew there was something about you. The monks taught you well. If they hadn't, I would have bled you dry. Now look at you. You've done well. You've learned all I have to teach you in this short time."

"I have a lot left to learn." Cesar found his attention turning back to Anthony and Kitten on the patio.

"Don't forget how well you survived with only your instincts. We'll speak after the dinner party." Harry left.

In all the years Cesar had known Harry, it still surprised him how Harry moved with such stealth, and he wondered if he would ever learn to move with equal stealth. Even Anthony could do it when he tried. Cesar turned his attention again toward the patio. Anthony's face remained close to Kitten's neck, a scene Cesar had witnessed countless times, but tonight Anthony acted with an affection Cesar hadn't seen before.

*****

David leaned against a tree, away from the constant stream of people walking back and forth along the street between the park, the Long Center, and the restaurants and bars. The Hunter had been easy to spot. He sat in a white rental car, texting, emailing, surfing the web, and sundry other fidgets to avoid the tedium of watching. Before the sun set, David got a good look at the man. Hispanic, clean-cut black hair, square shoulders with a peculiar eye. He didn't seem very tall, and his mannerisms screamed ex-military. David guessed the marines by his neatness and squareness.

Someone's pet Chihuahua walked up to David. The dog was lost and needed help. He approached with ears and tail down, nudged David's ankle and sat waiting with his tail brushing back and forth behind him.

"Who are you?" David picked up the Chihuahua. He scratched the little dog's ears. The dog's ears went up, and he rubbed his face against David's hand.

"Yes," said David. "I'll help you find your home, but you'll have to wait 'til I'm done here."

David was about to put the Chihuahua in his jacket pocket, but he set it on the ground instead. "How about you do a little favor for me?"

The little dog sat wagging his tail, kicking up dust around him.

The Hunter got out of his car to stretch his legs. He twisted and stretched and walked around the car.

"You see that man? Go over there and tell him who the boss is. Make sure you mark his car."

The little dog ran across the lawn and stood in front of Torres. Torres laughed as the little dog ran up to him, barking. He tried to bend down to pet the dog, but the dog barked with a fierceness he hadn't expected.

"Stupid dog."

David heard the Hunter and laughed. The Hunter tried again to pet the dog, but the dog darted away from him toward the street. A stream of cars, released from the stoplight, headed for the Hunter and the Chihuahua.

The Hunter called out, "Get back here!"

The dog ran around the car, stopped by one of the rear tires, lifting its hind leg and marking the car.

The Hunter yelled. "You little shit!"

David held back a growl forming in the back of his throat but relaxed as the dog ran away from the Hunter.

The Chihuahua dashed through the bushes to David's feet, his tail wagging as fast as he was panting. His ears perked up, and he danced back and forth in front of David until David picked him up.

David laughed. "You did good kid." The little dog licked David's fingers and face. "Come on. I heard someone calling for Plata on the other side of the park. Is that you?"

The dog yelped.

"Then let's go. Car's marked now. I can find it whenever I want. But we have to hurry. I've got work to do."

Plata barked again as David ran through the park faster than Plata had ever dreamed of running.

*****

"Seriously, is there anyone you like?" Isabella rolled her eyes and shook her head at Cesar.

"What?" Cesar's lips pursed together as he tried to keep his voice low and steady. "All I said was you shouldn't sit around gossiping with the help."

"The help? Gads! Cesar, what century are you in? Wake up and smell the twenty-first. We're practically the same age, but I'd swear you were like ancient or something. And I do not gossip. Ol' Mike was just telling me the hot spots I'd probably like to visit. He's friendly like. Wants to help the new girl get her feet on the ground. Which is a hell of a lot more than you've done."

"Mike is a chauffeur, an employee—"

"Right, chauffeur. And he's NOT driving any cars because? Oh, yeah, he's seventy-seven years old and lives rent-free above the garage. For a handsome salary, he wipes down the cars and sees they're parked in the right spot every morning. Technically, yes 'the help' but it looks to me he's a bit more than help. Just like you're ain't exactly the help." Isabella grinned, watching Cesar squirm as she argued with him. Few argued with Cesar more than once. "Apparently, Anthony thinks he's important enough to keep around, so why not talk to him?"

Cesar squished his lips together. "I'm not going to argue with you, Isabella. We have different ideas. Forget I said anything."

Cesar turned to walk away, but Isabella stepped in front of him. She smiled and batted her eyelashes. She took his tie in her hand and swirled it around her fingers. "Come on, Cesar. Let's be friends. We're going to be working together for a while. Why don't we have fun? Hummmmm?"

"What would you like to do?" He spoke each word carefully, enunciating as though he were afraid of showing emotion.

"Why don't you take me out? Maybe we can go to the dinner club Ol' Mike told me about. What do you say? We'll have a little fun, relax, let our hair loose. Get to know one another."

"Whatever you want. Just, please, let me go on with my work, and keep a close eye on the Carlisle woman tonight." Cesar did not look at Isabella as he spoke.

"There you go again." Isabella let go of Cesar's tie and put her hands on her hips. "Can't you be nice to anyone? When you're around her, it's like there's an iceberg right there in the room."

"I don't like being around dying people. They stink." Cesar's voice increased in volume but only enough for Isabella to notice. He kept his gaze across the lawn toward the river.

"Fiddlesticks!" Isabella stomped her foot demanding Cesar look at her. "Everybody's dying. There's something else. You don't see me plugging my nose around her, do you? You don't see Anthony or Harry doing that? No! You walk around her with your nose all scrunched like she's covered in dog poo. If I didn't know better," Isabella stopped talking, smiled, and crossed her arms. "Cesar, you're jealous."

"I'm what?"

"I so took you wrong. I thought you preferred girls, but—"

"I am not jealous. And I don't prefer girls. I like grown women." By now, Cesar was looking down into Isabella's face using his towering frame to loom over her, but she held her ground.

"It's ok, sweetie. I get it." Isabella patted his cheek with her hand. "So, you still taking me out?"

"Thursday. It's your night off. I'll show you how to get around town and follow the rules."

"Peachy," Isabella squeaked. It was one of those cute things men liked about her. "I'm putting my feet up till time to go. The Duchess had me running all kinds of errands last night. I'm beat."

Before Cesar could ask what the Duchess wanted, Isabella walked away. She had a long night ahead of her and wanted to talk to someone. Hopefully, Jenny was around. She had to talk to somebody about her upcoming date with Cesar.

*****

Anthony and Kitten moved among the donors, gathering checks, shaking hands, and hinting at a longtime love affair. Three photographers hired by the orchestra's fundraising committee continued to flash at the handsome, wealthy couple as they mingled through the crowd of Austin's elite and want-to-be elite. The right picture of the wealthy couple could earn a photographer extra cash on the gossip sites. Anthony ensured the hardest working and most sincere of the donors sat in his box when the orchestra played. The guest conductor shared a glass of Champagne with them after the performance. Cesar remained in sight of Anthony but always in the background.

At first, it bothered Kitten to be watched so closely by Isabella, but when she considered how much money she and Anthony took in, Isabella's presence gave her a sense of security. Kitten ignored her the rest of the night. When Anthony nodded, Cesar led them out a side door of the Long Center, away from the crowds.

Kitten breathed in the October air, filling her lungs with freshness after the stale air of the crowded rooms. She, Anthony, and Cesar waited near the door for the car. Isabella disappeared from Kitten's view. The light over the doorway buzzed but provided no light. Kitten looked at the night sky, searching for any stars that might outshine the city lights. Anthony massaged her neck. "Are you certain you can handle the dinner party?" he asked.

"Of course. Nothing like a moment of quiet before another two hours of smiling and begging."

"I need to get these people under contract tonight. They sign and we've got a strong foothold inside a powerful organization. If not, we work in the cold."

"I understand."

Anthony no longer appeared as the philanthropist playboy but as a man on a mission. All the smiles, all the flirting, all the pomp gathered people to him. He ruled without commanding. He gathered people to work together for one purpose. And Harry commanded Anthony. Kitten pondered the implications of their discreet hierarchy as they waited.

Kitten's thoughts were interrupted by the sound of tires screeching and the loud crash of metal hitting metal. A red Mercedes slammed into a shining gold Peugeot as it drove out of the parking lot's employee drive. The guest conductor stepped out of the car, yelling obscenities in French as a young man jumped out of the Mercedes. The young man pointed a gun at the conductor and began shooting. The conductor fell to the ground. The young man returned to the Mercedes and turned the car toward Kitten and Anthony. Isabella ran toward the Mercedes. Cesar stood in front of Anthony, who pulled Kitten close to him. Kitten saw Anthony's limo driving toward them from the street. It stopped in front of them, and a man who looked familiar—tall, long hair, moving with stealth—leapt from the front passenger door. Before she could place a name to the man, a hand pushed her forward into Anthony. Her beaded handbag snagged on her dress as something sharp scratched her arm. She reached to pull it toward her, when she saw a second man. He thrust a long knife toward her. She continued to pull on her handbag even as a trickle of blood ran down her arm.

Anthony wrapped his arms around her, preventing her from falling. Growling and wailing filled the air, silencing the sound of gunfire. The man who grabbed Kitten's purse flew as the man with the long hair and stealth-like build ran into him, pushing him away from Kitten and Anthony. He landed with a plop, fat and tissue skidding along concrete. The man with the long hair lifted the knife-wielding man and snapped his back in half. A death scream struggled to make itself heard but only dithered on the edge of sound. Kitten turned as Isabella pulled the other man out of the red Mercedes by the neck and lifted him, squeezing his neck until his feet stopped kicking and the sickly sucking sound stopped foaming from his mouth. Anthony guided Kitten into the back seat of the car. She felt her stomach churn until she turned to see Anthony following her with his eyes blazing in anger. Behind Anthony, she glimpsed the familiar form of Harry standing above them on the roof of the Long Center.

"You're hurt." Anthony's voice almost quivered as the door to the limo closed them in a cocoon of safety. "Let me see."

"It's only a scratch. I didn't even muss my dress." Kitten tried to smile, but her breath was erratic as her heart continued to race. She closed her eyes, willing her stomach to stop churning and her heart to return to its normal rhythm. Nothing she did stopped the shaking running through her body.

"I wouldn't expect you to be anything less than fine." Anthony's voice calmed, but the calmness belied the harsh look he directed out the window toward Cesar. "But let me look at your arm."

Anthony cradled her arm in his hands as he removed a handkerchief from his pocket and patted away the blood on her arm. Blood smeared the flesh along a less than three inch line between her elbow and wrist.

"Barely worth a mention." He smiled at Kitten and bent forward as though to kiss the wound. His tongue glided along the wound, sending a shiver through her arm and spine like feathers tickling her back. Images of Anthony moving his tongue along her neck and toward her lips flashed before her. The shaking of her body stopped as her breath paused.

With a sudden gush of breath, she smiled. "Barely anything at all. I suppose you knew something like this was going to happen tonight?"

Anthony tossed the bloodied handkerchief onto the floor and ran his hand along her smooth and scratchless arm. He raised his eyebrow, as if thinking of what to say.

She answered the question he saw in his eyes. "Cesar would never have had so many people there to guard you if you hadn't had suspicions."

"Another reason tonight is so important. Let me make excuses for you with my guests. You should go home and rest."

"Yes. Let me go sit in my room and knit something." Kitten rolled her eyes, but her heart still beat in panic. She took deep breaths to calm herself. She thought of going home, but an unexpected concern for Anthony overwhelmed her own needs.

Anthony's laugh filled the back of the limo with merriment. He kissed her hand, continuing to hold on to it. "You're marvelous, Kitten. You're going to make me pay for tonight for a long time, I'm sure, but it will all be worth it."

Kitten returned his laughter as the tension and fright of the attack left her. She allowed Anthony to continue holding her hand, and she leaned into him as the limo drove them to his house and the waiting dinner party.

*****

Cesar closed the passenger door and signaled the driver. Gunfire meant that police would arrive soon. His tech team had turned off the cameras in this part of the parking lot earlier in the day. He rehearsed his story for the police. He placed the bodies in the trunk of the Mercedes and told Isabella to get rid of the car. He positioned himself next to the guest conductor as consciousness stirred him to sit up. When the police arrived, Cesar provided them with the story of someone attempting to kill or kidnap the guest conductor. Luckily another car drove by. The potential kidnappers or killers ran away without hurting anyone.

As Cesar maintained the shocked yet expert witness persona, he looked into the shadows of the parking garage. Somewhere in those shadows, David stalked, searching for the scent of the Hunters.

Harry, however, remained an unforeseen factor. Eldests always did whatever they wanted. Harry wanted Anthony and Kitten protected from Hunters. He even told Cesar to send for Isabella to help guard Kitten. That he should make his presence known tonight remained unexpected, especially after their conversation before Cesar left for the concert. And then the anger in Anthony's eyes when he closed the door to the limo. Anthony didn't get angry when plans worked. So why tonight?

*****

Jenny entered the guest room from the open door leading to the garden behind the green velvet drapes to find Kitten sitting at the vanity, fixing her makeup. She glimpsed streaks on Kitten's cheeks, but Kitten moved quickly to replace the makeup that had run off. Jenny sprawled out on the bed, letting her long white hair cascade down the edge and pile along the floor. "I heard there was some excitement at the concert."

"Did Anthony send you to check on me?" Kitten turned and laughed despite herself at the sight of the pretty albino woman hanging her head off the side of the bed. Her long white hair shimmered against the green silk of the bedding.

"No. I saw Ol' Mike putting the car away. When I said hello, he scowled. Now, you don't know Ol' Mike, but he's the sweetest old man that ever was. Never has a bad word to say to anybody about anything. And then David didn't come home with you, so I figure Cesar's got him working. And that's not going to happen unless something's up." Jenny turned herself right side up crossing her legs underneath her white gypsy skirt. "So, tell."

"Not much to tell, really." Kitten rubbed her arm where the blade had scratched her. There was no mark. She turned back to the vanity mirror and put a tissue to her eye in case tears started again. She then put on more eye makeup.

Jenny jumped off the bed and moved behind Kitten, placing her hands on her shoulders. "Take your time."

"A couple of thugs tried to mug us, that's all. At least, they wanted to make it look that way."

"Oooohhhhh. Anthony won't like that. I bet he's in a huff."

"They did a shit job of it, but they're dead now." Kitten raised her head and put her hand on Jenny's hand. "Thanks, but I'm ok. Really. I should be upset, but look, I'm still standing. Besides, I signed up for tonight. Maybe when the night is over, I'll need someone to lean on."

Jenny bent over to pick up the beaded handbag lying on the floor. As Jenny tossed it on the bed, she noticed the intricate stains of blood dancing along the silk strap.

"Of course," Jenny grinned into the mirror, "but I don't think you'll be wanting my comfort. Too bad the bad guys spoiled the evening. It's hard to be pretty when there's so much ugliness around, and there's no pretty in death. All the poets like to make it sound pretty, but it never is."

"It never is."

Jenny tucked a lock of Kitten's hair in place with a pin. Silence filled the room. Kitten's shoulders relaxed, and Jenny asked, "Did you see my David there?"

"I saw him but couldn't place him without you next to him. I recognized his form. He was fine. What will he do for Cesar?"

The smile on Jenny's face returned. She bent down and kissed Kitten's cheek. "Whatever needs doing. There's a lot more to you than I thought at first glance. I like you. Seriously, I mentioned it earlier, but let's plan a girl's day out. How about Thursday? I'll show you my new exhibition on Fifth Street, a nice lunch, too many drinks. You know, the usual drill. Now, I've got to get back to the puppies. Did I tell you, one of them's an albino and a girl. What are the odds of that? Have fun tonight. And you look gorgeous. So stop fussing. You've cleared away the tears. Just smile and you'll do fine." Jenny left the way she entered.

Kitten left her room to find Anthony walking down the hall toward her room. "I heard the doorbell," she said, offering her hand to Anthony. "Did you find someone to make the number even at the table?"

"Of course." Anthony smiled his most charming smile. "Are you sure you're up to this?"

"I always do what I sign on to do."

Kitten and Anthony pulled their shoulders back and matched grins as the dinner guests entered the house.

*****

Cesar paced on the roof of the Long Center, waiting for the Hunters. The police and crowds had long left, quieting the area. He didn't believe the Hunters would come until the early hours of the morning, or even later in the day, to collect their recording equipment. Isabella had found their equipment when she scanned the parking lot in the afternoon. Smart to record and not be present, but that's why he brought David in. He would scent them out and find out where the Hunters gathered.

Isabella stood talking to a few docents and musicians smoking beneath the side door about all the excitement of the police earlier in the night. They waited for rides back to their homes or for friends and lovers in the orchestra to finish packing. Isabella mingled well. By morning, the docents would ensure everyone heard the details of the terrible attack on the guest conductor. Isabella only arrived from Chicago a week ago. Not much chance of the Hunters knowing her face. He might as well leave the waiting to her and David, but something about pacing the roof in the dark with a mild October breeze comforted him.

The bustle of life up and down the roads of downtown Austin overtaxed his senses, but the solitude of the roof let his mind focus on the job. Nothing about his early days had prepared him for the sights, sounds, and energy of modern city life. For a moment he allowed himself to remember the days of begging and thieving from the merchants in his village. He struggled to survive as someone's unwanted bastard roaming the streets. The village boys took every opportunity to beat him as their merchant fathers encouraged them, while the village wives chased him away from their doors with brooms, at the same time tossing the occasional old loaf of bread and greening cheeses for him to eat. Winters had been the worst, waking in the mornings under snow and ice, but he survived.

Brother Sebastian, the Hospitaler at the monastery, told him he was special. Did he know what Cesar would become? Perhaps he suspected, but he never said. Brother Sebastian convinced Father Abbot that Cesar should learn. In payment, Cesar worked for the monks, cleaning, digging, scrubbing, or whatever else the brothers needed. Cesar spent countless nights with Brother Sebastian in the gatehouse. Since Cesar naturally stayed awake at night, Brother Sebastian used the time to tutor him. He learned to read and write. He learned to speak beautiful Latin, Spanish, French, and German. He didn't understand why he wasn't allowed to speak his native Catalan in the monastery. Brother Sebastian told him that languages would save his life.

As manhood approached, Cesar planned to join the monks despite Brother Sebastian's reservations. "This life isn't for you, Cesar. Soon you will have to leave here. Better to go now. Besides, this bloody war will eventually make its way to our village. I hear in the cities, monasteries are being burned. Better to be elsewhere."

Cesar didn't listen. The strange urges and violent dreams were becoming worse. Despite Brother Sebastian's assurances that strange urges were natural, Cesar knew his were not. He wanted the solitude and strict lifestyle of a monk to control the urges. He didn't want to be the monster he feared he was becoming.

Father Abbot approved of Cesar taking orders, but the night before the ceremony, an explosion rocked the center of the village. Gunfire and sirens followed. Fire, smoke, screaming, and confusion filled the air in and around the monastery and village. Brother Sebastian pushed Cesar through a hidden side door of the confectionary to a tunnel leading outside the compound. When Cesar turned to help his old mentor, the door banged closed.

Three nights later, after all the soldiers had left and quiet smothered the remains of the town, Cesar wandered through the remains of the monastery. Bodies still littered the ground. The smell of rotting and burning flesh scorched his lungs. None of the brothers survived the attack. The Francos accused the village of hiding rebels. The village no longer existed. If anyone survived, they hid in the mountains and forest, more afraid of soldiers than dying of starvation and exposure. Cesar didn't die.

Cesar shook his head, bringing his thoughts back to the present. "The past is the only dead thing that smells sweet," he spoke the words to the poem aloud. He'd always liked that poem. He used it to guide him. One of Harry's first lessons: Learn from the past, but don't linger there. Always move forward.

The energy of the city no longer oppressed him. He soaked in the life flowing through the streets like a draught of good ale. Below him, the docents were long gone.

He signaled and Isabella leapt to the top of the building to stand beside him. "I leave this to you. Don't engage them. Just watch. Let David follow. We need information more than bodies."

"Yes, sir." Isabella smiled. She liked the hunt, but she followed orders. Her Eldest wanted her in this city, working with Cesar. And as Cesar was good-looking on top of being smart, she didn't mind working for him for now.

*****

Jasmine LeBrere's reputation for finesse in organization lived up to expectations. As guests arrived, servers appeared when needed with drinks the perfect size and food the perfect temperature. She remained in constant sight of Kitten allowing for them to keep the guest entertained while Anthony conducted business one-on-one.

Kitten noticed the even number of place settings and hoped someone would arrive to fill it. She felt Harry's presence but doubted he would show. As soon as Anthony nodded, she corralled the guests to the dining table. As if on cue, Cesar arrived smiling and making apologies for being late.

Kitten stared at him recalling the anger on his face as he pushed her and Anthony into the car when the gunshots rang out.

As he took his seat to her right, he placed his hand on hers. "I'm sorry I'm late. Some last-minute business, but it's all taken care of now. Nothing to worry about."

Kitten nodded and felt her shoulders relax. She didn't realize how tense she was. Cesar's smile and words provided more relief than she could have imagined. He had never spoken so many words to her.

"Cesar De La Rosa," Cesar's arm reached across the table to Lieutenant Diggers. "Nice to meet you."

Kitten's smile never waned. She sipped without drinking, ate without eating, and spoke with interest on subjects she cared nothing about. She watched Anthony doing the same at the other end of the dining table.

"You have a lovely house, ma'am." Lieutenant Digger's formality set him apart from the casually formal manners of his superior officers. It annoyed Kitten almost as much as Cesar's lack of contributing to the conversation.

"It's not my house, lieutenant. And please, call me Kitten. I'm neither an officer nor the queen."

"Yes, ma—Kitten. Please call me Diggers. Everybody here does."

"As you like. What is it you do for these generals?"

"Push papers, set appointments, arrange things. Basically, I'm an old-fashioned secretary with a uniform."

Kitten tried to like Diggers. He worked his handsome face and friendly smile expertly, dropping any suspicions anyone might have of his motives. However, he was too damn polite.

"Don't sound so humble, Diggers. Most secretaries I work with know more about the running of a company than their bosses. I bet it's the same with you." She pointed the stem of her wineglass toward the general leaning close to Anthony. "They may be over there working out business deals, but you're the one who'll make it work or not."

Diggers' smile straightened. His eyes narrowed. "Business?"

Kitten laughed. "Don't worry. I'm just window dressing. It's obvious there's business going on. I promise, you won't have to shoot me for stealing state secrets." She caught Cesar leaning forward in his seat as she laughed.

"I'll keep that in mind." Diggers forced a short burst of laughter.

"What are you two laughing at over there?" Anthony lifted his glass to Kitten.

"Just trading state secrets."

"Not something I ever worry about with Diggers on my team." The ranking general, who had been speaking with Anthony, interrupted. "He's number one in efficiency and discretion. A good man."

"Thank you, sir." Diggers toasted his superior officer with his water glass as his pasty cheeks reaffirmed the familiar smile.

Cesar leaned toward Diggers. "Hard to impress the brass most times. You must be doing something right. Most generals use colonels and captains as their aides."

"Hard work. That's all it takes. I come from a family of officers. I know what it takes to move ahead."

"You have an advantage," said Kitten. "You're working not only for yourself but for them."

"And God." Cesar surprised Kitten with the statement.

"My faith drives me to succeed." It was the first time since Kitten heard a conscientious tone from Diggers.

"Such faith provides many with what's needed to live well," said Cesar.

Kitten turned her stare at Cesar, willing him to change the subject.

"Exactly. Most people think they don't need faith to live well, and maybe they don't. But I recognize its worth in guiding my actions to a higher purpose than myself." Diggers' animated comments betrayed genuine belief.

Cesar sipped more wine before answering. "I was educated by a group of monks. They wanted everyone to succeed and believed faith and education were the two tools a man needed to do well in this life and the next. They didn't care who our parents were. As long as they had willing pupils, they taught."

"Jesuits provided the core of my education. With my father and mother in the army, I boarded at a school in upstate New York. Those were the best years of my life."

Cesar nodded his head. "They were good years with the monks. For a while I considered joining them, but it wasn't to be."

Kitten found herself unable to concentrate on the other conversations at the table. Cesar had never spoken more than a few words in front of her, but tonight she was learning much about him.

"I understand. The calling may be strong, but sometimes the world won't let us go. Is there a church in town you would recommend? I would like to take Mass in the morning."

"Go to St. Mary's, downtown. You'll like it, but check the schedule. They have masses in English, Spanish, and even one in Latin. Guess some folks just don't want to move ahead."

"I like to listen to the Latin mass. It's all I had in school."

"Yes, when you grow up with something, it's hard to let it go. But, I still prefer it in English."

Kitten stood, "Anthony, I think it's time we move to the patio for dessert and coffee."

"Excellent idea," Anthony's expression never changed, neither smiling nor frowning, interested and aloof. "It's a fine night to be out. Cesar, do you have the papers?"

"In the office, ready for signatures." Cesar stood. "If you'll excuse me, Kitten. It seems it's time for business."

"Perhaps I'll see you tomorrow—at St. Mary's?" Diggers asked.

"Oh, I don't go to church anymore. Outgrew it." Cesar left the room.

Kitten realized Cesar had learned something or done something clever. "Ignore him, Diggers. He's being contrary for the sake of being contrary."

The colonel sitting next to Cesar knocked her wineglass over. Kitten reached the spill first with her napkin, followed by Diggers.

"Please, ma'am. Let me take care of this." He set his napkin on top of hers and took her left hand in his. "I wouldn't want anything to get on your dress."

Jasmine and two servers took over under the apologies of the colonel and her husband.

Only Diggers remained at the table, finishing his water, as Kitten led the guests to the patio. Kitten turned to close the patio doors but found Isabella standing behind her.

"I got these," she said, closing the doors and remaining inside the dining room. For a moment, Kitten saw Isabella lifting the man with the gun by his neck, but the image passed as the doors closed and she heard her name mentioned.

*****

By Austin standards, the night was cool. Kitten continually mingled with the guests but always circled her way back to the fireplace and its burning logs. Leonard Bellini arrived as servers brought out the coffee. He surprised Kitten by making his way to her before speaking to anyone else.

"Ms. Carlisle, you look enchanting." He took her hand into both of his. "And may I add my thanks? You hosting tonight is invaluable. Anthony would be at a loss without your help." He continued to hold her hand.

"I can't imagine Anthony at a loss for anything."

A waiter appeared next to her. She took the opportunity to remove her hand from his. His hands were as cold and as slick as she imagined him to be. He took coffee and continued to stand with her.

"In business, I agree. Few can resist his persuasive tactics, but such a gathering as this needs a woman to finesse and convey sophistication. I only wish business hadn't kept me away from the dinner. I hear the chef is fantastic."

"He is." Kitten could find no reason not to like Leonard Bellini. He charmed his way through conversation as though he meant every word he said. Politeness formed his every move. In all appearances, he came across as a genuine man. He continued to impress Stacy and she continued to talk about him as though they might become an item. "A dessert tray is yet to come. I have every reason to suspect it will match the perfection of the dinner."

"I look forward to it." Before he could say anything else, Anthony called to him from across the patio. "Excuse me. Back to business."

✳✳✳✳✳

Kitten kicked her shoes off and slumped into the overstuffed chair on the patio.

"Well?" she asked as Anthony tossed his tie over his jacket on a hook by the door. "Get what you wanted?"

"Yes." He tapped on the screen on the wall near his jacket. Pink Floyd played over the speakers as lights dimmed. "Drink?"

"Of course." She stretched her body to peek into the dining room where the servers methodically picked up dishes. "Jasmine, will you bring out the tray, please?"

Jasmine appeared with a tray carrying two plates of sundry snacks and finger foods Kitten arranged for them before the party.

"Perfect." Anthony handed Kitten a bourbon and sat opposite her.

Kitten nibbled the food and sipped her bourbon, watching as Anthony leaned back in his chair and closed his eyes. Before the guests arrived, anger had oozed from his pores. He hid it well beneath pleasantries and business, but now they were alone, she could see it brewing within him.

Jasmine left the room as silently as she entered, closing the patio doors behind her.

"Are you all right?" Anthony sat up to look into Kitten's eyes.

"I'm fine. It shook me up more than I like to admit, but I'm okay. I may not walk alone in the dark for a while, but I'll survive. It didn't break me." Kitten meant to joke, but it didn't have the effect she expected.

"Good. I don't want you anywhere alone. I'll assign a driver for you."

"Anthony—"

"It's necessary." Harry interrupted Kitten before she could protest. "They went after you because they thought it would draw one of us out. They would have succeeded if we hadn't been ready."

"You didn't tell me you would be there." Anthony remained seated but stared at Harry.

"My movements don't concern you. Where's Cesar? I told him to come to me when he returned."

"He was working the dinner party," Kitten said. The anger over Anthony and Harry dictating her movements fanned the flames of tension growing inside her. She did not try to hide it from them. "He seemed concerned about Diggers. I'm going to bed. Please have your driver ready at nine o'clock. I won't bother you anymore."

She stood to leave, but Harry grabbed her arm. "I'm sorry about tonight."

"I'm not in the mood." Kitten entered the dining room to find her way blocked by a rolling tray stacked with flowers and spent candles.

"Sorry. I'll get this right out of your way." A redheaded woman with freckles rushed to shift chairs so she could move the tray.

"It's all right. Take your time," Kitten noticed the name tag on the woman, "Lisa LeBrere." The woman did not hurry, intent on listening to what Harry and Anthony said, and she did not have a cast on her leg nor did she have any physical characteristics of Jasmine LeBrere, Lisa's mother.

"You wanted me to ask her here tonight. How was I supposed to know they'd go after her?" Anthony controlled his anger but not the spike in the volume of his voice. "We both underestimated them."

"I'm too old for this," replied Harry.

Kitten had never heard Harry's voice sound so tired.

"Not again, Harry." Anthony's voice quieted. "Without you, the grand plan fails. We all fail."

"It's time for a change. You know it in your bones just like you knew it when you were young. As long as we can change, we live."

"But now?" Anthony pleaded.

"Soon."

Kitten's concentration broke as the sound of Jasmine's voice filled the room. "CC, get that thing out of here."

"Moving now." The red-haired woman smiled and pushed the cart out of Kitten's way.

Kitten meandered out of the room, watching the staff clean away all signs of the dinner. Cesar walked into her as she entered the hallway. "They're looking for you," she said.

"Assumed they would be. Thanks."

Before he could walk away from her, Kitten turned and reached for his arm. "Did you get what you wanted from Diggers?"

"Enough."

"Good. Before you meet with them, you should know that the red-headed woman gathering flowers isn't who she says she is."

Kitten continued to her room, having done enough work for one day.

*****

The numbers on the clock progressed from three zero seven to three zero eight followed by three zero nine. She shifted the pillows behind her head, again. The thick velvet drapes blocked all light from outside, so she got up from the bed and pushed them aside. The garden, lit by stars and a few security lights on the far edge of the house, glowed whites and blacks and grays in shapes both enveloping and bewildering.

Her fury over being attacked and finding out everyone except her knew the attack was coming continued to grow, despite the logical side of her reminding her that her fury was only keeping her awake and alone. Two large dogs walked one in front of the other along the edge of the lawn where the formal garden stopped. They kept their heads parallel to the ground and their ears pointed up. Jenny walked behind them, looking up at the stars and turning her head first one direction and then the other as though listening. The whiteness of her hair, skin, and dress almost glowed, reminding Kitten of Gothic paintings of ghostly maidens wandering the moors in search of their lovers.

Kitten allowed her mind to wander, attempting to pass the anger out of her. She heard Anthony knock several times on the bedroom door and finally called to her. She returned to the moment and answered, "Come in."

Almost at once, she regretted telling him to come in. The oversized T-shirt she liked to sleep in provided minimal coverage for her body, and it contained a number of immodest holes. As he walked into the darkened bedroom wearing only slacks and an unbuttoned shirt, Kitten felt an attraction for him she had not noticed before.

"Are you all right?" Anthony spoke softly, as though he expected her to be asleep.

"Will you please stop asking me that!" Kitten turned, pulling the curtains closed as loudly as she could, flooding the room with darkness. "Do you really expect me to become all weepy and faint in your arms?" As she spoke the words, she imagined what it would be like to fall into his muscular arms.

In the darkness, Anthony's laugh danced off the walls. A bedside lamp clicked on, and Kitten watched as Anthony moved away from the bedside table to stand in front of her. "No," he said. "I only asked because I heard you moving around. I thought you might need something. Besides, I'm supposed to be keeping an eye on you."

"I don't need a babysitter."

Anthony stood so close Kitten could feel coolness radiating from his body, which she found surprisingly warm.

"Is Harry still here?"

"He left. Business."

"When isn't it business?" Kitten attempted to move away from Anthony, but the movement only made him move closer to her.

"Harry is an important man. Great things are happening." Anthony moved one hand to Kitten's face. The other he placed on her shoulder.

Kitten found herself leaning into his body. "No doubt." She turned her head to find his head nudging into hers. "You can see I'm well and tell Harry you've done your job." Her breathing came fast and deep. She felt his left hand glide down her left arm and make its way up her torso. His touch was cool and warm, sensual and chaste.

He placed his mouth next to her ear as his hand stopped just beneath her breast. "Harry won't be back tonight."

"I can't let anyone else die." She closed her eyes and let herself relax into his body. She felt her own shadow slip away from her body.

"No one has to die." His hand began to fondle her left breast. "I'm not as old as Harry. My passions aren't bottled up."

From her mouth came her voice but not her voice. "Mi amerai?"

Anthony moved away from her. She turned to see him standing at the open bedroom door, staring at her.

"I'm sorry." He closed the door, leaving her alone in the dimly lit room.

Kitten lay on the bed, wrapping the covers tightly around her body, sinking into the warmth and comfort of the bed. Her head swam with shadows and light, fear and hope. Confusion settled in, even as her breathing returned to normal. She closed her eyes imagining what it would be like to have Anthony wrapped around her even as she considered why she felt so attracted to him.

When sleep finally overtook her, she walked familiar steps with unfamiliar shadows. As the images in her mind cleared, she saw Harry's studio, she saw the paintings, she saw Eddie bleeding on the floor, she saw Isabella strangling a man with one hand, she saw a large, white wolf stalking through the crowds on Sixth Street, the redheaded cleaner leaning on a signpost crying, and a black car speeding to her, and most confusing of all was the dream of kneeling before an altar with gold and sapphire sparkling in subtle lighting as a familiar man knelt and wept beside her. She should know who the man was. His distinctness stood out among men, but she had no name for him.

*****

From the moment CC arrived at the Mugello estate, she realized the plan was flawed. Jasmine LeBrere met the crew at the lot near the guardhouse where the crew checked in. She pressed her daughter's badge into CC's hand, but she looked nervous and her speech stumbled when clearing her crew with the security clerk. Then the man named De La Rosa checked all their bags and jackets before clearing them to drive to the house. He stared at CC before looking through her handbag. *Shit. He suspects. Or maybe not.* As he handed her purse back to her, he winked at her.

Once inside the house, things did not improve. Jasmine LeBrere referred to her as CC twice instead of Lisa. When the dinner party moved out of the dining room, Jasmine became busy with the coffee service, and CC had room to work. She planned to fill her cart, then wander to the next room that opened to the patio to eavesdrop on the dinner guests. However, when she arrived in the dining room, Diggers sat at the table. CC did her best not to notice him, but he glared at her. She hoped no one noticed and was glad when he left the room.

She took her time moving her cart to the patio doors, but when she reached them, she found the way blocked by a slim woman with a long brown ponytail who motioned CC to move away.

And then there was the chef. He insisted she clean in the kitchen. Whether he liked her looks or was suspicious of her, CC couldn't tell. The guests were leaving before Jasmine LeBrere reappeared in the kitchen. CC tried to talk to her, but Jasmine wouldn't look at her.

To top off a bad night, there was the Carlisle woman. CC had seen her at a distance in surveillance photos but never suspected her presence would precede her into a room. As soon as she found a good spot to listen in on the conversation on the patio, the Carlisle woman opened the door. CC knew her cover was blown.

The woman stood in front of her, smiling. For a moment CC thought the Carlisle woman was listening to the conversation on the patio when Jasmine LeBrere shouted her name, again.

And then, De La Rosa entered the dining room.

"You need to leave. Now, please." He didn't threaten, but CC felt his cold hand on her arm turn her away from the patio door.

"Is there a problem?" Jasmine's keen eye and entrance into the dining room diverted Cesar's attention.

"No problem. This woman is leaving the house." His smile gleamed in the bright lights of the room.

"Good. Then maybe I can get on with my work." Jasmine picked up a tray of dirty utensils and turned to head back to the kitchen. CC followed close to her.

"Ow!" shouted Jasmine as CC slammed into her. "You're trying to kill me, aren't you?"

The kitchen still buzzed with the sound of water flowing and splashing over pots and pans. A few of the cleanup crew turned to look at them as they entered.

Jasmine stopped and turned to CC. "I did my part. It's not my fault you got caught. Please let her know it wasn't my fault. I got you in. Maybe I slipped with the name, but it wasn't my fault. Please don't let her blame me." Jasmine handed CC the keys to the van. "Take it. I'll figure out how to get the rest of the crew home."

CC took the keys but couldn't move. "I don't understand—"

"Please? You know that bitch will ruin me. All my hard work, and she'll destroy it all if she thinks it's my fault you got caught." Jasmine rubbed her hands together and stifled tears.

"It was all my fault. I promise."

CC left the kitchen, her head spinning over a simple plan that went so wrong.

She counted her breaths in and out as she made her way across the service lot toward the parked van. Her heart was beating at a regular pace as the cool night air filled her lungs allowing her to think. De La Rosa hadn't threatened her. She'd be safe as long as she left without delay. She played the day's events over in her head to find out how either the Carlisle woman or De La Rosa knew who she was. And what did Anna do to make Jasmine LeBrere so frightened?

Because her mind was occupied, she didn't notice him until it was too late to change paths. He stood near the service lot, partially in the light of the house. The sound of his voice sent a wave of panic through her she hadn't felt in years. She froze, deciphering the sounds he made into words.

"You shouldn't have come. We agreed you'd stay away." His back faced her, and CC could make out the form of a woman standing too close to him.

"You don't want to make me angry, do you?" His voice, oozing passion and hate, slipped and glided through the air to the desperate, cowering woman.

CC almost missed the voice of a woman whispering to him. "You know I love you. It's the only reason I came tonight. I had to warn you." CC saw him bend over as a woman's arms wrapped around his neck.

"Show how much you love me."

"Not again, please." The woman's voice pleaded to resist but deepened in anticipation.

"You know you want to." He stopped talking as CC forced a foot toward the van. The man turned to face her.

The face she remembered from the photos and then the restaurant in Berlin stared back at her. CC's brain screamed at her to run, but she could not move. She'd never been so afraid. And then she saw the woman. The woman turned away from the light, but not before CC saw her face.

"Can I help you with something?" he asked. His gray eyes saw through her, but it was the kick she needed to move.

"Thanks. Heading home." She didn't turn to see if he heard her words or what he might do. She had to get away. He recognized her.

She didn't turn the headlights on until she turned the van around.

Her stomach turned flipped and flipped until she was ready to vomit. She turned the air conditioner to full force to blow in her face. Perhaps that's why she almost ran into a woman standing near the edge of the driveway. She was the whitest woman CC had ever seen, but it was the reflection of pink eyes that startled her stomach back into its correct place.

*****

James Earl handed Phillip a beer, but Phillip continued to pace the living room floor.

"It was weird," Phillip said. "I mean, it's like I wasn't there, but I was. One minute, Roger's all ... chill ... and the next he's running off just because Madeline sends him a text. He never used to be that way."

"We've never been this close before." James Earl picked up his phone again to check the time.

"You're hardly any better," Phillip grumbled. "What's so damned important you can't talk with a friend?"

"CC's in Mugello's house right now."

Phillip whistled. "When did this happen?"

"Earlier today," began Derek. "Rev got the call from Anna saying she could get someone in the house during this big meeting. Not sure the rev trusts Diggers to report everything."

"Told you. Anna's all right. She gets things done, she's ready to act. She's like Madeline, only sane."

"I guess." James Earl pulled out his laptop and started typing.

"What's so damned important you can't put that shit down and talk to a friend for a while."

"Sorry." James Earl closed his laptop. "Little side project. What the hell is that dog barking at?" He went to the door and opened it enough to look out. "Quiet!"

"Since when does the rev make plans and not include the whole group?" Phillip sprawled on the couch across from James Earl's chair.

"Since when does *Roger* make plans and not include the whole group?" asked James Earl returning to his chair.

"What plans?" Phillip sat up straight.

"The plan to record Mugello and his girlfriend vamping out by mugging them. You didn't know?"

The neighbor's dog continued to bark.

James Earl turned his head from the window to Phillip. "No. What happened? What went wrong?" He stood before Phillip could answer and slid the patio door open. "That damn dog! He never goes on like this. Ask Derek for the details. It was his cousins Roger hired to do the job. Quiet!" James Earl yelled in the yard's direction. He stood a moment longer in the doorway, listening. The dog stopped barking. He returned to his chair. "All I know for certain is I didn't get the cameras back. Something went wrong."

"Ha!" Phillip slapped his hands and pulled out his phone. "That's why I was stuck watching the place all day. Good thing I was too. I saw the mugging but didn't know it was us doing it. Good thing I had my phone with me."

"You got it?" James Earl picked his laptop. "Shoot it to me."

The neighbor's dog, as well as the rest of the neighborhood dogs, serenaded the night, sending more than James Earl to their doors.

James Earl leapt out of his chair. "Son of a bitch!" He stormed outside. Before he could yell, he felt his phone buzz in his pocket. He pulled it out, answering, "Babe, what's going on?"

An unfamiliar voice spoke. "They want her dead. She's seen too much. We'll do what we can for you and your redheaded friend, but hurry. David will contact you as soon as it's safe. Wait for him. Don't act without thought. Trust no one on your team."

"Wait," he said to the voice, but the call ended. The dogs stopped barking.

"What's up?" Phillip didn't look up from his phone.

"Nothing." James Earl locked the patio door. "Dogs stopped their yapping on their own."

"On its way." Phillip stood and put his phone away. "I told Morgan about it when I was with him. He's got a copy too. So, what do you want to do? Stay here 'til CC gets back and watch the fireworks when the rev and Madeline realize they've been working on separate plans, or what?"

James Earl walked from the patio door to the couch. He pulled his phone out, turned, walked back to the door, turned, and walked back to the couch. He continued doing this while staring at the phone's screen.

"Seriously?" Phillip finished his beer and headed to the front door. "That girl's got you whipped."

"Come on. She's working. She should have sent me a text before now."

Phillip walked out the front door. "Whatever."

James Earl's phone beeped. He read CC's message and ran out the door.

*****

CC stopped running as she turned onto Sixth Street. The noise and smoke of the crowd roared in her ears after the silence of the park where she had abandoned the van and the dimly lit streets of the residential area. Her lungs struggled to fill with air as her heart continued to thump against her chest. The bars were closing, but the college crowd continued to laugh and dance.

She felt safe in the crowd. A group of girls, just pretty enough to flirt their way into the bars, walked into her. The smell of alcohol, perfume, and vomit hit CC in the face as she bumped into them.

"Sorry," she said and moved into the center of the street to blend with the crowd flowing like a river along Sixth Street. The girls laughed at her and entered the river of flesh in the opposite direction.

CC pulled out her phone. Still nothing from Yasushi. She messaged James Earl this time. James Earl always answered texts. Once she figured out where she was and the direction the crowd was taking her, she sent the text.

"Pick up now. Trouble. Congress Street Bridge."

The heat of the crowd and the fear still coursing through her made sweat run down her face and neck. She saw the vampire everywhere and heard his slippery voice in her ear. How many times had she heard that voice while translating surveillance tapes when she was still a special agent? And his face. She would never forget his face. He still had that distant expression confirming there was nothing she could do to touch him.

It was the same in Berlin. She and her partner, Grimes, listened as the terrorist cell greeted their banker and his entourage. It was the break Grimes had been waiting for. With CC's help, they had tracked the meeting to a cheap, drug-filled brothel at the end of a row of darkened and mostly abandoned tenements. With the wires and cameras in place, they were ready to catch the mysterious banker in the act. They would bring down not only one of the most militant terrorist cells to date but the man who funded them.

CC listened to the voice of the banker for hours over phone calls and online meetings with the group. Tonight, they would have him. But it all went wrong. There was no plan to make arrests that night. It was a simple surveillance operation. The local police were skeptical about the meeting. Grimes's plan was to record the meeting, follow the banker, get names, and let the locals make the arrests.

Grimes spotted the anomaly first. While they heard the banker and his entourage enter the designated room, they had seen no cars driving along the road leading to the brothel. The brothel backed onto an abandoned warehouse. To enter from the back, the banker must have walked, which seemed unlikely.

The voice of the banker said, "What money?"

"You promised—"

"I never make promises I can't keep, and I never promise money to idiots who don't know they're being watched."

The screams started. CC lurched toward the door of the surveillance van, but Grimes pulled her back.

"Stay. Call it in." He leapt out of the back of the van and ran toward the sound of gunfire.

CC called in the code, but when she got out of the van and looked, she couldn't see Grimes. Flames poured from the windows as the popping and fizzing of an incendiary device flew past her head and onto the van. Flames engulfed the van within seconds.

The sound of sirens moving in her direction snapped her into action. She ran to the burning house. Hanging half out of the front door lay Grimes. Terror filled his face as he lay with his neck ripped open and flames covering his body. She bent over to pull him away from the burning building, but a small man or maybe a boy inside the house bent forward and pulled Grimes's body inside. Shadow covered his face, but CC saw clear blue eyes burning like the surrounding flames.

The mandatory psychiatric therapy helped. Talking about the incident with the doctor cleared her mind, but when she talked about the sounds of growling, tearing flesh, and the shouts of "monsters," the doctor told her she imagined the monsters to make her feel better about her feelings of helplessness. Her boss insisted she take a leave after the surveillance went wrong.

CC wouldn't change her story of the sounds she'd heard or the sight of the man in the doorway. The official report cited the terrorists arguing amongst themselves and setting off the incendiary device by accident or on purpose. No one survived that night, not the terrorists, not the hookers, not the customers, not her mentor. CC kept her job but pushed papers for six months. She might have kept her badge if she hadn't had dinner at that particular restaurant on that particular night. She sat with her mother, visiting for moral support, when she heard the banker's voice at a table behind her. She walked to the table to arrest him, but the army general with him stopped her. In the end, she lost her job. She might have lost her sanity and her life had Yasushi and Roger not found her.

She wished Yasushi or Roger, but especially James Earl, would come to her now. The crowd thinned out as it approached Congress and spilled onto the sidewalks. Cars drove along, spacing themselves for the many pedestrians. CC felt the vibrations of her phone.

"On my way," flashed on the screen.

"Thank you for being such a geek, James Earl," she whispered to herself.

Her safety relied on remaining in the crowd. She scanned the side streets, rooftops, and darkened corners, darting her eyes from one place to another, bumping into people around her. At one point, someone reached out from behind a bus stop, putting a hand on her shoulder. She shrieked despite herself.

"Got a dollar?" asked the man.

Three young men, buff from working out and brave from an abundance of beer, leapt to CC's defense. "Back off, tramp!" One of the young men yelled.

"Don't bother the lady," shouted another.

CC increased her pace. The tramp scuffled away from the young men, and the young men told the story the next day about the pretty redheaded woman they had rescued from certain peril.

Her heart beat at its regular pace as the crowd approached the lights of Cesar Chavez Street. CC leaned against the cool bricks of a retail shop. She needed to be seen easily by James Earl, but she didn't want to be seen by anyone else.

Her mind wandered over the events of the night: The vampire at Mugello's house, Why she hadn't recognized his voice on the surveillance tapes, The shadows outside the gates to the estate, and where was James Earl?

The guards at the gate had waved her through. She had relaxed, realizing she would be allowed to leave. But then she saw that figure across the street from the gate. It still sent chills through her. Barely discernible in the darkness, it stood alone, black against the blackness of night with hands slipped into pockets removing any distinguishing features. She would never be able to describe the prickly sensation she felt upon seeing the figure. Her heart told her to fear, but that feeling kept her calm. It was almost as if someone whispered comforts in her ear.

CC kept the Congress Street Bridge in her sight but meandered closer to the Radisson Hotel. The chase, the panic, the aloneness overcame her. Her tears flowed. She leaned against a signpost, keeping her face down. She didn't want James Earl to see her crying.

"Breathe in, two, three, four." She counted her breaths to calm her swelling emotions. "Breathe out, two, three, four." She stopped when she heard the honk of a familiar car horn. There were many car horns, along with music and laughter, on the street corner, but that horn she knew. *Roger.* She turned to see the black car moving slowly up Cesar Chavez toward her.

CC smiled and wiped the tears from her face. She stepped to the curb and waved as the crowd swelled to wait for the light to change. A pair of hands gripped her shoulders and pushed her into the street as the black car sped up. It hit her. She flew into the air. Her body hit the back of the car and rolled onto the street as it turned sharply and sped away from the scene. Her body rolled three times before stopping. A small blue car approaching from the other direction ran over her arm. She heard screams and yelling. She felt someone's hands on her head.

"Hang on, miss. I've called nine one one."

"Oh god! Oh god! I swear, I didn't see her."

"You'll be ok, just keep breathing."

"Don't try to move her."

"Did anyone get the plate ..."

The voices said more, but consciousness left CC.

* * * * *

The sacristy of the church offered comfort to those who sought it. Tonight, comfort didn't come to Yasushi. He sat in the pew, staring at the dark blue of the ceiling and wondered how long it took to complete. Once again, he pulled out his phone to check the time and for messages. CC might need him. One of the others might need him, but he couldn't tell anyone where he was. He wanted to be at the house, waiting for CC. Sending her to the Mugello house with so little warning bothered him, but the opportunity to infiltrate outweighed the risk. So, why did it bother him so much to be sitting in a church?

He felt the hairs on the back of his neck prick his skin and a chill ran through him. Harry's voice had never frightened him as it did tonight. "We had a deal" was all Harry said on the phone. Now, Yasushi sat in the church waiting for him instead of waiting at home for CC's call.

Yasushi settled onto the kneeler, clasping his hands so he could speak to Harry, who now knelt in the pew in front of him. "I intend to keep our deal," he said, keeping his voice as quiet as he could.

"Then why did you hire thugs to attack the woman?"

Yasushi lifted his head to look at Harry. "What? We didn't hire—"

Harry interrupted him. "Can you speak for everyone in your group? Who else would have done it if not someone in your group?"

Yasushi turned his eyes down as people entered the church for Matins. His mouth felt dry as thoughts raced through his head. "I can't believe any of my people would have done this. Is the woman all right?"

"It frightened her, but she's strong. We have little time left. There must be no mistakes." Harry sat leaning back to be close to Yasushi's face.

"It couldn't have been my people," Yasushi whispered. "We will not risk civilians. That's one rule I've always insisted on."

"And yet, your friend Diggers noticed the scratch on her arm from the attack had healed. How did he know about it?"

Yasushi closed his eyes. *It always comes back to Diggers.*

Harry turned to face Yasushi. "Someone set up cameras all around the parking lot. Someone wanted to see how Mugello and his people would respond to a threat. Who do you know who would do that?"

"Roger," Yasushi said without hesitation.

"Your Captain Morgan grows bold. Why?"

"I'll keep them under control, but you need to tell me everything. Why is Mugello meeting with the generals tonight?"

"Survival." Harry followed the directions of the priest and knelt again. He turned his head to look at Yasushi. "You know the army captured a young one. They know too much not to be monitored. Mugello has the resources to control their investigation. We need to stay invisible."

Yasushi listened to the methodical rhythm of the monks' voices. When he opened his eyes, he said, "We need to act soon. My people know too much to do nothing now. Bring me the killer I want, and we'll leave."

"Soon," said Harry. "I want him as much as you do. He risks everyone for his own gain."

Yasushi's head jerked up on hearing the venom in Harry's voice.

"There's one more thing," said Harry as Yasushi started to stand. "Are you prepared for your friends to know the whole truth?"

Yasushi blinked, but Harry was gone before he could answer.

*****

At nine o'clock, Isabella leaned against the town car parked under the shaded portico. She pushed her shades back up onto her nose. They didn't fit right, but the electric blue rims matched the electric blue of her new sneakers and the electric blue embroidered peace sign on her new jeans and the electric blue trim of her new wide-brimmed Explorer hat with an Austin bat painted on it. She caught her reflection in the car and pushed her long hair behind her ear and adjusted her hat. *A bit much? Naw!*

The Carlisle woman came out of the house, looking worn out behind her own wayfarer sunglasses. It might be a pleasant, sunny morning, but neither woman looked pleased about it.

Isabella smiled. "Ready if you are." She opened the back door and offered to take the overnight bag.

"Thanks, I'll keep it." Kitten said with a flat tone.

They drove in silence. Isabella monitored Kitten. Kitten sat without moving or sighing, too still. Something was bothering her.

When they arrived at the condo, Isabella turned around to ask, "You going to let me drive you to work tomorrow?" The answer was obvious, but a friendly smile cost nothing.

"No." Kitten said, opening the door. She stopped before exiting.

"Thanks for the ride. I appreciate it. Please tell Anthony I won't need you to drive me to work."

Isabella smiled and nodded. It took guts to stand up to Anthony Mugello. She admired Kitten for it, but it was clear the woman rejected the offer of a driver with trepidation. If she wasn't afraid, she'd be stupid. From what she had learned of Anthony and Harry, neither would concern themselves with a stupid woman, which brought her back to her first question. *Why is everyone so concerned with this woman?*

She drove the town car back to the house to get one of the sports cars. Ol' Mike gave her the pick of the bunch. She loved to drive, even on a sunny day, as long as the windows were tinted. She only had guard duty for a few hours this morning. Cesar had designated a good watch point: a large live oak tree near a park provided perfect cover and an excellent vantage point to watch Kitten's condo and Harry's house. The deep shade of the tree made being out in the day more bearable than chasing shadows around people's homes. After parking the car near enough to access if she needed to run, she settled into the branches, unnoticed to residents of the neighborhood, patrolmen, or Hunters. Just a few hours, and then she could get a good day's sleep, unless the Duchess called. She'd have to be back here tonight, but that was hours from now. For now, she enjoyed listening to the suburbs wake on a lazy Sunday morning.

*****

Frank sat at his desk in the office enjoying the quiet. Since the Feds took control of the murder of the bankers, his office contained the peaceful order he enjoyed. They were still investigating the other murders. Few except he and Renaldo and perhaps Hank connected them to the murder of the bankers. Today, they hoped to clear paperwork.

Frank set down the coroner's report on Sadie. "Sit down. You're wearing me out."

Renaldo stopped. "What?" He looked around him and laughed. "Sorry. Can't stand sitting for long. Never have. Drives Mama nuts too."

"You read the details?" Frank asked, holding the coroner's report. "Other than the rape and beaten face, little Sadie died just like the accountants and the others. Why go through all the trouble to let them bleed dry before moving their bodies?"

"Weird. Could be a cult thing."

"Can't see the same person killing our girl as killing the accountants. You get anything from your contacts in the Valley?"

Renaldo sat and pulled his phone out of his pocket. He searched through his notes. "Sort of, but it's a far stretch."

"At this point, I'd say a far stretch is our closest connection."

"A buddy of mine told me about an old crime outside Lackland Air Base some years back. It was before my time. An old brothel went up in flames one night. Killed just about everybody there, but a couple of customers got out of the house. They didn't get far. The bodies were found about a half mile away, faces beaten in, and their necks slashed wide. Coroner decided they were killed at the house since there was no blood anywhere near the bodies."

"Don't see how that helps us," began Frank. "But what do you see?"

"My contact said there was a cult operating on both sides of the border, killing for La Santa Muerte back then. Maybe the cult is active again."

Before Frank could answer, a deep voice boomed through the room. "Jarvis!"

"Hank?" Frank answered. "Thought you went home for the weekend. Houston not busy enough for you?" He grinned till he saw Hank's lips pursed and turning pale.

"Did you see the report from the Long Center last night?"

Renaldo lifted a file from his desk. "It's right here. We hadn't got to it yet."

Hank sank into a chair with a thud. "Read it."

Renaldo handed the folder to Frank who waved it back to Renaldo. "Tell me what you see."

Renaldo paced and read. "Someone went after the guest conductor. Gunshots, no one hurt. Everyone walked away." He handed the folder to Frank. "Cesar De La Rosa was the principal witness. You know him, owns the hot spot on Sixth Street. Nice guy."

Frank stared at both of them. "Shit."

Hank nodded his head. "De La Rosa works for Anthony Mugello. The accountants worked for Mugello, Sadie was last seen walking away from a party hosted by Mugello, and Mugello was at the Long Center last night."

"Fuck!" Fell out of Frank's mouth like his breath.

"You can say that again," said Hank. "I already called my boss. We'll need to tread carefully. Could be a big coincidence."

"Not likely," said Renaldo, stating what neither of the others wanted to and noticing that neither looked at him. "What are you two not telling me?" asked Renaldo.

5

❦

Judith With Holofernes

Tomas watched the river of life flow up and down Sixth Street. The smells of youth and life, love and lust ran like currents along his spine. The hunt, the chase, the prey, the bite, and life flowed tonight. He opened his eyes, listening, waiting for something to happen. The redheaded woman moved with care and purpose through the crowd. One moment her feet decided where to go, she'd falter, and he'd smell her fear. "Don't stop," he said, though no one heard him. High above the city, he digested the hunt. The wolf missed his mark, but so did the Hunter.

Screams, shrieks, sirens. Done. Or was it? Breath continued. Life flowed. He lost the will to hunt as a breeze caressed his brow like the loving hand of a cruel mistress, whose voice drifted from airwaves and earbuds. "Embrace the purpose," he said and left the scene.

The mists lift as Fall embraces.
Change is life while nature drifts to sleep.
From the sleep, death, to awaken, life.
And the seasons mimic our traverses.
You're listening to the voice of change.
I'm Mary Midnight online and in your mind.

Embrace what is for what it might become,
Or brace for what you never hoped to see.

James Earl squeezed CC's hand, placing it to his lips and kissing her fingers. The fingers of her right hand were black and blue beneath thick bandages with wires, bolts, and nuts sticking out. Her pale face turned blacker around her eyes with each hour. One thick red curl stuck out of the bandages wrapping her head.

The nurse standing on the other side of the bed smiled at James Earl. He used only his most practiced, comforting voice with patient families. "Don't let those bruises worry you. They're natural with head wounds. There's no change to her vitals. That's good."

James Earl heard little of what the nurse said. He closed red, dry eyes that refused to cry any more tears of rage or sorrow. He listened to his heart pounding in his chest and felt his blood coursing through his veins too fast.

He heard the nurse saying, "I'm sorry, my patient can't have—"

"Reverend?" James Earl cut off the nurse, recognizing Yasushi's large frame entering the room.

"May I?" Yasushi asked the nurse. "We're like family. And I'd like to pray for her."

The nurse, seeing the recognition in James Earl's face, nodded. "Not for long. She needs rest and quiet." He left the two men to pray.

Yasushi moved to stand next to James Earl and placed a hand on his shoulder.

James Earl shrugged it off. "Where the hell were you? She tried to call you."

"I'm sorry, James Earl. Something came up. I knew you would be watching out for her. I had no idea ..." Yasushi's voice trailed off. James Earl wouldn't look at him.

Yasushi closed his eyes and prayed. His face had paled upon entering the room, but the slow speech and the muffled sound of his prayer eased the worried lines around his eyes. He hadn't expected to see the face of the cheery, smart woman he had grown to love and respect so close to death.

"Doctors say she's holding her own." James Earl's mechanical speech hit Yasushi as soon as the words came out. "Had to lie and say I was her husband so I could stay with her. Don't call her family yet. She wouldn't want them involved until we know one way or another."

"Of course." Yasushi said no more but sat in a chair in the back of the room.

At last James Earl broke the silence. "She was frightened—of something. She didn't say what, only to pick her up. Someone must have been following her."

Yasushi listened as James Earl's speech ebbed and flowed from mechanical to sorrowful to logical.

"I headed for her as soon as I got the text. I wasn't in time." James Earl stopped speaking to clear his throat. "When I got to the corner to meet her, the police were directing traffic away from the scene. Investigators were all over the place. Didn't look like an accident to them. That was obvious. There was a man crying on the side of the street. I asked around. A guy who drives one of those bike cabs said he'd watched a woman fly off the sidewalk. He was sure the car that hit her sped up to hit her. The guy crying had been driving behind and in the other lane of the car that hit her. She flew into his lane as the first car pushed her into the air. The crying man didn't have a choice but to hit her. The bike cab driver said an ambulance had taken the woman. That's when I started looking for her."

"You did well, finding her so quickly." Yasushi watched James Earl focus on CC.

"Her phone was in her pocket." James Earl said. "I wiped it clean in case the police ask for it."

"Good."

James Earl opened his mouth, as though to say more, but turned back to CC.

Yasushi remained silent, staring at CC and then at James Earl.

"Why was CC downtown when she should have been at the dinner party?"

Yasushi felt the venom in James Earl's voice. He wanted someone to blame. *What's he not telling me?*

"I don't know. I'll see if I can get hold of the police report. That should tell us more about what happened on the street." Yasushi stood to leave. He wanted to stay, but James Earl wanted neither his presence nor his comfort.

"Why would they do this?" James Earl asked before Yasushi could open the door.

Yasushi turned back to James Earl.

"I mean," stammered James Earl. "They could have made her disappear. They could have drained her and left her for us to find. Why this? It's not their way."

Yasushi tilted his head. "Perhaps this has nothing to do with them."

"Bullshit! And you know it. Something is going on we don't know about."

"Indeed," Yasushi left the room. He needed to think. James Earl wasn't telling him everything, but he was right about something going on they were not aware of.

*****

Hank stood and looked out the window. Below him, traffic on the streets of Austin flowed with the regular consistency of the traffic lights. The morning rush hour was over. He felt the sweat on his palm slide beneath the base of the floral arrangement. He moved the arrangement to the other hand until it sweated, so he placed it back in the first hand. He tried to walk around the small waiting room, but he didn't want to wander away from his view of the door to CC's hospital bed in case he could go in. He sighed and sat, placing the small vase on the chair beside him.

Despite his badge and the phone confirmation the nurse had from the Austin Police Department, he would wait.

"You know her status, agent. She's critical and can have no visitors," the nurse said with that cheery smile and resounding authority all good nurses possessed.

"I appreciate that. And I don't want to be a bother. As I said, this is a personal visit. We used to work together. You said her husband was there. I just want to let him know I'm here if they need me." Hank, too, knew how to persuade, but the intensive eyes and determined chin of the nurse told Hank that he was having no undue persuasion.

"I'll tell you what. Their pastor is with them right now. When he leaves, I'll see if the husband will come out to see you, but honestly, I don't think he will. He hasn't left the room since she was admitted."

"I'd be grateful," said Hank and left the nurse to his work.

Hank stared at the flowers, little pink and white roses with lots of green looking things filling in around them and a "Get Well" note attached to a stick. He wondered if it was appropriate. Brandy, his wife, took care of this type of thing. Hank sighed, thinking about Brandy and the girls. He missed them. He pulled his phone from his jacket pocket, and then he put it away without calling.

"She's just getting to work now. After dropping off the girls to school, she's always frantic. Better wait 'til tonight." No one else waited with him in the room of chairs at the end of the hall, so he didn't mind talking aloud to himself. He noticed CC's nurse heading to the far end of the hall, pushing a medicine cabinet. Hank scratched his chin, then grinned and got up carrying the flowers to CC's room.

As his hand reached for the door, someone inside opened it as though to leave but stopped before pulling it wide.

A man's voice stammered, "They could have made her disappear. They could have drained her and left her for us to find. Why this? It's not their way."

Hank froze and turned his ears to the voices in the room.

A deep, melodious voice replied, "Perhaps this has nothing to do with them."

"That's bullshit and you know it. Something is going on we don't know about." Hank's eyebrows burst up at the venom in the response.

Hank had just enough time to take three steps backwards before he heard, "Indeed."

The man with the melodious voice was even larger than Hank. His bald head, dark skin, and clear eyes commanded full attention. Around the clear eyes, Hank saw worry lines engraved into deep recesses, but the astuteness and quickness with which the man took in Hank spoke of intelligence and caution.

"Reverend?" asked Hank. "I'm sorry if I'm intruding. The nurse said CC was in this room. I wanted to drop these off for her and ask her husband if there is anything I can do." Hank held out his free hand to shake, then reached inside his pocket. "I'm sorry. You don't know me. Special Agent Hank Williams. CC and I used to work together. I was at the PD this morning when I noticed her name come up on an incident report."

The serenity of the reverend's smile did not hide the keenness with which he studied Hank. "Yasushi Brown. Pleased to meet you. She doesn't talk much about her days with the Bureau."

Hank noticed how the reverend led him away from the door and lowered his deep, resounding voice to a soft, conspiratorial tone.

"I don't imagine she does," Hank said. "Those were tough times for all of us. She will be alright, won't she?"

"That's what I pray for, Agent Williams." The reverend stopped moving to ask, "Do the police have any idea yet about who did this to her?"

"Not as far as I can tell. Of course, it's their investigation. The detective in charge allowed me a cursory look at the report as a professional courtesy. Does her husband have any ideas?"

"None."

Hank wanted to smile but kept it concealed. The reverend lied as smoothly as his voice flowed. He wanted to burst in and talk to the husband now, but he saw CC's nurse coming toward them, and this wasn't his case. Still, a feeling that his case and CC's incident were connected grew with each breath.

"Nurse, I mean Justin," Hank asked, handing the flowers over.

"Would you mind taking these in when you have a chance. I need to get back to the office. Maybe later I can come around to talk to her husband."

"Of course," Justin said, casting the reverend a glance as though to protect him.

"With respect, Agent Williams," Reverend Brown began. "I don't think he would care to see you now. While she doesn't speak much about her time in the Bureau, she doesn't speak fondly of it."

Hank felt a lead weight hit his stomach, yet his curiosity continued to grow. *Who the hell is this guy?* "I understand," Hank said, offering his hand. "I really do need to get going. Hopefully, we'll meet again, reverend."

"God keep you safe, Agent Williams."

Hank didn't pretend to be in a hurry. Questions rushed through his head. Yes, CC had issues after her partner died, but she was a damn good investigator and too smart to let her setback with the Bureau hinder her career. He had to find out more about her incident and what she'd been up to since Germany.

*****

"How long has he been betraying us?" asked Diggers, sitting on the edge of the chair next to Madeline.

"We don't know he's betrayed us." Madeline looked at Roger sitting opposite her. "He has secrets. We all do. He'll tell us about meeting with the demons when he's ready. Have a little faith."

Roger wondered if Madeline believed what she was saying. The cracks he had seen forming in her stoic exterior over the summer flashed across her face.

Roger's years as a marine still flowed as the authority in his voice took hold of Diggers. "I have no doubts, nor should you. Leave this to us, Diggers."

"But with the contracts the generals signed, I won't be able to keep

Mugello's people out. And now this. How can we be sure about your brother?"

The waitress stopped at the table. "How we doin'? More coffee?"

"Thank you. Yes." Madeline smiled at the waitress. "And would you bring more of that honey sugar? I used it all in my last cup."

"Yes, ma'am. Be right back."

"Go home with your generals and leave this to me." Madeline's expression returned to its customary grim.

"The wound disappeared from the Carlisle woman's arm. There's your proof she's one of them. Then there's your operative working the party. It was clear they knew who she was. She's probably dead by now. And—"

"Enough!" Roger's sharp retort silenced Diggers. "Pull yourself together."

"Here you go, hon." The waitress dropped off the sugar as she carried a large tray of food.

Digger's face tightened. His eyes narrowed. "You trust me enough to give you information about Mugello and the generals. You send me the video proving what they are. Why are you pushing me away now?"

"Control yourself, lieutenant." Roger tightened the muscles around his mouth and eyes, squaring his gaze at Diggers. Madeline might drive the fight, but circumstances changed. Instead of watching and learning, it was time to act, but first he needed to get Diggers out of the way. "Phillip and Derek both worked with me to set up the surveillance without telling the reverend. There's no need to panic. I'll work on James Earl."

Madeline looked up from her plate. "Work on him?"

"He's not a marine—not even military. He doesn't take commands, but he listens to me. It's time to call the others in. Once we've done that, I'll approach James Earl. He has access to all the finances and can get our people here quickly and quietly."

Diggers rolled his eyes. "About time we did something."

"And you need to get back to your generals." Roger raised his hand before Diggers could object. "With the contracts signed, we need someone to monitor Mugello's people. And with this news about the reverend talking to one of them, we need everyone doing what they do best. There's more going on here than we thought."

Diggers stood, tossing his napkin on the table and nodding. "Ma'am. My plane leaves in two hours. The general wants me with him to review the contracts. I'll do what I can and keep you informed." He left without waiting for a response.

"Good riddance to him." Madeline sipped her coffee. "Is it finally time?"

"Yes. But we need to give Yasushi a chance to explain and let's see where CC and James Earl stand."

"My brother is under their influence." Madeline's eyes stared into nothing. "When we rid the city of the demons, he'll be back with us. Until then, we watch him. Pretend to follow him, but we're acting on our own now."

"Madeline," Roger shivered suddenly, afraid of the coolness with which she spoke of her brother. "When did you see Yasushi and the demon?"

Madeline took a final sip from her mug and stood. "We have demons to destroy. In doing that, we save my brother."

Roger swallowed the last of his coffee and stared into his cup.

"Now, let's call Anna. She was right when she said my brother wouldn't be much help to us."

Roger stood, "You're the boss."

*****

The warm air of summer refused to hand off to fall. Kitten lay on the lounge chair on her patio, allowing the breezes from the water to float over her. The sun grazed the tops of the hills across the water easing the day into night. Traffic noises ebbed as evening rush hour faded with the sun. She'd left work after lunch intending to sleep, but it didn't come. Strange images like paintings floated across her eyelids whenever she closed them. In one image, she held a tray with a head on it. There was something familiar about the face surrounded by blood and gore, but she smiled at it as though pleased with herself. In another image, Anthony stood behind her, or someone who looked much like her, caressing her bare shoulder. She saw Eddie/Harry leaning over her as his body thrust into hers. She saw the man from the red Mercedes at the Long Center as his eyes bulged and foam spritzed out of his mouth. Lack of sleep and too much vomiting coursed through her body, leaving her more exhausted than when she left the office.

As a last resort, she opened Stacy's novel to focus her mind.

The crowd parted and there he stood, lonely, desirous, ready to pounce. She wanted him right then, she longed to feel him pressed against her. Longed to feel his tongue in her mouth his penis between her legs. He felt her staring. He wanted her as much as she wanted him.

"No," she said to the cat in her lap. "This won't do." The cat rolled onto its back. "I need to know what it's all about."

She stared across the water. The cat's purr vibrated from her lap, along her spine, and stirred her mind to action. "Come on, cat. Let's find Harry. Let's see if he can make sense of it all."

The cat stood, leaping to the patio railing, swished its tail, and disappeared down the stairs.

As Kitten locked the gate on her patio, she glanced at the man across the street whom she had seen outside of Harry's house. He was tall, dark-skinned, with long dreadlocks. He stood near the road under a live oak, too far away to make out the details of his face. She assumed it was one of Anthony's security guards tasked with watching her. And there was Isabella sitting in the tree above him. It annoyed her and added to her growing feeling of doom. Then she laughed. "I bet that's the same man Leigh and I made a hero of in her romance novel."

The last of the day's heat and the slow, steady walk to Harry's house helped clear her mind. Her head hurt, but she had questions, and the looming feeling of death called her to seek the sense of security and comfort only Harry could provide. Even the man across the street no longer bothered her.

She opened the front door of his house without knocking, knowing he was at home as much from the sense of Harry's presence as by Bach's Concerto for Harpsichord and Violin serenading the evening. He stood bent over a large table cluttered with drawings and parchments. His hand rubbed one way and then another on a page before lifting a piece of charcoal to draw.

In the center of the room stood a young, naked man with long, golden curls flowing down a sculpted chest. His slight frame leaned on a circular table covered with cups, some spilling imaginary contents, an earthen jug, and a large pewter platter. The man remained frozen in his pose. His cherub grin smirked a secret twinkling in deep blue eyes that followed Kitten as she entered the room.

"I assumed you'd come by tonight." Harry didn't look up from his painting. "There's wine in the fridge."

"You shouldn't leave your front door unlocked. Someone unwanted will come in." Kitten found the wine and poured a glass. The cool, golden liquid eased her throat, coating it in coolness. She leaned over the bar, enjoying the wine and admiring Harry's model. She shook her head before settling into the overstuffed armchair near Harry.

"No one enters my house unless I want them to," said Harry. "Long day? You look tired."

"You don't have to pretend your people aren't reporting my movements to you." She hadn't intended to be sharp with Harry, but her head hurt and as long as the model was there, she would get no answers.

Harry set the charcoal on the table. "Tomas, take a break. I'm ready to paint now. Give me a few minutes to set up."

In a single exhale, Tomas's shoulders dropped, and he rolled his head around, crossing his arms to rub his shoulders.

"Okay. I could use some fresh air." He went out to the patio without covering himself.

Harry moved one of the large easels to a place near the circular table where Tomas had been standing and placed a canvas with forest-greens and blacks already painted in areas as a background. He moved back and forth from the easel to boxes of paints and brushes, setting up his painting station. As he moved his stool in front of the canvas, he paused to lean over Kitten, caressing her face with his hand. He said nothing but lifted the corners of his mouth in as much of a smile as he could.

Kitten allowed the coolness of his hand to calm her as she sighed. She would have to wait for answers.

*****

A different nurse came in to check on CC. She was short and fat with a grin that insisted on being returned. James Earl didn't want to smile at her, but he couldn't help himself. Her voice, quiet and soothing, required his full attention. She smelled good.

"I'm Margo. It's my shift now. Call me if you need anything." Margo wrote her name on the whiteboard near CC's head, logged into the computer, checked connections between machines and flesh, and left the room saying no more.

James Earl stood to stretch his long body and twisted his back into forgiving him the hours hunched over the bed and CC's hand. How many hours had passed since they arrived at the hospital? Nothing had changed in CC's condition, but perhaps the swollen, black eyes weren't getting any blacker. He thought the lights flashing on the machines flickered in a regular rhythm compared to the staccato beat he'd heard when he arrived. Perhaps CC's hand wasn't as cold as it had been.

Nothing would take James Earl away from CC's side. Someone wanted her dead. He couldn't tell Yasushi and he certainly couldn't tell the police who arrived to talk to him after Yasushi left. Based on witnesses, the police believed someone pushed CC into the path of the oncoming car. They were waiting on the traffic footage to determine if the first car that hit her did so deliberately, but they seemed convinced it had.

CC's *accident* happened exactly as the caller said it would. The woman's voice had been sweet, steady, and a little salty. "They want her dead. She's seen too much. We'll do what we can for you and your redheaded friend, but hurry. David will contact you as soon as it's safe. Wait for him. Don't act without thought."

"Wait," James Earl wasn't sure what to say. "Who wants her dead? Why? Who are you? Who's David?" He wanted to say, "Give me something to hang on to." He needed hope, but the call ended.

As he pondered the strange phone call, Torres's video, and the dogs suddenly stopping their barking, the emergency text from CC arrived, and he drove as fast as he could to get to her.

Now he stood looking at the parking lot. He felt eyes watching him before he noticed the long, lean figure, standing in the corner of the lot outside the rim of a streetlight. The man waved at him.

James Earl pulled the cord to close the blinds. "How could anyone know we're up here? Yasushi ..." He asked CC but the door to the room opened.

Margo entered, pushing her computer cart. "Sorry. What did you say?" She pulled out vials of medications, scanning them into the computer before administering them to CC.

"Talking to CC," replied James Earl. He moved as though to hold the door until he stood between Margo and CC. "Weren't you just here?"

Margo smiled. "Two hours ago, hon. You've been asleep."

James Earl looked up at the wall clock. Had he dreamed of the man in the parking lot?

"Would you let me have a cot pulled in here for you? You'll be more comfortable and still be right here when she wakes up."

James Earl inhaled the sweet floral scent of honesty about Margo. He felt his shoulders and the hair on his neck relax. "Nice scent. CC wears something like it when we're not working."

"I'm sorry," Margo turned a shade of pink below her walnut cheeks, making her look younger than she was. "Thought my perfume would have worn off by now. I was at a wedding today."

"No, it's okay. I like it, really. With all the chemicals around here, it makes a nice change."

Margo recovered her smile. "Good. What do you do? The chart says she's not from around here. On a work trip?"

"Yes, but we're thinking of staying around Austin. Assuming—" James Earl didn't finish his thought.

Margo injected the medicines into tubes. As she left, she placed her hand on James Earl's arm.

"I'm rooting for you two making this your home. Are you okay?" Margo's infectious smile turned grim. "You're burning up."

"I'm good." James Earl stepped away from her. "I run hot at night. Always have. No big deal. But thanks."

"I'm going to get you some juice. Got to keep your strength up," Margo looked back at CC smiling again. "For her."

The door closed. James Earl opened the blinds, but the man in the parking lot was no longer there. He returned to his position at CC's side, taking her hand into his.

"It's not as cold as it was, babe. You're going to pull through. You have to. I need you more than ever. Somebody knows our secret. I need to trace the woman who called to warn me you were in danger."

He pulled his laptop out of his backpack, realizing how much better he felt after just two hours of sleep. He told CC what he was doing; his voice remained steady and strong as he explained how he created the secure network and searched for the phone number that contacted him the night CC was run over. CC liked to hear how he did what he did.

"For a smart woman, you're incredibly naïve to the ways of a good hack, babe. Lucky for you, I'm here. From now on, no going on assignments without backup. I'll listen more when you tell me how to work under cover. I'll get good at it. If the rev don't want anyone going with you, I'm going anyway. Shit!"

His first attempt to track the phone number failed. He kept his fingers moving and his mind whirling with techniques to find the source of the call he was sure would change his life.

When he heard the door to the room open, he didn't look, assuming Margo was back with the orange juice he suddenly wanted. The faint smell of flowers and honesty and orange juice did not fill his senses. Instead, a masculine, wolfish, and somehow comforting essence filled the room. He turned his head to see the long, lean man from the parking lot standing in the corner of the room.

Margo opened the door, carrying a glass of juice. The man hid in the corner behind the door and put his finger to his lips as he melted into the shadows.

James Earl leapt to stand between Margo and the man to take the glass of juice.

"Thank you." He tried to smile.

"Sure. Call me if you need anything else, hon."

When James Earl turned around, the man was standing at the foot of CC's bed. "You're David," he said. Who else would have been able to enter the room without James Earl knowing it?

David kept his eyes on CC. "Pretty. You want to keep her alive?"

*****

Of all the things that upset Isabella, sloppy work topped the list. It took so little effort to do a job right. She counted on her fingers the little things that made surveillance work. "Like it took so much time to park my bike in front of a house so it looks like it belongs there. Like staking out a place in this comfy tree was a bother. And why the hell does everyone feel the need to be always on their phones? Really? Oh shit! I sound like Cesar."

Evening shifted into night, and Kitten was now inside with Harry. Her replacement would arrive soon, but curiosity over the dreadlocked Hunter and what Harry and Kitten were doing ate at her core. Since no one told not to pry, she decided it was worth the little trouble it took to snoop well. There was the Hunter: annoying, sloppy, but kind of cute. In her hippie days, she developed a liking for a man with long hair. She needed him distracted to move across the street.

The dreadlocked Hunter walked toward Harry's house as soon as Kitten entered. He sent another text, then he put his hands in his pockets and strolled along the road as though he belonged there.

"At least he's trying to fit in," Isabella said to herself, "and there is that ass. Nice."

Isabella smiled and was about to leave her tree when a black Tesla slowed on the road and stopped in front of the dreadlocked Hunter. An older white man with gray hair stepped out of the driver's side. Isabella turned her ears toward them.

"She's been in about fifteen minutes. Spent most of the day inside her condo or on the patio. I saw a young guy with blond hair go into the artist's house about an hour ago."

"Is that it?" The window on the passenger side of the car framed a woman with angular features.

Before she could say anything else, the older man interrupted her, "Any sign of Mugello?"

"No one else." The dreadlocked man tried to hide the annoyance in his voice.

"Good work, Woods," the gray-haired man spoke too fast. "Text me if he shows up. We're meeting at the church later."

"I don't know, colonel. You sure about—"

The woman in the car cut him off. "Of course he is. It's time to act. Let's go, Roger."

The window rose as the colonel turned back to Woods. "We're just talking. Join us when Torres takes over for you."

"Whatever." Woods rolled his eyes. As the window of the passenger door closed, Woods bent over to stop it. "You had a chance to talk to James Earl?"

"We went by the hospital earlier. He's pretty torn up over CC. Better to plan without him for now."

Woods pushed his hands further into his pockets.

Isabella leaned against the trunk of the tree and looked at the sky. Too close to the heart of the city to see many stars, but those she could see flickered bright. Her impression of Woods changed. "Not sloppy. Torn. Could be useful."

With Woods distracted by his own turmoil, she left the tree and moved to a tree close to the river where she could see the inside of Harry's studio and still keep an eye on Woods. Turmoil of her own raged through her mind. Her assignment from Cesar was to keep an eye on Kitten, but she could break Woods with a few kind words and gentle strokes of affection. He wasn't a happy man. The Duchess would want to know what Isabella had overheard. Harry also needed to know.

She sighed. "Focus, Isabella. The Duchess is always reminding me to focus. One thing at a time." Hearing her own voice reminded her of the current task—watching Kitten and Harry's house. At least from this vantage point, she'd get a look at the man who had entered Harry's house earlier in the evening. He arrived in a taxi and kept his face hidden behind a high-collar jacket and cowboy hat.

Through the open curtain to the studio, Isabella saw Kitten snuggling in an armchair. Harry moved around the room, gathering paints and brushes. The French doors opened, and the golden-haired man walked onto the balcony. He stood naked at the railing. He looked at Isabella, turning the edges of his mouth in a cocky grin.

Isabella startled. "Jinkies!" she exclaimed as a smile spread across her lips.

*****

"He doesn't like you," Kitten said as Harry's front door closed.

"He's afraid of me, and that will due for now." Harry continued to paint.

Kitten tilted her head toward Harry. She stood behind the table Tomas posed next to. She sighed and shifted her weight to her other leg.

"You're fidgeting again," Harry's eyes darted between her and the painting.

"Not used to standing for so long. Who am I this time?"

"Judith. And if you stood the way I told you, you wouldn't be uncomfortable."

"No costume?" Kitten returned to the straight-backed, balanced leg pose she'd started with and sighed. "And which Judith?"

"The one who kills Holofernes. No costume. You and she are so much alike costumes would look ridiculous."

Kitten said nothing. A throbbing in her head pushed against her eyes. For a moment, she thought she would fall. She gripped the edge of the table and took a deep breath.

"Why is Tomas afraid of you?" she asked as the pain subsided.

"Does it matter? At present, he needs to be afraid." Harry stopped painting and stared outside. "In some ways, he's very brave, which doesn't negate the fact he's a fool. Sometimes you need a little foolishness in you to be very brave. Would you like to take a break?"

As Harry set his brush down, Kitten sank into the cushions surrounding the table and drowned in their softness. She covered her eyes with her hands. "Will you turn the lights down?"

"If you like. Rest. I'll make the toddy."

Kitten didn't listen to anything in particular. She heard Harry moving around the room and a pot touching the stove in the kitchen, the wind blowing outside the closed doors of the patio, an owl calling. She listened as her heart beat the blood through her veins, cooling her skin.

"Why does he need to be afraid of you?" Kitten asked without opening her eyes as Harry sat beside her.

"I told you, he's a fool. He did something that made me very angry." Harry stretched his arm behind Kitten and helped her sit up. "Now I need him to do something very foolish and very brave. If he succeeds, he'll live a long life."

Kitten leaned against Harry and took the large cup of warmed, spiced port. She let it linger under her nose, savoring the spices, the wine, the history in the grapes, and the now-familiar other flavor she could never place. "If he's not very brave and very foolish, you'll kill him, won't you?"

Harry kept one hand on the cup. "Yes. He accepts my proposal. What's wrong?"

"How many more have to die?"

Harry tilted his head to the side as though listening. Finally, he placed his lips near her ear and whispered, "Drink and we will always be together. There will be no more pain. I can promise nothing more."

Kitten sipped from the cup. The familiar warming spread through her body as the drink passed her lips and down her throat. She tipped back the cup, emptying its contents. The warmth, the erasure of pain, the ease of seeping into sleep overwhelmed her. Before the deep sleep embraced her, she tried to repeat his answer but only managed, "Together, no pain, death."

*****

Tomas stepped outside Harry's house, glad to be leaving. He knocked a speck of dust off his lapel and walked to the street, stopping at a parked car to check his hair and the placement of his hat in his reflection in the side-view mirror. He jerked his head around at the sound of a breaking twig across the street. The corners of his mouth twitched up. He continued walking toward the condo building. As he neared a large live oak casting its shadow across the road, another shadow flew from across the road, knocking him off the sidewalk and almost into the brush beside the river.

"Tommy!" squealed Isabella.

"Issy!" shouted Tomas, as he twirled her around in the air.

"Damn! You're looking good, old man." Isabella laughed, finally breaking her embrace and settling her feet on the ground. "Last time I saw you ... well, never mind ... I thought you were dead for sure. And look at you. Standing there bare naked just for me."

"I missed you too." Tomas hugged Isabella again. "I'd say let's go get naked together, but I've got work to do, and I'm betting you do too or you wouldn't be in Austin."

"Shit! You? Responsible and working? Thought I'd never see the day." Isabella stood on her toes and kissed Tomas on the lips.

"Easy, girl. I'm toeing the line these days. On probation. Sort of pissed off the bosses."

"The Duchess was ready to let you to burn," scoffed Isabella. "You must have done one hell of a lot of sweet-talking."

"It's my boyish dimples and sweetheart smile. Gets them every time."

Tomas wrapped one arm around her, and they moved deep into the shadows. "I suppose the Hunter is still in front of the house?"

"How obvious can he be? I mean, seriously? But he's not paying attention to you. Besides, David's watching too. Come on, tell me. What's going on? What are you doing here?" Isabella straightened her grin, looking directly into Tommy's face.

Tommy raised the corner of his mouth in disgust at the sound of David's name.

"Get over it, Tommy," said Isabella. "I'm sure he doesn't like you either, but he's a nice guy and damn good at his job. Don't change the subject."

"That guy," Tommy turned his head toward Woods, still standing across from Harry's house, "This Hunter group has some serious muscle behind it. Supposed to see if they can spot me. And, hum, well ..."

"Señor Tomas." Isabella interrupted. "You're holding something back. I know Harry and the Duchess are too. What gives? Why we gotta play this cloak-and-dagger game?"

"You know I want to tell you, Issy, but if they haven't said, I shouldn't. But listen, do me a favor. Don't let on we talked. Like I said, I'm sort of on probation. If they think I'm screwing around, I'm toast." Tomas put his hands in his pockets and looked over the water. "And, um, if you should see me around, and I don't seem to notice you, do me a favor and don't notice me either."

Isabella scratched her ear as she followed Tomas's eyes across the water. Nothing was there that shouldn't have been, yet the shadows of the night grew darker, longer, more menacing. Tomas could be an ass, more often than not a dangerous ass, but if he was afraid, she should be too. "Sure, Tommy. Just scratch your ear when I'm not supposed to notice."

"Take care of yourself, kid. We really gotta get naked again, and soon."

"Sooner the better." Isabella smiled as Tomas slid further into the shadows and disappeared. She returned to the tree where she could watch Harry and Kitten.

Isabella tried to focus on the Hunter as he paced back and forth. She thought she saw David running between houses. The neighborhood dogs were certainly barking a lot at something. Inside Harry's house, Kitten stood still while Harry painted, but even from her vantage point, Isabella could sense something was wrong. Kitten fidgeted too much, what little color she had blanched against the black shirt she wore. Harry kept painting but looked as though he wanted to jump off his stool. The tension in the room eased its way to her.

She counted the cars on the street. She counted stars in the sky. She watched an owl on the roof of a nearby house swoop to the street and grab a mouse. The owl flew to its nest and ate with glee. Finally, she could bear her curiosity no longer. The street was clear, but Isabella scanned it first to make sure no new Hunters had arrived as she eased out of the tree and sauntered toward the balcony of Harry's house. The French doors were closed and the lights dim. She watched through a break in the curtains as Harry settled close to Kitten, raising her head with his hand. They whispered back and forth. Isabella resisted no longer and focused her hearing. She held back the gasp as she heard the words and witnessed Harry giving her the drink. She understood too well what it meant.

*****

Isabella tried to stay still but had to pace between the street and the water in the shadows of the trees to calm her mind. She wasn't supposed to know what she now knew.

Possibilities about the future exploded in her mind, which is why she didn't notice the icy fingers boring into her shoulder and the total blackness surrounding her until it was too late. Her back hit the bushes as her arm slapped the water and moist mud oozed into her shirt and jeans. She stared into Harry's face as he leaned over her holding her in the mud with one hand, his lips a malicious snarl, his fangs bare, and oh-so sharp above her.

Isabella closed her eyes. "I'm so sorry. I didn't mean to eavesdrop.

Really, I was just keeping watch. Tommy left. You closed the doors. I know I didn't need to be so close. It's not like I meant to pry in your business. I know better than—"

She opened her eyes to see the palm of Harry's hand. He let her go. She remained on the ground, frozen in place, realizing one hundred and three years old was too young to die. Nothing happened.

Harry continued to glare at her, but he no longer snarled. "Tell me about the Hunter watching the house."

"Name's Woods." Isabella tried to slow her speech, but fear still coursed through her. "Please don't kill me. The black Tesla you said tried to run you over pulled up. Older man, named Roger, got out to talk to him. Woods referred to him once as colonel. Looks like a marine. A woman was in the car too. Odd woman. Really," Isabella found herself not looking at Harry and analyzing what she had witnessed. "Woods didn't seem to like her much. Seemed pretty snotty if you ask me. I wouldn't like her. He mutters a lot to himself. Sloppy surveillance work. Something's wrong in that group. No idea what, but I'd bet my neck on it." Isabella grinned but twitched as she looked back at Harry's face and feeling them biting into her neck.

"It may well cost you your neck." Harry no longer looked at her. His gaze drifted across the water.

Perhaps it was the shadows, but Isabella would have sworn Harry aged a hundred years in front of her. She massaged her neck with her hand. "Again, Harry, I'm really sorry. The Duchess taught me better than this. I mean, she taught me enough—"

Harry lifted his hand again. "You understand why you must not speak of what you saw to anyone. Your Duchess already knows."

"Of course not! I wouldn't dream of it. That would be interfering with—"

"Enough. I'm not going to kill you, but I will have extra work for you to remind you of your place."

Isabella relaxed her shoulders. She allowed her head to lean back into the bushes as wet mud cooled her neck.

"And do stand up, Isabella. We're not animals." Harry's words may have sounded severe, but Isabella sensed amusement in them. "What is your task from Cesar tonight?"

Harry offered his hand to Isabella, and she took it. She dusted off leaves and debris and tried to wipe the mud off her pants. "Watch Kitten, keep an eye on her place, and report suspected Hunter activity. I sent Cesar the plates for the Tesla and my notes about Woods. I'm sure he's on it."

"And Tomas?" Harry raised his eyebrow as he spoke the name.

Isabella closed her eyes and clenched her jaw, realizing she had promised not to mention she had talked to Tommy. "I know him from my early days in Chicago. I approached him, but don't worry, the Hunter didn't see us. I swear I won't tell anyone about him. I promised him too. He knows you're not happy with him. Seriously, I've known him for—"

"Learn to think before you speak, Isabella. If you do, you'll live a long and happy life."

"You're really not going to kill me, tonight?" Isabella hesitated a moment. "You're not going to tell the Duchess, are you?"

She pictured what the Duchess could do to her. Isabella shivered.

"Not tonight, and the Duchess speaks too well of you to kill you for one infraction, but she will know about it. Perhaps it's time ..." Harry's gaze drifted far away as his words faded, but she stopped paying attention at the realization that not only would she not be killed tonight but also that the Duchess thought well of her.

At last Harry's gaze returned to his house. "Remain here tonight. My friend is sleeping. See she's not disturbed and make sure she reaches her home safely in the morning. I won't be back tonight."

And Harry was gone.

"You are so incredibly stupid, Isabella," Isabella said to no one.

She moved from shadow to shadow around the house, checking the doors and windows were secure. At the patio door, she peeked through the curtains and saw Kitten sleeping on the cushions with a dark green velvet cover over her. If Isabella hadn't noticed the rising and lowering of her chest and heard her labored breaths, she would have assumed Kitten was dead.

"You stupid shit!" Isabella whispered aloud. "Peeking is so going to get you into trouble again—or worse." With that, she moved to the roof of Harry's house and sat in a crevice, keeping watch. The Hunter remained across the street, leaning against a tree, oblivious of her presence. He continued to mutter from time to time. She wanted to find out what was troubling him, but she would not leave the post Harry had prescribed for her. Besides, David lounged nearby, curled up safely next to a parked car. He would follow Woods when he left.

"On the bright side," Isabella said aloud as a grin broke across her face. "I know something Cesar doesn't. That's going to piss him off. Yes." She put her hands behind her head and leaned back against the roof. "It's good to be sneaky."

*****

David enjoyed walking neighborhood streets late at night, listening to the everyday moments people took for granted: the kids complaining about bedtime, the teens sneaking out of the house and getting caught, the couples snuggling in front of the television, the dogs patrolling their yards. Walking suburban streets reminded him of normalcy, complacency. Suburban houses contained the ordinary people who mattered most, without whom the world would crack and whither, without whom his kind could not survive.

Few of those who walked the night as he did understood the power of these ordinary people. The Eldest of the vampires did. Anthony and Cesar? He shook his head.

David wanted to laugh at Isabella, sitting in Harry's house looking gloomy and smug, but he had a new respect for her. She remained unnoticed by the Hunter, despite flying across the street to tackle Tommy. Seeing Tommy had been a surprise for both David and Isabella. Isabella liked Tommy, and David held no grudge. If the Eldest of the vampires allowed him to live despite what happened in Galveston, it was no business of his. Isabella spying on Harry and Kitten had surprised him. He wouldn't have done it, but Isabella was young.

He neither saw nor heard the exchange between Isabella and Harry, but from his position sitting against a fence behind some bushes with the pup sleeping at his side, he had felt Harry's shadow as it thundered over Isabella.

The pup yawned and stretched his head onto David's lap. David scratched the pup's ears. "Don't interfere when vampires quarrel, pup, especially if one of them is an Eldest."

The pup leapt to stand at attention in front of David.

"No," said David, unable to contain a laugh at the eagerness of the young German shepherd. "I'm not playing with you now." But David stood. He tossed the tennis ball. The pup barked once and dashed away with tongue hanging from his mouth. He reached the ball as it rolled toward the gutter. The pup continued to run down the road away from David.

The neighborhood dogs barked as he passed. David followed the dog until he spotted Woods slow his pacing and move toward his car. David raised his hand and the neighborhood dogs stopped barking. His pup returned and sat at his side.

"Let's go," David said to the pup. "We know where he's going, and I have to meet a couple of new friends." David sent a text to Cesar about the Hunters' meeting at the church as he made his way to his own car. Jenny had done all she could for the young wolf and the redheaded woman on the night of the dinner. It was up to him to save them.

*****

"How much longer we gonna wait?" Karol asked while biting a hang-nail. He and Karol leaned back in the pew they occupied at the front of the church. Five more soldiers sat in the pews behind them, looking bored but talking amongst themselves.

"Until he gets here," replied Madeline. She and Anna sat next to each other near the baptistry, chatting about ordinary matters.

"This is bullshit," said Karol, rising from his seat.

"Soldier!" snapped Roger, standing behind Madeline.

Karol stiffened to attention. The other men and women of the group sat up straight, looking at Roger.

"We're in a church. You will show respect." His voice left no doubt to his authority.

"Yes, sir. Apologies, sir." Karol sat without a snarl or rolling his eyes. He kept his eyes forward and said nothing to Torres or anyone else.

Anna's lips curled up for a moment but returned to normal as she continued talking to Madeline about her dress with the large tropical floral print.

Roger stared into the eyes of each member of the group. All were good soldiers, fit, well-groomed, attentive, but Roger looked beneath the appearances. Not one pulled away from his stare. In them he saw action. Unlike the others he and Yasushi kept close to them, these men and women would follow orders with the fortitude of the faithful. They were killers.

Madeline touched his hand nodding toward the door. Woods entered, hesitating as he scanned the unknown faces until his eyes fixed on Roger.

"Gather up!" Roger's voice vibrated through the church with no need to yell.

The soldiers quieted and looked at Roger.

Anna stood centered at the altar. "There's no need for introductions. We all know each other, if not by face then by reputation. We're all Hunters gathered for one purpose: to kill demons. Derek Woods has been surveying our chief suspect, one of the leading demons and most likely the one who appeared in Galveston over the summer to the detriment of colleagues and family." No one spoke, but two of the soldiers crossed themselves. "Thanks to Derek's surveillance work, we have a plan in place to take down this king vampire through his weakness, a woman he's converting into a vampire."

Everyone looked at Woods, but he said nothing. His gaze jumped between Roger and Madeline.

"The artist is the key." Madeline stood. Her hand clutched her right side for a moment and her face paled, but she shook her head and stood tall, towering over Anna even though they were near equal in height. "We know when he arrived at the dinner party on Saturday our operative's cover was blown. When she left the house, someone ran her over. The local police suspect a deliberate hit-and-run. As we know, they're cunning. They attacked her in public. It was a warning. We know if we work as one unit, we can kill them."

Woods took in a deep breath. Roger put a hand on his shoulder, gripping it.

Madeline continued. "The time to act is now. Each of you has special skills, and we have special knowledge of the target. Because of Woods's work, we know how to get close to them and wipe them from the face of the earth."

Roger watched as the thrill of the kill raced across the faces of the soldiers he now commanded. "We must act with speed and determination. If anyone has any doubts about our purpose, speak now."

Madeline stared at Woods. He dropped his gaze to the floor.

Karol stood up. "When do we start, ma'am?"

"You were there when they killed the captured vampire in Galveston." Roger recognized the name.

"Yes, sir. Vamps don't die quick, and they don't look all that much like we expect vamps to look. Took out a couple of them with my flamethrower when the fighting got thick. They're hard to kill. You're sure about who we're going after?"

"I'll never forget his face." Madeline's eyes waxed pale as though she forgot who was around her. "I woke to find it leaning over me. I had to watch as it killed my family. I'll never forget it." Madeline's usual icy stare returned.

Karol turned to look at Woods. "What do you say, Woods? This artist the vamp of vamps or just a crazy ol' fruit loop who likes to wear black?"

Woods shrugged. "He seems to get around with no one noticing, and he scares me." He paused and took in a deep breath before adding,

"I know he's one of them. Not about the others. Until we catch one, we can't know for sure."

"Catch one?" exclaimed Anna. "We're not here to—"

Madeline interrupted Anna. "We're not here just to kill. We're here to destroy the demons. Let no one here think any different. Mercy is as unknown to them as it will be to us. If any of you have doubts, walk out now."

No one in the room moved.

"Settled." Anna smiled. "To flush out the artist, we need the Carlisle woman. She's a key in this. Woods, work with Karol. You know her habits. Find the best way to grab her. I'll get the safe house ready. The rest of you, get your gear ready. Once this starts, there won't be time for rest 'til they've all gone back to Hell."

"I think it's best if we put Torres on this," said Roger, without looking at Derek. "Wood's been our point man with surveillance. He might be recognized."

"Good catch," said Anna. "Karol, Torres, work out the details."

"Roger that." No emotion crossed Torres's face.

"The rest of you, let's get the safe house ready."

The group dispersed. Woods remained standing near Roger. Roger watched him out the corner of his eye as the others chatted and dispersed. Madeline and Anna walked side by side toward the door, looking at no one.

"Did you hurt yourself?" asked Anna.

"Stupid," Madeline lowered her voice as she spoke. "I slipped walking out of the house on those fucking steps. I'll be glad to leave the place."

From his periphery, Roger caught sight of Pastor Pete near the window to the sanctuary. Roger smiled but moved to stand next to Derek, putting his hand on his shoulder. "I know it's sudden, Derek, but it's time. Madeline is right. And you know how the rev feels about involving civilians, especially since we know nothing for certain about the Carlisle woman, but she is a key between the artist and Mugello. We won't kill her unless we have to."

Derek spun to look Roger in the eye. "Gotcha" was all he said as he pushed his hands further into his pockets.

Madeline called to Roger from the door. Roger nodded before leaving Derek's side. "Get some sleep. We'll talk more in the morning."

Woods, with hands still in his pockets, followed them out of the church.

*****

"How thick is she?" Tomas stopped pacing along the edge of the swimming pool on top of the Westin Hotel. This late at night, hotel patrons were not allowed on the floor. "And why didn't you take care of the redhead? She was right in front of you."

"With Harry and Anthony in the house? Until one or both are gone, I must appear to play by their rules."

"But if the woman recovers and tells her friends about you and—"

"I'm perfectly aware of the repercussions." Leonard's stern reply caused Tomas to stiffen.

"We can use this to our advantage," continued Leonard as he watched Tomas. "The Hunters don't trust each other. They'll trust each other even less now. That will make them easier to control. They will take care of the killing. All we have to do is poke them a little."

"Go on," replied Tomas, squinting his eyes as though looking at something far away.

"You told me one of the Hunters felt your presence. Check out these others. They're meeting at the church down there. I have a feeling they won't be as sensitive to us."

Tomas strode to the edge of the building where Leonard stood looking over the city. The church Leonard pointed to was only a few blocks away.

"If you know so much about them, why aren't you working on them yourself?"

Leonard smiled. "And risk the trust I've worked so hard to earn with Anthony? He knows you're in town, by the way. You should stay clear of him."

"This from the man who let that woman wander onto Anthony's grounds," sneered Tomas.

"I let her do nothing," snapped Leonard. He paused for a moment before shrugging his shoulders and grinning. "I let her get a little out of control, but she won't do it again. I've made certain of that." He sneered and held up the back of his hand. "Finish off the Hunter at the hospital—just in case. Can't have her waking up and letting anyone know what she saw."

Tomas looked down at the church. "No problem. I'll check out the Hunters first?"

"Yes. The woman was in critical condition last I heard. She's not much of a threat for now. Make sure her death looks like part of her accident."

Tomas snorted, "I know what I'm doing."

"We can't afford mistakes, Tomas. It's almost time."

"Later, boss." Tomas stepped off the edge of the building. At this time on a weeknight, there were not enough people downtown to watch a man drop from the roof of a high-rise hotel and walk away.

*****

James Earl lifted his face from his hands. He concentrated on returning his breathing to normal. The sweat from his brow cooled him. "How did you know?" he asked.

"Saw you the other night. I followed your friend, Woods, to your house after the killings at the concert. Knew right away." David sat opposite James Earl. "No one had helped me when I changed. I had a blade to my wrist when Mary—*she* might be a vamp, but she was a good friend. I return the favor when I can."

James Earl considered David's words. "How much do you know about our group?"

David sighed, recognizing torn loyalties. "I suspect the vamps know a good deal about your group, but I'm here for you and her. You need help. I've seen your group. They'll kill you if they find out what you are. Luckily, they're not looking for us, this time."

James Earl rubbed his chin and stared at CC. His face twisted as acceptance settled over him.

"She's safe as long as we're watching her," said David.

"We?" asked James Earl suspiciously.

"Think." David smiled. "Have you seen anyone here you felt particularly at ease with? Anyone make you feel relaxed?"

James Earl's eyes widened. "Margo? She's like us?"

"Werewolf. Say it. It's what we are."

James Earl looked back to CC's face. Her breathing came easy now. Her face looked almost normal except for the bruising.

"If you want to save her," said David. "You have to accept what you are. Learn to use your skills. There's a war coming, James Earl. Your friends might think they know what they're doing, but they're in over their heads. They want to kill, and they don't care who gets in their way. The Eldest who runs this city wants peace. You don't have to believe me, but you do need me. Very soon now, your wolf will force its way out. You're on the verge of a change. I can help you through this, or you can risk killing everyone you love. It's what happened to me. It almost destroyed me."

David watched as James Earl sat up straight and closed his eyes. His chest rose and lowered with large gulps of air. The hands that had shaken sat calmly on James Earl's knees.

"I don't want to hurt anyone, especially CC. She knows I'm different, keeps going on how we need to leave the group 'til I feel secure, but these guys are my friends. They—"

"What will they do to you when they see what you are? You know the answer. Sounds like she does ..."

"The rev and Roger helped me out when no one else would. I owe them something." James Earl stood, looking out the window. "I'm afraid what will happen if me and CC up and disappear."

"The moon will be full in a few nights. Will you be able to control—"

Before David could finish his sentence, both men turned as CC coughed.

James Earl rushed to her side, taking her hand. "Babe, it's ok. I'm here." Tears filled his eyes as a smile spread across his face.

CC moved her mouth to speak but coughed. David poured a glass of water and gave it to James Earl, who placed the straw in her mouth.

"Don't try to talk, babe. You're ok."

"Listen," CC managed a coarse whisper. "Listen to him. Help the rev or we're all dead."

*****

Within an hour, Margo unhooked CC from the monitors and helped roll her to the loading docks where a windowless black van waited. CC grunted once as David lifted her off the bed and into the back of the van where the whitest woman James Earl had ever seen sat placing pillows and blankets around CC. Margo sat in the bucket seat next to CC and reconnected a bag of fluids to CC's IV, hanging the bag on a hook on the side of the van. James Earl sat in an empty seat near CC as David closed the door and started driving.

"Jenny," smiled the too-white woman as she extended a hand to James Earl. Despite her cool appearance, Jenny's hand was warm and welcoming. "Glad we can help."

CC sighed as her head leaned back against the pillow of flesh that was Margo's leg. Her eyes remained closed, but a smile rested on her lips.

"She's fine." Margo winked to James Earl. "Her poor body's all worn out. Jenny, toss over a couple of those pillows. I want to keep her arm elevated and keep this safe." Margo handed her a large purse. "Some of those meds need to be in the icebox when we get to the house."

"Yes, ma'am."

James Earl watched Margo as she moved with precision to make sure CC rested comfortably.

"Where are we going?" James Earl asked as the lights of the city grew fewer and dimmer.

"The vineyard," replied Jenny. While David hunched his shoulders in concentration, Margo shifted her girth in the bucket seat that seemed too small for her. James Earl remained sitting straight while Jenny remained smiling as though out for a Sunday drive, her body swaying with the van. Only her hand, resting on CC's knee, betrayed any concern for the sleeping passenger. "It's Anthony's, of course, but we use the cottage when the moon is full. Your friend will stay in the big house. She'll be safe there. No one's following us, are they, my love?"

"Not that I can see." David said, as his head continued minute shifts from rearview mirror to side-view mirrors. "Going to take a long way just to be sure. Easier to lose tails on country roads."

"Oh, Lord," said Margo, rolling her eyes. "Why did I pick this bra to wear tonight? The wire's going to be the death of me."

"Take it off," replied Jenny. "No one will mind."

James Earl felt heat rushing to his face when Margo pulled her top over her head. He stared at the floor as the very large black bra fell onto it in front of him.

"Oh, that's better." Margo laughed. "Son, you're going to have to get used to it. We shed our clothes before changing. You never want to get caught in your own knickers while running out to hunt."

"Don't tease him," said Jenny, still smiling but with concern in her voice. "He's new to this, and he has other things on his mind right now. You'll be fine." Jenny reached over and patted James Earl's knee.

"You're a werewolf too?" asked James Earl, staring at Jenny.

"We all are, except your friend here. There are only a few of us in Austin. There would be fewer of us if it weren't for vamps like Anthony and Harry. They keep the peace. Maybe they're a bit strong sometimes, but they help anybody who needs it."

"Amen," said Margo. "You young ones come in with your silly notions and get everyone all riled up. It nearly cost this little one her life."

James Earl had begun to relax but sat upright and looked into Margo's eyes.

"It's okay, hon," began Margo with a smile. "She's going to live. She looks bad, I know, but I'm not going to let anything happen to her."

CC opened her eyes and looked to James Earl. She tried to reach her hand to his, but the weight of it tugged her arm back to the floor. James Earl took her hand in his.

"You were right, babe. We've got a lot to learn."

*****

Tomas kept to the shadows of the exterior of the hospital until he recognized a windowless black van circling the parking lot. Within a few minutes, the lights outside the receiving dock went dark.

"Curious," he said to no one in particular. "What are the odds I arrive just as my prey is about to spring?"

Tomas found a tree in the parking lot in front of the receiving dock, far enough away to not be noticed. From his perch, he saw the beautiful white wolf emerge from the van as Margo and James Earl wheeled CC down the ramp. David leapt out of the driver's side of the van and lifted CC into the van. The escape completed in only three minutes.

"Impressive," Tomas leaned back in the tree resting his head against the trunk. "No one will think twice about a wheelchair sitting outside a hospital. But someone might notice when shifts change."

Tomas dropped from the tree and made his way along the ramp to the wheelchair. A tub of used scrubs sat ready for pickup. He changed into the least bloody of the scrubs and pushed the wheelchair into the hospital. He meandered down halls until he found an empty office labeled Human Resources. At his touch and with a few twists of the handle, the door opened. At the second desk, he found an identification badge hanging by its lanyard for a blond woman named Meg.

"Tsk, tsk. You shouldn't leave IDs hanging around Meg. That's how you lose them." He continued through the neat office stopping as he approached a closed door. It wasn't locked. Inside the office, he lifted the keyboard and read several sticky note phone messages. Next he lifted the trophy, World's Best Dad. A picture of the family smiled at Tomas from their embossed images on the side of the trophy.

"Nice-looking family." Tomas looked back at the nameplate on the desk, "Carl. And kudos for not keeping your password written under your keyboard, but under a trophy? Really, Carl, and you call yourself head of HR."

Username and password secured, Tomas searched the hospital's databases for information about female accident victims. There was only one: Catherine Carson. In from out of town, the husband remained at her side, critical but expected to make a full recovery. Tomas read all he could, turned off the computer, and headed for the south wing.

As he pushed the wheelchair through the lobby, the security guard at the front desk waved to him, "Quiet night?"

"Thank God," replied Tomas. "Had enough excitement for one day."

On the fourth floor, Tomas noticed the security camera wasn't blinking. "Broken." He laughed and smiled, making a note of the cleverness of wolves. He looked in CC's assigned room.

"Oh, my. No one here. They must have escaped." Tomas smiled as he meandered down halls and elevators, as the graveyard shift stirred to make way for the first day shift.

A nurse in pink scrubs and dancing ballerinas got into the elevator with him.

"You got the time?" he asked.

"Five after seven." She smiled back at him. "Long night?"

"Pretty slow for the most part. I'm ready for home. Have a good one." Tomas nodded as the nurse stepped into the pediatrics ward. "Where did all the time go?" he said to himself. "Where did they go? Moon will be full. Catherine needs rest and someone to take care of her."

Tomas was still laughing when he stepped off the elevator on the main floor. As he prepared to follow others to the parking lot, he passed the chapel where he heard a familiar voice. He stopped and sat outside the open door, bending over to tie his shoe.

"They figure if they grab the woman, it will force the demons out."

Tomas recognized the voice of the Hunter, Woods. "I don't like it, rev. I never signed on for kidnapping or murder."

Tomas stretched his neck around to peek into the chapel. Woods sat with his head hanging low, dreadlocks falling over his face. A large man sat next to him. "Reverened Brown," he whispered to himself.

When he heard the reverend speak, he felt a comfort few people were privileged to convey with their voices. "We'll make this right, Derek."

"Madeline says you're working with *them*, that you've been talking to *them*." Derek turned to look at the reverend, his eyes full of water, but no tears ran down his face.

"I have been, Derek. That's how I knew to come to Austin. He, too, wants justice."

Tomas jumped moving away from the door as the reverend stopped speaking. He noticed the reverend's shoulders shudder as he cocked his head to turn around and look behind him.

Tomas moved away from the door before the reverend could see him. He stopped only to pick up his clothes from behind an old box in the receiving doc. As he waved to the security guard near the door, he stopped and looked back at the hospital. "So many webs."

*****

It seemed too obvious a place to find the rev, but that's why Derek thought of it as the first place to look. He entered the hospital chapel, noticing first the nun arranging flowers. Yasushi knelt in a pew to the side. The nun looked at Derek but said nothing. Derek sat in a pew next to the door until the nun walked to the front of the altar, genuflected, and left the chapel pausing to smile at Derek.

Yasushi lifted his large frame to sit in the pew and motioned Derek to join him.

"CC's gone." Yasushi lifted his gaze to Derek.

Derek gripped the pew in front of him and sank into the pew beside Yasushi.

"I'm sorry," Yasushi said quickly. "I don't mean she's dead. She's just not here anymore. Neither is James Earl."

Derek stared at him for a minute breathing deeply. "Rev, you're supposed to be a man of words. Pick them more carefully."

"I'm sorry," Yasushi repeated. "My mind is twisting and turning, trying to understand what happened. It's all my fault. I don't know how I could have been so stupid as to act without consulting all of you. But the opportunity was too great. I was greedy for knowledge. It's all my fault. Now two of our group are missing."

"There's more you need to know." Derek looked into Yasushi's eyes, seeing a guilt-ridden soul. "It's not your fault they're gone. Roger, Madeline, and Anna have their own agenda. I'm afraid I helped them."

Derek put his hands over his face as he felt his eyes water. Fear washed over him even as he felt Yasushi place his arm around him.

"So much has and is happening, Derek." Yasushi's voice filled Derek's head. "We'll get through this together. Tell me what you can."

*****

"Dude. Seriously?" David's voice caused James Earl to jump as he stood next to the vineyard, cell phone in hand. "I thought you were a geek. Rule number one 'Don't use your cell phone if you don't want to be tracked.' Assumed you knew that."

"I haven't turned it on. It just feels good to hold it." James Earl lifted the phone to show David. "The Rev's a good guy. I'd hate it if anything happened to him. He needs to know the truth. I'm useless without my tech."

"You've got a lot to think about before deciding who the good guys are. I need to get into town. Margo's staying. Do what she says."

David passed James Earl without saying more. He opened the door to the van as Jenny came out of the house. "Get some sleep, James Earl. You'll want your strength to help CC."

The sun bloomed over the vines. James Earl took in the natural beauty surrounding him. He had never been in the Texas Hill Country with its rolling hills, vineyards, trees, and blanket of blue sky. The house was huge, with large-shuttered windows open to the coming day. At the other end of the vineyard, a white pickup truck followed a dirt road to the winery. David told him the vintner and his staff would be in and out of the winery but assured him they wouldn't come to the house. James Earl pushed his phone deep into his pocket and went inside the house. He stopped to make certain the front door locked behind him.

He walked up the long curved staircase, following the sounds of a television to find the room CC slept in. The curtains were drawn, hiding the morning sun. A small lamp lit the room, casting a hazy shadow across her face. For the first time in days, she looked as though she slept and dreamed and wasn't battling death.

James Earl felt his days without sleep creeping over him. Margo sat watching a small television. An old movie flashed on the screen, something familiar, with the volume at a whisper.

"Take the room next door," said Margo, speaking just loud enough for him to hear. "She made the journey here fine. That arm will take some time to heal, but otherwise, she looks good."

"You'll call me if anything changes?"

"Of course," she answered, grinning.

James Earl walked through the connecting door and saw the bed. He wanted to ask what she was watching, but as soon as he sat on the edge of the bed, sleep overwhelmed him, and he fell into a deep sleep without taking off his shoes.

*****

Thursday arrived as it always did, by following Wednesday. Since Monday night, Harry had avoided Kitten, saying he was painting. She remembered going to his house Monday night. Something important happened, but she couldn't remember what. She couldn't even remember getting home. Kitten wondered if his avoidance had to do with the danger he and Anthony were in. However, since that night there had been no headaches, no fatigue, no guilt, and no fear gnawing at her. Between her daily work routine, she wrote and wrote as though the deadline for the book hung over her head like Mademoiselle le Guillotine.

But if Harry did not wish to be with her, Anthony did. On Tuesday, it was a call from him for an uptown drinks party. On Wednesday, it was dinner and the opening of a local independent film he produced. After the events, he sat on her couch while they sipped bourbon and talked in the quiet of the night about life and art and love. They flirted but resisted following through. When he left for the night, she stayed up writing and imagining what lovemaking with Anthony would be like and putting those thoughts into the pages of Stacy's book. She kept herself away from friends and coworkers. They all said the same thing. "Are you ok? You look pale." She could not remember feeling so well. She wondered at her growing affection for Anthony.

Thunder woke her this Thursday morning. Lightning preceded the sunrise. She lay in bed, watching it dance across the sky over the houses on the hills. There were no lights at Harry's house. Today she would meet Jenny and play hooky from work and writing. She looked forward to something different, a day to relax. She'd liked Jenny, but Jenny was one of those people everybody liked, assuming they didn't gawk at her albinism, feel left out with her tendency to dream as she spoke, or take offense at her penchant for stating the obvious faults of those she was with. Kitten laughed at herself and got out of bed. Despite plans to do no work, she pulled out her tablet and wrote the next chapter of the book featuring a woman much like Jenny.

The cat sat on her desk, staring at the rain and swishing its long, fluffy tail back and forth. The screen flashed Jenny's name and a message, "On my way. Meet out front."

"Damn it, cat! You were supposed to watch the time." She rushed to dress and had just enough time to email Leigh the latest pages of the book. Before leaving, she looked at the cat she had not named. "I suppose you want to stay out of the rain. Don't make a mess of my stuff." The cat didn't bother to look at her or reply. It curled its tail around its body, nuzzled its head under its arm, and went to sleep.

Kitten hurried to the front of the building where she could watch for Jenny and stay dry.

"Hey, lady! Looking for a ride?" Jenny leaned out the window of one of Anthony's town cars. She held a martini glass in her hand, filling it with rain. "This is all we get until lunch. Isabella won't let me drink and ride."

Kitten laughed at the sight of white, colorless Jenny leaning out of the black car with tinted windows and Isabella in her hot pink overcoat with matching hat and rubber shoes, standing by the black car with the large pink umbrella. Despite the heavy storm clouds, she wore pitch-black wayfarer sunglasses. Kitten was the only one dressed to match the car. It reminded her she'd dressed too quickly and, once again, in black.

*****

Isabella smirked. Cesar was certain it was the same smirk she had on her face when he told her he would be at the gallery. Harry never publicly chastised those of authority unless he intended to kill them, so she couldn't know how Harry had berated him over not providing his personal protection to Kitten. Harry didn't say why he, alone, must hold the responsibility, and Cesar didn't ask.

"If you love me," Harry said, "protect her as you would protect me."

Cesar pushed aside his personal animosity for the woman and kept his attention fixed on her. When duties called him away, he left Isabella in charge of Kitten's protection. Fortunately, Anthony was spending more and more time with Kitten, so Cesar could provide security for both with Isabella assisting. And still, Isabella smirked.

When the car arrived late at the gallery, he wasn't concerned. The storm would slow even the best of drivers, and Isabella, for all her flightiness, was the best driver. When he opened the back door holding a large umbrella for Jenny and Kitten, Jenny stared at him, eyes wide with curiosity until they reached the front door.

As Kitten opened the front door, she took hold of Jenny's arm. "You can't walk through walls, you know. Time to get to work." Jenny gave Cesar a little smile, or was it a smirk?

Cesar signaled Isabella to park the car before following the women into the gallery. Rows of art hung from stands zigzagging across the once open warehouse space. Mobiles hung at varying heights from open beams that once housed rails to move crates of merchandise from trucks to storage and back to trucks to stores and eventually to homes across Central Texas. Windows cut in the old concrete walls near the ceiling allowed natural light to fill the space on sunny days and keep the public from looking in. Today, only gray with flashes of brightness entered from the windows.

"Jenny," shouted Margaret Smythe, the manager of the gallery, from her office.

"Hi, Margaret. Hope you don't mind. I brought a friend to browse while we work."

Margaret eased her way across the gallery. "Nice to see someone looking around. With this weather, I doubt we'll get many visitors. Good day to rehang those pieces we talked about."

"This is Margaret. I told you all about her," said Jenny. "This is my friend Kitten Carlisle."

"Named for the actress?" Margaret shook Kitten's hand.

"There aren't many people who know who Kitten Carlisle was." Kitten raised her eyebrows in surprise. "Was your mother a fan too?"

"I had to sit and watch that one game show she was on every day with mother. Can't remember what it was called now. But mother insisted we watch just to see what Kitty Carlisle was wearing." Margaret stopped talking as her eyes and mouth softened. "She was glamorous. Wasn't she?"

Kitten beamed. "I've got to give Mommy credit for recognizing true glamour."

"Who are you talking about?" Jenny's confusion rushed across her face.

"Kitten Carlisle. She was an actress and singer from back in the day. She was wonderful." Margaret reminisced about the long-gone actress.

"I'll have to find the game show or one of her movies now and look for her," Jenny, ever practical, decided.

Cesar studied Kitten. Her face lit up when talking about her parents. Her fondness for them showed itself in every slide and twitch of muscle in her face. He wondered why he didn't notice before how expressive she was or her sincerity in her affections. Never having parents of his own, he could not suppress the surge of jealousy flowing through him.

"Where do you want me, boss?" Isabella slipped in behind him, standing on her toes to whisper in his ear.

The interruption shook Cesar out of his contemplation.

"Take perimeter," he said without taking his eyes off of Kitten. "I'll stay with her."

Isabella pursed her lips together, looking between Cesar and the three women. Before she could say anything, Cesar handed her the wet umbrella.

"Hang this up and get to work."

*****

It wasn't the worst way to spend a rainy day. Cesar preferred the modern art pieces, but Kitten preferred the more traditional pieces and lingered in those sections of the collection. He didn't mind. He would come back another time to enjoy the art. Today, he worked. Margaret and Jenny still chatted, dropped pins, twisted wires, and occasionally gasped as a framed photo slipped from fingers. For all her chattiness, Jenny loved her art and spoke deliberately on the best ways to hang it. Margaret, just as serious about art, countered her arguments well. Cesar decided each woman matched the other's logic, and in the end the two found the best solutions and continued as friends.

Kitten meandered through the gallery, oblivious of the chatter. She moved from piece to piece, examining the art. In some places, she stood still with the piece centered in her vision. Other times, she paced forward and backward, examining details within a painting or photo. Sometimes, she glanced at a piece and moved on. Cesar found her interest in the art refreshing. So many of Harry's models lacked interest in anything other than themselves. They posed for pay, and moved on, unconcerned whether Harry's art captured them. Many of them posed for Harry because they wanted something from Anthony. With his good looks, charm, and unlimited finances, Anthony had no problem acquiring models for Harry, but Anthony had not found Kitten. Harry found her.

Cesar noticed Kitten rolling her eyes as he once again intruded on her solitary stroll. He stepped back to give her space. He might need to guard her, but he didn't want her complaining he was doing his job too well. Until today, he had not wondered why or how Harry found Kitten.

Harry's art was so literal there had to be a meaning in his choice of model. It bothered Cesar not to know something. The answer had to be obvious, or why would Isabella be smirking so much?

A shoe squeaked. The shoe that made the squeaking was moving close to him. Cesar stepped around the corner, expecting to see Kitten, but she wasn't there. The squeaking shoe was almost in the center of the gallery. The rows were broken here, allowing viewers to turn in three different directions. He clenched his fist as he saw two men and a woman walking away from him on his right. One of them wore the shoe with the squeak.

Isabella's description was good. Cesar recognized one of the men as the Hunter named Torres who had been watching Harry's house. The other two were unknown. David had reported seeing Torres talking to a military-looking group yesterday. Torres wore an oversized denim jacket, which hung loosely at his shoulders. His fists were plunged into the pockets. The other man, a little taller, dark-skinned and muscular, wore a military haircut. The third person, a woman, equal in height to the men, also sported a military haircut. None of them pretended to look at the art.

The three Hunters turned to the right. They must have seen her go that way. He pinched his lips together, blowing a whistle imperceptible to ordinary ears. Immediately, Cesar heard Jenny stop speaking. If she heard, Isabella did too.

He gave the Hunters another ten feet of distance before following. There were plenty of shadows in the odd corners of the display racks. He smelled Kitten. She was unaware of anyone near her. The men walked past the turn she had taken. Cesar slowed his pace to be near Kitten when he heard and saw Jenny approaching Kitten.

"There you are," she said. "I'm ready for you to see. Margaret and I have rehung the pieces I was telling you about, the ones I made when I was still in Galveston. Come see."

The Hunters turned down an aisle parallel to the one Kitten and Jenny walked. Cesar remained in sight of the two women until a bend in the aisle at a large support pillar. The pillar also blocked the security camera's view of Cesar. He leapt over the art into the Hunters' aisle, landing with only the slightest of thuds a few paces behind them. He followed them.

At an intersection of aisles, they turned toward the voices of Jenny and Kitten. Cesar watched the women walk past them, neither of them looking up from their conversation of black-and-white versus color photography for the best night work. The Hunters followed but stopped. In front of them stood Isabella. Leaning against one of the support pillars with her bright pink high-tops and hat, skinny jeans, and baseball shirt, she was just another artist or admirer of art. But the dark wayfarer glasses and white-toothed grin provided enough warning. The Hunters reversed direction.

Cesar stood face-to-face with them. No one moved. The unknown man's mouth twitched with irritation. Torres's face betrayed a flash of relief and fear. Only the woman hid her emotions. Cesar listened. The Hunters' heartbeats increased, but their lungs slowed as they forced their breaths to slow. Torres removed his fists from his jacket pockets. He put a hand on the shoulder of the other man, nudging him away from Cesar. The three left the gallery with the same deliberate pace they had entered it.

Cesar and Isabella took turns remaining in eyesight of the Hunters until they left the building. Only then did Cesar pull out his phone and call for backup as he moved in sight of Jenny and Kitten, now talking to Margaret. Isabella disappeared from sight as she checked the rest of the building for more Hunters.

Kitten looked up from the picture Margaret was holding in front of her. Cesar thought he saw a shadow pass over Kitten's face, and then Jenny reached out as Kitten crumbled to the floor in a faint.

*****

Tomas leaned against the building a block away from the Phantom's Menace. Three blond women passed him. "Ladies." Tomas grinned showing off his dimples.

All three looked at him and smiled. The tallest turned back to give him an extra smile, winked, and nodded toward the Phantom's Menace.

Tomas sighed and waved but didn't move. "One of the few places I can't go." He sighed as he straightened himself to walk away from the bar.

Before he stepped away, a woman's voice he recognized roared just over the chatter of the gathering crowd. "What the fuck were you thinking? Let me tell you: you weren't thinking."

"You didn't see that little shit with his prick of a smile because he knew there was nothing we could do." The man's voice was young and as full of venom as the woman's.

Tomas allowed himself to meld into the shadows of the building. The Hunters stood not ten feet in front of him. He recognized them all and smelled the alcohol and anger emanating from them. The woman, Anna Leitz, plump and neat as usual, demonstrated her firmness as she led them away from the bar's door and gathered them in a circle around her. He turned his head to miss nothing they said.

Anna's voice, hushed, reminded them who was in charge of their group. "This morning was a flop. I understand. I'm disappointed too, but that's no reason to put yourself out here where they could be looking for you. The place across the street is owned by one of Mugello's minions."

Tomas snickered, "Anthony's minion. Cesar's going to love that."

"This morning was my fault," Torres said. "He knew my face. He must have seen me watching the house. Maybe they read my mind. I don't know, but we should have been able to take them."

Tomas put his hand to his mouth to avoid laughing out loud as his eyes rolled.

"It's not your fault, Torres," Anna said. "But I need you all to think ..."

"Look!" Karol interrupted Anna.

The suddenness with which the group became silent and moved close together caused Tomas to follow their gaze across the street. Cesar stood outside a black town car. As the door opened, Isabella stepped out, sparkling and dripping of sex. Tomas's gaze remained fixed on her as they entered the Phantom's Menace.

Karol's voice broke his reverie. "Motherfuckers! Look at them. Rubbing our noses in it."

But it was Anna's calm, steady voice that frightened him. "Perfect. We've got them where we can take them. Follow me."

Tomas shook his head, wanting to warn Isabella, but instead followed the Hunters. He'd find out what they planned. Hopefully, he'd find a way to warn her of their plans.

*****

Cesar's eyes scanned the busy street. Music blared from the bars, and cigarette smoke wafted through the humid night, coating the air with a smoky fog. Anthony had insisted he take his night off, and Isabella refused to work despite the Hunters' foray into the gallery in the morning. Cesar adjusted his tie and paced a few feet away from the car. Two college students dressed for a night out walked past him, giving him their best smiles. He didn't look at them.

"Are you always so uptight?" Isabella asked. She pushed her hand out the back door of the car.

Cesar continued to scan the street.

"Hello," she said, louder this time, wiggling her fingers in his direction.

Cesar took her hand as she glided out of the car. Her toes emerged first, catching his attention. They twinkled with gold rings and purple toenails studded with rhinestones inside gold spiked sandals. Long legs shimmering in purple satin followed. The high heels gave her so much height, her head almost matched Cesar's. Gold loosely covered her torso, revealing hints of cleavage. In his hand, her small hand glistened with long purple fingernails and more gold.

On the way to the bar, Isabella had leapt into the back seat to change her clothes. "I can't go to dinner in work clothes," she said. Cesar shrugged and shook his head. They were hungry, and too much was happening to make a night of it.

"You're dressed for a frat party?" Cesar told Isabella as she posed for him.

"This is a college town. Why not?" replied Isabella.

"You don't look like a college student any more than I do."

"Flattery's not one of your stronger attributes." Isabella rolled her eyes but smiled and tossed her head back to sway her hair out of her face. "But that's okay. It's more fun being Mrs. Robinson."

Cesar walked toward the Phantom's Menace, his club, scanning the crowd for faces that didn't belong. This was one of the hottest clubs in town, particularly for the college crowd. Hunters should be easy to spot.

A long line stood outside to get in. As they walked to the door, many of those waiting to get in scowled until one of the doormen silenced them with, "He's the owner." The scowls turned to awe. Cesar wondered if they were for the owner or the woman he escorted. The doors opened and the full force of the music brushed through them. He led Isabella up steps and around to a dais near one of the bars, offering them a view of the dance floor, two large swirling bars rising to a second floor, and the multiple video screens projecting the dancers on the floor, bar patrons, music videos, and psychedelic colors.

They stood for a moment in silence, taking in the scene. Isabella turned to him. He still held her hand.

"Oh, Cesar, it's a buffet!" Isabella squealed.

Cesar removed his hand from hers. "Remember the rules," he said.

"Who needs rules when you've got a smorgasbord?" Isabella giggled and slid onto the dance floor, swaying and shimmying with the dancers.

Cesar watched her glide around the floor, enticing and refusing offers of favors according to her whims. He might have continued watching her, but a buxom blonde at the bar with a skirt much too short caught his eye. When she saw him, she grinned, crossed her legs, and stoked the neck of her beer bottle with her little finger. He gave the dance floor a final look. His security personnel stood in their places—some obvious, some not obvious—so he signaled the woman to follow him upstairs to his office.

At one thirty, the alarm on his phone beeped. "Time to go," Cesar told Tenisia, the political science student sitting next to him on the couch in his office. "It's almost time to close shop."

Tenisia smiled as he handed her the pass card. He didn't hand them out often. Her golden brown eyes sparkled from the glitter stoking her dark brown skin. Red fingernails on perfectly petite hands took the card and slid it into her bustier, which revealed just enough cleavage to tempt. He didn't hand out cards often, but Tenisia was both beautiful and intelligent. He enjoyed his conversation with her as much as her blood. She wobbled a little as she walked out the door, so he escorted her down the stairs. The club was still full. His bartender would ensure she drank plenty of juice, and one of the doormen would place her in a taxi for the ride home. The Phantom's Menace was famous for its selection of organic juices and helpful servers, not to mention student-priced local beers and Texas Moonshine.

The crowd still danced and drank, and the music still blared as Cesar's manager gave the thirty-minute signal to the staff. One of the video screens changed to an old-style clock face. It was the first notice to patrons that closing time approached.

He found Isabella leaning against a bar. Roses glowed in her cheeks as energy oozed out of her.

"What do you think of the place?" Cesar asked, bending close to her ear as patrons in a loud bar will do.

"Peachy! Never thought you'd have a place like this." Isabella's smile rubbed off onto Cesar. She leaned close to his face. "You're really not the old stodgy sort you make yourself out to be."

"It's just a club. A place to attract the young and healthy and a place for us to feed." Cesar did not move away from Isabella's face. Her scent reminded him of a cool autumn morning along a lush and lazy river. It provided a sharp contrast to the throngs of heavy floral perfumes, colognes, and sweat.

"Good clubs reflect their owners." She allowed her fingers to rub the hand he had set on the bar. "All the best ones do."

"That was in the day." Cesar did not remove his hand. He studied Isabella's green eyes. "Today, it's only business. Nothing romantic about running a bar anymore."

Isabella turned her head as though to flirt but suddenly stood to attention. "Problem."

Cesar followed her gaze, first to one of the video screens, then to the entrance. Tomas leaned against the upstairs railing over the dance floor. He looked toward Isabella as he scratched his ear. He nodded to Cesar and pointed his head to two men out of place among the throng of dancers. They wore their hair too short and their clothes too drab.

"What the hell is he doing here?" Cesar said aloud, not intending to get an answer.

"He's not who you need to worry about." Isabella took Cesar's hand as her eyes narrowed. "They've got convincers."

"The one on the left with the mismatched eyes, Torres, was in the gallery this morning. So was the woman." Cesar looked at the faces of the Hunters flash across one of the video screens.

"Let's get out of here," said Isabella.

"They're looking for blood. Protect the patrons." Cesar leapt over the bar and reached below the surface. Red lights and sirens blared over the music as soap suds poured from the ceiling. As one, the crowd screamed with glee as they slipped and slid across the floors. The faces of the two men Tomas had pointed out to Isabella and Cesar appeared on one of the video screens, growling. Their hands reached inside their coats as the bright lights went out, leaving only enough light to see figures.

Gunshots smacked through the air over the roar of sirens, turning roars of glee into screams of panic and sparking a rush for the exits. Cesar pulled Isabella over the bar to him and ran, pushing the bartenders to an exit. Cesar remained by the door, guiding patrons out until one of his security guards took over and he followed the patrons outside. Isabella was no longer near him. He ran down the alley and jumped up to the fire exit on the second floor, where he forced open the door. He pulled on arms until the patrons spilled out two by two and then pushed his way inside.

From the railing of the second floor, he searched the building. On the dance floor, three patrons lay dead. Two wounded women huddled behind the upstairs bar. For now, they were safe. A woman and two men, neither of them the original two from the dance floor, roamed the second floor with weapons drawn. One of the men, carrying a shotgun, saw Cesar and aimed. Cesar leapt to the side before the bullet left the barrel. The man turned in the wrong direction to look for Cesar. Cesar pounced, grabbing his head and twisting until the snap and tear of bones and ligaments issued from the man's body. Before he could move away, the familiar double click of another shotgun pumping issued from his right. Cesar turned toward the sound as Isabella rushed the woman with the gun, pushing her into the far wall. Her head broke through mirrors, shattering with the glass. Another shot blared through the emptying and burning nightclub. When Cesar turned to look for the shooter, he watched as Tomas lifted the man and dropped him over the railing to the second floor, into flames.

"There are times I really love my job," Tomas smiled as wide as his eyes. Blood dribbled down his chin. "That's it. We left one alive." Tomas disappeared as smoke filled the air.

"Fire?" Cesar asked as he stood.

Isabella smiled with the same thrilled expression Tomas had. "The one we left alive had a flamethrower. Afraid he started it as soon as he saw me. Who knew they could make them so small these days?"

Cesar reached for Isabella's arm. "Are you okay?" Black and red marks scarred her bare arm from her hand to her shoulder.

"Only scorched." Isabella smiled at Cesar. She had tossed away her shoes when she jumped over the bar and once again had to tilt her head up to look into his face. "The live one is down here. Better get him out before the flames get him."

"Boss!" Cesar's security called. "Boss!"

"Over here," yelled Cesar. "Any of us down?"

"No, but I've got three guests dead on the dance floor. Just took out two wounded. Emergency folks are here. Better get out now. Stanly's got you leaving two hours ago."

Cesar looked to Isabella, "Where is he?" He growled when he asked, as hate soared through him.

Isabella turned to the security chief and pointed behind her. "I heard some moaning over there. Better check it out." She led Cesar to an unconscious Torres with bound hands and feet lying under a table.

"I got this," he said, tossing the car keys to Isabella and swinging Torres over his shoulder. "Let's get out of here. And I want to know what that fucking little cherub was doing in my bar with Hunters."

*****

"Kitten, are you sure you won't sit down?" asked Harry as he continued to paint. "You look exhausted."

"I am not made of glass," Kitten rolled her eyes and shifted her stance. "I wish everyone would stop telling me to relax. How did I know those men were after me this morning?"

"We don't know that," Harry put his brush on the table and looked outside the patio doors.

"Bullshit. Why did I become so afraid and angry at the same time? I hate fainting. It's so embarrassing. And what's so important outside you can't hold a conversation?" Kitten walked out the French doors to stand behind Harry.

Harry turned. They were standing close. Kitten could feel the coolness of his body radiating toward her. He brushed a strand of hair away from her eyes.

"You're very beautiful when you're angry."

Kitten started to pull away from him but changed her mind and drew herself closer to him. She placed her hands on his chest. "Why?" she asked.

His lips touched her forehead. Her breath deepened, and he put his hand to her chest. The lead of guilt pushed its way through her. "I can't kill another man."

"You don't have to." He reached for her. This time, she allowed him to wrap his arms around her. He stroked her hair and brushed her cheek with his. They heard the front door open.

"Harry," called Anthony. He didn't wait for an answer before walking into the studio. "Problem."

Kitten walked to the bar and poured a glass of wine. She intended to look away, but the sound of Anthony's voice pulled her eyes to face him. His hair was loose about his head instead of slicked into place. The button-down shirt, while neat and starched, had an extra button on top undone, exposing his exquisite chest. No belt held his slacks.

Anthony looked at Kitten and Harry without speaking.

"Go on," said Harry.

Anthony kept his eyes on Kitten as he spoke. "One of Cesar's nightclubs was attacked by gunmen. It's burning now."

"The men from the gallery," she said.

"I believe so, although I'm waiting for confirmation."

"Casualties?" asked Harry.

"None of ours, but several patrons died, either shot or from the fire." Anthony finally turned away from Kitten. "They're stepping up their game." This time Kitten heard anger in Anthony's voice.

"Perhaps." Harry turned back to the patio.

"It's time to act," said Anthony.

"Not yet," began Harry, but Kitten interrupted him.

"This morning they were calm and rehearsed. Why would they suddenly set fire to a nightclub full of people?"

"Exactly." Harry walked to Anthony, placing a hand on his shoulder. "Patience, Anthony."

"How much am I supposed to have? Innocent lives were lost, and we lost a prime location for our people."

"More patience than me. I'm not holding you back, Anthony. I'm only saying let's know the facts first. Take Kitten home. I have work to do."

Harry walked through the French doors and vanished from the patio. Anthony picked up a glass ball paperweight and threw it against the wall. It shattered.

Kitten set her glass on the bar, picked up her purse, and held out her arm for Anthony.

"If enemies are shooting nightclubs full of innocent people, they can hardly bother us for a nice stroll in the moonlight. Andiamo?"

Anthony stared at Kitten. She felt his gaze burn into hers. She had never noticed how brown his eyes were, how they reflected as much as they took in, or how gold twinkled behind his irises.

"Si. Camminiamo. I need to think." He took her arm and led her out.

Anthony's car followed them at a distance as they walked toward Kitten's condo. Four guards walked in the shadows around them. One man took Kitten's keys and secured the condo before they arrived.

Kitten sat Anthony on the couch and poured them bourbons before walking behind him to massage his shoulders.

"It's Cesar's nightclub or yours?" Kitten kept her voice quiet.

"Cesar's. It was his idea."

"Cesar is alive?"

"Yes. He called me to let me know what was happening."

"Wait for him. He knows what he's doing. I assume you've taught him well."

"I couldn't function without him." Anthony took Kitten's hand and kissed it. "Thank you. I needed a reminder to think before acting."

Kitten bent over and kissed his cheek. "What are friends for?" She ran her hands up and down his arms, breathing in his scent. She felt her chest heave as she took in a long draught of his scent; masculine, woody, earthy.

Anthony turned his head to look at her. "You're different," he said. He stood pulling out his phone. It vibrated in his hand.

"Where are you?" he asked without saying hello.

Kitten picked up her drink and lounged on the couch as Anthony paced. She admired his physique. She hadn't noticed before how nearly perfect he was. His muscular chest swelled as he spoke. The cuffs of his sleeves were rolled up, giving hints of strong arms. She already knew his hands were smooth and caressing. As he turned his back to walk toward the patio, she admired his backside, smooth and tight.

The cat jumped into her lap, and she sat up, shaking her head. She scratched the cat's ears, listening.

"Bring him to the compound, then head to police headquarters. Be cooperative. Yes. She should go too. I'll be there as soon as I can."

Anthony looked at Kitten with the cat in her lap. "I have to go," he said. He almost smiled.

"Have a drink. Collect yourself." Kitten stood and set the cat on the couch.

Anthony sat on the couch, picking up his drink from the table.

Kitten put a hand on Anthony's face. "Be careful," she said, bending over and kissing his lips, savoring his taste mixed with bourbon and authority.

Anthony placed his hands on her waist, and she straddled his lap as she inhaled his essence. His hands caressed her body as she wrapped herself around him. The muscles in his arms tightened, and his chest rippled with the slightest of tension as he lifted her and laid her on the couch beneath him. His hands pushed at her skirt as her hands dove into his shirt to press into his chest, smooth and strong. They rolled off the couch and onto the floor. She pressed her body into his before pushing herself up. She pulled her shirt off as his hands grabbed her bra straps and slid them down until he could fondle her breasts. He rolled the two of them over again pushing himself into her. She gasped for breath as shadows danced before her eyes. He thrust again. She wrapped her legs around him tighter, feeling his strength, cold, hard like steel, and tight. She felt herself breaking under his strength. Her heart pounded in her chest as though it would burst and then ... release.

Her breath slowed as her heart returned to its normal rhythm. His head lay on her stomach. Their sweat mingled as it cooled. Neither moved nor spoke. Kitten closed her eyes, picturing *The Lovers* and recognizing herself and Anthony in the figures.

Anthony broke the silence as his hand traced curves in the sweat around her breast and belly button. "Any regrets?"

Kitten put one arm behind her head and stroked the hair on his head. "No. You know what's in my head. We won't last."

"I know, but we have now." Anthony leaned forward and kissed her lips. "I have to go soon. My people need me."

"You're an important man, Anthony. I won't pretend to understand everything, but I won't regret being with you. Take a shower. Look your part."

While Anthony showered, Kitten wrapped her favorite white robe around her and poured herself another drink. So much was happening with her and around her. The only thing she knew for certain was she would regret nothing she did for the last of her days.

As Anthony opened the door to leave, she gave him one more lasting kiss.

He whispered in her ear. "Someone will be watching you. You don't have anything to worry about."

"I know," she said, smiling at him.

As she closed the door and locked it, she felt safer than she had in a long time.

*****

"What the hell are we missing?" Frank plunked back in his chair, rubbing his temples.

Renaldo scratched the stubble on his chin and looked up at Hank pouring himself another cup of coffee. "It doesn't make sense. First the accountants and now the fire. What do your *experts* say?"

Hank shrugged. "Wish I had an answer for you. The team in Washington is looking over the same information we are, but they're scratching their heads too."

Frank opened a manila folder. "If it were just the bar fire, we could bring in the usual suspects and chances are one of them would be guilty. But there's no way we have a mass execution and an attack on a bar and they're not connected."

Renaldo tossed a stack of papers from his desk to Frank's. "We don't *know* these others are related, Frank. Each looks like the work of the cartels, but they aren't."

Hank picked up a report that had fallen off Renaldo's desk. "I'm with the kid, Frank. We're eating up resources looking for a connection when maybe we should look at each incident on its own."

Hank stopped himself from laying the report on Renaldo's desk. A name on the report caught his eye. "Why'd they send this to you?" he asked, handing it to Frank.

Frank took the paper, scanning it before setting it down. "Sorry, forgot all about it. Davis says you had asked about the victim. She and her husband disappeared from the hospital the same night as the bar fire. Since she was in a coma, she didn't check herself out. Davis thinks the husband maybe ..."

Hank jumped out of his seat. "You mind if I take a look?" He was holstering his revolver before Frank could answer.

Frank raised his eyebrows, "What do you see?"

Hank shrugged his shoulders, "Maybe nothing. Maybe something."

Frank handed the report to Renaldo. "You go with him. He smells something, and you know Austin."

Hank was already walking out the door when Renaldo jumped out of his chair to follow him.

*****

Karol paced in front of the picture window. The view overlooking the river glowed gold with autumn's morning bloom, but he didn't notice.

"So where the hell are they?" he said, agitation oozing from his pores.

Roger sat in the faded armchair, watching him. Karol was key to keeping this group of soldiers under control. He was loud, obnoxious, too-wired for this kind of operation, but he provided Roger with a good pulse for the rest of the soldiers.

"Those that made it out will make their way here or signal for help. Everyone knows what to do." Roger kept his voice calm, letting Karol vent while they were alone in the house.

"The news only talks about three gunmen entering the bar." Karol's fists clenched, and the muscles in his arms contracted and expanded.

Roger watched. "Woods is on it. He knows the right questions to ask. He'll discover what the police know, and then we'll know. Trust nothing you hear in the news."

"This is bullshit!" Karol flung himself onto the couch, allowing the golden rays of sunshine to flow over him.

"It's the bullshit we've got," said Roger, watching Karol drifting into sleep. Since Anna's disastrous attempt to kill the demons at the art gallery, they were all as agitated as Karol. Anna seemed to think they were there to pursue her course of vengeance, but Roger understood these former soldiers had their own agendas. They liked to kill, and Anna had given them a purpose and a target they could pursue with enthusiasm. As he sank further into their motivations, he realized the team he and Yasushi had formed were broken souls seeking redemption more than revenge. The demons had touched each of them, and Yasushi made them whole. Each member of the team worked with purpose to understand, heal, and conquer. They had killed but with stealth and purpose. The killing at the bar was brash, unplanned, and damaged their goals.

Madeline sat at the table drinking coffee and staring at nothing. Roger insisted she come with him to the new safe house. He insisted they stop at the store to purchase beer and whiskey. She showed no concern for the civilians who died in the ill-planned attack on the bar. She didn't even watch the television's almost constant news coverage of the search for the attackers.

Roger walked to the couch. Karol's eyes were closed, and his facial muscles twitched uncontrolled around his mouth and chin as his eyes danced behind their lids.

He went to the table and sat in front of Madeline. "What happened at the hospital?"

"Nothing," she replied and poured a cup of coffee for Roger.

He raised an eyebrow, waiting for her to say more.

"Madeline," he began after checking once more Karol was asleep. "We're in deep shit. I need to know everything if we're going to win this war."

"Nothing," she said again. This time, Roger thought he saw confusion in her face.

"Is CC dead or alive?" he asked.

"I don't know," she replied. Roger opened his mouth to speak, but she finished her statement. "No one knows. She wasn't there."

"James Earl?" he asked.

"Also missing. I finally found one of her nurses. He said they were both in CC's room a little after midnight. On the next check, before two, no one was in the room. The administration filed a report with the police, but no one knows where they went. Now you know as much as I do." Madeline slammed her cup on the table.

Roger turned to make sure Karol did not wake before leaning back in his chair.

"Shit just keeps getting deeper," Roger said. "If we had—"

A knock on the front door caused them to turn. Karol leapt off the couch, grabbing the handgun he had placed on the coffee table.

"Stand down, soldier," Roger placed himself between Karol and the front door.

Karol kept the gun in his hand and moved to the blind side of the door. Roger looked through the peephole.

"Woods." He sighed and opened the door.

Karol remained in the blind spot until Woods entered. With a smirk on his face, he moved back to the couch where he set the gun back onto the coffee table.

"It took a while, but I got inside to look at the bodies. Torres wasn't there. Three were." Woods's eyes scanned the room, watching Karol, Roger, and Madeline.

"They have him! Fuck! I told you they got him," shouted Karol, jumping off the couch again.

"We don't know that," retorted Roger. He turned back to Woods. "What else did you learn? Where's Yasushi?"

Woods took a deep breath, but his eyes continued to survey the room. "Police know a fourth man was with them from the video surveillance, but they can't find a body. Witnesses talk about a man with a flamethrower being knocked down by a bouncer or maybe a patron. It's pretty confusing. They found the flamethrower but not the man."

"Can't trace it to us," interjected Karol.

Woods's attention turned to Madeline. "Didn't find the rev. Looked everywhere he should have been."

"What about the girl in the hospital?" asked Karol. "Did you look for her, or did you help her get out of town?"

Woods looked to Roger, about to say something, but Karol jumped between them. "I heard you talking. What about the woman and her boyfriend? I thought your team were hot shit with tech and surveillance, but you can't even keep up with your own people when they're dead."

Karol stepped close to Roger, leering at him.

"I went to check on them this morning," Madeline stood. "They were gone. They've been gone since Tuesday morning. No one in the hospital knows where they went, but CC was stable, which means she could have been moved. I'm going to make more coffee. Would anyone else like some?"

"Roger?" asked Derek.

"They'll be in touch. James Earl must have believed they were in danger. I'm not worried about them," Roger lied. "I'm going to find Yasushi. We need him now."

"No," Karol said, taking Roger's arm. "Anna says he's compromised. It's probably his fault—"

Before Karol could finish, Roger turned and threw his fist into Karol's nose. Karol fell to the floor, blood spewing from his nose. "Never question me again, soldier. Woods, clean him up. Nobody leaves the house till I'm sure the area is clear."

"Yes, sir," replied Woods, looking with no pity at Karol.

Madeline returned from the kitchen and looked at Karol. "We're not getting our cleaning deposit back."

*****

"Here it is." Carl Tang wrote down the address of Margo Titler and handed it to Renaldo. "Her next shift starts at eleven, but she always comes in early. Very dedicated and one of the best nurses this hospital has. I'm not sure what else she can tell you that she didn't tell Detective Davis."

Renaldo took the slip of paper and smiled at the administrator with the smile that always set people at ease. "You'd be surprised, Mr. Tang. Often all it takes is asking the same question with a different voice, and suddenly a witness remembers all sorts of things they didn't think important the first time they were interviewed. Thank you for your help."

"Let me know if there is anything else you need. We've had patients get up and leave without signing out before but never one in a coma." Carl's fingers traced the edges of the trophy his kids had given him. "If Margo hadn't gotten sick that night and had to leave, I bet that poor woman would still be safe in her room. I hope she's all right."

"So do we, Mr. Tang." Renaldo left and headed upstairs where Hank said to meet him.

It annoyed him that Hank said nothing on the way to the hospital and then ordered him to the administrator's office. When the elevator door opened on the fourth floor, Hank stood opposite the doors, staring out the windows. Down the hall, a technician in a blue uniform stood taking down a security camera.

Renaldo cleared his throat, but Hank showed no sign of recognizing him. "I've got the info for the nurse that got sick the night your friend went missing. She won't be here 'til after ten. You want to catch her at home or come back here later?"

Hank's shoulders slumped. "I'm an idiot, Renaldo."

Renaldo said nothing. Hank continued looking out the window.

"Agent Williams?" The technician Renaldo had seen with the security camera walked up to them. Hank turned. "You were right. If you hadn't suggested it, I wouldn't have looked for it." The technician held the camera in his hand and pointed to the connector.

Hank pulled his shoulders back. "Thanks, Lewis. Detective Sanchez will take the connector in for evidence."

Renaldo pulled out a bag as Lewis handed him the small connector saying, "I'll be damned if I ever seen it before. Who would have thought to look for a connector so small nobody would notice?"

"Appreciate your help," Renaldo said, pretending he knew what Lewis was talking about. He had never seen a connector pulled apart and wondered what was unusual about it.

When Lewis walked away, Hank looked at Renaldo. "I take it back, Renaldo. I'm not an idiot and an ass." He walked to the elevators.

"What?" Renaldo asked. "What does this tell us?"

"CC was onto something. Nearly got her killed, and she ended up here. I don't know if she's dead now or if she got away, and it's my fault."

The elevator doors opened. Hank banged the ground floor button, almost cracking it. "Son of a bitch!" came out of his mouth in a loud whisper.

Renaldo said nothing but smiled at the woman with gray hair wearing a volunteer vest.

Outside the elevator, Hank thundered across the parking lot to the car. Renaldo jogged to keep up with him.

Before they reached the car, Renaldo caught up with Hank and grabbed his shoulder, turning him around. "Are you going to tell me what the hell's going on or are you going to storm around like a jackass the rest of the day?"

Hank stared at Renaldo. His chest expanded and then he nodded his head as his shoulders relaxed. "That trick with the camera connector's one that pros use when they don't want to be seen or let anyone know they've been around. Whoever took CC from the hospital knew what he was doing. I stood there and talked to that Reverend Brown, knowing he was lying, and I did nothing."

"Reverend Yasushi Brown?" he asked.

Hank's face lit up. "You know him?"

"Most in the department do. He's been a chaplain in PDs throughout the county. Kind of famous for it. I met him a few weeks ago at a community event. Told me he was in town for a while on business. Want to talk to him?"

Hank grinned but looked out across the parking lot. "Yes," he said at last. "But let's talk to that nurse first."

Renaldo unlocked the car doors, relieved Hank's mood had shifted.

As Hank fastened his seat belt, he said, "You're not as dumb as you look, kid. I can see why Frank keeps you on."

Renaldo shook his head, whispering under his breath, "Stupid old men running around half-cocked." He pulled the car out of the parking spot.

* * * * *

No dreams troubled Kitten's sleep. She woke in the morning feeling well and whole. Her blankets cradled her in warmth and softness. Her breath came easy, and the sun streamed through her windows as it should. And then her stomach rumbled. Kitten stretched herself out of the bed and meandered into the living room. On the table sat a basket of fresh kolaches, still warm, a pot of coffee steaming its aromatic charms, and a single red rose in a vase. The cat walked in from the patio and wound itself around Kitten's feet. She picked up the cat and cuddled it as she walked outside to feel the sun on her face.

No one was on the river. Singing birds, lapping water, rustling leaves filled the air. Kitten laughed. "A glorious day, cat. Too nice a day for work, but I suppose I should go in after playing hooky yesterday." Memories flashed before her of men glaring at her from behind paintings, flames bursting in her face, and a golden-haired face, bloodied and laughing as flames surged around him. She set down the cat and poured coffee as she felt Anthony's touch on her brow and felt their lust surge through her body. She caught her breath and sat as her knees weakened. "Oh, cat," she said as it curled on her lap, purring for attention. Kitten stroked the cat without looking at it. "What a strange world I'm leaving."

Her phone vibrated on the desk, shocking her and the cat into the present. Kitten took the cat with her to check her messages. A long list of text messages from Stacy, her mother, Leigh, Carol, and other members of the publishing house reminded her she still had work to do. And there was the pile of papers known as Stacy's book. "Come on, cat. Let's get to work."

6

Rape of Europa

Ring in the season of death with lights and songs.
Sleep and dream for Spring's lust and Summer's gild.
Let the moon release the beasts to guard against the blasphemous light.
Bathe in the sun to heal old wounds.
Death walks this town tonight under shadows long and dark.
Peace in sleep brings hope and life.
Dream, my children, of netherworlds and Gods forgotten and unloved.
Dream, my children, to walk in hope.
Patience, Peace, and Paradise wait for all who obey the laws of nature.
Be bound and escape to live again.
Release and die a thousand times, for no peace will come to you.
I'm Mary Midnight.
You're listening online and in your mind.
Mourn, my children, this loss of innocence.
Know that I see all.

Roger and Anna snarled at each other for an hour before the yelling started. The soldiers lingered downstairs or in the boathouse waiting to find out who survived the attack on the bar.

"I told you—" Roger began.

Anna interrupted, "And I told you we needed to act. If your man hadn't been so trigger-happy, it would have worked."

"How many civilians died because a plan wasn't in place?" Roger gave up containing his anger. The latest news broadcast listed six dead including the three gunmen. Law enforcement locked down the city as they searched for a missing suspect. Downtown Austin held an unearthly silence as residents remained in their homes.

"Necessary casualties. The place was a den for demons. How many more people would have died if we did nothing?"

"We don't—"

"Enough!" Madeline stood between Roger and Anna. Her normal bitter face softened as she looked from face to face. "Let's review what we've learned." She motioned for Roger and Anna to sit on the couch.

She leaned into the old-fashioned rocking chair and looked at Roger. "You agree Karol saw the two vampires from the art gallery entering the nightclub." She turned her face to Anna. You agree Roger oversees operations." Madeline held her hand up as Anna opened her mouth to speak. "I, too, might have acted as you did. We had little warning where they would be or who would be in danger because of them. It's only natural you wished to act, but we must maintain control. Is that right, Roger?"

"Yes, but ..."

Madeline raised her hand again to interrupt Roger. "We have one enemy. Destroying them is our only goal."

Roger placed his hands on his knees as though to stand but instead rolled his shoulders. "Yasushi needs to be involved. He can keep us working together."

"I'm afraid my brother has been compromised. You're well aware of his situation." Madeline kept her voice quiet. The others leaned in to hear her. "I witnessed him talking to one of the demons. We decided it's best to keep him out of direct decision-making until we know he's safe from their influence."

"Without him," said Roger, "We have no one for the troops to rally around."

Anna straightened her back. "You're a captain. I'm a deacon. We can rally the soldiers if we work together."

Roger said nothing, looking first to Madeline and then out the window.

"We'll bring him to the safe house." Madeline turned her attention to Anna. "We can keep him safe from the demons and still involve him with the day-to-day matters so critical for continuity."

Anna nodded. "We'll still be able to use his vast knowledge of the creatures."

"Roger?" Madeline raised her eyebrow. "Agree?"

Roger waited before turning his attention back to Madeline and Anna. "We'll have to make it work. Until the city is back to normal, there's not much we can do in the field. I believe I know a way to set the reverend free of the demon's grasp and deliver a damaging blow to them. We can use this quiet time to our benefit. Yasushi will want to be here."

Madeline stood straightening the folds of her floral dress. "Excellent. I think you would prefer to fetch my brother here."

Roger stood. "After I talk to the soldiers. They need to know the fight continues despite a rift in the timeline."

"Let me do it." Anna bounced off the couch and headed to the door. "I recruited many of them for this. It should be me."

Madeline nodded approval. "I'm going to the store. We need more groceries."

"Be careful," Roger said. "The police are desperate to find their man. Be sure to cooperate with them if they stop you."

"They're not looking for a middle-aged woman, but I'll be careful all the same." Madeline picked up her purse and rifled through it.

Madeline stopped to watch Roger and Anna walk out and heard Roger calling for the soldiers to gather downstairs. She listened at the inner door as Anna rattled on about how brave the dead were. She cringed her nose, "Sanctimonious bitch. They're not stupid. Roger's losing his touch if he lets her prattle on." She resisted the urge to open the door and set the soldiers straight about what was happening.

*****

Cesar sat across the table from Detective Frank Jarvis, who kept putting his coffee cup to his lips but not drinking. Detective Sanchez sat beside Isabella, who continued to droop her head and sniffle. "It still hasn't sunk in, you know? I keep thinking I'll wake up and this will all be a bad dream."

"Cartels are getting bold, Cesar," said Frank. "Nothing prepared me for this though. Shit! I thought I'd hit retirement without ever having to touch 'em."

"I just don't get it, Frank," said Cesar. "What did they think would happen? Austin's a loose place, I give you that, but to pull this kind of shit, just to scare us? I mean, you're proof this city isn't going to take this kind of shit from anyone. I bet you and every detective in the city were on the case in what, an hour? It's a miracle so few died."

Isabella's shoulders shook as a tear again streamed down her face. Detective Sanchez placed his arm across her back. "It's okay, just let it out."

Cesar cringed, but he had to admire Isabella for playing her part well.

The police station roared, stuffed with police officers, police employees, federal agents, and government watchdogs working around the clock to find the missing suspect and identify the three dead suspects.

"Let's give credit where it's due. If your security folks hadn't acted so quick, it could have been a bloodbath."

Isabella let out a long groan, and more tears flowed. "Those poor kids. They just wanted a good time, and now their mothers—" she didn't finish her sentence as she turned to bury her head in Cesar's shoulder.

A young police officer opened the door, grinning ear to ear. "We got a break," he said while trying to catch his breath. "The lone guy on tape leaving just walked in the door. Says he works for De La Rosa." The officer closed the door.

"What the hell?" asked Jarvis as he and Sanchez headed out the door.

"Overplaying it?" asked Isabella, looking at Cesar winking.

Cesar winked. "Perfect performance as you know. Anthony must have gotten my message."

The door opened. Detective Sanchez entered, asking Cesar to join the others in the viewing room. As Cesar stood to leave, Detective Sanchez added, "I'll stay here to look after Ms. Iandanza."

Cesar resisted smiling and patted Isabella on the back. "I'll be back as soon as I can. You stay here."

Frank Jarvis stood with two FBI agents outside an interview room. "Cesar," he called out. "Agents Williams and Jones. We want you to see if this is one of your people."

The door opened on a middle-aged man sitting with shoulders slumped in a chair behind a small table. His hands were handcuffed behind him. His head hung low, but when the door opened and he saw Cesar, his eyes widened. "Señor De La Rosa. I'm so sorry. Debería haberte dicho."

Before Cesar could answer, Agent Williams walked into the room. "Que deberías haberle dicho a Señor De La Rosa, Ramon?"

Ramon's face sank even lower. "My papers. They're fake. I knew if you checked, you'd find out and send me back to Venezuela. That's why I ran out when the shooting started. I'm a coward. I left Venezuela to get away from the gangs. I didn't want to get involved, but when I saw me on the news, I knew you'd find me."

Frank pulled Cesar back into the hall. Cesar shook his head. "Poor Ramon."

"He came forward on his own," said Frank. "Look, if you want to take your friend home, go ahead. You can't do more here."

"I don't want to step on any toes, but—well, Ramon's a decent guy with a family. Would it be alright if I got him a lawyer? I can't imagine him being in on the shooting. I'd hate to see him deported."

"Give us a couple of hours to make sure he doesn't know anything, but looking at him right now, I'm inclined to believe you."

Cesar nodded his head. "Thanks, Frank. And please, call me when you know anything. This happened in my bar. I feel responsible. Surely there's something else I could have done."

"No, you did everything right. Go home and stop beating yourself up."

Ol' Mike pulled the town car to the door inside the garage, away from reporters. Cesar and Isabella, surrounded by detectives, left the building. As he drove away, Ol' Mike said, "Anthony wants to see you."

"How are things?" replied Cesar.

"Locked up tight, just the way you like it. No one's getting near the house."

"My feet are killing me," interrupted Isabella. "I don't suppose you have any spare shoes in here."

Ol' Mike laughed. "No, ma'am. But I'll have you at the house soon. Might want to wait 'til after you've seen Anthony before changing though. He's a bit miffed about the whole thing."

Cesar leaned back in the car. Isabella remained sitting very close to him, but he didn't object. They had survived a fire and an attack by Hunters. Now, they had to face Anthony.

*****

"Oh my god! You should have seen him. He's adorable. No, he's incredibly sexy. I don't know a woman who wouldn't look at him with those golden curls and polished dimples and not want to jump on top of him. If I could get him on the cover of a few books, they'd sell in a flash. There was nothing wrong with Fabio, but girls, you should see this man." Stacy's animated description of Tomas continued for several minutes.

Kitten, Leigh, and the other managers sat smiling into their cameras as their boss obsessed over a young man she had seen earlier in the week. The city might be locked down, but Stacy was no tech novice. The weekly project list meeting went on as scheduled. Their task now was to find a man worthy of their boss's praises or there would be no rest for any of them.

"And," Stacy continued, "you know how I rarely go for the golden boy look. I mean, it's passé, but this boy will melt your tits off."

"So," Leigh took advantage of the momentary break in Stacy's praises to channel the discussion back to this week's project list. "I'd say your book is around the halfway point, Stacy. Kitten and I may yet have it edited in time for the Romance Writers' Conference this summer."

"If we could get him for the cover ..." Stacy's eyes glazed over. "It would be perfect."

Kitten held her hand over her mouth to hide her smirk. "You'll have to talk to your new friend about recruiting him." They prepared to steer Stacy's fascination for the young man back to business. "In the meantime, I've got three possible new textbook writers desperate to pitch their ideas. Two of them are worth listening to."

"Carol, set it up. What else is new?" And Stacy was back to business. "Leigh, sales are falling on your latest fall series. Find someone to say something fresh about it, or let the author go."

"Got it," Leigh scribbled on a notepad ignoring most of what Stacy said.

"Kitten, no playing hooky without me knowing about it. Thought I'd have a heart attack trying to find you yesterday."

"It's not playing hooky if the boss knows I'm not going to be around," replied Kitten. "What did you need me for?"

"You've got to get your artist friend to get Anthony to convince Leonard to convince Tommy or Tomas, whatever the hell he's called, to pose for cover."

"I'll get right on it," laughed Kitten.

"The rest of you should have a hooky day now and then. Look at her all smiles and glowing like a woman in love. Oh, I like that line. Use it in the book. We're not already using it, are we?"

Leigh and Kitten typed "parallelism" in a private message to each other and tried not to giggle on camera.

*****

"You were right to stay away." Yasushi sat on the open deck of the river house. The late afternoon sun beat on the wooden planks creaking underneath Roger's weight.

Roger said nothing until he sat opposite Yasushi. "It was a mistake to think the demons could be killed in such a public place. We lost three good soldiers, and we can't find Torres. He hasn't made contact. We have to assume he's dead or worse."

Yasushi continued to stare across the meandering river, empty of human life on this day of mourning in the city.

Roger waited, but when Yasushi made no sign of speaking, he continued. "I'm sorry. I should have told you about the change in agenda, but the opportunity to act arrived. We had to take it." Roger walked to the edge of the deck. "Damn it, Yasushi! You should have told me you were talking to one of them. Madeline won't trust you again. I don't think anyone will."

Yasushi remained silent.

Roger paced back and forth in front of him. "We've been friends a long time. I deserve some sort of explanation from you."

"Police were here about midday," said Yasushi. "They're searching all the homes and boathouses along the river, particularly the rentals. I didn't hinder their search, and they were thorough. Fortunately, Derek and Phillip were also thorough. The police found no weapons or anything suspicious." Yasushi stood and turned to walk into the house. "About time for a cup of tea. Would you like one? This is not a conversation to hold outside where anyone might hear us."

Roger wondered why he hadn't noticed the furniture sitting askew, the magazines stacked too neatly on the coffee table, and the amount of shoeprints in the carpet. He had dreaded finding Yasushi as much as he wanted to find him. He needed the spiritual strong arm he had depended on over the years. And now Yasushi's distance from him felt like a part of himself was missing. He felt a tug in his chest as he sat on the couch.

Yasushi entered the room carrying a tray with a teapot and two cups. "We've always agreed that civilians must be protected."

"I wasn't there to tell the soldiers not to enter the nightclub." Roger rubbed his neck as an ache drifted down his arm.

"I'm not talking about the nightclub." Yasushi poured steaming tea into the cups. "Why attempt to take the Carlisle woman? She may be involved with the demons, but there is nothing to suggest she's one of them."

Roger licked his lips as he put the cup to his mouth. He breathed in the soft aroma and steam. "You've been talking to Derek."

"He's troubled as much by your actions as he is by the demons'. If you had told me you no longer had faith in me, I would have stepped aside. There was no need to hide your actions."

Roger leaned back on the couch, still holding onto his cup. "Derek is a good marine—"

"He's a good man who no longer considers himself a marine," interrupted Yasushi.

Roger nodded. "Yes, a good man. I should have talked to you about my suspicions, but you were seen talking to the artist, a known demon, and you disappeared. I couldn't take any chances. We know they can manipulate people."

"I see." Yasushi smiled at Roger.

"I still believe in you, Yasushi. I do. I need to know I can trust you."

"I've never lied to you, Roger. I've been here since CC's accident. My source of information was a secret only to protect Madeline. Clearly, she doesn't need me protecting her anymore. She has you." Yasushi lifted his hand to prevent Roger from speaking. "I'm happy she has you. I'm happy you have someone to care for. You know how her mind works. It's now your responsibility to lead the group and Madeline to complete our mission."

They drank their tea in silence. Roger saw Yasushi watching him, waiting for Roger to say something, but Roger didn't know what to say.

"Your end goal has changed. You were content, as I was, to find the demon responsible for the lives of so many servicemen and women caught in those dens of inequity and destroyed by them. We know it's one demon leading those raids. Justice draws close for us all. What do you want now?" Yasushi looked into Roger's eyes.

"After the reports I've read, I know there are more of them than we thought. They all need to die. We need to cleanse the world of their influence. No longer will demons like Mugello ruin the lives of ordinary people."

"You sound like Madeline." Yasushi set his cup on the table. "If that's what you want, you must strive for it."

Roger pounded his cup on the tray, breaking the cup and toppling the teapot. Its contents filled the tray. "It goes against everything you've ever said. Why the hell are you so compliant? What do you know you're not saying?" yelled Roger.

"All I ever wanted, Roger, was justice. My mother may have been a whore who mistreated her children and pimped out her daughters, but she didn't deserve to have her throat ripped out. My siblings never had a chance to grow up, perhaps to climb out of the cesspool we were born in. I gathered together those who, like me and Madeline, found themselves broken. We found hope in the search for justice. You've taken over the group and expanded that justice. Who am I to resist?"

Roger slumped his shoulders, placing his face in his hands. He wanted Yasushi to argue with him, to fight him on this, but Yasushi wouldn't. "We've moved to a new safe house. If you come with me, you can't come back here. We can't run the risk of the police or anyone else noticing us. You're known, so you could move around the city, get us supplies, and see what's happening in the streets, but you won't be included in the planning anymore. And Madeline won't leave you alone after dark."

"I'll just clean this up first." Yasushi stood and carried away the tray filled with spilled tea. Before he left the room, he asked, "When did Madeline see me with the demon?"

Roger said nothing, wondering the same thing.

*****

Margo stood on all fours in the shadows behind the hospital. No Hunters approached her hospital or threatened her patients. She padded her way through the parking lot, avoiding the security cameras and sniffing the cars for anything unusual. Satisfied the lot was secure, she made her way back to the corner of the loading bay where her clothes remained folded and stacked under a chair. Shift change would start soon. No one would question her being at the hospital outside her shift. She was always there.

The television in the break room continued its round-the-clock vigil for the search for the terrorist that got away. Video of the burning nightclub repeated over and over.

"No good to keep watching," she said and turned the television off. The two nurses drinking coffee opened their mouths to object but stopped when she held up her hand. "DeeDee, I know you've been working extra hours. Either get back to work or go home. You look like shit. What good are you to your patients like that? And Ben, I hear two bodies not related to that fire came in to the morgue. You get downstairs and process them for the doctor."

"Yes, ma'am," they both said. They glanced at the television but looked less dejected at the purpose Margo had given them.

Margo laughed to herself. "Kids!"

She drove home. The city was too quiet. It irritated her. She slammed the door of her car closed. "Sons of goats! Going around killing for the sake of killing. What's the world coming to?" She murmured even as she tried to smile and wave hello to old Mrs. Sanchez, working in her garden next door. Maybe her growing anger at the Hunters' audacity distracted her. She didn't notice the two men sitting in a car across from Mrs. Sanchez's house. She walked into her kitchen and didn't notice the smell of strangers in her house and gas leaking from the stove until it was too late.

*****

The whimpering stole into Tomas's ears, again. She had been in the box for most of the evening.

"Aren't you afraid of some hotel guest hearing her or the police coming back for another search?" he asked, moving from the couch to sit at the table with Leonard.

"No one else can hear her. Those stupid police officers didn't even ask to look inside the box."

Tomas raised his eyebrow.

"She knows better than to make herself known." Leonard sat at the table in the living room of his suite at the Driskill Hotel, stretching out his legs and sitting back. "I can't believe she had the gall to come here." Leonard rapped his fingers on the tabletop.

Tomas watched Leonard's face. "The werewolves took the redheaded woman. There's no doubt. I could smell them all over the hospital."

"There haven't been werewolves in Austin since Kennedy was president." The rapping of Leonard's fingers on the table increased.

"They're here now," replied Tomas. He moved to stand in front of the window overlooking Sixth Street. "I assume you know about the ones Anthony keeps at the compound."

"I know about him. His wife is one too? Why didn't I know that?"

From the box in the bedroom, Tomas heard the whimpering again. This time she tried speaking. "Leonard?" she whispered. "Leonard? My love? Please. Let me out. I promise to be a good girl. Leonard?"

Tomas wanted to sneer but focused on Leonard's face, amazed to see his old mentor confused. Leonard prided himself in knowing everything about everybody. His face contorted as though seeking the right descriptor.

"She's a freak," snarled Leonard. "I can't have creatures I know nothing about wandering the streets, upsetting plans."

Tomas returned his gaze to the quiet street below him. Emergency vehicles remained parked up and down Sixth Street but fewer now than there had been. The police had already been through the suite when they inspected every room in the hotel. He still smelled them. Sweaty, worried, anxious, ready to kill. "Leonard?" echoed through the room into his ears again.

Tomas cringed. "You don't think the she-wolf could be useful?" he asked, trying to focus on his purpose.

"No. Do it as soon as Harry and Anthony are dead." Leonard walked to the sofa, picking up a book as he sat. He opened the book, but almost as soon as he sat and opened the book, he set the book down and moved to stand next to Tomas.

"What's wrong?" asked Tomas.

"I can't stand being stuck in one place. I'm going out."

"That a good idea? The police are trigger-happy, and Anthony said he wanted everyone to stay hidden for now."

Leonard rolled his eyes. "I'm tired of his excessive caution and placating. Soon," Leonard placed his arm on Tomas's shoulders, "soon, this city will be mine, and we won't remain hidden."

The woman's voice creeped into the silence of the room. "I promise to be a good girl." Leonard and Tomas turned their heads toward the bedroom.

"Should you leave her in there much longer?" Tomas asked.

"She needs to learn her place," replied Leonard. "She's another reason to get out of here. Her bawling is pathetic. How I hate these creatures. When this is done, Tomas ..." Leonard trailed off as though his mind were already on a killing spree.

Tomas smiled and looked at Leonard. "I'll find out where the werewolves are hiding. Can't be too many places in a city this size where they can run when the moon is full."

"Good man. I knew I was right in bringing you here."

✳✳✳✳✳

The smell of food woke him. Sunlight streamed in through cracks in the heavy curtains. James Earl sat up as his stomach growled. The sound of CC laughing, though hushed and coarse, reminded him where he was and why he was there.

He jumped off the bed and ran to her room. CC lounged against large, fluffy pillows. "Hey, sleepyhead, you decided to wake up."

James Earl bent over CC to look into her face. Black and gray, but glimmering green eyes reflected his face. A smile pushed up the corners of her pale lips.

"You're beautiful, babe." James Earl kissed her but kept his lips a whisper's breath away from the blue bruises.

"I look like shit," she said. "Margo let me see a mirror, but I feel better."

James Earl bent over to kiss her again.

"Easy does it, lover," said Margo. "My patient is recovering from major trauma."

"Oh!" James Earl jumped away from the bed.

Both women laughed. "I'm only a little broke, babe, but I'll be okay." CC squeezed James Earl's hand. "Margo's a terrific nurse."

James Earl looked at Margo. He tried to smile as his eyes scanned her face.

"She's healing well. Relax. I'm going to check on the soup."

CC sighed and gazed out the window. "It's a lovely place. You should go outside and take it in. We'll be here for a while."

James Earl sat down beside CC. "I'll stay here with you."

CC smiled. "Margo explained a lot to me, babe. Out here in the country, you'll be able to let go, to become what you're meant to be."

James Earl turned his eyes away from CC to stare out the window. "I suppose."

"Babe," began CC. "When I first realized I was fighting a vampire, I thought I would lose my mind. I didn't want to believe it. Once I accepted that vampires existed, it was easier to live with myself. We've both known you're different. So, maybe we're both cursed a few days a month. We'll live with it, understand it, and make it work for us."

"Your curse won't kill me."

"Oh, babe. Come here." CC laughed and motioned him to her side.

James Earl felt a lump forming in his throat and his stomach turning. "I almost lost you, Catherine. I don't know what I'd do if that happened. And now this. How can you be so calm about everything?"

CC stroked his face. "I'm relaxed because I'm on heavy-duty pain meds, hon. But everything makes sense now. Margo and I had a long talk this morning. I'm still digesting a lot of this, but she's been able to tell me about a world we never knew existed. Babe, we don't have to be so afraid all the time."

Jenny, entered the room like the ghost she was. "But be a little afraid. It helps you stay alive. You won't believe the day we've had." An albino puppy jumped out of her arms and ran around the room barking. "Fluffy! See what I mean. Just as I'm about to sit down for a nice chat, Fluffy decides it's time to run around."

Fluffy preened as people in the room watched her. She moved to the corner of the dresser and bent her legs to squat.

"Don't you dare!" Jenny yelled, pinching her lips into a stiff frown. She picked up the dog and dashed out of the room. "Be back in a few."

CC laughed. "See what I mean. We're with the right people. It feels right to be here."

James Earl stood picking up a pillow and hitting it. "But you nearly died to get us here."

David entered the room. "Margo said your wolf would show itself soon." He sat on the window seat. "Looks like we're all together just in time."

"In time for what?" James Earl's stomach growled, and he moved to stand over David.

David stood, towering over James Earl. "Settle down. Don't make me regret helping you."

"Let's have dinner." Jenny entered the room carrying a tray for CC. "We'll all think better with food in our stomachs. It's been a stressful few days, especially for CC. She doesn't need the two of you growling for dominance."

James Earl flopped onto the window seat burying his face in his hands. "I'm sorry," he said looking at CC. "It's just so damn hard to take in."

"That's why you're here. You have a few days left to think about it," David said, placing his hand on James Earl's shoulder.

*****

"Isn't it exciting," began CC between sips of iced tea. "You can let go tonight and be what you're meant to be. No more struggling to be what you're not."

James Earl snuggled next to CC. "I suppose."

CC smiled at him and relaxed into the pillow beside him. "Everything's changed. When this is over, and you're comfortable dealing with your wolf half, you'll want some time—"

"Don't even think that," James Earl interrupted her. "I need you more than ever, babe. Let me have a sip."

"You can say that again." David entered the room with Jenny carrying Fluffy behind him. "You two are hotter than I thought. Neither of you will leave here for a while."

Jenny sat at the foot of the bed. "It's a good thing we got you out of the hospital when we did. More than a few people are looking for you."

James Earl sat up. "Who?"

"Your reverend friend is looking for one, but so is a certain golden-haired vamp, and a mean-looking woman in a floral dress, and an FBI man." Fluffy barked, and Jenny turned her attention to petting the dog.

"An FBI agent?" asked CC. "But who—"

James Earl interrupted her. "Hank something. I forgot all about him. Justin, the day nurse, brought some flowers into your room saying the agent dropped them off. He was there to check on you but had to leave."

"Hank Williams?" CC laughed. "I'll be damned. So, the son of a bitch heard I was in the hospital and came to see me. Never would have thunk it. Who's the vamp looking for me?"

"What about Madeline?" James Earl jumped up. "She can't find CC. We can't trust ..."

"Relax, you two." David held up his hands. "No one will find you here. And if someone should show up, we can take care of them. Had to tell Anthony you're here. It is his house. He's hot under the collar right now. First, your Hunter friends tried to kidnap his girlfriend, and then they burned down the nightclub Cesar runs."

CC shook her head to stop James Earl from speaking. "Makes sense. Roger's good. He knows the Carlisle woman is important to both Harry Reign and Anthony Mugello, although we never figured out why, but what's this about burning down a nightclub?"

James Earl shook his head. "The rev wouldn't allow anything to happen to civilians."

"You sure, James Earl?" Jenny continued to play with Fluffy. "Someone tried to run over CC and kill her. We've established it wasn't one of Anthony's people. You already seem to think it could be one of yours."

James Earl said nothing. David cleared his throat to get everyone's attention. "All these questions need answers, but tonight, we have pressing business of our own to deal with."

Everyone in the room looked at James Earl.

"Babe," CC squeezed his hand. "The moon is full tonight. They expect you to change with them."

"Right." James Earl didn't know what else to say. "I don't even know if it will happen tonight."

"It will, but instead of being able to run as we like, we need to patrol. Dangerous times. I want to stay close to the house."

"CC can't be alone." James Earl shuddered, recalling all the visions and urges he had when the moon was full.

"Not a problem." Margo entered the room pushing a cart loaded with food and pitchers of water and iced tea. From under the trays, she pulled out a sawed-off shotgun. "It's loaded, and I'm not afraid to use it on any man or beast that tries to get into this room tonight." Her smile faded as she looked around the room.

"She knows what she's doing." Jenny placed a reassuring hand on James Earl's shoulder. "David and I know what we're doing too and how to control the urges. You don't. We'll do what we can to help you. She's here just in case."

"Chill." Margo winked at CC. "These shells won't kill a wolf, though it will hurt like all heck. This is for human problems. You didn't notice the steel door to the bedroom?"

James Earl stared at the shotgun. "But you said I'd change tonight whether I wanted to or not. I assumed that meant ..."

"I've been around for a long time, sugar." Margo placed the shotgun under the tray and pushed it to the side of the room. "Even longer than my young friends here. I change when I want. One day, you will too—if you live long enough."

"It's time to head out." David stood, ending the conversation. Jenny left Fluffy on the bed with CC. The puppy jumped onto CC's lap and curled into a ball to sleep. "We have a hike ahead of us to keep you away from the house and vineyard."

"See how well protected you are?" Jenny said to CC. "Sleep easy. We'll take care of your man here."

James Earl kissed CC before getting up. "I think I looked more forward to the day my family insisted I stand up at church and say my catechism."

As he walked out of the room, he heard Margo talking to CC about the food she had prepared as she closed windows and shutters. The door to the room closed behind James Earl with three loud clicks and bangs as locks bolted the door shut.

David put a hand on his shoulder. "Even if you got into the house, which is unlikely, you won't make it through the door. And if you did, Margo would shoot you."

James Earl found little comfort in David's words.

*****

"You should meet Ezra," Jenny said and walked ahead of James Earl and David.

David kept his eyes forward, watching Jenny. "Ezra is Margo's son. She has a daughter named Emerald who lives in San Antonio. They're good people."

Jenny turned back to look at them. "Emerald's not a wolf."

James Earl opened his mouth to speak, but David interrupted him.

"No one knows why some in a family are wolf and others aren't. Emmy's a good nurse and helps when we need her. She volunteered to come help CC, but I told her she was safer in San Antonio."

"Why safer?" Too much was happening for James Earl. His mind raced with all he knew about his friends or those he had thought were their friends.

"The Hunters, silly," replied Jenny, walking backwards to look at him. "They're not very particular about who they kill. If they have suspicions about you or Margo, they'd probably kill you both just because you're different."

David stopped walking to look at James Earl. "I know you're confused and afraid. It's okay to be both, but these are dangerous times. I don't have time to explain everything you need to know right now. After tonight, you'll have more questions, but you'll also understand more."

James Earl sighed and looked around him. The trees would hardly make a forest, but they had walked at least a mile from the house. "Do you know why I'm like I am?"

For the first time, he saw David smile. "That's the six-million-dollar question. Nobody knows. Some people have it. Some people have it and never manifest it. They're often not nice people when they hold it in." David turned, continuing to walk. "According to some legends, it's the earth calling us back to our roots, reminding us we're all connected to each other. The first time I changed, I felt like the earth was calling me, so I went with it. There's nothing like it, James Earl. Don't fight it. Savor the experience, and you'll live a happy life."

"There's nothing like it." Suddenly Jenny was beside James Earl, smiling as she always did.

James Earl felt a wave of heat push through his core. Sweat formed on his back, under his arms, and on his brow. He noticed the sun sinking below the horizon.

"We patrol tonight," said David, not looking at anyone. "And be careful. It's not likely Hunters will show up here, but they could."

James Earl wondered when they would stop walking. The sun set and still they walked. The moon peeked above the horizon. He didn't know if his hot flash was the heat or the fact both Jenny and David were removing their clothing as they walked toward a copse of trees. Inside the trees, the heat in James Earl's core burned hotter and hotter. Sweat ran down his face. This was the time CC would lock him in the extra room after a healthy dose of phenobarbital. A thirst he hadn't felt before stuck to the back of his throat. He wanted to be locked in a room, alone, to wait for the nightmare stirring in him.

When he looked around him, he was on his knees. David knelt next to him placing his hand on his shoulder. "Breathe." David was naked. James Earl looked at the ground. "If you feel sick, let it out. Accept what happens. It will make the change easier."

With permission given, James Earl vomited until nothing remained inside him. The heat at his core continued to pulse, shooting out through his limbs. Someone was helping him remove his shoes. He wanted to fight the heat, the sickness, but his mind pushed him forward. Margo's words echoed in his head, "You don't want to get caught in your own knickers when you're ready to run."

He looked up. The moon showered the woods like a cool embrace. He'd never noticed how bright the moon could be.

"That's it," David's voice sounded distant and different, as though he were growling. Or was he howling? "Bathe in the moonlight. Let it flow through you."

Jenny, cool and blue like the moon, floated before him. And then she wasn't there. Or was she? A great white wolf leapt in the air, landing in front of him. It howled. Another howl answered, and James Earl realized he too howled. A great brown wolf with a snowy muzzle pushed at his side. He ran, following it through the woods, over hills, splashing in streams.

He saw the house. He saw the lights on in the rooms where CC recovered. He smelled her, even at this distance, and lust filled him. He wanted her as he had never wanted her. A growl behind him caught his attention, but he ignored it. As he stepped out of the woods toward the house, the great brown wolf leapt in front of him, baring its fangs. James Earl tried to step forward. This time the great wolf bit his snout, sending a sharp pain through his body. He dashed back into the woods, forgetting the pain as a rabbit ran out from a hole in front of him. The smell of blood and flesh took over the lust for something else. He forgot CC.

After he and the others fed on rabbit and feral swine, they gathered in a clearing near the vineyard and curled on the ground to sleep. James Earl remembered seeing the large brown wolf standing on a log nearby, watching. He drifted into a blissful sleep.

*****

CC opened her eyes, aware of movement around her. Fluffy stood at the end of the bed near her feet, a tiny growl vibrating in her throat. CC listened and heard howling outside the house. It was far away, but Fluffy remained standing and staring toward the shuttered window. Slivers of moonlight lit the bedroom and Fluffy with tiny streams of blue light. She listened as a deep growling moved close to the house. Fluffy's hair stood up along her back.

A loud, high-pitched yelp echoed through the night, and Fluffy turned to look at CC. Her pink, albino eyes burned red in the moonlight, but the hair along her spine relaxed. Fluffy walked to CC's face, kissing her lips. CC petted Fluffy with her good hand.

They listened but only heard the occasional howl. Fluffy curled up under CC's good arm, content with CC's hand stroking her despite sleep driving CC further away into dreams of running and trees and wolves.

*****

Dawn signaled its arrival with birdsong traveling in the morning breeze. Harry stood under the large live oak tree on the street, watching Kitten's condo. No Hunter had walked the street since the fire. Harry growled to himself whenever he thought about the men who had stood here for so long watching and how they had the audacity to burn down a building full of people. He spent most of his days and nights painting, but still he returned to this spot, close but not too close. He didn't want her to know he was there, but the ties binding them continued to strengthen.

Windows in surrounding houses glowed with early risers. A jogger ambled along the road not noticing Harry. A shadow fluttered in his periphery, and Tomas stood next to him.

"I need to talk to you," he said to Harry. His usual dimpled smile failed to precede his speech.

"My house," Harry replied. Together they moved from the shadow of the tree to the shadows of the cars parked in the road to the shadows of the house, until they entered Harry's studio. Human eyes did not see them as they moved. Once inside, Harry touched a button, and the curtains closed as the sun's rays pushed away lingering shadows between night and day.

Tomas stood in front of an incomplete painting studying the images forming in the paint. Tomas felt small and disproportionate against the enormous canvas. Storm clouds smashed into a tumultuous sea where a great tortoise struggled to lift itself above thrashing waves. Great swaths of the painting were missing.

"Why does he want the wolves killed?" Tomas asked, at last turning to look at Harry.

"Perhaps he's seen too many teen movies."

Tomas did not smile. "I've never liked David, but I don't see the point in killing him or his wife."

Harry allowed his knowing grin to grace his lips. "He might try to kill either of them, but he wouldn't succeed. And if he did kill one, woe be unto Leonardo when the other one finds him."

"Why is she so special?" Tomas asked.

Harry sat in the overstuffed chair waiting for Tomas to tell him why he had come. "What's troubling you? You never used to ask questions."

"I'm doing what you've asked of me. I won't fail you." Tomas walked around the room, examining other canvases, some complete and others not. "One of the Hunters. You've seen him on the street watching, though he doesn't do it very well. The one with the dreadlocks, called Derek Woods."

Harry said nothing.

"Should all the Hunters be killed?" Tomas asked.

"It goes against The Rule." Harry closed his eyes.

Tomas stopped walking around the room and looked at a canvas with flames smothering the air with soot and smoke. "I can make him whole again."

"When a mind breaks, Tomas, nothing makes it whole again. It can only be patched."

"Then let me patch it," Tomas knelt in front of Harry. "Let me help him, ease his mind. Please."

Harry reached out and touched Tomas's face. The face before him had spent four hundred years as the sweet-faced cherub of destruction and selfishness. The eyes of the face before him now anguished for answers. His brows twisted in pain as he fought to understand.

"Tell me what you think you could do for him."

"California. You know what happened there. You know Leonard's appetites. Derek Woods saw me at the brothel. I swear, I killed no one there. I didn't even want to be there. I tried to get him out of the house." Tomas's shoulders collapsed into himself. "Leonard heard he was asking a lot of questions. He thought it'd be fun to teach him a lesson. I went with him to the man's house, but Woods wasn't there. His wife and child were. She screamed when she saw us. Leonard killed her so Derek Woods would know it was him. He told me to kill the child."

"But you didn't." Harry's voice neither rose nor fell.

"No. I hid the child until the house finished burning. Afterwards, I took her to some people I know in Colorado. They're good people who love and protect her. If I could show him his child—"

"He won't forgive you," Harry leaned toward Tomas.

Tomas shook his head. "I don't deserve it. I could have saved his wife.

I should have saved his wife, but I didn't. Won't knowing his daughter's alive give Derek peace of mind?"

Harry stood and walked toward the painting with the flames. He saw his own face looking back at him as flames reduced him to dust. "Perhaps. Or perhaps he is beyond saving."

Tomas did not answer. His eyes fixed on the painting.

"We must complete the work we've started," said Harry to his own image. "When it is over, we'll see about the child. Hold on to her. Leonard is more powerful than you imagine. She may need your protection."

Tomas stood, straightened his lapel, and moved toward the door. "I won't let you down, but I will do all I can to save Derek Woods."

*****

"Mommy," Kitten tried to break into her mother's monologue on safety. "But Mommy—"

Stacy sat across from Kitten at one of the patio tables at their favorite lunch spot trying not to laugh. November's sun sparkled in the soft breezes making outdoor tables the best place to be in Austin in November.

"Mommy, seriously? We see the same news reports. It's perfectly safe to be at work today. Yes, I stayed in all weekend. I had a lot of work to do. Stacy will tell you. She was with me most of the weekend."

Stacy took the offered phone from Kitten. "Hi, Barbara. Here, look around." Stacy held up the phone, scanning the packed restaurant. "You see, we're in good company. The police chief, the mayor, the FBI all say we're safe. And the only place I went this weekend was to your daughter's. You know I never keep food in my place, and I wasn't going to go out when the authorities said to stay home. Here, talk to your daughter again."

"See, Mommy, I told you. No, my artist friend did not call me this weekend. No, I didn't see Anthony either. I worked. Stacy came down, and we worked. I'm okay. Turns out there was never any real danger. There were no terrorists. Relax."

Stacy signaled the waitress for another bottle of wine. Many people were drinking today. The arrest on Sunday afternoon of several suspected cartel members accused of orchestrating the nightclub shooting as part of a racketeering scheme allowed the city to relax. Everyone was at work, but therapy called for long lunches and lots of talk with little work.

"I love you too. Can't wait to see you next week for Thanksgiving. Tell Daddy I'm sorry, I missed him. Bye." Kitten set the phone on the table and drank the rest of the wine in her glass. "I love Mommy, but sometimes she can drive me nuts."

"It's the curse, Kitten. Gotta love them even when they drive us nuts."

"Thanks for not letting on you didn't see much over the weekend."

"After seeing how much you did on the novel? Honey, I'd lie to God."

They laughed and enjoyed the sunshine and fine weather. Stacy, released from the courtesies of listening to Kitten talk to her mother, picked up her discussion on the need to get Leonard's friend on board as a model.

"Please," exclaimed Kitten as she took a long sip from her wineglass. "Can I not hear any more about your new favorite toy boy?"

"You don't suppose he's Leonard's toy boy, do you?" Stacy gasped. "That would explain why we still haven't had sex."

"Have you been out with Leonard enough times to have sex yet?"

Stacy's laugh burst over the conversations all around them. "Sometimes, I forget how innocent you are. Seriously? At my age, hon, I get it whenever I can." Stacy stopped laughing and leaned her face over the table lowering her voice. "You don't suppose his age is preventing him from having sex? I know he's older than me, but men usually don't have as many problems as women do when the change sets in."

"Now who's being innocent," replied Kitten with a grin. "We came to lunch to talk about your book. Remember?"

"I just can't get him out of my head. He's so young and fresh, but at the same time he's not. He knows what life's about. There's almost something wicked about him."

"Galveston," said Kitten, to force the conversation away from the golden god of Stacy's infatuation. "I've placed it in Galveston instead of some unknown Eastern European city. More realistic, I think. Leigh agrees. Any problem with that?"

Stacy forced her lips together. Kitten watched as the cogs in Stacy's brain churned over this change to her book. "I suppose it's okay. Might be better on some white sands beach, what about Florida?"

"Disney," replied Kitten. "If it's in Florida, and they're traveling around as much as you want, they'd have to go to Disney sooner or later. That's not a place for a ravishing romance novel the way you like them."

"I suppose—Galveston." Stacy rolled the name of the city over her tongue and stared off in the distance. Kitten took the time to look around her. It had been a long weekend. She wrote through most of it. Harry wanted to paint alone, whether to prevent her from walking alone back and forth from his house or not, she wasn't sure. Anthony called her every few hours. His concern for her since she'd fainted teetered on obsessive. However, he never asked to see her.

As she watched the surrounding people, she realized she was missing the woman who always wore the floral dresses, who had the tightly bound steel hair, who always sat within sight of her. She was not in the restaurant. There was a peculiar man in the far corner who seemed familiar. Something about his large frame, dark skin, and Asian face reminded Kitten of someone, but she couldn't remember who.

"I like it," Stacy interrupted Kitten's survey of the man in the corner. "Galveston it is, which means I've got the Texas readers. Texans love their romances. When did we order more wine? Are you becoming a lush, Kitten?"

"Just following my boss's lead," replied Kitten, lifting her glass to Stacy. "Just don't tell my boss we drank two bottles in one meal."

They laughed and Kitten spread out the point plots of Stacy's novel.

She didn't realize until much later how sad the odd-looking man in the corner looked.

*****

"He was never my boyfriend," Isabella said again, this time rolling her eyes. "I know him. He knows me. We had a good time, and yes, he's a friend. Will you give it a rest?"

Cesar continued to look forward as he drove his new Mercedes toward Harry's house. "Then why all the eye contact? What gives? Is the Duchess planning something?"

"That's like asking if Harry's planning something. Who the hell knows? They're Eldests. They'll do whatever they want, whenever they want, and I for one stay out of the way when they decide to do anything at all."

"You haven't answered my question, what is your old *friend* doing in Austin when he's supposed to be anywhere except in Texas right now?"

"I don't know why Harry wants him here, and if I did—"

"Harry wants him here? I thought he belonged to the Duchess."

"So do I, but you're not questioning me being here." Isabella bit her lip and turned to look out the passenger side window.

They drove in silence until they turned on the street with Harry's house.

"He may not be alone," Isabella said without looking at Cesar.

"Probably not. I'll go in first. Can you handle it?" Cesar turned his head toward the trunk of the car.

Isabella rolled her eyes and snorted as she got out of the car. She leaned against the trunk with arms folded. Once Cesar went inside the house, she pulled her hand to her mouth to bite her nails. "Always saying too much. You stupid girl!" she whispered to herself. "Just keep your mouth shut."

Cesar opened the front door, signaling her. She opened the trunk where Phillip lay, clean, naked, and securely bound. "Come on, kid. Time to talk to the boss."

Phillip's eyes widened as she bent over him and lifted him over her shoulder. She settled him on her shoulder and couldn't resist a quick pat on his buttocks with her free hand. "Always a sucker for a nice ass. Too bad you're such an asshole."

Inside the house, the smell of paint and wine mixed with the fear emanating from Phillip. She laid him on the ground in front of Harry and stood back to wait. Harry was Cesar's Eldest.

She stood silently, listening as Cesar told Harry what they'd learned from him and wondering if Harry would kill him or if one of them would. Realizing her mind wondered, she closed her eyes. That's when Kitten's scent flooded her nose. Curious, she shifted her eyes to scan the room while keeping them respectfully averted from Harry. The stillness of the curtain gave Kitten away. Harry must know she's watching, yet he did nothing to secret them from her. Remembering the night she had watched the two of them when she wasn't supposed to be watching so closely, she averted her eyes back to the floor until Cesar nudged her arm to follow him back to the car.

Cesar looked up and down the street with practiced accuracy before getting into the car.

"No one's watching." Isabella pulled her seat belt into place. "We should go. I don't think Harry wants anyone around."

"He doesn't, but it doesn't hurt to take a look just in case."

Cesar did not look at Isabella, and Isabella would not look at Cesar. They drove in silence the half mile to the coffee shop. Isabella turned to Cesar, wondering why they had stopped, but he said nothing. He got out of the car and walked into Mozart's. Isabella followed.

Despite the all clear from law enforcement, many places, like Mozart's, entertained few crowds at night. The great hush left by the horror of the nightclub assault would take time to lift. In the meantime, those who did go out remained somber. Only small groups sat with heads close together, speaking in barely audible tones. A sprinkling of laughter shattered the great hush on occasion and danced across the water. It, like the November breeze trickling in the first cool weather of the year, lightened hearts just enough to enjoy the laughter even if it didn't spread.

Cesar ordered two espressos and sat at a table on the glassed-in portion of the building. From this vantage, Isabella could see both Harry's house and Kitten's condo. The other patrons sat outside, enjoying the cool breezes from the water. Neither Cesar nor Isabella spoke until the lights in Harry's house went dark.

"Did I ever tell you about the first time I met Harry? I was sure he was going to kill me. He pulled me out of a hole I was living in, held me up like the filthy mutt I was." Cesar closed his eyes and smiled. "Good thing I remembered the lessons Brother Sebastian taught me. He was always on about the importance of appearances, so even though I was filthy, I spoke immaculate Spanish and commanded him to put me down."

"Would like to have seen that." Isabella leaned back, sipping the rich black liquid in the cup. "I was lucky, I guess. I mean, I was on the street and all, but I hadn't changed when Tommy found me. I used to go around painting pictures on buildings. Back in the day, graffiti wasn't considered art, at least by most folks. Tommy said he liked my stuff and knew someone who'd pay me for it. I figured he was just some swell, hanging around the meat district looking for cheap sex. You know the type. But he was persistent. Found my brother, Jesus, and convinced him to bring me to see the Duchess. No matter how much Jesus cleaned up, he was still a slaughterhouse butcher. Anyway, from then on, I had the Duchess watching over me. Helped me make the change when it came. Always felt sorry for folks who had to do it on their own. It was scary enough for me, but for you—"

"Thought for sure the Devil had taken my soul. No telling how many I killed, but I remember every face. Once I was over the revenge thing for the death of the monks, I hated myself every time I killed, but I wanted to live."

"The Duchess said I was the first she knew to make the change without killing. I've had to kill since, but only when it was necessary."

They returned to silence. Isabella thought about her big brother, how he looked in his best church suit. She missed her brothers and sisters. Even after their parents had kicked her out of the house, they'd remained true to her. Little Felix still lived but in a monastery in New Mexico. To all who remained, she was strange, old Aunt Isabella who never seemed to grow old.

"Tomas didn't try to make you turn when he found you?" asked Cesar.

Isabella appreciated the lack of accusation in his voice. Whatever brought on this strange, reminiscent mood of Cesar, Isabella didn't question. "No. I know he usually tries to. He always liked being a kid and being around kids, but I don't know if it was because the Duchess sent him to find me or he had other ideas, but he was good to me. Helped me say goodbye to my family."

"Strange times we're living in." Cesar leaned his head into the window. "Don't see anybody watching. We should go."

"Sure." Isabella finished her espresso, feeling relaxed for the first time in days.

*****

"You're going to the funeral with Anthony tomorrow?" Harry asked. He stood behind his easel as Kitten lounged on the cushions. A white silk sheet draped across her body, concealing little and highlighting her curves.

"Why do you ask when you already know the answer?" Kitten sighed and shifted her neck, looking behind her.

"Why do you keep looking behind you when you know we're the only ones here?" The smirk on Harry's face made Kitten laugh.

"You're terrible," she finally said. "I don't know why I keep looking around. It seems like something I ought to be doing. That's all."

Kitten sat up, hearing a car stop in front of the house. "Expecting someone?"

"Yes. Would you mind going upstairs?"

Kitten narrowed her eyes and opened her mouth. Harry stared at the front door. She shrugged her shoulders and wrapped the sheet around her. Upstairs, she sat on the floor behind the curtain concealing the loft from the studio and amazed herself she could sit so still and quiet. She forgot, for a moment, even to breathe as she listened to Cesar and Harry.

"We went to the house where they were staying, but no one was there. Looks like they abandoned it, although the police had been through it. He knows there's another safe house but doesn't know the location."

"What else did you learn from him?" Harry asked.

Kitten heard a faint grunt and wondered who else was downstairs, but she resisted opening the curtains to look.

"The group is growing, but not all are on board with it. Two members are missing. They think we have something to do with their disappearance." Cesar laughed. "Like we're the ones going around killing indiscriminately."

"Remove his gag."

Kitten lifted her hand to the curtain's edge. This time, she pushed it aside just enough to let in a small portion of the room beneath her. Harry stood with his back to her. Cesar knelt in front of him, before standing to reveal a third man. She couldn't see much of him until Harry stepped aside, revealing a naked and bound man on the floor.

"We know what you sons of bitches are. There's nothing you can do to stop—" He ended with a grunt as Cesar kicked him in the gut.

"We're not the ones burning down nightclubs, asshole." Cesar's voice spouted venom sending a shiver through Kitten. She pulled the white wrapper tighter around her shoulders as she looked at his face, noticing its details for the first time. Not naturally a handsome man, Cesar stood distinguished in his uniqueness. His sharp facial features contrasted with round, kind eyes. At the moment, those kind eyes squinted contemptibly toward the bound man. She felt a sudden empathy for Cesar she hadn't before.

Harry looked up toward the curtain Kitten hid behind. "Go. Leave him to me."

Kitten looked back at him. A spark ran up her spine.

Neither Cesar nor Isabella made any noise as they left the house.

Kitten waited till she heard the front door close to walk downstairs. Harry had closed the doors to the patio and drawn the curtain. He stood again at his easel, painting as the man lay on the floor. He had given up trying to free himself, but the moment he realized Kitten was in the room, he squirmed again to pull away from her.

Kitten studied the man's face. It was unremarkable except for his different-colored eyes. She knelt behind him and put her hand on his face near the lighter-colored eye.

"Can you see from this eye?" she asked.

"Get away, bitch!" He pulled his head away from her hand but couldn't move away from her touch.

"I see you can," she said, studying his face.

Harry continued to paint. He looked mostly at the man on the floor and his canvas. Occasionally, he looked at Kitten.

Kitten smiled. "He's one of the men from the gallery. One of the men who wanted to hurt me."

Phillip bit his tongue, wanting to say something but unsure what to say.

"Yes, he is," replied Harry. "What should we do with a man who wants you dead? With a man who will kill whoever gets in his way, just because he can kill?" Harry still held his paintbrush, but it no longer moved along the lines on his canvas. He stared at the painting.

Kitten, once again, felt that tingle run up her spine. Her breath deepened. She found her hand stroking the man's arm. He had a plain face, but his arms were strong. His muscles tightened as her fingers glided down his chest along his side. His hips tightened as her fingers drifted over his thighs. His sweat wetted her fingers, and her gaze went to Harry, standing, not painting, and not looking at her.

She breathed in deeply. The smell of the man beneath her filled her with fear and lust, hate and love. She wanted Harry, but she wanted more than Harry. Memories of *The Lovers* in the gardens at the gala filled her. Harry alone provided her with the means to the passion she wanted.

"Take him," she whispered.

Harry knelt over the man. She looked into his eyes, the eyes that captured her imagination at the gala, those dark eyes where she saw through vast ages, the eyes as timeless as they were fathomless. Their darkness calmed her beating heart, slowed her breath as she relaxed, accepting her desire. She watched as he leaned closer to the bound man. She listened as his teeth broke his skin, tore through ligaments, and gulped his blood.

She closed her eyes, feeling the life drain from the bound man. And the man was no longer bound. He reached his hand to her face. She looked into his eyes, seeing Harry's eyes. A rough, warm hand stroked her face. With his other hand, he pulled away the silk sheet covering her body, and he rolled on top of her. She wrapped her legs around him as their bodies pressed together. Coarse lips kissed her neck as hands stroked her body. As her excitement grew, abandon filled her, and she rolled the two of them until she sat on top of him. She measured her thrust to thrill as he pulled her to him, engulfing first one breast and then the other with his mouth.

Kitten turned her head to see Harry's body, still, kneeling, frozen in a moment of ecstasy. His right hand lifted toward her. The realities of the world fell away as she floated above the world, her body reverberating like thunder with each thrust of their bodies. With each breath, she neared exploding like the thunder pounding inside her chest.

Just like the last time they were together, a great hammer thrashed upon the anvil in her head. Her breath halted. Her heart pounded against the wall of her chest, demanding to be let out. Pain soared throughout her body. Screams would not escape her mouth. At last a cold, smooth hand caressed her brow. Another cold hand pushed on her chest.

"Breathe." Harry's voice echoed from a distance and reverberated in her head.

A gulp of air forced its way into her. She gasped.

Harry's hand lifted her head. "Drink."

The warm spiced port flowed down her throat, calming her, but this time there was no port, only Harry as it always had been. Her heart beat with a distant timbre as though it belonged to someone else. She reached up, touching his chest, feeling for a heartbeat that was not here. Her body cooled and sleep wrapped itself around her aching body.

"Almost over," Harry whispered. "I promise."

Kitten relaxed into Harry's arms as he lay beside her. She neither feared the coming of her death nor Harry's, only the mystery of what might be.

*****

CC set the book on her lap and closed her eyes. The sun heated her skin and eased soreness in her muscles. The vineyard was beautiful; the house was beautiful, and when the vintner or one of his aides came near the house, they were beautiful in their friendly waves and total avoidance of her and the house.

"You're going to sunburn your good arm, and then you'll complain about both arms itching." James Earl lay still on the grass next to her. He didn't open his eyes.

"At least scratching both arms will give me something to do." CC sighed. Neither James Earl nor Jenny allowed her to do more than walk around the house and yard. She felt stiff but well. "I want to know what's happening, babe."

"I do too, but you know we can't be seen in town, not if what David says about Roger and Madeline is true. I still can't get over Roger being involved with anyone who'd just start killing in hopes of hitting a target."

"Me neither." CC closed her eyes, hoping the sun would warm her spirit. "Damn it! I'm bored and this damn cast itches."

James Earl laughed. "I'm sure you'll get used to wearing the cast about the time it's ready to come off."

"You're no help. What time is it?"

Fluffy came darting from the house and jumped onto CC's lap, licking her face.

"If you're up to complaining, you're probably up to helping me in the kitchen." Jenny followed Fluffy from the house. She wore a large white hat, covering her face in shadow. For a November afternoon, the sun was bright and warm.

"Please," said CC. "Anything. I just can't stand lying around doing nothing."

"What do you need me to do?" asked James Earl, helping CC to her feet.

"Play with Fluffy. She's at the naughty stage and won't listen to anything I say."

James Earl sat in CC's chair and dropped his chin.

"Now who's moping?" CC bent over and kissed James Earl.

CC's usefulness in the kitchen amounted to pouring water into the coffeepot and pulling items from the pantry or fridge for Jenny, who stood at the stove making stew. The television blared until the local news broke into live coverage of Austin's official memorial service for the victims of the nightclub ambush, as it was now being called.

CC stopped moving when she saw Anthony Mugello and Kitten Carlisle exiting a car.

"It's them," she said.

Jenny turned to look. "Kitten looks good in black, don't you think?" She continued to stir her stew.

"She looks different." CC sat and watched as the couple walked the steps leading into the cathedral. The couple following them were also familiar.

"That's Cesar and Isabella. It was his nightclub the Hunters went for. Makes you wonder what they're up to. Do you like sweet potatoes?"

"What are they up to? Why didn't they go after Mugello?"

"I should think the attack on him at the Long Center would have put away those kinds of thoughts. You're okay with chipotles, aren't you?"

"The hotter the better. It doesn't make sense." CC sat at the table, withdrawing from the conversation.

Jenny, comfortable with silence, continued the day's cooking.

"It's not right at all." CC stood. "I'm such an idiot! I have to see Anthony Mugello."

"That's not going to happen," replied Jenny without looking up from her stew.

"Why?"

"Last week you were with a group trying to kill him. Kind of started off on the wrong foot, don't you think?"

"Shit!" CC sat and tapped her good arm on the table.

"Continually tapping on the table won't make him want to see you." Jenny sat at the table, placing a cup of coffee in front of CC. "If it's really so important, maybe David can talk to Cesar."

"The gray man, I think his name is Leonard, he didn't show up for the dinner party until late. Is he a vampire?"

"Of course, he's one of Anthony's oldest friends."

"He was the one I saw with Madeline that night. I remember it all now. Seeing Cesar reminded me. Cesar scared me, but I didn't feel threatened by him. He just wanted me out of the house. But Madeline was all over Leonard. It was disgusting. I'll lay odds he's the one who raped her when she was a kid. He controlled her then, he's controlling her now. We have to let Anthony know what Leonard's up to."

Fluffy ran into the kitchen, barking, and sat at CC's feet. She didn't look but reached down with her good arm to pet the dog. James Earl walked in a moment later.

"The funds," began CC, seeing James Earl. "Did you have a chance to trace the funds?"

"No. I started back on it when I could see you were going to make it, but David took my laptop and phone. Too much temptation for me."

"Jenny, we have to get to James Earl's computers."

"Not going to happen." David walked into the kitchen. He kissed Jenny before sitting at the table. "I've been watching your house. The shits hit it early this morning. What they didn't take, they destroyed."

"Leonard's behind all the troubles," Jenny poured a cup of coffee for David. "CC's memory is coming back."

"Whatever you had on those computers is gone. I can talk to Anthony about what you think, but without evidence, he won't move against Leonard, not with your friends shooting college students and burning down bars."

CC coughed, "Not my friends anymore, and you don't know much about computers, do you? Babe, you want to explain?"

"I told you, computers are my thing. No one will get anything off my hard drives. I set precautions. By now, whoever they got to hack them has burned them. If I can get back online, I can find the proof."

Fluffy yelped an agreement, placing her paws on CC's lap.

"You're really as good as you think you are?" David asked.

"Better. Took the Feds five years to find me, and they wouldn't have if I'd not been so careless. I learned my lesson."

Jenny rubbed David's arm. "I believe him."

"Let me make a call."

*****

Roger kept his arms folded and sat up straight in the overstuffed chair in the corner of the room watching the others watch the television. Limousines and town cars stopped at the front of the cathedral, and people in black stepped out of them looking somber as they posed for the cameras. Someone in the room turned the television's volume off.

"Why the hell would any of us want to watch this farce?" Madeline exclaimed when Anna announced Austin's memorial service for the victims of the nightclub fire was starting its live telecast. Madeline returned to the kitchen, supposedly to prepare lunch. Anna said they should all watch to remember their fallen comrades.

Roger wouldn't object in front of the soldiers.

Yasushi said nothing when Roger looked at him. He sat closest to the television screen. The soldiers sat around the room, mostly looking bored. Karol's nose, bandaged and broken, made squeaking noises when he spoke, so he said little and wouldn't look at Roger. Only Derek showed any interest in the broadcast. His left leg bounced nonstop, and his hands continually massaged his thighs.

Getting out of a limousine, Anthony Mugello stood holding the door open as Kitten Carlisle stepped out of the car. Roger noticed how Mugello's face turned, scanning the onlookers. He imagined Mugello's eyes, hidden behind dark sunglasses, darting through the crowd, looking for the Hunters. Roger leaned forward, looking for tells to help him develop his plan of attack.

Kitten Carlisle also wore dark glasses and a black suit. She looked every part the mourner. A town car pulled up next, and Cesar De La Rosa stepped out the back door. The woman, also dressed for mourning, who came out after him was identified as Isabella Iandanza in the closed captioning. Roger felt the now-familiar pressure pushing against his chest. He caught his breath as he realized the room was unusually silent.

The soldiers in the room stared. The two demons responsible for the deaths of their comrades stood before them. Cesar, being interviewed by a reporter, stood calmly, almost mockingly before them.

Roger recognized the wheezing voice of Karol, "Sons of bitches."

"Ridiculous!" came another voice.

"Murderers," came from more than one voice.

Anna remained silent. The noises from the kitchen stopped. Madeline entered the room with a dish towel in her hand. She stared at the screen. Roger recognized the twitch on the right side of her mouth, the glaze over her eyes, the shallow breathing. A tirade about the evils of the demons, their undue influence on ordinary people, and the need to destroy each of them brewed just beneath the surface. Roger grabbed the arms of the chair and braced for the verbal onslaught.

Yasushi stood. In his most ministerial tone he bellowed, "Brothers and sisters. While the city mourns the loss of innocent young lives, let us remember our fallen heroes. Let us pray for their souls." He reached for the remote and turned the television off.

All the soldiers bowed their heads and clasped their hands. Three knelt. "Heavenly Father," began Yasushi.

Roger watched Madeline's face reform. She pursed her lips and snorted, returning to the kitchen. Anna closed her eyes and whispered her own prayer. Roger remained sitting but lowered his head for the sake of the soldiers. For the first time since Yasushi's return, he was glad for his presence.

*****

"Thanks for coming today. You made it easy to stay calm. I swear those bastards were watching. When I find them—" Anthony didn't finish his sentence as the waiter entered the private dining room with dessert.

"La pazienza, Antonio," Kitten sipped her coffee while watching Anthony as he smiled politely at the waiter.

"That's what Harry keeps saying."

"It's good advice. They're not going to do anything right now. They've gone to ground. Put your plans in place. Be ready, and all will be well."

Anthony looked at Kitten. His eyes bore into hers. She could feel him thinking. Finally, he looked away. "Tell me about your family. Distract me with happy families."

Kitten laughed. "We are a happy family. I never thought about running away, although we had our share of squabbles. Daddy is my daddy in every way except genetics. Mommy was fiercely independent and instilled that in me. Did I tell you she was one of the first Dallas Cowboys Cheerleaders. When you meet her, be sure to comment on it. She loves to talk about her year doing that and dancing for Ms. Texie. She and Daddy met when she was dancing in Vegas. I was almost eight when they married. Best daddy a girl could have."

Anthony leaned forward smiling, "And when will I be meeting the happy parents?"

"Thanksgiving. Yes, that will do. After dinner. Meet us at Mozart's. We always go to see the light show."

"A date," Anthony grinned, raising an eyebrow and leaning closer to Kitten.

"A date," said Kitten, leaning toward Anthony.

Their lips hovered near each other just as the door opened, pulling

Kitten and Anthony apart. Kitten narrowed her eyes as the hairs on the back of her neck stood up. Leonard entered with Stacy on his arm.

"Anthony. When we heard you were here, we had to stop in and say hello. You remember my friend, Stacy Ghoode?"

Anthony stood, taking Stacy's hand. "Actually, I don't think we've met, although I know you and Kitten work together."

"Don't believe a thing she says about me." Stacy laughed. "It's all lies"

Anthony smiled and kissed Stacy's hand. "You are every bit the woman Kitten described to me."

"Anthony, may I have a quick word?" Leonard placed his hand on Anthony's shoulder and led him away from the women. "Excuse us for a moment, ladies."

"Oh, Kitten, you weren't lying when you said he was good-looking. And look at you. Very lady of the manor. You two are a good fit."

Kitten rolled her eyes. "Chill. We're not in one of your romance novels. So, you and Leonard are out again. Things getting better?" Kitten raised her coffee cup to her lips, "In the bedroom department, I mean."

"I know what you mean, but no." Stacy sighed. "I only agreed to come out tonight because I was tired of being cooped up at home. Did I tell you, my new history professor has an idea for a book."

Kitten raised her eyebrows. "Do tell."

"We're heading out to Gruene for the weekend to discuss the details. What sort of business could Anthony and Leonard have to interrupt a nice dinner date?"

Kitten and Stacy both turned to see Leonard speaking quickly and physically to Anthony. "You're making a spectacle, Leonard. Calm down," he said.

"How can I be calm when all our plans are turned upside down? You should have told me."

Anthony's voice didn't rise, but the force of his words hit both Stacy and Kitten. "I will tell what you need to know. I will decide what happens for the safety of all of us."

Leonard clinched his mouth and looked away from Anthony. After a moment, he relaxed his face and turned back to Anthony. "You're right. I presumed too much on our past friendship. I'm accustomed to knowing everything going on around me. May I ask what the plans are now?"

"I'm going to finish my dinner, then go home. I suggest you do the same. She's a lovely woman, by the way, and strong. She could make you a very happy man. Now, if you'll excuse me." Anthony walked back to the table. "So sorry, ladies. I promise, Kitten, no more business tonight."

Kitten pressed the button for the waiter. "Will you two join us for dessert?"

Leonard produced a forced smile as he took Stacy's hand. "Thank you, no. Stacy and I have dinner arrangements downstairs." He looked at Stacy. "All right with you?"

"Sounds good. Catch you later, Kitten," said Stacy with a wink to Kitten.

Waiters entered the room and cleared the table. Another waiter entered with dessert and drinks. When they left, Anthony opened the door to the patio. He looked down on the street where life was trickling back to normalcy.

"We have little time left," he said.

"We have tonight." Kitten stood next to Anthony, allowing her arm to rest against his. "Let's enjoy what we have while we have it."

*****

"I loved this monitor," James Earl held the broken frame of what was once a large computer monitor. "The others were good, but this one had perfect resolution."

"Why so many screens?" David smirked at the mess of what was once James Earl's computer setup.

"Asks the man who doesn't even use a smart phone." James Earl tossed the broken frame on the floor. "I should get some clothes for CC and me while we're here. We got time?"

"No one's watching the house, but move quick." David had already walked through the house. He stepped onto the small patio. The neighbor's dog barked at him once before curling up and going back to sleep. David found a broom lying behind a deck chair and brushed away the broken glass from the window the Hunters had broken to enter the house. In the garage, he found an old board big enough to cover the window.

James Earl emerged from the house carrying two small suitcases. "Thanks. You don't think it's a lost cause trying to keep anyone out?"

"Never hurts to try."

"I found this pinned to one of my shirts." James Earl handed David a scrap of paper with a note scratched on it. *Stay hidden. I don't know who to trust. God bless and keep you both, Y.*"

"Nothing you didn't already suspect." David returned the note to him.

James Earl folded the note and slid it into his wallet. "CC will want it. It was pinned to my favorite shirt. The rev would know which is my favorite. I'm worried about him."

"Betrayal's one of those things that always hurts. For what it's worth, I hope your reverend friend is okay. Ready to go?"

"Just need to grab my hard drives." James Earl pulled a small palm tree out of its pot and pulled a plastic bag from the soil.

"You keep your drive in a potted plant?"

"I was in a rush to get to CC. Didn't have time to properly hide it. You think Mugello will listen?"

David shook his head and led them toward the van. "He's a good guy, for a vamp. Be straight with him, he'll be straight with you."

James Earl placed the bags in the back of the van. Now he was on his way to talk to the person that until a week ago he'd considered an enemy. He felt a pit forming in his stomach, his palms began to sweat.

"Relax," said David. "He's not going to bite you. I explained your situation."

"Will he protect CC?" Until now, James Earl had not considered what Mugello could do with her.

"You trust me, don't you?"

"CC and the rev are the only people I've trusted for a long time," said James Earl. He looked at David. "I'm trying."

"Fair enough," laughed David. "Anthony won't let anything happen to you or CC. In case you've forgotten, you're currently living in one of his houses."

James Earl filled his lungs with air and pursed his lips to let it out. He allowed his heartbeat to slow back to normal. He wanted the meeting to go well.

*****

The city woke to a clear and cool Thanksgiving morning. Kitten stood on her balcony, breathing in the freshness of the autumn sun and sipping her tea. Stacy arrived an hour ago and fussed over the capon roasting in the oven. Kitten didn't argue over one less thing to do. The morning was perfect. All would be perfect today.

Harry's house stood dark in the rising sun. He told her he would be out of town for a while, but she suspected he stayed away from her in a chivalrous attempt to protect her from someone. No doubt Anthony knew where he was, but Harry was the one subject they never talked about. Anthony continued to take her out to dinner, and they continued their flirtations late into the night when she wasn't writing. Cesar remained near her whenever she walked out of her condo building, either walking along the road, sitting in his car, sipping coffee in the shadows, or sitting on a roof across from her office. The times she didn't see him, she missed him. Yet, there had been no sign of the men from the gallery or even the feeling of fear and anger that accompanied them.

She wondered where Cesar was this morning. Under the clear, blue sky there were few shadows to hide in. But, she felt no fear or concern. Santa Claus crossed the television screen at the end of the Macy's Thanksgiving Day parade.

"There he is," shouted Stacy. She walked out to the patio handing a glass of sparkling wine to Kitten. "Time to toast in the book buying season."

"To lots of eager readers," said Kitten, lifting her glass.

The doorbell rang. Stacy sighed. "That will be the parents. Ready to face them?"

"Of course." Kitten beat Stacy to the door and opened it.

"Mommy!" Kitten reached through the door to embrace her mother, Barbara.

"My little Kitty! Look at you," Barbara grinned so large, Kitten was afraid her face would break. "You've lost weight."

"A few pounds, maybe," started Kitten but Stacy jumped in for her share of embraces.

"She's working too hard. Wait till you read the book she's helping me with. Without her, it would go nowhere."

"She's already told us all about it." Beau, Kitten's stepfather, bent to hug Kitten.

"Daddy!" Kitten clung to him for an extra moment. "I'm so glad you two came down to see me this year."

"It's been ages since we've been in Austin," Barbara said as she sailed through the living room and into the kitchen. "Did you get new cabinets, Kitten? The bird smells wonderful, Stacy. How long has it been in the oven?"

Stacy winked at Kitten mouthing *I've got this*, as she followed Barbara into the kitchen.

"Now, I remember," began Beau as he walked out to the patio. "This is why you liked this place so much. What a view! And such a fine day too."

Kitten handed Beau a flute with the sparkling wine. "It is fine today. We can eat out here in the sunshine."

Beau put his arm around Kitten, and she rested her head on his shoulder. "Good to see you looking well, but you have lost a bit of weight."

"Just working hard, Daddy. I want to finish the book. It's good. Leigh's helping me with it."

"I know it's important, princess, but you need to take care of yourself."

Kitten felt the concern building in her father. "I'm okay, Daddy. I'd tell you if things had changed."

"I know, princess." Beau kissed the top of Kitten's head. "It's Daddy's job to worry. You know that."

Beau sniffed and set his glass down to pull out a handkerchief.

"What are you two conspiring about out here?" Barbara waltzed out to the patio, commanding the attention she was always given. "What am I missing? You know I have to know everything going on around me."

Kitten laughed and moved to stand next to her mother. "Just enjoying the sun and the breeze. I'm thinking we eat out here today. What do you think?"

"Perfect!" Barbara exclaimed. "When did you start wearing taller heels than me? You're too old to grow taller than me. Oh my word! I've finally started shrinking."

"I think so, Mommy. I'm not getting any taller."

"I know I promised to be good," Stacy said, entering the patio with a tray, "but I couldn't resist fried macaroni and cheese balls. Picked them up last night. Who thinks they can resist a little sin?"

"Ooooooo," said Barbara. "I can feel them on my hips already."

*****

"I can't believe I'm saying this, Kitten, but I'm glad we walked. Will you look at all the cars?" Barbara held on to her daughter's hand as they maneuvered their way over the parking lot and down the stairs leading to Mozart's Coffee.

"It's always popular this time of year." Kitten ducked as a toddler sitting on the wall next to the stairs tossed a ball to his father. The young father grabbed the ball just before it hit Barbara in the head.

"Sorry," he said and picked up his child.

Kitten laughed. As the four of them walked from the condo to the coffee shop, Kitten felt a tingle up and down her spine. Cesar, as usual, shadowed their walk. His presence allowed her a moment's security, but the tingle lingered. She thought it might be the excitement of the crowd, the lights, and the loud music. She noticed Isabella sitting high in the old tree above the patio. Her head bobbed to "Jingle Bell Rock." She looked lost in the music and lights.

As soon as they landed on the patio, Anthony appeared beside her, leaning close to her and kissing her cheek.

"Anthony." Kitten smiled at him, deciding he was the spark she'd felt.

"I was afraid you weren't coming. Beau, good to see you again. And this can only be Barbara Parker. Between Beau and Kitten, I feel I already know you." Anthony was all charm and grace. He kissed Barbara and led her to a table on the water's edge. "I hope you don't mind, but I thought cocoa would be perfect on a cool night like this."

"Absolutely, Anthony. So thoughtful of you. Cocoa and Christmas lights. A perfect night."

Kitten smiled appreciatively at Anthony, who sat beside her with his arm placed around her waist. As comfortable as the moment felt, she realized he was not the cause for the spark turned itch running along her spine. She tried to follow the conversations between the bursts of loud music. Stacy talked about unveiling her book at the Romance Writers' Convention next summer. Beau talked about fully retiring and the work he wanted to do on the ranch. Anthony talked about a new art foundation he was forming for low-income students. Barbara's opinions and advice flowed on every topic, and still Kitten felt that tingle turned itch flowing from her back of her neck.

"What's wrong?" Anthony whispered in her ear as they all drew quiet to listen to the latest burst of music and dancing lights.

"That odd feeling I told you I had at the gallery, like darkness was crawling all over me." As Kitten spoke, she turned her attention past the dazzling light show. She felt her heart stop. A coldness wormed its way through her body and out her fingers. From Harry's house, a flash and a spark and flames poured out of the windows. "Fire," she said just loud enough for Anthony to hear.

Anthony stood, facing Harry's house.

"Go," Kitten said, looking at him. "But he's gone." Only Kitten noticed the subtle signal he issued to Cesar and Isabella. They were gone before the audience at Mozart's noticed the blaze lighting the night sky near them. The roar of the crowd overwhelmed the music.

"Isn't that where your artist friend lives, Kitten?" Beau asked.

"It is," replied Stacy. Barbara and Stacy both placed a hand on Kitten's shoulders, but she didn't cry. Harry was gone, but he wasn't.

*****

"Go with God," Yasushi said, but only Derek listened. He wondered why Yasushi said it.

The artist, the big bad vampire, lay in the chair sleeping like any old man would at the end of a long day. Boats crowded the river with families laughing and enjoying cool weather after their Thanksgiving feasts. The music from the coffeehouse sailed over the water toward them. Christmas carols sung by choirs of children got stuck in everyone's head. Though Derek tried to ignore the tunes, familiar melodies cracked through memories of happy times.

"Go with God, and have a good time tonight," his mother had said that November night so long ago. He had brought Babs home for the first time to meet his mother. They married as soon as he got back from his tour and were already pregnant. Mama was so happy to become a grandmother. He sailed on this very river with Babs bundled up on one of the rare freezing November nights in Austin, but she sang all the words to all the songs wafting from the coffeehouse. He remembered the joy of knowing everything in his life was perfect. He loved, and he was loved.

Tonight he sat in the boat, alone, waiting for the others to kill the old man. Karol didn't trust him, and Roger had made no objections when Karol suggested Derek remain with the boat as a lookout. Derek saw how the others looked at him, always muttering to himself. He didn't like the idea of killing the artist. The artist, even if he was a vampire, hadn't killed his wife and child. He would never forget the face of the gray man standing just outside the flames of his house. Even now he saw those burning eyes that were not on the face of the old man the others were about to kill.

"Are you happy?" Babs asked, looking up at him from the bow of the boat. Her eyes reflected the stars in the sky.

"Yes," he said. "Are you happy?"

Babs rubbed her burgeoning belly. "Very happy. We're so blessed." A tear drifted away from her eye and down her cheek.

Derek heard another round of "Jingle Bell Rock" storming up the river as Karol and three others climbed to the balcony of the house, their black clothing blending into the shadows before they pounced on the old man. Karol pulled him off the lounge chair and onto his knees. The old man's head remained bowed as Roger, Anna, and Madeline walked onto the patio from inside the house. "It's the Most Wonderful Time of the Year" began as Madeline slapped him across the face. The sound of flesh beating flesh inched its way into Derek's head. The old man drooped his head a little more. Laughter erupted from the crowd of the coffeehouse as Madeline laughed and stood looking toward Anna.

"It is the most wonderful time of year, isn't it?" Babs smiled at Derek.

"Next year will be better. We'll have our baby and maybe it won't be so cold."

Anna raised her arm. A gleam of something long reflected the light from the house as her arm hurled down. "Rocking Round the Christmas Tree" couldn't hide the noise of steel through flesh and bone. Madeline still laughed. Roger turned back to the house. Two of the soldiers went with him. Derek didn't have to see them to know what they were doing: turning on the gas appliances, turning off the safety switches, setting the timers on the igniters. They would be miles away from the crowded road and river before the fire started.

"One day, we'll have a house on the water," Derek said.

"Not till the baby learns to swim," said Babs.

The lights went off in the old man's house. Derek heard his compatriots running toward him.

"Done," whispered Karol as the others jumped in the boat and he pushed the boat away from the shore. "Son of a bitch never saw us coming. That will show the army shits what real soldiers can do."

Derek drove the boat upriver while the soldiers removed their hoods and black jackets. They looked like so many others out enjoying the water on this holiday night. He steered clear of a small sailboat carrying a young couple. Between the man and woman sat a little girl, perhaps five years old.

"Oh! Oh, look, Mommy! Look at those lights."

Derek steered the boat a little farther from the sailboat, remembering the baby girl who should have been five years old now.

"Old enough to swim," he said, but the soldiers didn't hear him.

*****

Cesar didn't like it. Anthony was too exposed in the crowd on the coffeehouse patio. He wanted more men to guard Anthony, but Anthony insisted on keeping numbers low. He'd have to make do with Isabella. Isabella had been especially nice to him lately. He wondered why. The Hunters would attack soon, but none of them imagined they would take on a full crowd of holiday revelers with news crews around. Then again, Cesar never assumed they'd attack a nightclub full of college students.

"Nothing really changes," he said to Isabella as they drove to the coffeehouse. Anthony followed in his town car with a driver and one other guard.

"How so?" Isabella was already humming holiday tunes, nodding her head to the beat only she heard. The nodding made her Christmas wreath earrings sway and twinkle on either side of her face. At least they didn't have flashing lights on them.

"The fighting," replied Cesar. "We kill, they kill, it doesn't matter who's killing for what anymore. They just like to kill."

Isabella said nothing, but she stopped humming.

"Why does everybody have to be right all the time?" Cesar asked, breaking the silence. "All we want to do is live our lives and not bother anybody."

"Once upon a time, our lot did an awful lot of killing."

"We changed. Why can't they?"

"I don't think it's in their nature to change. The Duchess says, change or die. And she should know. Eldests don't survive by always doing things one way."

"Harry says the same thing." Cesar frowned and his eyebrows joined together as he thought.

"Cesar," Isabella asked but hesitated. "Nothing, just a passing thought. Already out of my mind. We're here. Want me to get out and scout the place out first?"

Cesar pulled the car to the entrance of the coffeehouse. Groups of people lined both sides of the entrance ropes placed to keep the crowds under control. "Sure. Find a good spot. I'll send the town car to Harry's for parking."

Isabella had been unusually quiet and contemplative since their talk the other day, but things had been so busy since the arrival of the new werewolf, they hadn't had time to continue their talk. Now, it seemed things were happening too fast.

He watched Kitten arrive and realized he was jealous not of Kitten or Anthony but of the chance they seemed to be taking in forming a relationship. When he and Harry left Spain for the battlefields of France, he relished the knowledge he wouldn't die like all the men he helped take off the battlefields. He hated living off their distress. He comforted himself by saying he eased dying men from the agony of a long death, but it didn't help. He didn't like to kill, even when the hunger came on him so hard he had to. That's when Harry told him about the idea he and the Duchess had for creating a place of peace. He learned how the Duchess ran speakeasies as places to gather healthy humans so unhumans could feed from multiple people without causing harm. It sounded far-fetched and improbable at the time. He had only just begun to think it would work when the Hunters attacked his bar. Now, it was a blur. They were starting over.

Reminiscence bothered him. It caused mistakes, but as long as he was thinking, where was the Duchess? Why did they hear nothing from her?

Cesar saw Kitten's eyes focus sharply up the river. He turned and saw the flames as soon as Anthony did. Isabella saw them last but was first to head toward the house. The crowd made it easy to move without being seen.

He rushed to Anthony, who seemed determined to walk into the flames. Cesar pulled him back before jumping onto the railing of the patio. There was no way to enter the house, but he didn't have to. A few feet from him, Harry's face stared up at him from where he lay on the ground. Flames were almost upon Cesar when Anthony pulled him back.

As he stood staring into the flames, he remembered the look on Harry's face when he'd pulled him out of the hovel he hid in. Harry snarled. His fangs gleamed in the moonlight, and his eyes burned. All Cesar could think of saying was, "Put me down, now." Harry laughed and dropped him.

"A fine example of a vampire you are, my friend," Harry said. "It's time you looked as civilized as you speak. Come. You're mine now. Act like it."

Cesar heard Isabella's motorcycle drive away and wondered why she had kept it at Harry's, perhaps she suspected it would be useful. She was not the silly girl she pretended to be. The Duchess taught her well.

And where was the Duchess? *Why the hell doesn't she make herself known?*

The coroner's van pulled in behind the fire trucks. The firemen must have seen the body and called it in. He cringed imagining strange hands lifting Harry's remains and placing them in a body bag. He would follow them to the coroner's office and take them before any tests could be run. Tests would cause more questions than a body that disappeared.

The coroner and her aide leaned against the van, talking to a uniformed police officer. Cesar turned and watched as Kitten and her friend walked into her condo from the patio, drinks in hand. The French doors remained open as lights dimmed. The coroner's aide pulled the stretcher out from the back of the van. Cesar waited.

*****

Anthony moved faster than either Cesar or Isabella. He stood behind the burning house near the patio. Even though flames leapt out the windows and over the patio, Anthony braced himself to leap onto the patio, but before he could leap, Cesar grabbed his shoulder and pulled him back. Cesar leapt onto the patio. He held one arm in front of his face and tried to lean into the flames, but Anthony leapt onto the patio near him and pulled him to the ground.

"I saw his head," Cesar said as they pulled each other away from the house.

Anthony stood still, looking around him. They could be seen, so he helped Cesar stand and moved them to the front of the house. Isabella stood next to Anthony's town car. His driver stood next to Isabella, waiting. Neither of them looked at Anthony.

The music from the coffeehouse ceased, but the roar of the crowd grew close. People were coming. Down the road, the flashing red lights of a fire truck marked the arrival of officials.

"Isabella!" Anthony nodded his head.

"Right," she said, more to herself than anyone else. She ran to the end of the driveway where her motorcycle waited behind the bushes. She pressed the speed dial button on her phone before starting the engine. "Lock it down," was all she said before clicking off and tapping the other speed dial button, making a call Anthony didn't know she would make. "It's done," she said and ended the call, started the engine, and drove away.

Anthony's driver opened the door for him. He turned once to look at Cesar, still standing frozen, staring at the house. "Cesar!" Anthony barked.

Cesar turned and walked to the car, "I've got it here, Anthony."

"I know this isn't what we thought would happen, but we have to stick to the plan."

"I know," was all Cesar said.

*****

From his vantage point, Leonard watched the coffeehouse and the crowds gathering beneath the rambunctious lights and blaring music. A turn of his head and he watched Derek steer the small boat to the shore beneath an overhanging tree and bushes. In front of Harry's house, the black Tesla pulled to a halt.

Leonard grinned and licked his lips. He didn't bother to hide behind curtains, not tonight. As Roger walked with Madeline and Anna to the front door of Harry's house, Leonard rubbed his hands together. His feet could not stay still. They bounced him up and down. Karol led his black clad soldiers from the river to the patio wall as Roger and the women entered the house.

A fresh wave of synthesized Christmas carols filled Leonard's ears. Leonard faced the coffeehouse. Somewhere in the crowd, beneath the blazing lights and snuggled with all those humans, sat Anthony. "Almost over, Anthony. You'll wish you had kept me a friend all those years ago."

A moan from the floor to his right disturbed his moment of glee. "Shut up!" He yelled at the prostrate woman bound on the floor beside him. Her husband, already dead, stared at her. She wept as acceptance of death crept into her.

He reached over without removing his eyes from the scene on the patio, lifting her by her neck. In front of him, Harry fell to his knees with sudden perfection. "Don't spoil this for me, sweet little Madeline. Do this for me."

The bound woman in his grasp choked, unable to see the people on the patio, unable to imagine who Madeline was. She only wanted to be free of his steel-like grip.

Leonard pulled the woman's face close to his. "Look. See the great and powerful Harry Reign destroyed. No one, not even Harry Reign, tells me to know my place. I'll rule this city. Me!"

The woman cried. Leonard filled his nose with her fear. Anna lifted the blade and swiped. Leonard closed his eyes for a moment. He laughed out loud, filling the house with the echo of joy.

"You're next, Anthony."

Leonard stopped laughing, but his grin extended beyond the edges of his mouth. Teeth, starkly white, reflected the growing flames across the street. "What's the matter?" he asked the shaking woman. "You should be happy. A demon is dead! Isn't that what you call us?" His grin turned to a snarl. "Why aren't you happy?" He shook the woman until her neck snapped.

"Useless!" He spat and tossed the body on top of the man's.

He rose to leave when he heard the cry from behind a closed door, "Mommy?" A new grin spread across Leonard's face.

*****

"I thought they'd stay here all night," said Stacy as she rinsed out coffee mugs in the kitchen sink. "Don't get me wrong. They're great, and I love them to death, but parents can get in the way sometimes."

Kitten leaned against the railing, watching firemen walk around the remains of Harry's house. Though the remains looked nothing like a house, Kitten imagined his house standing tall against the darkened horizon. Emergency lights still flashed, and people with flashlights combed through the remains.

"They'll probably be at it most of the night." Stacy walked outside handing a glass of bourbon to Kitten. "It could be days or weeks before we know what happened."

"He's dead. That's all I need to know. I'll miss him." Kitten didn't look at Stacy.

"Likely, but we don't even know for sure."

"Don't you have a date?" Kitten appreciated Stacy's attempts to console her, but she didn't want the company.

"Already canceled. Leonard's such an old fuddy-duddy. He's boring. Better off sticking to my cover boys. At least they know how to have a good time, not just sit around and talk all the time. A girl my age needs action. I can't afford all those pleasantries like I used to."

Kitten smiled and leaned into her friend. "Thanks," she said and nothing more but drank her bourbon in one gulp. "I'm ready for another."

"Good girl." Stacy laughed. "When things go bad, a little lubrication loosens the knots all tied up on the inside."

She walked inside Kitten's living room and noticed the front door swinging open.

*****

Isabella sped around the parked cars and pedestrians on Lake Austin Road making her way to the bridge. Everything depended on perfect timing. She had to get to the house, make sure the gates were locked, seal the tunnels, let the dogs out, and wait for the Hunters to act. The plan was brilliant, but no one had expected to have to do it tonight. She hoped David was at the house and Jenny wasn't. Not that Jenny couldn't take care of herself and be useful in a fight, but she had become a good friend, and Isabella didn't want to worry about Jenny.

She sped through a red light and soon crossed the river, making her way to Anthony's house. How she managed to make it this far without at least one patrol car pulling her over, she wasn't sure. She could move through the shadows without being seen, but not on a motorcycle. She wondered if the Duchess could travel by motorcycle without being seen.

"Head on the plan, girl," she mumbled to herself.

Most of the houses along the road had lighted gates. Isabella looked in the shadows around each gate as she passed, making sure no one waited for her to pass. At last, she reached the main gate to Anthony's house. The gate was closed and locked. Three armed security guards stood behind the gate. They halted their pacing and pointed their shotguns at her. Young Mike stepped out of the guardhouse and waved to them when he saw it was Isabella.

"Anything?" she asked, stopping only long enough to check.

"Nothing. We're locked up tight. No one's getting in."

"Watch for Mugello."

Isabella drove through the gate going slow to make sure the gate closed behind her. The long drive snaked toward the house. The lights were out except for a few perimeter lights. Human eyes would have difficulty seeing the house. She was pleased to see the security guards not using flashlights. Being human, they would want to, but being highly paid and specialized, they performed their duties expertly.

She stopped the engine in front of the service garage. Ol' Mike stepped out of the door.

"Who's there?" he yelled.

Isabella could see the revolver in his hand. "Isabella. And what are you doing here? I told you to head to your townhouse when we went on lockdown."

"And who's going to make sure the cars are in the right place with full tanks if I'm not here," he answered, daring her to answer him.

Isabella smiled to herself and wondered if she would ever be able to count on such loyalty from anyone. "Suit yourself, but stay inside. I don't want one of our own folks shooting you."

"You want your bike out or can I put it away?"

"Leave it here. I'll probably need it again tonight."

Isabella turned and walked to the house, listening and relaxing as Ol' Mike turned her bike around. *He will have his vehicles his way.*

She heard dogs barking along the perimeter near the river. As she looked up, David ran across the hill toward them. At the same time, gunfire erupted near the front gate along with a boom and a flash. She ran back to the service garage as a dark car sped toward it. Its bright lights blinded her. Ol' Mike stood in the doorway when a loud bang from the car and a red-orange streak issued from one of the rear passenger windows. The garage doors blew open, and fire filled the garage.

Isabella ducked as security forces ran toward the garage from behind her, shooting. The car turned and sped down the hill and through the broken gate. Gunfire from the river perimeter ceased after a loud scream and a long, low howl. As Isabella reached the garage, Young Mike pulled Ol' Mike away from the flames. His eyes stared up at nothing.

"Oh, Mike," Isabella sniffled as tears formed in her eyes.

"Fuck! Shit! Where the fuck are they?" Young Mike bent over as though to be sick but picked up a stone, stood, and threw the rock into the burning garage.

Isabella turned to see Young Mike dropping to his knees again. Blood flowed from a large cut on his head. Burn marks blacked the left side of his face, head, and arm, but tears issued from his good eye on the right. "Old man," he cried. "He was one of the good ones, you know. Knew more about cars than anyone I ever knew. I swear I'll kill the motherfucker who killed Ol' Mike."

"Not if I find him first," Isabella told him.

7

Cleopatra before Cesar

The river ran smooth with quietness and purpose. Joggers flowed along the paths. Walkers meandered, stopping to examine small flowers and let their dogs play. Cars drove along the roads high above the river, and still the river ran. As the moon faded and stars brightened, fewer people jogged, walked, or drove along the river, and still it ran. At one point, a young man lay his pack on the ground and unrolled a sleeping bag. He was past hungry. He didn't care. Aloneness smothered him in the bag, so he gave up sleeping and sat, leaning against the tree. Later tonight, he'll hear raised voices, a shot in the dark, feet running, and he'll feel a coldness that brings death. No one will miss him, but one man will mourn him. And the river will run.

Winter breaks the horizon.
Spring sleeps and dreams.
In the night the war of ages rages.
Power, lust, hunger batter the night with pain and grief.
But we know ourselves and we stay true.
Love and life are fleeting.
Let winter bloom and warm your heart,
Then spring will lift your eyes to nights of stars and joy.

I'm Mary Midnight, online and in your mind.
Dance with me in step with light-studded night,
And walk into dawn with life in blooming visions of green and gold.
Fight me on this, and die forever lost.

Barbara's voice reached the condo door before she did. "I can't believe you slept so late. It's almost nine o'clock. She'll be wondering where—the door's open."

Beau stepped in front of Barbara and pushed the door open. "Kitten?" he called out in a loud but not yelling voice.

Barbara followed him inside. "Kitten," she called as she bumped into Beau's back. "What—"

A sharp, high-pitched scream issued from Barbara as she pushed herself in front of Beau and ran to kneel beside Stacy, who lay on the carpet with blood pooled around her.

Beau rushed forward stepping over Stacy while pulling out his phone and dialing nine one one.

"Stacy's alive. Kitten! Baby!" Panic pushed its way out of Barbara's voice. "Beau, where's my baby?"

Beau yelled out one more time, "Kitten!" Beau stepped on the patio and tripped on an overturned pot.

"Yes," he said, assuming the control that had made him a successful banker. "I need an ambulance and the police. One woman's been shot. Another missing. I think she's been kidnapped."

Beau felt his hand tremble as he saw the gate at the foot of the stairs broken and swinging open.

Inside, Barbara applied pressure to the wound on Stacy's stomach. "Stacy, dear. It's Barbara. I'm here with Beau. You're going to be okay. I promise. Beau!"

Beau wiped his face with his handkerchief and walked inside the living room to face his wife. "She's not here, Mommy."

A faint groan issued from Stacy's throat. "Stacy, honey. I'm here. Don't speak. Help is on the way."

Beau stood outside the front door to signal the paramedics when they arrived. While he waited, he called Anthony Mugello.

*****

"We were right," Renaldo said, setting down his phone and sipping his coffee. He sat across from Frank in the coffee shop next to HQ. Downtown gleamed in the morning sunshine. Few cars or pedestrians passed by the windows early on a Sunday morning. "My friend went back to look at the Titler explosion. He thinks there might be something to Hank's suspicion."

Frank kept his gaze out the window. "Thinks?"

"He won't commit to more than that right now. Says it will take a few days to confirm."

"Shit." Frank didn't move or change expression.

Renaldo sat back in his chair. "You can say that again."

Neither man said anything. They sipped their coffee and stared at the street. Renaldo watched subtle shifts in Frank's expression.

When Frank let out a long, quiet sigh, Renaldo sat up. "You've decided something."

"It's complicated." Frank didn't move but studied Renaldo. "We're in over our heads on this one."

Before Renaldo could answer, three squad cars zoomed past the coffee shop with sirens blazing. Renaldo's phone buzzed as Frank's rang. They each answered the phones and replied, "On my way."

Renaldo jumped out of his chair, but Frank took a long sip of his coffee. He set it on the table in front of him with both hands. "And now, it's even more complicated."

*****

Sunshine streaming in woke CC. She stretched, feeling resistance from cracked bones, sore muscles, and bruises but enjoying the stretch. Outside her window, the glare of the sun reflecting in the dew from the vineyard blinded her. She reached for the latch to the window, but a pain in her side reminded her she had much healing left to do. Fluffy yawned as she woke and stretched on CC's bed.

"Come on," CC said, scratching Fluffy's ears before leading her downstairs. "Time for you to go outside, and then we'll have breakfast. Don't stay outside long. You don't have your sunscreen on."

CC opened the outside door in the kitchen. Fluffy ran outside. The crispness of the morning filled CC's lungs. She enjoyed the healing in the fresh air. "Time for coffee."

She heard nothing out of the ordinary in the house. The morning breeze blew against the chimes hanging outside the kitchen window. With the coffee brewing, she sat at the table to wait for the dinging melody to tell her the coffee was ready. She noticed a photograph on the table. She didn't remember it from the night before but decided Jenny must have been looking at it after she went to bed.

A little girl with a toothless smile grinned as wide as her tiny face allowed at a cake in front of her with five purple candles on it. It was a white cake with purple flowers, purple edging, and purple writing. The purple matched the bright purple flowers in her dress and the shiny purple beads at the end of her rich, brown braids. Her brown eyes sparkled with the light of the candles on the cake, and her cheeks sparkled as only a little girl's cheeks can sparkle. The woman helping the girl blow out the candles could have been her mother, but the features didn't match the little girl's. Her sky-gray eyes glowed with happiness at the moment. The man holding the cake and smiling into the camera could have been her father, but again the features were wrong, and his light brown skin contrasted to the little girl's rich brownness.

The coffee machine sang its Coffee Ready tune, and Fluffy barked to come in. CC held on to the picture, admiring the joy in a family moment preserved on the small piece of paper. She opened the door. Fluffy dashed in barking. CC turned to see what Fluffy was barking at and felt her heart sink into her stomach.

She tried to turn and run, but her sudden twist sent spasms of pain down her side. The cast on her right arm slammed into the door, sending a shooting pain up her shoulder.

"I'm sorry. I didn't mean to frighten you, but you wouldn't have let me in if I asked, so I just came in." Tomas lifted both his hands toward CC showing his palms.

CC stood frozen, her mind whirling and her eyes darting around the room. She wanted to call out, but there was no one except Jenny. If she was healthy, she might have been able to outrun him in the sunlight, but this was the vampire who tried to kill her all those years ago. Five years of hunting hadn't prepared her to face him, but now that he stood in front of her, she wanted answers more than a fight. "What do you want?"

"Talk, that's all. I just want to talk to you. I need to talk to you. Please?" Tomas sat at the far end of the kitchen table outside the light of the window. He pointed to a chair, but CC stood firm.

Fluffy stood between CC and Tomas, growling. Her hair stood up, but she lowered her growl to an audible snarl and stared at Tomas.

"Talk," CC said.

"I'm sorry I attacked you the last time we met, although I had no intention of killing you then and have no intention of killing you now. I made sure your enormous preacher friend and his old soldier found you first. Technically, I am supposed to kill you now, but I'm not going to, and I don't want to."

"And I'm believing you because?" CC found the handle to the kitchen door comforting.

"You're a good fighter. I had to make it look good. You don't have to believe me when I tell you I'm sorry, but I hope you will. It will make things easier if there is at least a little trust between us."

"Convince me." CC loosened her grip on the door handle but still refused to get close to the blond-haired vampire with the pretty eyes and pink lips. "What's with the picture?"

"Darcy," replied Tomas, turning his pink lips into a smile. "She's the daughter of your friend, Derek."

"She's dead." A lump formed in CC's throat. She turned it into venom.

"No! That's her. I swear. I hid her. Then I took her to a safe place. They're good people with other kids they've fostered and adopted. Darcy is happy there. I check in on her when I can, but it's getting harder to do. If Leonard suspected I kept her from him, he'd not only kill me, he'd kill the whole family. I need you to let her father know she's alive and well."

CC's mind swirled with possibilities. She stared at the picture. The little girl's features had the familiar forms she recognized in Derek's face. "Why did you keep her alive?"

"I've never been afraid to kill, too old to change my ways overnight, but I've never killed a child. And a baby? No way. That's just—ick."

CC registered the disquiet in the vampire's voice, but this was the same vampire who attacked her in the airport parking lot. It had been sudden and fierce. He threw her across the lot into a parked car. Several bones broke, but then the rev and Roger were there and the vamp ran.

Fluffy barked, and CC jumped as she felt Jenny walk past her. "You holding the door open to let the chill in?" she asked. "Hello, Tommy. What are you doing here?"

Jenny walked in and washed her hands before grabbing two coffee mugs. "Glad you made coffee. I so need a cup. You?"

Tommy's expression changed. His shoulders relaxed, his smile widened, and he nodded his head to Jenny. "I'm not here to kill anybody."

"Of course you're not." Jenny poured a mug of coffee and handed it to CC. "You wouldn't dare do anything like that in one of Anthony's houses. You can relax, CC. He's a bit of twit now and then, but he's really not that bad."

Tommy rolled his eyes. "Hardly a glowing recommendation."

"It wasn't meant to be." Jenny shook her head. "I know what happened in Galveston. You were so sure you could one-up Max that you nearly got a lot of vamps dead."

"A mistake." Tommy straightened his tie and tugged at his shirt cuff.

"Do we have to talk about that now? The Duchess has forgiven me, you know."

"More like put you on probation, and only because Harry thinks you're worth saving. Speaking of, does he know you're here?"

"Not exactly. But he didn't say I couldn't come. Darcy's father needs to know she's alive, and I can hardly walk up to him and tell him. Once I figured out you two were here, I thought she might help."

"By sneaking in on me?" CC couldn't keep the anger out of her voice.

"Point," said Jenny. "But let's not argue 'til after breakfast. My girl here is healing and needs to keep up her strength."

Tommy jumped out of his chair, bending his head first one direction and then another. "Where's your boyfriend, Catherine? I thought he would be here."

Jenny turned from the refrigerator. "He's in town with David. They're working with Anthony."

"Shit!" Tommy's angelic white face paled even more.

"What?" replied both Jenny and CC.

Tommy turned his head to the front of the house. "Someone's pulling up. Expecting anyone?"

"No," replied Jenny and set the carton of eggs on the countertop. "Let me deal with it."

"No! If I could figure out you're here, so could—"

The sound of someone running through the house froze the three of them. The door from the dining room burst into the kitchen.

"They killed Harry!" Ezra Titler's body shook and would have fallen over if Tomas hadn't sped with vampire speed to grab his arm and sit him at the table. His head fell in his hands. "First Mama, now this. It's over. They've won."

Jenny leaned over Ezra with her hand on his back. "Slow down, Ezra. What happened?"

"They killed Mama, the night after the fire. Clay found me and told me. And then last night. They killed Harry. It's over Jenny. Everything we hoped for."

Jenny looked at Tomas. "No. It's not over. Is it Tomas?"

CC turned to look at Tomas standing in the darkest corner of the kitchen. His face, so small and cherub-looking, aged before her. His pink lips grimaced and he shook his head.

"It's just starting," he said and turned to the hall. "I can't do anything today. Tonight, I'll go to town, take care of what needs to be taken care of. You should all stay here. Leonard wants you all dead."

Silence filled the room. Before Tomas could step into the hallway, CC broke the silence. "We're not staying here. I can help."

*****

The wetness of the place made the chill colder than it was, but knowing that did not help her feel any warmer. The smell of mold, humidity, and old fish filled her nose. Kitten wanted to cough, but the gag in her mouth choked her when she tried. The constant lapping of water against wood below should have mellowed her. Now it haunted her into thinking the sound hid someone watching. Yet, if any of her captors were near, they remained silent.

She tried to shift, but the plastic ties on her wrists cut circulation to her hands. Her arms ached, especially the right one as she lay on her right side. The bindings on her ankles cut off feeling in her toes. She managed to kick off her shoes. It relieved some pressure in her feet but did not help warm her.

Unable to move or see anything more than the rough wooden post in front of her, she closed her eyes to recall details of how she came to be in this place. Daddy had always worried someone would kidnap his little princess. Anthony must also have feared it, or Cesar and Isabella wouldn't have always been nearby. She found little comfort in knowing that Anthony probably had Cesar and Isabella looking for her. They must have been preoccupied with the fire at Harry's house to not see the strangers break open her gate and rush up the stairs. They didn't hear the shot. Kitten remembered Stacy falling to the ground.

"We're not afraid," said a voice in her head, Harry's voice.

A door opened and slammed shut. A hand reached over, grabbing her shoulder.

"Sit up," the voice, masculine, young, and as rough as the force used to pull her to sitting, barked. "I'm supposed to make sure you're not suffocating to death."

Able to see around her for the first time, Kitten realized she had guessed right. She sat in a boathouse near the edge of a boatlift. A boat dripped from its bottom plug. The boat had been used recently, but the boathouse sat in remarkable disrepair. Part of the roof over Kitten's head was covered with a tarp. Wooden slats covered the window over the boat door. The remnants of a garage door opener hung from only one set of metal brackets, its chain missing. Rusted fishing buckets rested on their sides, and moldy fishing poles dangled from warped nails along one wall.

The man smirked as he looked at Kitten. "Look around all you want. You're not going anywhere."

Kitten felt the cold in her feet spreading up her legs. She pushed her feet closer to the man, hoping he would loosen the ties. As his eyes narrowed, she regretted the gesture, also, wearing a skirt. It inched up her thighs.

She watched the man's eyes meander from her ankles up her legs. He pulled a switchblade out from his pocket and opened it with a flick of his wrist as he knelt in front of her. He grabbed her ankles with one hand and set the blade against her shin.

His smirk changed to lust. "Bindings too tight?"

Kitten tried to pull her legs back and hold her knees together. He slid the knife up her leg. She wanted to turn her head and close her eyes, but a rage burned inside like she had never felt even as the cold in her limbs continued to creep closer to her torso. No man had ever forced himself on her. Her vision faded as a blackness closed in around her, and then she heard a familiar voice.

"Enough! I may not have a say in much around here, but I will not condone molesting this woman." An odd-looking man with a deep bellowing voice filled the doorway. Kitten was certain it was sunny outside, but the shadow of the man filled the boathouse. "Get out."

"Relax, reverend," the man said with a snarl. "Just loosening the ties. Can't you see? Her feet are swelling." The knife cut the ties, and the pain of a thousand pins filled Kitten's feet, but at least she felt something other than cold in her toes, even if coldness still oozed its way through her. The younger man took his time replacing the ties, making sure they were tight.

Kitten watched him as his eyes remained fixed on her raised skirt. She felt her stomach turning and wondered if he would take the gag out if she began to vomit. Doubting it, she bit harder into the rag.

When he was satisfied she was secure, he left. The large man carried a thermos and cup. He turned one of the old fishing buckets upside down and sat next to Kitten.

"I'm sorry," he said. "Let me get this out of your mouth. My sister said it was okay if I brought you some tea. It's one of my favorites, and I've put extra honey in it to give you strength."

Kitten said nothing. The gag had filled her mouth with cotton and oil. The fluff from the cotton and slickness of the oil remained when the man pulled out the gag. He held her head up as he lifted the mug of hot tea to her mouth.

"Slowly," he said. "Take your time."

The smell of the leaves warmed Kitten's head, and then the taste of sweet sunshine flowed down her throat. The warmth of the tea spread through her. Though still cold, it was now bearable.

The man removed his hand and pulled the cup away. "Let that settle. My name is Yasushi. I know your name is Kitten. When I first heard it, I thought it was odd, but I've grown to like it."

His voice was kind but melancholy. He tried to provide comfort, but hot tea was all he could muster.

"I've seen you before, but I can't place where." Her voice croaked, but moving her jaw relaxed her.

"I've been one of the people watching you for some time. I am truly sorry you're here. It was never part of the plan."

Kitten looked up into Yasushi's large dark eyes and saw only sadness. "Thanks for keeping that creep away from me. I suppose he'll be back when you're not around."

"Not if I can help it." Yasushi's sternness and urgency alarmed Kitten. Her temporary savior was as much a prisoner as she was.

"Are you going after Daddy's or Anthony's money?" she asked.

Yasushi stared at her. She could see the struggle in his face. The man before her was accustomed to controlling, but he did not control here. His helplessness frightened him. It frightened her too, knowing the other man was near.

"They're not asking for money from anyone," Yasushi said. He looked across the boathouse, staring at nothing in particular. He placed the cup back to her lips and tipped the cup for her to drink. "I've wanted to talk to you for some time, but they said it would do no good. Why did Harry spend so much effort protecting you?"

Kitten forgot herself and where she was. She saw only Harry's house burning. Once again, she leaned against her balcony, watching the flames leap high into the black night, and in those flames she saw Harry looking at her. She saw him painting Mars, who lay on the floor with blood dripping from his neck. She saw him standing overhead as Anthony kissed the scratch on her arm and Isabella picked up the thug at the Long Center and crushed the man's neck. She saw him in the eyes of Holofernes as he lay beneath her, fondling her breasts.

When she woke, Yasushi was gone. His jacket was wrapped around her shoulders. It covered most of her body. His scent lingered in the jacket. The coldness continued to radiate from her core, and she knew more than death waited for her.

*****

The sedative worked. Kitten fell into a deep sleep. Yasushi removed his jacket and wrapped it around her, making sure it was tucked tightly under her chin. He wanted to save her, and the only way he could think of was to appear to cooperate. The bile in his stomach churned. As soon as she was asleep, he vomited into the river. Then he knelt beside her to pray, but the words in his heart would not issue from his mouth.

The others hated her because she was involved with the vampires. He couldn't hate her, but he couldn't understand her. Harry had been adamant nothing happen to her but wouldn't say why. Yasushi needed answers, but his first priority was to keep her safe. For that, he wanted her to sleep. The others would not be able to question her if she slept. Karol could not torture her if she slept.

He tried again to pray for guidance. When he failed to find the words, he opened his eyes. She looked back at him but not with her eyes. Blackness in depths he had only seen in one other person stared up at him. He fell backward, slipping off the bucket.

"What's the matter, *reverend*? Have you so abandoned God that you can no longer seek solace in your prayers?"

"Harry?" Yasushi closed his eyes, shaking his head. When he opened his eyes, Kitten's eyes were closed.

Yasushi stood up, shaking. "No," he whispered. "You won't take her, Harry. You promised no harm would come to her."

Even as he spoke the words, he remembered Harry's warning, "If anything happens to the woman, all is lost."

*****

Barbara's eyes remained dry, but only because they were too swollen to cry anymore. She sat on the sofa in their suite, continually rubbing her hands down her thighs as though to straighten her skirt. Beau sat next to her. He would take her hand to stop her, but then she'd start to sway back and forth. He loosened his tie and looked at Anthony.

Anthony held the document wrapped in a plastic evidence bag in front of him. Finally, he set it down on the table and placed his head in his hands.

"It's all my fault," he said without looking up. "If I hadn't liked her so much, she'd be here with you now."

"No, Anthony. It's those sons of bitches' fault for taking her. Lord knows I've always done what I could to protect her. You know how it is. You have money, and there's always someone around who wants you to give it to them." Beau stood, pacing back and forth in front of the glass doors leading to the balcony.

Anthony stood up and moved to sit beside Barbara. "I will find her. My people are already on it. I don't care what it costs or who gets in the way. No one is going to take her from us."

Barbara clasped Anthony's hands in hers. "Oh, Anthony, I know you'll do your best."

Anthony stood to leave. "I'll keep you informed. The note came to me, but that doesn't mean they're not watching you too. I'm putting some of my people outside your door. Please let them know if you need anything or go anywhere, and wait for my call."

Beau shook his hand. "Don't worry about us, Anthony. I know you'll do the right thing."

Anthony left. Beau went back to sit next to his wife. "We gotta hang on to hope, Mommy. Our little Kitten is depending on us."

"Anthony believes she's already dead," Barbara said, standing. "His hands were so cold. He's so angry. I hope this doesn't kill him too. It's time I got back to the hospital."

"We should stay here—"

"No. I can't do anything to help my baby sitting in my room, but I can help Stacy."

Beau nodded and watched his wife go into the bedroom, where she would wash her face and change her clothes. The shock was wearing off of both of them. She would take charge of Stacy's care and demand attention from everyone around her. He wanted to stay in the hotel. He wanted to do something, but instead went to the door to tell the security guard their plans.

While waiting, Beau poured himself a bourbon. "Good man Anthony. Just wish he wasn't lying about that kidnap note." He finished the drink, then went to change his shirt.

*****

Isabella leaned against the door of Anthony's limo. Despite the perimeter guard, she continued to scan the area for Hunters. Harry was dead. Hunters had attacked Anthony's compound, but when they realized their surprise attack wasn't such a surprise, they'd dispersed.

"Stupid shit," she said under her breath looking again at the text Cesar had sent her in the morning. "Body recovered and on its way. Following lead to Hunters."

Not knowing what he was doing bothered her, but worrying bothered her more.

Anthony's guard walked out of the hotel, signaling her. She opened the passenger door for him as he exited. She tapped on the roof of the car and followed Anthony into the back seat.

"Good job on the note," he told her with his usual cool control. "Vague about who took her. That will buy us time. I don't want the FBI or local police stumbling on the Hunters while we're looking for them. Anything from Cesar?"

"Nothing new." Isabella gave up trying not to bite her nails. The manicure was long gone. "Why all the secrecy?"

To her surprise, Anthony laughed. "We survive on secrets, Isabella. I thought you realized that by now."

"It's one thing to know secrets, it's another not knowing what the fuck is going on." Isabella sat up straight, pulling her fingernail out of her mouth. "Sorry, sir."

Anthony kept the smile on his face, but Isabella noticed the lines around his eyes tracing his weariness. "Stressful," he replied. "I knew what I was in for when Harry came up with the plan for a safe place where we could all live. Just thought Harry would be here to share it."

"Is it okay for me to ask why you changed plans? I thought the whole idea behind the big house and compound was to hide everyone in a safe place. I mean, with the bunkers, the dogs, the gates, it's the safest place in Austin."

Anthony continued staring out the window as they made their way through rush hour traffic back to the house. He hadn't been there when the attack came this morning, and that puzzled Isabella too.

"Do you know why you're in Austin?" Anthony asked.

"To learn. Mary said trouble was coming, and Cesar needed help."

Anthony looked at her. His eyes widened. "She mentioned Cesar by name? Interesting."

Isabella sat on her hands. "Have I said something I shouldn't have?"

"No. Mary and Harry have always done exactly what they wanted, and they both want this place to work." Anthony remained silent for a while. "You're too young to remember the old days."

Isabella tried to lean back in the seat, as Anthony did, to relax.

"When I was young, before I changed, I watched my cousin go from simple farm boy to a grand Duke. I was jealous, but he was my cousin and my friend, so I was also happy for him. He took me with him to Florence as a servant. It was a magical place filled with magical people. And then one day, I looked around and realized all that beautiful art, all that money, all that power being wasted on petty people. Then came the change. Fortunately, Harry was there. He guided me.

"I could have been a king, almost was, but Harry held me in check. 'Don't waste your time ruling,' he'd say to me. 'Learn what you can from these people. Why wear a crown when you can lead from the shadows?' Still, I wanted the glory. I wanted to be a king.

"We were always moving around. In those days, people died so easily. It was easy to kill when everyone around you expected death, but even the dimmest of peasants recognized signs when too many people were dying and you were always healthy-looking. Then I met Leonard. He's a little older than me. We both wanted to rule.

"One day, Harry left us, saying he had business elsewhere. Leonard and I let loose on this little village. We feasted, reveled, and ruled that village without regard for anything other than our own pleasure."

"I've heard stories like this before," Isabella said, taking Anthony's momentary silence for an invitation to say something. "They always end with lots of deaths."

"As did our story. Hunters came. They killed everyone in the town, every man, woman, and child. I heard an infant being burned alive in a house. I wanted to save it, but the flames were too great. Leonard ran off as soon as they arrived, but I stayed, wanting to keep my territory, protect my people. The Hunters nearly got me. I would never have killed everyone. What would have been the point? I would have let them kill me to save the villagers, but they believed the entire village was contaminated. If Harry hadn't arrived and taken me away, I wouldn't be here now."

"Maybe the Hunters won't kill Kitten Carlisle." Isabella no longer wondered why Anthony worried about her.

Anthony shook his head. "It's always the same with zealots. Kill first, pray for forgiveness later. Just like Margo. They couldn't have known what she was, only that she helped someone associated with us. Any word about Ezra?"

"Margo wouldn't leave her shift at the hospital when you sent out word about the Hunters and told everyone to scatter. They got her at home. Made it look like a gas leak. Ezra's alive. He was at a party given by the mayor. It was the safest place to be for him last night. Three vamps died before they got the message, but everyone else went underground. I've had a few 'unknown caller' texts asking when they can come home. And then," Isabella paused as she felt a lump in her throat. "Ol' Mike. They killed him this morning at the house."

"Shit!" Anthony let out a long sigh. "He was such a good kid. Always had to do things his way." The limo drove through the damaged gate of the compound. "There will be calls for blood, Isabella. Keep your head clear. I need you in control while Cesar's away."

Before Isabella could ask anything else, the car stopped. Leonard was at the door waiting for Anthony.

Isabella watched as Leonard hugged Anthony. They both wore long faces and angry eyes, but Leonard's actions roared with anger. Isabella stepped out of the car and noticed David on the hill near the house. He waved for her.

"Mary," she said to herself as she headed for the tunnel leading to the kennels, "what have you gotten me into?"

*****

"Have you totally lost your senses?" Isabella paced in the secure room under the kennel. "Do you have any idea what's going on around you? You're not stupid, David. Are you siphoning the giggle water or what?"

David leaned against the door, his long, thin frame contrasting with the bulky steel door. He neither smiled nor frowned. His brown eyes followed Isabella's pacing, but he remained silent.

James Earl, sitting on the desk chair in front of the computers, turned his head first from David then to Isabella and back again. "I know what I'm doing. It's no problem—"

"Amateurs!" interrupted Isabella. "You want him to follow money transfers, fine, but what is he doing here?"

"I can do this anywhere, really. All I need is—"

"Harry's dead! Don't you get it? Hunters are openly attacking us. They killed Margo, you know, and they killed Ol' Mike. He was just an old man. Kitten's missing, her friend's been shot, Cesar's out running around doing who knows what, and Anthony's reminiscing about the old days. Are you going to say anything or just stand there all day like some chump?" Isabella stopped pacing and sat on the chair next to James Earl. She closed her eyes and let out an audible sigh. "So, James Earl. Do you actually go by James Earl? Can I just call you James? It seems like a long name. Never mind. You're tracking money heading in and out of accounts used by your little vampire murder club?"

"Let him talk, Isabella." David moved to lean over Isabella and picked up a water bottle from the desk. After he gulped down the contents, he continued. "He's come around to our side by a long route. You'll like him when you get to know him."

James Earl turned back to his monitors and grabbed his mouse highlighting a series of numbers. "This account here. The rev had me set it up years ago. From here, I pull funds to pay the group's expenses. We have multiple accounts, but this one the rev said to keep an eye on. When I first tapped it, it held about fifteen thousand dollars. With all the traveling we do, it didn't take long for the amount to dwindle, then one day I go in, and there's another fifteen thousand dollars in it."

"Where's the money coming from?"

"Well, that's where this gets a bit sticky. The rev didn't want me following the source. Told me specifically not to, since he knows it's the type of thing I can do, so I didn't look. I just moved funds around—"

"Don't you think it's time to look?" Isabella rolled her eyes at James Earl.

David placed his hand on Isabella's shoulder. "Let him talk, Issy. You'll find it worth your while."

"Sorry, a little preoccupied, so if you could get to the good stuff, please."

James Earl grinned. "You sound like CC. Made the same argument to me. That's why I started tracing the money. I was making good headway, and then the account disappeared. I chose this account because the amount was always steady and replaced quickly. Other accounts fluctuate normally, the way donations and installments should. A single entity has been maintaining this account. And this is where it gets interesting, the source of the money was not constant."

James Earl stopped talking and looked from Isabella to David. "Don't you see? Whoever was putting money in the account was making it as complicated as possible to find the source. Someone doesn't want me to find him."

"Him?" asked Isabella.

"Could be a her, just a figure of speech. What's so cool about this, since it looks like I'm losing you, is that this is how I manage money, a man on the run who doesn't want to be traced. I'm still wanted by the Feds. You don't think I have a checking account or credit card that can be traced to me, do you?"

Isabella stood to once again pace the room. "We're all constantly revising our identities. The more complicated it gets, the easier it is to hide."

"Exactly." James Earl's eyes widened, and his grin grew. "Whoever is on the other end is almost as smart as I am."

"Name," said David, leaning over James Earl to look at the computer screen running algorithms. "Who is almost as smart as you are, James Earl? We need a name."

"Don't know yet, but I will." James Earl's fingers raced over his keyboard, while his head turned to look at a different monitor. "But now there's a new player."

David and Isabella both looked at him.

"This account here. It's Madeline's. Normally, I put money in there to cover her expenses. She likes dresses with lots of flowers on them and high-heeled shoes. Anyway, that's about it. Well, and basic supplies for the group, but someone dropped over fifty thousand sometime yesterday."

Silence filled the room until Isabella said, "One of us is killing us."

"Told you he was worth it. We need that name, James Earl." David headed toward the door, guiding Isabella out with him.

"I need time, but I'll find it. We've all been played."

David turned at the door to face James Earl. "Don't leave the safe room. Even the vamps can't get to you here."

James Earl nodded. "Got it. I won't let you down." James Earl returned to his work.

David and Isabella were about to close the door when James Earl cleared his throat. "Before you go, can I ask a question?"

"Shoot," she said.

"Are you into the whole Harry Potter thing, or what?"

Isabella raised her eyebrows and started to answer, but David laughed and touched her shoulder.

"Giggle water."

Isabella's eyes widened. "What?"

David's laugh matched his rich, melodious voice as it echoed in the hall leading to the safe room. "Sorry, kid. Don't mean to laugh at you. She's a lot older than she looks. When she was your age, they called booze giggle water. She's really just a little old-fashioned lady."

"I am not old-fashioned! I happen to like the expression."

"Let's go, Isabella." David pushed Isabella through the doorway. "And you, buzz me when you know something, and do NOT open this door for anyone except me."

"Got it." As the door closed, they could hear James Earl saying to himself, "Wow. She really is a lot older than she looks."

David closed the door and stood listening for the clicks as James Earl sealed the electronic door from his side.

"I'm not old." Isabella huffed and walked up the stairs to the kennels.

*****

Derek walked out of the house as the last of the soldiers fell asleep. Most had been drinking and their snoring reverberated through his ears like an airplane in flight. At first, all he wanted was clean air and silence, but he found himself walking farther away from the house. The morning dew clung to the grass on the side of the road, wetting his bare feet and ankles. The coolness felt good after the stuffiness of the house, or maybe it was the heat in his body burning with questions that appreciated the cool vacuum seeping into him.

At some point, he turned his body to walk backwards and lifted his thumb for a ride. It didn't take long for someone to pull over. When he arrived on Lake Austin Boulevard, he thanked the driver and walked down the road to the remnants of the house that had belonged to the old artist.

A fire truck remained, and firemen walked around with hoses, dousing areas. Others carried shovels, turning over hot spots. Investigators were also there. There was not more crowd, but a few neighborhood residents gathered nearby, drinking coffee and talking about their luck that the fire had not spread and how odd it was another house burned down on the same night.

Derek walked to the river, keeping his head down but his eyes on the house. A reporter stood in front of the house lit by a camera and talking about the apparent death of the artist. Derek dashed behind a tree near the water and vomited. He heaved until nothing else would come from his stomach.

The cold of the hand on his shoulder startled him. The hand remained firmly on his shoulder and lifted him up.

"Come to gloat?" said the man Derek recognized but couldn't put a name to.

Derek stared into the man's eyes, but they were cold and lost. The face, so familiar, twisted with rage and sorrow. A moment later, the hand on his shoulder released him. Derek fell to the ground. His butt splashed into muddy water.

Derek leaned over and splashed water on his face and then stood watching the water flow. He saw Yasushi sitting in the corner of the living room he had just left. "Wasn't him. Rev, you said we're getting justice. We killed the others but only when we saw them killing. The old man was just an old man."

Cesar placed his head next to Derek's. "Where are you, Derek?"

"At the river, all sins are washed away, but they're not really washed away. The blood remains. Why does the blood remain, rev?"

Cesar sent a text to Isabella.

"Come on, Derek. We have work to do."

Derek lay in the back seat of a car. He tucked a blanket under his chin. "Sleep when you can. You don't know when you'll get a warm spot to sleep in again. You think I'll ever break that habit, Babs?" Derek muttered to his wife who died so long ago, but only Cesar heard him.

*****

No one ever questioned a hearse arriving at the medical examiner's office. They might question why he and not one of his helpers was picking up a body, but everyone liked Clay. All he needed to do was smile.

Cesar stood in the shadows of the docks. Clay took his time removing the gurney before addressing Cesar.

"Only the one camera," he said, not looking at Cesar. "If you're here, the rumors are true. Harry's dead."

"Yes," Cesar said, watching as Clay dropped his head.

With a shudder, Clay lifted his head and turned the gurney toward the ramp. "I'll get the body."

"Can you do this by yourself? I have a ..." Cesar hesitated a moment. "I have a problem that needs my full attention."

"No problem." Clay took a tablet from his jacket pocket and tapped. "I'm due to pick up today. I've received notice of a few others that will need my services. Amazing it wasn't more from what I heard."

"I want to see him before you leave."

"Wait here," Clay said and waved to a guard opening the door for him.

Clay chatted up the clerk outside the refrigerator as she pulled up paperwork for him to sign just like he always did. As soon as he entered, he located Harry's body, removed it from the body bag, and placed it on top of the body he was scheduled to pick up. He adjusted his gurney. He'd had it made specifically for stealing bodies. Today, it paid for itself.

Finally, he reached inside the body bag and removed Harry's head. Someone had closed his eyes. Clay trembled as he lay Harry's head in the bag where it should be. Knowing Cesar wanted to look, he pulled out his handkerchief and placed it where the head and neck should have met.

"I'll miss you, old man," he said before closing the bag. Pulling his shoulders back and stifling a sniffle, he pushed the gurney out, smiling and waving to the clerk.

Outside the loading dock, he stopped where Cesar could come out of the shadows to see Harry without being seen by the camera. He pulled back the purple cover and unzipped the bag low enough for Cesar to see Harry's head. Cesar unzipped the bag further but said nothing.

An ambulance drove up to the dock. Clay placed himself between the driver and the gurney, zipping the bag up and replacing the cover. "Never dreamed I'd be doing this for Harry. I'm sorry, Cesar. You two were together for many years."

"Take him to Anthony's." Cesar turned and left.

The ambulance driver waved to Clay, who smiled and waved back as he loaded his hearse. As he pulled away, he saw Cesar pulling out of the parking lot. A head popped up in the back seat. A young man looked at him, then lay back down.

"Harry, what is your boy up to?" Clay said aloud. "Always thought Cesar liked girls. At least he has good taste, Harry. Always thought I had the best-looking dreads in town."

*****

Derek was lost. It was the only thing about him Cesar knew for certain. He drove him to the apartment he kept downtown when he wanted to be alone. Even Anthony didn't know about it. The easy part of his day was getting Derek into the apartment without being seen. The difficult part would be convincing Derek to tell him where the Hunters hid. Cesar considered calling Isabella but decided she should remain protecting Anthony.

Derek sat at the table, starting at a plate of scrambled eggs and toast in front of him. That and coffee were the only things Cesar knew how to cook.

"Eat it while it's hot, Derek. You'll feel better. You want coffee?"

Derek stared at Cesar.

"Shit, Derek. Eat the damn food." Cesar hadn't intended to yell, but it did the trick. Derek shoveled food into his mouth and at all on his plate. "Good. I'll get you some coffee."

Cesar kept an eye on Derek, not daring to turn his back on him. Derek's eyes fixed on Cesar's face as Cesar placed the mug of coffee in front of Derek.

"Feeling better?" Cesar asked.

"Yes, sir," Derek said and put the mug of coffee to his mouth.

"Where are you, Derek?" Cesar kept his voice calm and low.

"Mess hall, sir."

Cesar pursed his lips and stood up to walk around. Derek stood at attention.

"As you were, marine."

Derek sat and continued to eat his toast. Cesar paced the room, recalling all the information they had gathered on Derek. He was a marine. He didn't trust all the Hunters. Derek had been touched by a vamp, and the result was the madness haunting him now.

Cesar watched Derek drink his coffee. "What the hell happened to you, Derek?" Cesar asked expecting no answer, so when Derek spoke, he stopped pacing.

"He's not the one who killed my Babs and my baby girl, rev. I know that. You know that too. And what are they going to do with that woman? She's not a demon. I don't understand. Why keep killing those we know didn't kill?"

"What woman, Derek?"

Derek didn't answer the question. "I'm sorry. Babs. You didn't sign on for this. But those guys were my buddies, my squad. I couldn't let them go and get themselves in trouble. I had to try to stop them. But demons showed up and killed everybody. I'm not crazy, Babs. I swear. I saw demons."

Derek jumped out of his chair. "They're everywhere. They keep killing. We have to stop them. I met a man, a man of God. He knows what I'm talking about. I'm going to meet him later. Please, stay inside and lock the doors. Don't let anyone in. I've got to meet the rev. He'll help me clear my name."

Derek turned as though he would walk away but stopped. He turned again and looked at Cesar as though he were seeing him for the first time. "Who are you? You're not the rev."

"The rev sent me to help, Derek. I'm going to take you to the rev. Are you ready to go?"

"I don't know you. My family needs protecting."

"I can help you with that."

"No, you can't." A look of panic spread across Derek's face. His eyes widened. Drool fell from his lower lip. "They're all around. They killed my family. I have to warn the rev."

Derek sprinted forward. Cesar caught him as he fell, tears pouring from his eyes. "They've killed everyone. They killed the old man last night, and the others took that woman and locked her down in the boathouse. What am I going to do?"

Cesar wrapped his arms around Derek, allowing him to shake and moan. "It's all right, Derek. I'll protect you, but you need to tell me where they are."

Getting answers from Derek would take time Cesar didn't have. Isabella would know how to talk to him, but he couldn't risk her coming here and leaving Anthony unprotected.

Derek drifted to sleep. Cesar placed him on the couch. He picked up his phone but put it away. He needed help, but who to call and how to call without making his position known? That's when he realized that he hadn't searched Derek's pockets. As soon as he put his hand in Derek's back pocket, he felt the phone.

"Almost blew that, Cesar," he said to himself. "Afraid I have to leave you for a little while, Derek. No offense if I lock you in? Good. I'll be back soon."

Cesar grabbed a hat and made his way to the parking garage. Standing in a dark corner, he looked at its history. "Not much of a talker, are you, Derek?" He memorized the most common numbers before dialing.

David answered with the first ring.

"David, meet me at eight near Harry's." He turned off the phone and crushed it without waiting for David to answer.

In the apartment, Derek still slept. Cesar stretched out on the recliner to wait.

*****

Jenny pulled the van up to the gate. Mike's shoulders softened and his lips turned to smile at Jenny.

"What are you doing here?"

"I live here, silly." Jenny smiled the way she always did.

"You know David isn't going to like you being here." Mike pointed his head at the damaged gate.

Jenny turned around in her seat as barking erupted from the van. "Quiet, I'll let you out in a minute."

Jenny turned back to Mike, "It's okay. He knows I'm coming."

Mike signaled to a camera, and the gate opened. He watched the van drive through and shook his head. "Who are you hiding in there?"

Jenny pulled the van up to the side of the kennels. As she got out of the van, she looked around her before walking to the passenger side and opening the sliding door. The shadows of the day were lengthening as the sun set over the trees.

"Stay," she said and opened the door to the kennels. She looked around one more time. "Come."

Fluffy and two Rottweilers bound out of the van and ran into the building. CC followed, stretching her limbs and moving as fast as her sore limbs allowed.

Jenny pointed the Rottweilers to an empty kennel. "There you go, sweeties," she said. "You'll like it here, but you're going to have to work for your meat. How you feeling, CC?"

CC placed her good arm behind her and twisted her back. "Tell me again why you didn't want anyone to know I'm here."

David stood at the top of the stairs, looking down on the two women. His voice caused CC to jump and turn. "Because this place is about to be filled with vamps looking to kill whoever's associated with the Hunters."

"Hi, sweetheart. Did you miss me?" Jenny smiled as David walked down the stairs and wrapped an arm around her, pulling her close to him.

David placed his face in front of hers and stroked her hair. "Always," he said and kissed her.

CC looked around the kennels, looking at each dog as each dog looked at David and Jenny. Fluffy sat next to her, so she bent down to pet her.

"I told you to stay at the vineyard," David said, moving away from Jenny but keeping hold of her. "It's dangerous around here, and not just for you, CC. It's dangerous for everybody."

"That's why I'm here." CC stood as tall as she could. David still looked down on her, but she kept her eyes steeled to his. "You need me. I know James Earl is here hacking, but I know things about Madeline, Roger, even the reverend that will help."

"That was before they were joined by their militant brethren. I'm afraid you're just a liability now."

"Listen to her, my love," Jenny said. "She might be a little broken, but her mind works just fine. Use what she knows about them."

"Anybody see you bring her in?"

Jenny laughed, "Oh, please. Safe room?"

"Follow me. I'll see if I can get Anthony down here later to talk to you. Shit!" David looked around him and stepped away from Jenny. "I have someplace to be. Let's get you downstairs."

David let go of Jenny and opened the trap door leading to the stairs. Jenny and CC followed.

CC's eyes widened as she walked down comfortable stairs to a massive steel door. This was not a safe room with minimal amenities, it was a luxury apartment for the apocalypse.

David's fingers tapped numbers into a keypad. A red light on the keypad glowed. "It's me. Open up, quick."

A moment later, the door opened and James Earl stood with his mouth hanging open as he saw CC. He ran to her and hugged her.

"Sorry," he said as she grimaced at a sharp pain moving up her broken arm.

"It's okay, babe. I'm good."

"What are you doing here?" began James Earl, but David cut him off.

"I've got someplace to be. Anything for me yet?" David asked.

"No, but I'm getting close. I can feel it."

"Back inside, show her how it works, and remember: don't open the door to anyone except me or Jenny." David leered at both CC and James Earl.

"I don't suppose I can convince you to stay with them?" David leaned in close to Jenny.

"Silly man," she said. "Go. You've got work to do. I'll find a way to get Anthony down here. He should talk to CC."

"Be careful." David kissed Jenny's lips. "Don't know when the others will be here."

Jenny reached up to give David a long kiss. CC and James Earl closed the door, securing it electronically.

"We'll be safe in here," James Earl said.

"Yes, we will." CC removed the large handgun from the holster on her belt. "I haven't worn one of these in ages. Time to get my groove back."

*****

Cesar sat. He watched Derek walk back and forth in front of the remains of Harry's house. When the wind stopped blowing, Christmas music from the coffeehouse drifted across the water. Derek would stop, stare out at the water, and pace again. David was late, but given the situation, it didn't worry Cesar. He knew Derek would make his way back to the reverend, and when he did, Cesar would know where the Hunters hid.

There was nothing on the news about a kidnapping, but he had learned enough from Derek's rantings to assume that the Hunters had kidnapped Kitten and Anthony would do anything to get her back. Not only was Anthony a proud man, but Cesar realized if Harry needed Kitten, then Anthony would too. Odd images of Kitten and Harry, Anthony and Harry, and Kitten and Anthony played out in his mind. Something connected the three. He just didn't know what it was.

The sight of Harry's face, lying wrapped in that body bag, lifeless, formless, no longer Harry remained burned in Cesar's eyes. He saw the face that rescued him from living in caves and feeding on animals, thieves, and Spanish Loyalists. Harry taught him his humanity was not lost. His soul survived. He had a purpose. They roamed Spain, feeding off the dying on battlefields, and then they roamed the battlefields of Europe. Harry taught him to mingle with ambulance drivers and medics, how to help those humans who could be helped, and how to ease life away from those dying miserable deaths.

"So many wars," Cesar said to himself as he listened to Derek ramble about the life he lost. "Too many wars."

Derek stopped mumbling and looked around him, his eyes clearing. Cesar watched in the shadows.

"The rev will know what happened," Derek said to himself.

Derek wrinkled his brow and took a deep breath in. "What does the rev say? Breathe in, slow. Blow it out. Count your breaths, Derek." It's what Derek did.

Behind him, Cesar heard the soft footsteps of David. He lifted his hand to keep David quiet.

Derek walked away from the remnants of Harry's house.

"We need to follow," Cesar said, audible only to David.

David nodded, taking the lead.

They followed Derek as he wandered down the road and hitched a ride. David took off his clothes, handing them to Cesar before morphing into his wolf and running after the car. Cesar ran to his car, easily finding the car carrying Derek. He pulled back, leaving enough space for Derek to not notice him.

Derek didn't remain in the car for long. He got out only a few miles away. He stood, muttering again. Cesar parked the car and walked to stand next to David, still a wolf, hiding behind a clump of trees.

Cesar looked at David, about to say something when they heard an enormous voice shout, "You can't!"

"Keep him safe," Cesar whispered to David and slid through shadows toward the source of the shout.

It wasn't hard to find them. The river was lined with homes, most with their lights out. The Hunters stood in darkness on a molding deck with a dilapidated boathouse. Cesar recognized the reverend by his size. The shadows of men and women stood huddled in a semicircle around the reverend.

Cesar leapt into a tree overhanging the house where he could see and hear all.

The reverend pleaded, "Please, Madeline. You can't do this."

"You have no say in this, brother. You, who gave in to them, who's been plotting with them behind my back." Cesar wanted to shrink further into the shadows at the venom in Madeline's voice.

"All I've ever done is seek justice, not murder."

"Go somewhere and pray, brother. Bring her out!"

Cesar watched a man in a well-worn army jacket and short hair emerge from the boathouse pulling Kitten by her arms. Her hands were bound behind her. She stumbled as her feet failed to keep up with the pushing and pulling of her capture. Despite the darkness, his eyes could make out her face, lethargic but not beaten. She was cold and dirty, but otherwise unharmed.

The man pulling Kitten took her to the end of the boat dock and pushed her to her knees. Kitten's head drooped.

Cesar turned to find David, but Madeline's voice froze him.

"We know she's being turned. She's been helping them from the beginning. She dies tonight."

"Madeline—" Before the reverend could say anything else, the man standing next to him punched him in the stomach, causing him to double over. Then the man hit the reverend's head, and he fell to the ground. He wasn't unconscious, but Cesar could see the reverend's head swaying side to side.

"Anyone else object?" Madeline asked and turned to face Kitten and the young soldier. "Kill her."

The young soldier pulled out a handgun, pointed it at Kitten's head. He froze. The young man bit his lower lip.

"Kill her!" shouted Madeline.

The young soldier still waited.

"Kill her!" Madeline shouted again, this time walking with lightning speed toward them. "Kill her!" she continued to shout.

Cesar leaned forward. He would need to get between Kitten and Madeline before Madeline or the young soldier fired. He could just make it.

Kitten lifted her head, looking past her kidnappers at Cesar. Cesar's jaw fell open. The eyes were like the night - all darkness and fathomless. He froze. He heard a slow growl coming from behind him. David, as wolf, stood with hackles raised. Cesar lifted his hand to quiet him.

Then Kitten turned her head, smiling at Madeline before slumping again.

Madeline stood beside Kitten, her face gleaming with erotic satisfaction as she pointed her handgun and shot Kitten in the head.

Madeline looked toward the deck where the rest of the group stood. No one spoke. "We kill them all."

The young soldier standing next to her put a second bullet in the back of Kitten's head, then pushed the body into the river.

"Let's get out of here," Madeline said, joining the group. "Leave nothing behind."

Madeline stopped at the prone form of the reverend, looking down on him. "Stay or go. I don't care anymore."

Cesar leapt to the ground and headed for the river's edge. David joined him, sniffing the shoreline.

"Find the body, but don't go near it." Cesar said. "We'll deal with them later."

Before Cesar looked away, he saw Derek kneeling beside the reverend, consoling, helping the large man to his feet. They were quiet. Derek's senses appeared to have returned, at least for a while. He led the reverend off the deck and away from the house.

* * * * *

Frank continued to scrawl on the whiteboard in the darkened office at the end of the hall. Hank sat in the old, wooden swivel chair. He tried to lean back, but the chair squealed every time he moved, so he returned to hunching over the battered desk. Renaldo leaned against the door, not moving except to part the metal blinds with his fingers to see who walked past the unoccupied office/storage closet they were in. Only one of the fluorescent light bulbs in the ceiling worked. A bright

LCD bulb lit the desktop and provided enough light for them to see each other and most of the writing on the whiteboard.

Frank stopped writing, stood back, and sat on the desk's edge. He folded his arms saying nothing.

Hank broke the silence. "You're right. It's crazy." His face remained stern.

A grin broke across Renaldo's face, but he didn't laugh. "We could be in a movie— talking conspiracies in an undersized, unused, and darkened office. I don't know whether to laugh or run."

Hank didn't laugh, "If we're smart, we walk away right now saying it's just a joke."

On the whiteboard, the initials for Anthony Mugello sat in the center of a diagram surrounded by circles containing: execution of accountants, terrorists attack a bar, murder of HR, disappearance of CC and husband, kidnapping of KC, and murder of MT. Hank circled the initials. "His is the only connection between all events."

Frank shook his head. "We've got nothing solid on the connection to the nurse."

"Catherine was investigating Mugello. She disappears and the nurse who helped get her out of the hospital is dead. What other connection do you need?" Hank raised his hand as Frank opened his mouth to speak again. "I know. No proof she helped, but think about it. Everyone says she was an exceptional nurse. If she didn't get sick and go home that night as she claimed, and I can't find anyone who saw her go home that night, she must have helped."

Frank shook his head. "I know it makes sense, but ..."

Silence filled the room until Renaldo asked, "What did you get from Mugello when you talked to him?"

"Too much cooperation," Hank replied. "He's upset about the kidnapping. No doubt about it, but something else is going on. He might as well not have been there. His lawyers did all the talking."

Frank nodded. "Did you see his face when you asked if he thought the murder of that artist was related to the kidnapping? Something was there. And when you asked if he knew the name Catherine Carson? He acted like he's never heard the name before, but from what you've said, she was never one to hide her suspicions. And when I talked to that chef from the dinner, he mentioned a woman the caterer fired whose description sounds a lot like your old colleague."

Renaldo nodded his head asking Hank, "What do your people think about all of this?"

Hank and Frank laughed. "Get back in the real world, kid," said Frank. "Why do you think we're talking in the closet rather than out there where everyone can hear us?"

Hank stopped laughing and stared at the floor. "CC was a good agent, green and ambitious, like you, Renaldo. Talk like this got her kicked out of the Bureau. I remember wanting to believe her when she mapped out the details of the connection to Mugello and some other banker—that Italian fellow—Bellini or something like it. But she was explaining a complicated conspiracy and complicated conspiracies don't exist."

"There is one hiccup in your map, Hank." Frank stood up and picked up a marker, drawing arrows of his own. "All these things are happening *to* Mugello, bringing him more and more into our radar. Somebody wants us to look at him. Do we focus on what Mugello's doing to make him a target or look at who's making all this happen?"

A knock on the door made each man jump. Hank pulled himself up to stand in front of the whiteboard with Frank, who nodded to Renaldo.

Renaldo cracked open the door, "What?"

"Urgent message for Agent Williams." The faceless voice handed Renaldo a piece of paper as the door closed.

Hank took the paper. His eyes widened and jaw dropped. "I've got to take this," he said.

Frank looked at him with raised eyebrows. "What now?"

"Catherine Carson's on the phone asking for me."

*****

From the balcony, Anthony watched another car arrive through the gate. It picked its way to the service parking lot. Guards would ensure the passengers found a safe place. Reporters and investigators left hours ago satisfied with the story of the attempted forced entry. In most cases, they would have left officers, but with Mugello's security it wasn't necessary. In all appearances, Anthony Mugello cooperated with law enforcement for the locating of the woman he held in special regard. But Mugello would do what he wanted.

Leonard stood near him. "It's nearly midnight. How many will come?"

"A few tonight," Anthony said. "The funeral will be tomorrow night."

"Tradition dictates—"

"No choice. I scattered everybody when the Hunters killed Harry." Anthony walked into his study. "Besides, my people will have the Hunters gathered up soon. For such a large group, they're remarkably unorganized."

"You think so?" asked Leonard, adjusting his tie.

Anthony stopped in front of his desk and looked at Jenny. She sat in his chair, wearing a thin white robe that exposed her frail white torso and tiny breasts.

"Anthony," she said, smiling up at him. "You look like you need a little diverting." Jenny walked around to the front of the desk and put her arms around Anthony's neck. He pulled her toward him and they kissed, entwining their bodies into one.

"I'll leave you, but we should talk soon," Leonard said, closing the doors to the office.

Anthony placed his hands on Jenny's buttocks and lifted her onto his desk as she wrapped her legs around his waist. He leaned into her neck putting his head next to hers.

She turned her head, "He's gone. You should have seen the sneer on his face." Jenny couldn't help but giggle.

Anthony stepped away from her but remained close enough to whisper. "What's all this for?"

"I have someone you need to meet." Jenny jumped off the desk, unconcerned with Anthony's wandering eye.

"I know about the wolf in the safe room. Does he have something for me?"

"You only know half of what's in the safe room." Jenny removed a book from the shelf and pulled a latch opening a hidden door. She replaced the book, "Coming?" she asked and led Anthony out of the room.

The corridor from Anthony's office to the kennel safe room wasn't like the others with their plush carpet and comfortable sleeping arrangements. It was a last-minute addition Cesar insisted on, allowing Anthony to get to the safest room in the compound without being seen by anyone. Anthony followed Jenny's white figure with her flowing robe glowing like a ghost in the darkness. When they reached the door to the junction room under the kennel, Jenny held up her hand and peeked around the door before signaling Anthony to follow.

The steel door stood massive and impenetrable. The red glow of the camera bathed Jenny's whiteness with red. Anthony felt a shiver down his back. For just that moment, he saw the blood that would soon spill.

The door glided open. The light that poured out of the room blinded him for a moment, but soon he saw the young man he had heard about from David. James Earl stood pointing a shotgun at him. He smelled the woman standing to the side before he saw her bright red hair and pale face.

"It's okay, he's with me," Jenny said and walked inside.

James Earl lowered the shotgun. The woman still held the gun ready, but as he moved closer, he saw her right arm bound in a cast.

"Put it down, CC. This is Anthony, your host."

"You were the woman from the party?" Anthony asked, looking at CC. "I'm sorry you were hurt. I didn't order it."

"I know who's responsible," CC said.

Anthony nodded, admiring her directness. She kept her left hand on the handgun even though she had placed it in its holster.

Jenny closed the door, locking it behind them. "Now, we can talk with no one hearing. Close your mouth, James Earl."

James Earl turned his head to look at the screens. Anthony wondered at his shyness until he recalled David telling him James Earl had just come into his wolf. "We don't have a lot of time. You have something for me?"

Despite her battered look, CC's voice was firm and controlled. This was a woman sure of herself and whom he could respect. "Whoever was giving money to Yasushi to run the group was good. James Earl hasn't been able to trace where the funds came from. So, I suggested he check on Madeline's accounts."

"As soon as CC told me about seeing Madeline with your friend the night she was here, I began following all Madeline's accounts." James Earl nodded to CC.

"Someone deposited a large sum of money into Madeline's account the day after I was run over. She's been spending it fast for weapons, vehicles, houses, and transportation. One of the houses she rented is on the river. That's where she'll be. She likes being on the water. We're working on the locations for the others. She's trying to hide them by using multiple aliases, but I know most of the aliases used by group members. As soon as she spends the money, it's replaced."

For the first time since Harry's death, Anthony felt hopeful. "You've traced who's giving her the money?"

"That's the delicate part, Anthony." Jenny placed a hand on Anthony's shoulder. "It's all coming from your banks."

Anthony sat down. "Which accounts?"

"Pull them up," CC told James Earl.

Three account numbers appeared on the screen. Anthony stared at them before speaking. "Only four people have access to those accounts, and one of them is me."

"One more thing you should see, Anthony." Jenny pointed to a small monitor above the two large ones with numbers running across them. The small monitor ran surveillance footage from the night of the dinner party.

CC's voice filled with ice. "That's the man I saw that night with Madeline. That's the man I've known as Leonardo Bellini. He's the one who killed my partner in Berlin. I hunted him alone for a long time before he tried to have me killed and I joined Yasushi's group. He also matches with the description the reverend gave me of the man who killed his family. The way Madeline was hanging on to him, pawing him ..." CC shook her head, unable to continue.

The disgust on CC's face matched the disgust Anthony felt. He looked at the image of his old friend and wondered why he didn't suspect him long ago. "Seen it before," Anthony said. "She lost her soul long ago. I knew Leonard's ambition surpassed my own, but this? I should have seen it before and done something about him."

CC sighed. "We don't have a lot of time. Madeline's purchased over sixty plane tickets for flights into Austin, arriving between now and tomorrow night. She's bringing in reinforcements."

"Then I have a lot of work to do." Anthony stood up. "This fight isn't yours. You'd better get out of here. I can arrange—"

"We're not going anywhere," CC said. "We've already talked about it. Because of us, these people are coming to kill you. Despite that, you're helping us. We're staying. Besides, I've got an idea how to take care of the troops. I've made a couple of phone calls that will keep you in the clear." CC smiled as Anthony raised an eyebrow.

"I told you it was good to have her around." Jenny smiled at Anthony. "We might as well do all the planning we can now. If either of us are seen upstairs now, our reputations as fantastic lovers will be blown. I mean, me and you in only thirty minutes? I don't think so."

*****

"Rev," Derek bent over Yasushi, trying to help him stand. "Rev, we need to go, now."

"Madeline killed her." Yasushi stared blankly until Derek's shaking made him move.

"I know. I saw. The others are leaving. I think we should too."

Yasushi stood, shrugging Derek off. "All this time, and I never realized ..."

"We'll talk about it later. Come on. Let's go." Derek pulled on Yasushi's arm.

Yasushi allowed Derek to lead him to the river's edge away from the deck, away from the house and those who had been his friends. Derek pulled, moving forward. They stepped off the stairs leading to a footpath. Karol stood on the path in front of them.

He sneered at Derek. "Where the hell have you been?"

"I'm taking the rev home with me."

"The hell you are." Karol pulled out his gun and pointed it at Yasushi. "Traitors get what they have coming."

"Soldier! Stand down." Roger's voice boomed from behind Karol. "That's an order."

Karol holstered his gun. "Yes, sir." He walked toward the house, knocking against Derek as he passed. Yasushi stood aside.

Roger stared at Yasushi and Derek. His face contorted for a moment as he coughed, then he shrugged his shoulders. "Find someplace safe." Roger walked back up the hill toward the house.

"Come on, rev." Derek said, heading down the path that ran along the river. "We'll be safe at the house. Babs's dad is a minister too. He'll help us."

Yasushi shook his head. A tear ran down his cheek as he followed Derek.

*****

David stalked the river's edge, sniffing for any trace of the body. He knew her scent, but all the people on the river, the trash, the fish, they all glommed together. Her scent was there, but it wasn't. He returned to the dock where she was shot. He needed to restart, get a fresh scent. It confused him; he couldn't detect her specific scent. Was it something wrong with him or her?

He found Cesar standing in the shadows near the footpath. David sat and watched. The man he knew as Derek walked past, leading the large man away from the house. Derek muttered as he always did. The large reverend looked sad.

The house and the pier were dark. Only traces of light from other fishing piers provided any illumination to the pier and the dark stain of Kitten's blood. He didn't need to get close to smell the blood. It smelled like Kitten, but it didn't smell like her. David circled Cesar, about to transform when the scent changed. David growled. His hair stood up. A threat loomed near, maybe from the water. It was all around them.

Cesar heard the growl and turned in the direction David stalked. He ran, overtaking David. A body floated from the water to the shoreline.

"Stay back," shouted Cesar, bending over the body and holding out his hand. "I left your clothes over there. Get the car, and make sure no one's around."

David stood lifting an eyebrow. "Not dead?"

"No." Cesar didn't need to say anything else.

David ran, allowing his long legs to outpace any curious eyes. At the car, he paused only to put on his clothes. Two women joggers came into sight. He gave them his most charming grin. They turned to continue their jog in the other direction.

He drove down a closed service road, stopping as close as he could to Cesar, found a blanket in the trunk, and made his way down a path toward Cesar.

A scream, loud but stifled, filled the air. He froze, smelling fresh blood. "Shit," he muttered and picked up his pace.

As he cleared a bush, Cesar's arm stopped him. Cesar put a finger to his lips. The woman David had known as Kitten Carlisle knelt over the body of a man. She turned her head to leer at David. The blood spilling from the vagrant's neck filled David's nose. It stirred the beast in him. A growl formed in the back of his throat, but he held it back as he held out the blanket to Cesar.

"We have to go now." Cesar spoke with careful, metered words to the woman in front of him. He took a step forward. "David will clean this up."

The woman stood. She looked from Cesar to David as though trying to recognize them. Her face melted from anger to confusion. "Cold," she said.

Cesar held out the blanket. "A blanket to warm you."

The woman's eyes fixed on David. He recognized the black depths of those eyes. He recognized them from another face.

"You know who you are." Cesar took another step forward, unfolding the blanket.

She looked at Cesar. A snarl formed on her lips. David thought she might pounce. Cesar froze.

"Cesar," David spoke the name with care and respect. "What do we do?"

The woman flashed her dark stare at David. He lowered his head.

"We stand together." Cesar took another step forward. "Or we fall apart."

"Cesar?" The woman asked as the fierceness of her gaze turned to confusion. "Donde estamos?"

David recognized the face of Kitten Carlisle, the woman he had watched, and now he knew why he had protected her.

"Why am I wet?" Her eyes focused for a moment, then her lids closed, and she collapsed.

Cesar caught her, wrapping her in the blanket. "Sorry to involve you, David. I didn't understand." Cesar knelt on the ground, holding the body of the woman. "He'll need to feed again. I didn't think ..."

"I've heard stories about how the Eldest survived, but I never believed them." David reached the body of the man. He rummaged through pockets but found nothing. "How do you want me to deal with this?"

Cesar stared at the dead man. He shook his head. "We don't kill like that anymore. We live with these people. Shit!" He stood up, carrying Kitten before him. "Can you make it look like a drowning? If not, he'll have to disappear. A few days underwater will explain the blood loss. We need to get—" He stopped for a moment, looking at the face of Kitten, "*her* somewhere safe."

"Get to the car. I'll be there in a few minutes."

David watched Cesar carry Kitten toward the car, then looked around him. The man had been alone. Nearby, he saw a sleeping bag rolled out and an old, patched backpack filled with cans and bottles.

"Sorry, friend. It looks like you died as you lived." David stopped talking and shook his head. "You're getting superstitious, David. Jenny would tan me if she heard me talking to a corpse."

David gathered large stones and long vines and tied them around the body. He then dragged the body into the river. Once a foot of water covered the body, he took out his knife and sliced the man's head almost off. He cut away the skin around the wounds in his neck and threw that skin farther into the water. Finally, he pushed himself under the water and pushed the weighted body as far out as he could go. When he thought the depth of the water would protect the body from boat engines, he let it sink to the bottom.

When he reached the car, Cesar sat in the back seat with the woman's head on his lap. His own head leaned against the window as David got into the driver's seat.

"The vineyard has a dark room and supplies," he said to David.

"You think it's safe? The Hunters seem to know a lot about us." David backed the car up the service road. He turned as they approached the main road and slipped into the lane heading out of town.

"This is my priority now," Cesar said sitting up. "Isabella will keep everyone safe."

David grinned, recognizing the business face Cesar was famous for.

*****

Midnight passed them by as they drove up the road to the house at the vineyard. Several lights were on in the house.

David jumped out of the car. "Let me go in first and see who's here. Jenny and CC arrived at the compound this afternoon."

Cesar sat up straight. "What are they doing at the compound?"

David didn't answer. He froze as the front door opened and a shotgun loomed out of the shadows pointed at him.

The voice behind the shotgun was deep and frightened. "Who's there?"

David raised his hands. "Ezra, it's me."

Ezra lowered the shotgun. Even though the light was behind him, Cesar could see relief spread over Ezra's face as his shoulders relaxed, and he opened the door wide.

Cesar thought he felt Harry stir in his arms as he shifted to carry her to the house. "Stand clear, Ezra. Business."

Ezra's chin dropped. "Sweet Jesus! How bad is it in town? Have you heard anything about Emmy? They killed Mama. You know they killed Mama, and I haven't heard from Emmy."

Cesar saw David's face pale as anger filled his face, but David continued to follow Cesar. "I know about Margo. I'm sorry. Emmy must have gotten the warning. I'm sure she's. Nothing I've heard so far indicates the Hunters are in San Antonio."

"Mama wouldn't leave mid-shift unless she had someone to cover her. Emmy wouldn't either. But I haven't heard from her."

"Later," barked Cesar, carrying Kitten down the hall.

David tossed Ezra the car keys. "Put the car away."

Cesar made his way to a door leading to the basement. David pushed himself forward to lead the way. Once in the basement, he turned on a light and pushed a shelving unit to the side revealing a steel door.

He opened the panel on the lockbox. "Code?"

"Five, eight, four, nine, one, two, seven, one, one, nine, two, four, three, six, six, six."

The steel door opened and soft light from three lamps glowed, illuminating a plush bedroom with no windows. Cesar lay Kitten on the bed, then opened a freezer on a wall near the head of the bed. He pulled out six bags of frozen blood.

"I'll warm these up." Cesar walked over to a table containing a microwave oven and fondue pot. "It won't be safe for you or Ezra here."

David remained in the doorway. "What about you?"

"He'll need a live donor." Cesar clicked switches until the burner under the fondue pot came to life.

David raised his eyebrow. "She didn't get enough with the vagrant?"

"She," Cesar repeated the word. "Yes, *she* took a life. She may not kill again, but she'll still need a live source. I can provide enough."

David turned his head listening for a sound from the hall upstairs. Cesar continued warming the blood and not looking at David. "You better go, now. He'll wake up soon ..."

Cesar stopped talking as he turned to see Kitten sitting up. Next to her stood a familiar shadow looking down on Kitten, who was also Harry, but who wasn't either.

"Duchess," began Cesar, but Mary lifted her arm, silencing him.

Cesar stared. She reminded him of Harry, with the dim lights of the room, the large, floppy hat, and loose fitting duster hiding her figure. Only the pale hand, whose palm faced him, betrayed her. Long nails, red and sharp, swished in the air, issuing Cesar out of the room.

He hesitated, opening his mouth to speak, but before the words would exit his mouth, David's hand gripped his shoulder and pulled him out of the room.

"We'll seal the room," David said, nodding his head. Cesar looked back once to see Mary remove her hat and sit next to the person who was not Kitten but not Harry either.

With the door sealed, David leaned against it staring at Cesar. "Have you lost all your senses?"

"I had no idea." Cesar continued to stare at the door.

Ezra's voice echoed from the top of the stairs. "Is it okay for me to come down now?" He poked his head around the wall separating the stairs from the rest of the basement.

"It's good," replied Cesar. "Door's closed."

Ezra's eyes darted between David, Cesar, and the steel door. "I should have stayed in the city, done what I could to help. I'll go with you when you return."

Cesar walked past Ezra without speaking. David followed but stopped to put a hand on Ezra's shoulder. "You did what we planned to do in a Hunter attack. If you come back with us, you'll have to fight."

Ezra nodded. "I know. I owe it to Mama to help. And maybe Emmy too."

Cesar stopped halfway up the stair and looked at David. "Did you know?" The shock of the night's events hit him like a rock. He felt anger taking control of him. "Did she tell you what was happening?"

"Mary tells no one anything they don't have to know." David stepped onto the stair and looked Cesar in the eyes. "I never asked why she wanted me and Jenny to come to Austin, and I never asked why she wanted Jenny to make friends with Kitten. I also never asked Harry why he let you and Anthony run this city as though he wasn't here. You know better than to ask an Eldest questions. Don't get sore at me and Ezra because we're here. I like you, Cesar, but not enough to take shit from you."

Cesar glared at David and David glared back.

Ezra coughed. "Mary said we should rest here this morning but be at the compound for the funeral. They're tonight. That's another reason I want to go back. I need to be there for Mama. And if Emmy's okay, she'll try to be there."

Cesar and David stared at Ezra.

"What?" Ezra asked. "You think she's too grand to talk to a civil servant like me?"

Cesar shrugged his shoulders and walked up the stairs to the main hallway. "I don't know anything anymore. I'm grabbing a drink and then going to sleep. Wake me when it's time to go."

As Cesar sat in the darkened kitchen drinking a cup of warm blood, the others ate eggs and steaks. No one spoke until the first rays of the sun made their way into the sky and the kitchen glowed gold and pink.

Cesar was the first to get up. "Everything's different now. We can't count on Harry or Mary to help in the fight."

"We can handle it." David set his plate in the sink. "We work well together, Cesar. Ezra, keep watch till noon. Then wake me. If we leave here by four, we can be at the compound before the funerals start. If the Hunters are going to try anything, that's when they'll do it."

*****

"He's not going to call." Roger walked up to Madeline who stood on the top level of the parking garage overlooking Seventh Street and the Driskill Hotel. He'd noticed her as he pulled in from picking up supplies.

Madeline jumped and turned as Roger approached. "What do you mean?" Madeline spit her words.

Roger stopped mid-step. "Yasushi's not going to call. You realize that, don't you?"

Madeline turned back to face the Driskill Hotel. "Yasushi. No, he's not going to call me." She massaged the phone in one hand and then the other. "Just thought I'd be ready in case he did."

Roger sighed. Her words were expected but not her actions. Something troubled Madeline. He placed a hand on her shoulder. "Let's get inside."

"Sure. Just give me a minute."

Roger turned to the elevators as Madeline mumbled, "Why won't you call?" Roger shook his head. He knew Madeline and Yasushi were close. He didn't realize how traumatic the separation would be for her.

By the time he reached the elevator, Madeline caught up with him. "Sorry about that," she said. "All this excitement. I can't believe that tonight it will be over."

"Yes," replied Roger, watching as Madeline used her hand to smooth stray hairs, but she still massaged her phone with her other hand. "What will you do when it's over?"

Madeline closed her eyes. A smile reached her lips. She shook her head as though realizing Roger was beside her. "There will always be demons, always more work to do. This is only one group."

Roger nodded. He felt more tired than he should have, and the pain in his arm throbbed down to his fingertips. He rubbed his left arm as he attempted to draw Madeline out of her reverie. "Anna called. She said the others are almost all here. We'll have a force behind us. No way any of the demons are getting away from us."

"Excellent. We want them all dead."

"She's arranged for someone to come and bless the troops before they head out."

"What the fuck for?" Madeline spat her words again. This was the Madeline Roger knew, and he couldn't help but smile.

"Most of them are in this because they believe they are doing God's work, Madeline. You know that." He instantly regretted mentioning God, since it would remind Madeline of Yasushi's abandonment of the group. "With Yasushi gone, they'll want someone to assure them of the righteousness of our cause."

"If they need that kind of reassurance, I don't want them." Madeline's mouth firmed its tight, angry line that Roger admired.

"Not everyone has your faith, and it costs us nothing."

"But time." Madeline loudly let out a long breath. "As long as we stay on schedule, they can gather and pray to whoever they fucking want to pray to."

Roger smiled as the elevator door opened to the lobby of the hotel. He felt relief that Madeline was herself. He just wished the pain in his arm would lessen and he weren't so tired.

*****

"You sure you're ready for all this, babe?" CC looked at James Earl as he helped her tuck her shirt in. "You've only changed once. You don't even know if you can do it just because you want to. And even if you can, you don't know that you'll be able to control yourself."

"It's ok, babe." James Earl leaned close to CC and kissed her ear. "I'll be fine. It's you I'm worried about. You're going to be surrounded by guns. Even if you surprise them, there's nothing to say they won't put up a fight."

"I know Hank Williams. He's a by-the-book son-of-a-bitch special agent, but my plan is good. It'll work, and an arrest this big will earn him a promotion."

"But you haven't seen Hank since Germany. How do you know he'll follow your plan?"

"He was one of the agents that wanted me out but not because he thought I'd lost my marbles, but because I refused to follow protocol. He never treated me unfairly and always worked hard to do the right thing. That's something you don't forget to do." CC tugged at the closed neckline of her blouse. "How do I look?"

"Like a badass G-woman, but sexy."

"I'm not supposed to look sexy." CC bunched her eyebrows.

James Earl smiled. "You're always sexy, babe."

The beeping of the outside door made both of them turn to check the monitor to see who wanted in. Jenny stood outside the door, grinning into the camera. James Earl entered the code to open the door.

"Don't you look all business like," Jenny said to CC.

"And you're wearing clothes."

"A little nakedness makes most people uncomfortable. I find it a very good distraction. Here are your papers." Jenny handed CC a stack of documents. "Your investigator's license was issued three months ago. You took up residence in Texas eight months ago. And the top one is your permit for a concealed weapon, also issued three months ago. You had a near-perfect score on your firearms test. Congratulations."

"Damn," James Earl whistled as he looked over the documents with CC. "I thought I was good. How did Anthony manage all this so quick?"

"I don't know." Jenny shrugged. "He asks, he gets. That's just the way he is. Are you ready to go? Anthony has everyone at the house right now, so it's a good time to move around without being noticed."

CC wrapped her good arm around James Earl. "Be safe, babe. Love you."

"Love you too. Be safe."

"Let's go," CC said to Jenny. James Earl closed the door, shutting himself inside with a sigh.

In the kennels, Jenny introduced CC to a man in a dark suit. "This is Mike Young. He's going with you. You need someone who can drive."

"Ms. Carson," Mike nodded to CC.

CC looked at Mike and pursed her lips, trying to figure out how to ask a question.

Mike winked at her. "I'm as human as you are. Anthony said it would be more believable if a known security consultant for him was working with you, and it's easy for me to spot the vamps."

"Okay." CC scratched her chin.

"Car's ready."

"Take care." Jenny gave CC a hug. "You want to check it's clear, Mike?"

Mike nodded and walked out the door. He looked around and motioned for CC to get into the car.

Jenny leaned close to CC's ear. "Be careful. And I'll keep an eye on your man."

CC laughed. "You be careful."

CC got in the car and buckled up as Mike started the car.

"You okay?" Mike asked.

"As okay as I'm going to be." CC shook her head. "As long as we're working together, tell me about yourself. And call me CC."

*****

"Thank God. I was afraid you were dead." Tears fell from Yasushi's face as he hugged CC, wrapping her in an enormous bear hug.

"I've been so worried about you." CC looked up into the reverend's face. She had never seen him looking so tired. "A lots happened since I saw you last."

"Yes," Yasushi took a seat across the table from CC. "Madeline," he began but looked away and became silent.

CC placed her good hand on his. "I know. She's gone. I saw her the night of the party with the vamp I've been looking for. I'm pretty sure he's the one you're looking for too."

Yasushi's head and shoulders dropped. "Dear God" was all he could say.

CC nodded to Mike, and he pulled out a picture of Leonard Bellini standing next to Anthony. He placed the picture on the table.

CC pointed to Leonard. "That's him, isn't it? You've been looking for him while Madeline steered us away from him."

Yasushi nodded. "Yes. I remember him handing me candy during some of his visits to the house. He's the one who came that night, with the others, killing everyone. I've hidden the details of that night for so long, I've forgotten the truth. Seeing Madeline kill Kitten Carlisle brought it all back." Yasushi looked up at CC. "She's gone, CC. I've lost my sister."

"You don't need to relive it. Plans—"

"But I do. You deserve to know the truth about that night. It may explain—why."

CC looked around them. Mike kept his head down as though afraid to hear. There were only a few customers in the coffee shop. They played board games, worked on computers, or read books. Only the barista behind the counter moved, and she talked in her headphone to someone unseen.

"Go on," CC said, squeezing Yasushi's hand.

"We lived with several other women that we called aunties. They worked in the front of the house. At any one time, there were twelve to fourteen children living in the house. We slept, ate, and played in that back room. The number fluctuated depending on how many women came there to work and how old the children were. Once the boys were about twelve, they were either kicked out or ran off. If the girls didn't, their mothers turned them into whores. That's what happened to Madeline.

"She was twelve. I couldn't have been more than four. Never have been sure of my right age. Anyway, one night Mother comes into our playroom with this man, who I now know as Leonard Bellini. I remember how he smiled at all of us, giving us candy and tossing a green ball I used to play with. When he left, Mother took Madeline. I didn't know what was happening, but I knew it was bad when the big kids went to the front of the house, and I know that night I heard Madeline screaming until she didn't scream anymore.

"Early in the morning, or maybe late that night, I don't know, she was back in the room where she should be, sleeping next to me. She held me tight and cried. I remember hugging her and telling her everything would be okay.

"Each time he came, there was candy and toys for all of us. Each time Madeline went away for the night. She started staying away for days at a time. When she came back, she always wore a new dress. You know the ones she likes, with lots of flowers on them. And she would spend time talking to me, pointing out the different flowers to me. She'd laugh and tell me about seeing all sorts of wonderful things.

"Then one day, she didn't come back 'til very late. She pulled me out of the blankets from the floor where I slept with my cousins, brothers, and sisters. She took me out back to the outhouse and lowered me into one of the holes. That's when the screaming started. She told me to stay put, but I wanted to see, so I pulled myself up to look out the crack at the bottom of the wall. The house was on fire. The flames were so bright, it was hard to watch. Several men, none of the regulars, ran in pulling out children and women. They'd pick them up, bite into their flesh, and throw them back into the burning house. So much laughter and so much screaming.

"I saw Leonard coming out of the building, carrying our mother, his face covered with blood and grinning that same damn grin he wore when he tossed me my favorite green ball. Mother tried to get away, but he held on to her. That's when I saw Madeline.

"She had been standing near the outhouse, out of the way of the fire and the demons, wearing one of her favorite dresses covered with flowers. Leonard walked up to her. Mother kept screaming, trying to get away. She saw Madeline and screamed even more.

"'Kill her,' Madeline screamed. 'Kill her.'

"Leonard kept hold of Mother, pulled a knife out of his pocket, and handed it to Madeline.

"Madeline took it and stabbed. She stabbed and stabbed and stabbed. And Leonard laughed.

"Then I heard sirens. Leonard and the other demons stood still. Madeline jumped into Leonard's arms and kissed him. He dropped her on the ground and laughed at her. She began to cry, but then one of the other demons took Leonard's arm and they left. Madeline crawled her way to me. I dropped myself into the hole to wait for her. That's where the firemen found us.

"Madeline told them about the house being attacked and someone killing our mother. I believed her."

Yasushi said nothing else.

"I'm sorry, reverend. Leonard used her," Mike said. "I've heard about a group of renegades who let loose on brothels and drug dens to satisfy their appetites for killing. No one asks too many questions when one of those places burns down. I didn't even know him 'til a few weeks ago. Ol' Mike didn't like him, but then he didn't like a lot of folks. Always said you had to be careful which vamps you work with."

"This group?" CC asked, surprised that Mike knew anything. "I thought you were just a security guard."

"I do a lot of things for Anthony, and when you work with vamps, you learn to listen to survive. Anthony's been looking for a group of rogue vamps for years. This place, Austin and the compound he built, was meant to protect the vamps so they wouldn't fall into that sort of thing."

"So Leonard's group attacked and killed others," Yasushi said as his eyes focused and cleared of tears.

"Anthony thinks it's one group. He knew, well, Harry knew, that Leonard was gathering a following out in California. Maybe he suspected. There was some sort of trouble there last year that moved here to Texas, Galveston I think. Harry went down there. After that, Leonard showed up in Austin. It makes sense that Leonard would be suspect, but he's powerful. I think Harry wanted to be sure he got Leonard and everyone working with him. The group is careful to cover their tracks. Most humans see a burned down whorehouse and don't think twice about it. It was only when the people in your group, reverend, started asking questions that Harry got involved."

"It makes sense." Yasushi leaned back in his chair. "I read the army's reports about Galveston. A scientist confined a vampire and was experimenting on him. Vamps gathered to rescue him, but there was this one in particular. A young vampire died. The reports make sense now. The colonel in charge was vague." Yasushi pounded the table. "He knew. He must have known who he was dealing with. Just like Harry was dealing with me. They both wanted to find who was doing the killing."

"Roger discovered a series of brothels and drug dens around military bases that had burned down," said CC looking up at Mike. "There were never any survivors. It'd been going on for years. If the vamps suspected Leonard was the leader, why haven't they done anything about it?"

Mike stared at her before answering. "Justice. It's important to Anthony and Harry. They want justice, and there are ways the vamps deal it out. But something else is going on too. Something went wrong with the plan. Harry died. He's known as an Eldest, a vamp so old nobody knows how old he is. They're mean and powerful. You don't want to meet one, trust me." Mike shuddered.

"Yet, Anna Leitz killed him," CC said.

"That's what's so weird," Mike became excited, pulling out a chair and sitting down to lean close to CC's head. "He must have let her. That's all I can figure. No way you, me, or any army walks up to an Eldest and kills him. It can't be done."

"Is Leonard an Eldest?" Yasushi's voice shocked them. The deep, troubled baritone voice resonated with purpose.

"No way," replied Mike. "I hear he and Anthony are about the same age. Anthony's a lot smarter and richer. The Eldests like him. Ol' Mike said he figured Leonard's jealous of Anthony."

"Then we can kill Leonard." Yasushi grinned.

"Only if Anthony lets you. If Leonard is leading the rogues, Anthony will want his head." Mike grinned back.

"Why attack tonight?" CC asked Mike.

"Funeral," said Mike. "Vamps have their rituals for dealing with the dead. Every vamp in the area will be here for it, especially since Harry is one of the dead."

"How many?" asked CC.

"Never more than twenty in town at a time. I know the Hunters killed two or three of them when they attacked the other day. There could be one or two staying hidden, but they feel safe at Anthony's compound."

"Not enough," said CC. "If our plan doesn't work, there will be at least sixty soldiers attacking the compound."

Mike whistled. "We should get back and—"

"Yes," CC interrupted, raising her hand. "Timing is everything tonight. We have a plan to take care of the soldiers. And we need to get moving. Rev, will you stay put?"

CC looked at Yasushi and wondered what he was thinking. "Rev?" she asked again. "I know you want to help Madeline, but if this is going to end tonight, then I need to know you're safe."

Yasushi sat up straight, his shoulders squaring. "I'm coming with you. I just got you back in my sight. I'm not going to lose you again."

"But," CC started and looked around the coffee house. "Where's Derek?"

"I took him to his mother's house," Yasushi said standing. "He's gone, CC. I don't think he'll be joining us again."

CC nodded and let the way to the car.

*****

"Mike Young, representing Anthony Mugello. Pleased to meet you." Mike shook hands with Hank Williams. "CC tells me this is your show. Glad to be handing this over."

"Yeah." Hank nodded before continuing. "You're involved, how?"

"Lead security for the Mugello compound, and one of the lawyers. Threats had been made against Mugello, and we take them all seriously. We hired CC a while ago to look into this terrorist group." Mike oozed charm, his smile never faltering. He turned to CC and winked. "But tonight, I'm simply her driver. Got to keep all our people safe."

Hank raised his eyebrows and looked at CC, who smiled back at him. He looked behind Mike to the car where Yasushi Brown sat in the back seat not watching them.

"Anyway." Mike coughed to regain Hank's attention. "When CC found out Anna Leitz made contact with Pastor Pete, that's how she discovered they were meeting here tonight. He was more than willing to help out when we told him what this group was. He volunteered to lead us to the meeting. He wants to avoid any scandal that might come from Anna Leitz's arrest, particularly as she's a fixture at our church."

"Told you," CC said, enjoying how Mike's nonstop banter kept Hank from asking questions she didn't want to answer. "Working for a man like Mugello means I can hire people who know what they're doing."

"Right." Hank shook his head. "I still don't know how you found out these guys were connected to the kidnapping."

"It was the note." CC said nothing else. Hank wasn't a bad guy, but he had worked to get her kicked out of the Bureau. She'd make sure he squirmed for the big arrest she was handing him. "You don't think a man like Mugello would hand that over to you without first making sure his own people saw it first?"

"He said he brought it to us as soon as he got it."

"And he did. I was in the car with him as he drove to the police station with it."

Hank raised his eyebrows. "I don't recall seeing you there or your name coming up."

"Didn't go into the police station with him. SWAT team about ready?"

Hank looked to the SWAT commander who nodded. "They're ready. You sure they're in there."

Mike looked up from his phone. "Pastor's arriving now. Key phrase is 'All the king's men.' When you hear that, they're in position."

"And, him." Hank nodded toward CC's car and Yasushi.

"Spiritual advisor and old friend." CC held up her cast. "He's also been helping me get around."

"OK." Hank turned to signal the team. Before walking away, he bent over speaking into CC's ear. "You're not telling me everything. I know the good reverend in your car is involved."

"Maybe I am a little mad, but you'll have a hard time proving anything against him or anyone I don't want you to know about." She grinned at him and winked.

"Shit! I've seen you pissed off but never mad. I'll play along for now. I suspect I'll get an earful from these weekend warriors once I get them in custody."

"No doubt." CC said, moving to stand next to Mike. "You sure none of them will say a word about vamps, Mike?"

"You know what happens to people who talk about vampires. Besides, I bet they have stories planned. Most will get off with a warning, and they'll have their weapons confiscated."

"Will it be enough to make them not a threat?"

"Wish I knew, CC."

CC took in a deep breath and kept her eyes on the equipment the law enforcement officers were using. Things had changed in the five years since she left. It was time to get back into the game.

*****

Pastor Pete stopped inside the door of the warehouse. The sight of so many men and women in military attire shocked him even though he'd been told what to expect. "Oh, I see what you mean."

"As I said," said Anna, smiling and pushing him forward. "They're here for exercises."

"Ms. Leitz." A captain walked up to Anna and shook her hand. "Can't tell you what it means to be here tonight. I was thrilled when I got your call. Everybody's here."

"Good. This is Pastor Pete. He's come to bless the troops before we engage."

"Excellent." Captain Blake turned and shook Pastor Pete's hand. "Thank you for coming out tonight. It means a lot to know God's on our side."

"Of course." Pastor Pete could think of nothing else to say. He wasn't nervous, although he felt he should be. That afternoon, Mike Young explained what would happen. All he had to do was what he always did, except that tonight there were many guns involved. His days as an army and a police chaplain came in handy. He recognized the weapons the soldiers were carrying. He imagined he was coming to the aid of a group of police officers after a shooting. How many times had he offered support in such cases? He'd lost count. But this time, he was doing this for men and women who wanted to kill. He tried to wrap his mind around the plan.

"Are you all right?" Anna asked.

"Focusing." Pastor Pete closed his eyes for a moment. "You'd think after so many sermons, I wouldn't have stage fright anymore, but I do."

Anna rolled her eyes and turned to Captain Blake. "Would you call everyone together? Follow my lead, Peter."

Anna led Pastor Pete to the far end of the warehouse. Almost sixty men and women formed a half circle around them. In the corner of his eye, he could see soldiers standing away from the group with weapons at the ready.

"Thank you all for making it here on such short notice. The event we've been waiting for is finally here. Demons gather, but the righteous also gather. In our numbers is the strength which we acknowledge comes from God. I've asked Pastor Pete to say a few words to bless our endeavors. Please give him your attention."

Anna smiled at Pastor Pete, motioning him to stand in front of her.

"Thank you," he said, then looked into the mass of faces. These men and women believed they were here by divine decree. "Please kneel as we bow our heads in prayer." The soldiers knelt. Anna remained standing behind him. He stepped close to the soldiers and knelt with them. "Let the Divine shine down upon us and guide us in its wisdom. Here kneel all the king's men and all the king's women—"

Pastor Pete said no more. Shouts broke the silence of the warehouse and black-and-gray-clad officers filled the empty spaces with shouts to lie down, drop weapons, and don't resist. Pastor Pete lay down on the ground and closed his eyes. He prayed no one would die, that all would be safe. He heard guns shooting, bodies hitting the ground, fists hitting flesh. Gun smoke, sweat, fear, dirt, and hate filled his nostrils.

From Anna Leitz, he heard a loud, "NO!"

Feet tripped over his outstretched legs. Oaths that a deaconess should never utter screamed in his direction. A hand grabbed his shoulder and helped him up. He saw Anna kicking and screaming and most of the soldiers kneeling on the ground as law enforcement officers handcuffed them before leading them away.

"It's all over, Pastor." Mike Young stood next to him, keeping his hand on the pastor's arm.

Paster Pete's knees shook and his stomach turned, but events wound down faster than he expected.

"Good job, Pastor. Thank you for your help." A man shook Pete's hand.

"This is Special Agent Hank Williams, Pastor. He's in charge of all of this."

"Yes," replied Pete. He could think of nothing else to say.

"If it's okay with you, we'll take you to the office tonight and get your formal statement."

"Yes, Agent Williams. That will be fine." Peter took in a deep breath as he realized there was nothing else for him to do.

He followed Hank and Mike Young out of the warehouse. Anna Leitz still fought as two agents put her into the back of a car.

"You son of a bitch! You idiot! I'll destroy you!" She yelled as she saw Pastor Pete. "You've ruined everything. The demons will destroy us all now. It's all on you. You stupid—"

Anna continued to yell, but with the doors closed he no longer heard her.

"By the way," Hank said, claiming Peter's attention. "Your bishop wanted you to call him when you finished with us. He said he won't sleep well until he knows you're home safe. Might want to call sooner than later."

"Uncle Phillip's always been a worrier," Peter replied with a smile.

As he got in the car with Special Agent Williams, he watched Mike Young and a red-haired woman get into a car a little apart from all the official cars. As it turned to leave, he saw Reverend Brown in the back seat. Peter felt a wave of grief for the man. He had never seen a man so sure of his own death.

*****

Mike shifted his position while looking out the corner of his eye at CC. Neither of them were sure what to do next. Plans dictated they oversee the arrest of the soldiers to make sure they were no longer a threat. They discussed nothing else. Both hoped it was safe to return to the compound, but no one called to say it was, and they had no way of contacting anyone inside once the funerals started.

When Mike asked the reverend where he wanted to go, he said he'd go to the compound with them. "That's not a good idea, reverend. With the funeral going on and not knowing where Morgan and your sister are—"

Yasushi interrupted him. "I need to be there in case they show up. Besides, you said it's safe for you and CC. And you say James Earl is there. No one should mind my presence."

CC turned her body as much as she could with her cast to look at Yasushi sitting behind her. "You realize you won't be welcomed."

Yasushi nodded as Mike pulled into one of the back gates to the Mugello compound. "We'll wait in the gatehouse to see what's happening. Don't expect more than that. Everybody's worried about Hunters."

"That's fine," Yasushi said. "I'll sit with you. Madeline will come, if not tonight, then soon. I need to be here when she does."

"Rev," CC's mouth pursed. "I'm not sure this is a good idea. Anthony knows you killed vamps. They were all rogues, so nobody cares, but if you were there, the night Harry died ... That's different."

"Why is James Earl in the compound?"

CC turned back to face the front licking her lips. Mike cleared his throat. "He's a hacker, reverend. He's the one who discovered the soldiers arriving tonight and where they were gathering."

CC said nothing but nodded her approval to Mike.

Yasushi said, "I see."

CC hoped he believed that was the only reason. She wasn't sure what he would do if he found out James Earl belonged in the compound. She pulled down the visor and looked in the mirror at Yasushi. He didn't look back at her.

*****

Clay made his way around the perimeter of the room, inspecting flowers, candles, and chairs. Everything was placed where it should be. He felt the sun setting outside the windowless room. In a few minutes, he would open the door. In another time, Harry would have needed an enormous room and a massive pyre, but with Hunters in the area, only a few would attend. The coffins for two of the vampires killed by the Hunters lay at the far end of the room. Their caskets closed, as little remained of their battered and burned bodies. Clay used a handkerchief to rub a spot from one lid. A third coffin sat apart.

He made sure the lid for Margo Titler's coffin gleamed. The damage from the explosion left her face unscathed. He did a fine job selecting the makeup that gave her a special glow in the candlelight. He made one final adjustment of the silk sheet he had tucked under her hands—there was too little of her torso left to reconstruct in such an insufficient time—and smiled, pleased with his work.

A photo popped up on his phone displaying the funeral pyres his people had built. "Perfect," he typed and sent. *Finished in good time.* He lifted his long coat from the back of the chair and put it on, buttoning the silver buttons with care. Walking to the mirror in the corner, he adjusted his lapels, tugged at his cuffs until they matched, buttoned black cotton gloves over his long fingers, and reached for the red rose boutonniere. Satisfied with its placement, he picked up his top hat, placing it on his neatly pulled back dreadlocks. "Old-fashioned, perhaps, but stylish," he said to himself.

Clay stood in front of the double doors leading to the hallway. He looked over the room once more, composing his face, and then he opened the door.

Anthony and Leonard stood a few feet away from the door.

"You can't turn your phone off for this, Leonard?" Anthony glared beneath heavy eyelids. Clay wondered at the level of stress showing on Anthony.

"Sorry," Leonard said with little meaning. He read the text message and turned the phone off.

Clay bowed his head as the two men entered. He wondered at the expression on Leonard's face. His mouth may have formed the traditional line of the mourner, but Clay noticed an arch to Leonard's eyebrows and a lifting of his shoulders, almost a spring in his step. Next to Anthony, Leonard looked happy.

Clay allowed his head to turn to look down the hall. No one else waited to enter.

"Really, Anthony," began Leonard, standing on the far side of the room, looking down on Margo. "This is too much."

"Margo was a good woman and a friend to all of us." Anthony stood for the last time near Harry. "Get with the times, Leonard."

Leonard said nothing but smirked, shaking his head, putting his hands in his pockets, and leaning against the far wall.

Years of experience allowed Clay to maintain his expressionless face, but he felt his blood boil. Margo was a wonderful woman, he wanted to say. She had helped him out of a few jams in his junior years. He felt others arriving in the hall. He listened to the silence in the room, but he still felt the tension between Anthony and Leonard.

Anthony stood at the doorway, greeting the arrivals. Clay counted ten already. He hadn't expected more and wondered if he should get more chairs. A hand lay on his shoulder. It was Anthony's.

"Thank you, Clay. Everything is perfect."

Clay nodded his head to Anthony. Neither of them expected Clay to say anything, so he didn't. He was, however, surprised by Anthony's grip on his shoulder. Firm, not the grip of someone worn out and stressed. Still, Anthony's eyes remained heavy and his pale olive skin paler than it should be.

The wolves arrived, breaking Clay's study of Anthony. Clay liked Jenny. He had only met her a few times, but they delighted each other with their company. They laughed and danced, and when she and David ran in the wild, he often went with them, just for the sake of running naked in the woods.

"Anthony," David asked, "I assume it's all right if we pay our respects?"

Anthony smiled. "Thank you for coming."

Clay watched, concerned about what Leonard would do when David and Jenny, Ezra, and a young man he didn't know came in. David and the young man were conspicuous in black jeans and shirts. Ezra wore his usual suit, but tonight a black one. Jenny, as always, stood out in her whiteness. She had, for the occasion, covered her white dress with a sheer black cape and hood. They made their way past Harry, stopped to bow their heads, then moved to the other coffins. As they approached the far wall, Leonard stood tall and walked out of the room. The wolves paid no attention but moved to stand next to Margo. Ezra's shoulders shook and his head fell into his hands. Jenny and the young man put their hands on his back and held him close.

Clay's earbud beeped. The voice of his helper told him they were in the kitchen. Anthony followed Leonard out to the hall, but Leonard didn't wait for Anthony. Clay slid into the hall to head for the kitchen and check on his people. They knew to ask no questions, but it was always best to monitor them, just in case.

"Leonard, this has got to stop." Anthony reached for Leonard's arm.

Leonard turned to face Anthony. "I know your intentions to make one nice happy family, but there is only so much I can take."

At least they kept their voices lowered. Still, Clay assumed the others could hear the argument. He stepped into a nearby doorway to avoid passing the arguing men.

"You will accept the new ways." Anthony reached for the door to his office and opened it. He and Leonard stepped in and stopped. Clay passed them but stopped himself when he saw them both bowing and heard the voice of the ages, sweet, melodious, and frightening. "Good evening, gentlemen."

He removed his hat and bowed his own head before running to the kitchen.

Before opening the kitchen door, he composed himself. "Madame Midnight," he said to himself with a grin. "All arguments will be settled tonight. I can't remember being so afraid." Clay realized he was smiling and straightened his mouth before entering the kitchen.

*****

Roger coughed again before he got out of the car. "I can't reach Blake."

"He said he was in position. He's not going to answer a text if he's ready to move." Madeline didn't hide her annoyance.

"Madeline, we have set signals so everything goes according to plan." Roger pushed himself out of the car but fell back into his seat with a grunt.

"Something wrong?" asked Karol.

"Just getting old," Madeline said and reached her hand over to help Roger.

He took her hand, wondering if the woman he knew was still before him. He coughed and rubbed his chest to avoid saying anything awkward. "Too old for this type of thing. I trust Blake. He'll move on schedule. Let's go."

He led Madeline and Karol to the boat they would take downriver to the Mugello house. Karol pushed the boat away from the dock and jumped on board. Three soldiers followed them.

Christmas lights decorated the homes along the water. As they passed the coffee shop where he had spent time watching the artist's house, the noise of the music and bright lights hit him in the face. At least the pressure in his chest lessened. Fishing boats, sailboats, and small motorboats passed them.

As the river rounded a bend, the lights and noises faded. Few boats were on the water as they approached the Mugello compound. He knew from the attack on the house that this was a weak point in security. Surveillance on the place revealed what looked like funeral pyres being built that afternoon. A gathering of the demons meant that they would be able to kill many.

Roger wiped the sweat off his brow. He looked up at Karol sitting in the bow. Karol pulled his jacket up close to his neck. Madeline sat in the middle of the boat, her head faced straight ahead with one hand brushing loose hairs away from her face. She always had remarkable control. It's what he first admired about her.

When they met, he'd assumed Madeline and Yasushi were just another pair of evangelicals who believed in demons. That night they convinced him to meet them outside a brothel near the base. His life changed. He's spent years studying the facts about the brothel fires and murders. He'd kept his theories to himself, although his colonel remarked more than once his obsessiveness about old cases was interfering in his work.

They stood outside the brothel. From their position in a neighboring yard, they could see soldiers and civilians entering the house while girls and children came in and out of the back door. It was all he could do not to sound the alarm when flames first appeared from a window on the top floor of the house.

"Wait," whispered Yasushi, holding on to Roger's arm and putting a finger to his lips.

Madeline pulled out an old but shiny Bowie knife and crouched close to the fence.

The screaming began. A man leapt out of the second-story window as though he'd stepped out of a car. He was a big man, pale white with whiter hair. His large torso glittered in the firelight and his flame tattoos mirrored the flames licking the roof of the house. He laughed and grabbed a girl running out of the house. She was only a kid. Terror filled her face as her large eyes took in the half-naked man laughing and pulling her toward him.

Roger felt the pressure in his chest tighten its grip as he remembered the details of that night. The girl's scream, the blood spilling down her, spilling from the mouth of the man as he tossed her limp body into the flames now pouring from the door. He recalled watching as Yasushi dashed forward, faster than a man his size should move, and grabbed the man's arms. The man laughed until Madeline's knife sliced through the sinews of his neck and his head fell to the ground.

Yasushi walked back to Roger, wiping his hands with a towel he had in his belt. "Another demon sent back to hell, colonel. We were able to track this one easy enough, but there are others. When they get together, there's even more death and mayhem. At least some poor souls tonight will live."

"No telling how many there are," Madeline said, cleaning the blade of her knife. "They need killing. Are you in?"

Roger took in a deep breath as the pressure in his chest eased.

Madeline turned her face toward his. "Are you in the game? You look like shit. Maybe you should sit this one out."

"I'm good." That was the same reply he had given her all those years ago. Tonight would be the pinnacle of their fight. Tonight would be his last fight. His heart wouldn't last much longer, but he would do what he could for Madeline one more time.

＊＊＊＊＊

The biometric scanner at the door was the only indicator that the single-story red brick house was anything other than what it appeared to be. CC nodded her approval as she walked into the darkened hall from the front door. It still looked like any other house in the neighborhood, but then they walked past a room filled with electronic monitors.

One man sat alone in the room. He nodded his balding head at Mike and said nothing.

The living room, on their right, spread out wide and filled with an overstuffed couch and recliners. Masculine and clean crept into CC's head. When they turned the corner into a bright, white kitchen, CC squinted her eyes. A woman in a black pantsuit sat at the table in the center of the room. Her brown face was as frazzled as her graying hair. Large, black eyes swollen from tears lifted to look at CC. Her red lips lifted into a forced smile.

"Emmy," Mike said, moving ahead of CC and taking the woman's hand. "I'm so sorry. If you need anything, let me know."

Emmy nodded at Mike. "Clay told me to wait here. He'll take me to Mama."

Mike nodded and pointed to CC.

"This is CC—I mean, Catherine Carson. Let me see what I can find out," Mike said and moved to leave the room before stopping and adding. "CC, this is Emerald Titler, Margo's daughter." Mike walked out the back door.

CC stared at Emerald. She didn't know how old Margo was, but this woman must have been the same age, if not older. While Margo had some gray in her hair, the steel gray in this woman's hair dominated the dark brown hair. Fine and not-so-fine lines crossed her face. Her eyes sunk into their sockets. Even her hands, thin with spider-like fingers, wrinkled. But then she studied Emerald's face, Margo's understanding eyes and her determined nose looked back at her.

"I didn't know your mother for long. She took good care of me, and I liked her." CC took a deep breath, unsure what Emerald knew.

"She told me about you and James Earl." Emerald sighed, blotting her eye with a tissue. "She always wanted to help every lost pup she found."

Yasushi stepped forward to stand beside CC. "This is all my fault, Ms. Titler. I didn't know your mother, but I've no doubt she was a lovely woman."

"She was, reverend," Emerald said, dropping her head only to twist her mouth and stare at Yasushi.

CC noticed. "Have you been here long? I thought you lived in San Antonio."

Emerald nodded to CC and pointed to the chair next to her. "Mama taught me what to do when there was trouble. I thought those days were long gone, but ... I hid like I was supposed to when word got out. I didn't know till this morning that Mama was dead. Got here as quick as I could. Please sit down, reverend. You'll frighten anyone looming like that."

Yasushi pulled a chair out from the table and sat as far from Emerald as he could at the small round table. "Thank you," he said and bowed his head.

Emerald put her hand on top of CC's resting on the table. "I'm glad you got to know her."

Mike entered the kitchen from the back door. Another man came with him. CC raised her eyebrows at the tall, thin black man with long dreadlocks.

"Emmy," the man said. "I'm pleased you can be here."

"Clay," Emerald said, taking his hands and standing next to him.

"Everything is ready," Clay said, looking from Emerald to CC. "If you ladies wish to pay your respects, now is a good time."

"Me too?" CC asked, standing.

"Of course," Clay said. "You are family." Clay stood aside, nodding his head as the two women moved to the door.

CC put her arm around Emerald and looked behind her to see Yasushi with his head in his hands. She tried to smile at him, but he wouldn't look at her.

Mike returned in a few minutes. "They're all inside. But your mother's already at the pyre."

"Perhaps," began Yasushi.

"No, reverend," Emerald said. "Please don't."

Yasushi sat down.

CC tried to look at him again, but his enormous shoulders slumped and shook.

CC followed Clay along a gravel path, then over a hill. To their right, the river flowed and sparkled in the city lights. The sounds of boats moving up and down the river, even at this late hour, comforted CC. They were the sounds of normality. From the top of a hill, even the sounds of the city, car horns, alarms, murmurs, laughter, and music drifted through her. Below them, four pyres surrounded a fifth larger pile. Torches encircling each and a coffin lay next to each, except the pyre close to them. Three men in dark suits stood aside for them.

Emerald gulped and shouted, "Ezra." She ran down the hill, and he ran up it.

CC stopped to give the brother and sister space. Mike moved up beside her.

"You sure it's okay for us to be here?" she asked him.

"The wolves are here because of Margo. You and Emmy are family, so you're here."

"And you?" asked CC looking at Mike.

"The vamps don't know you. If there's trouble, I'll get you and Emmy back inside, safe. Besides," Mike rubbed his chin and gazed over her head. "There's a lot going on you don't know about. You'll be—surprised, probably confused. Better I stick to you tonight."

CC wrapped her arms around her chest as a shiver touched her shoulders. She and Mike made their way down the hill.

Emmy and Ezra embraced near the coffin. CC watched as Ezra led her to the coffin where Clay stood and lifted the lid. CC slowed her pace. Clay lowered the lid and signaled the other men to lift the coffin on the pyre.

"We can bury her if you prefer," Clay told Ezra and Emerald as CC approached. "Anthony only asked she be part of this because he didn't know where either of you were."

Emerald looked at Clay with watery eyes. "This is good, Clay. Thank you. It's what Mama would've wanted."

Clay nodded and noticed CC and Mike drawing near. He stretched his neck to look around him. "I suggest you two stay with Emerald a little apart from the others." He paused as though listening, then added, "Ah, the gathering has begun. More turned up than I expected."

CC looked around her, surprised she heard no one approach but all around her stood figures dressed in black. At least two dozen men and women stood spaced around the hills as though protecting the pyres. Behind her she felt a hand touch her shoulder, and James Earl was there. Behind him, David and Jenny stood unique in that they were, as usual, pressed together.

Anthony walked down the hill, taking a torch offered to him by Clay. He didn't acknowledge CC's presence, but then she didn't expect it. She clasped James Earl's hand, wondering what would happen.

Anthony kept his face toward the pyre as he lifted the torch. "We say goodbye to friends tonight. Remember them. Remember their hopes and dreams. Remember why we gather. We are one and not one. We live with the sun and we live in the night." Anthony touched the torch to the pyre. Others, including Ezra and Emerald, did the same to the other pyres. The pyres flamed, lighting the surrounding night.

The heat of the fires blew CC's hair away from her face. The roar drowned the noises of the city. CC turned her head to look around her and saw Roger. He stood on top of the ridge, pointing a gun toward the people and the pyres. All the training she had done to be a special agent and all the training she continued when she joined the Hunters kicked in. She pushed James Earl away from her and used her good hand to reach for her gun. "Down," she yelled as loud as she could and shot at Roger.

Roger managed one shot that went wild as CC's bullet hurled toward him. It grazed his shoulder, forcing him to drop his shotgun and fall backwards. More gunfire erupted around her. She fell forward as James Earl pushed her down and lay on top of her.

"Stay down, babe." Next, she heard a deep, guttural growl and knew he was changing. And then, he was no longer on top of her and she realized her arm in the cast, below her, hurt.

"Babe," she yelled, lifting her head. The flames of the pyres silhouetted a great wolf that growled and sneered as its hair and hackles raised. Another wolf soon ran alongside the one she saw. She rolled over to sit up and found a massive white wolf growling in front of her. "Got it, Jenny. I'm staying down." The white wolf turned and attacked as a man in military clothing ran toward CC. The man lifted his shotgun to shoot the wolf, but CC shot him, hitting him in the chest.

She'd hoped when they'd arrested the soldiers at the warehouse Roger and Madeline would leave town. CC looked for James Earl. She didn't know which wolf he was.

"All you had to do was listen, Anthony. I told you this would never work." Leonard stood over Anthony, pointing a long sword at his chest.

Anthony leaned on one arm. His loose hand gripped a burning torch.

"Letting the dogs in? Letting humans in?" Leonard turned and snarled at CC, Emerald, and Mike. "You're too soft. Harry's gone, and it's time you were too. And then they all die." Leonard lifted the sword to strike, but a figure dashed down the hill and knocked him down.

Tomas held Leonard on the ground with his knee. CC stared at the golden-faced cherub with glaring white teeth. She never thought to see such a beautiful face filled with so much hatred.

"Tomas?" Leonard's eyes widened as he stared at Tomas.

"Never was your man." Tomas's grin sent a shiver of fear down CC's back. "I've always been hers."

CC turned to look where Tommy looked. A woman stood on top of the hill. The vampires knelt. She recognized the man known as Cesar and the woman known as Isabella standing behind the woman. The white wolf ran up to her and howled. The woman nodded. Tomas lifted Leonard from the ground.

Pins and needles shot through CC's spine, up her neck, and into her head. The woman was all shadow. Even the flames of the fires wouldn't light her face, but CC knew she was as beautiful. This was the woman with the voice CC heard in dark corners at night coming from radios, computer speakers, and leaking out of earphones. Pieces of the puzzle she played moved into place.

"No!" cried Leonard, spitting his words. "Harry's gone. His place is mine. Those are the rules." Leonard pleaded more than demanded, but Tomas didn't pay attention as he pushed Leonard through the crowd.

A single gunshot stopped Tomas. CC saw a hole in his side. He crumpled to the ground, but Cesar ran forward with Anthony and grabbed Leonard before he could move. And then the familiar double click of a shotgun and then an all too familiar voice.

"Let him go," Madeline shouted and walked toward Leonard. She fired again.

Anthony and Cesar looked up at the woman on the hill, who raised hand. They let him go. Leonard fell to his knees but pushed himself up.

Madeline threw herself into Leonard's arm. "It's over," she said. "We've won. We can be together now."

Leonard raised his eyebrows and opened his mouth to speak, but as he looked around, no voice came out. The eyes of everyone, even the wolves, glared at him. Some vamps shook their heads and looked away.

Silence screamed into CC's ears. She found it hard to breathe until Leonard said, "Get off of me, you stupid cow." Leonard tossed Madeline to the ground the way a man tosses a cockroach off his shoe.

"Leonard, you said we'd be together. Leonard!" Madeline continued shouting his name as he walked through the crowd toward the woman on the hill.

"You know I'm right. With Harry gone, I'm next in line. There's nothing you can do to stop me."

CC wondered why no one moved. Leonard walked around the vamps between him and the woman, but as he drew close to the woman, a second figure appeared beside her. CC's jaw fell open. The baggy slacks and long jacket were familiar. It was the artist, but the artist was dead. It couldn't be him. Then the figure took off the hat, revealing long, thick curls scattered over her shoulders. CC watched Kitten Carlisle long enough to know what she looked like even at a distance, but Kitten Carlisle was dead. Yasushi witnessed her execution. She forced air through her throat to ask how, but Mike's hand on her shoulder stopped her.

Leonard turned to face the crowd, his face red in a sudden rush of flames from the pyres. His eyes widened as fear took hold of him. "This can't be. You told me you killed them both," he shouted to Madeline. "You promised me they were dead! You fucking, useless—"

The first woman lifted her arm again. En masse, the vampires hurled themselves on Leonard. CC closed her eyes. Emerald pulled CC to her and they put their heads together to not see the carnage or hear the agony of his cries as flesh ripped from bone and bone from tendon.

When silence returned. CC sat looking around her. The vampires were gone. She, Emerald, and Mike stood next to each other.

"Leonard?" Madeline's voice called out, though a whimper. "Leonard?" she called again.

"No, sister mine," Yasushi stood above her, weeping.

CC's heart wanted to break. Tears rolled down his face. His shoulders drooped, and he turned his head side to side.

"Brother?" Madeline reached up for him.

Yasushi knelt in front of her. "I'm here, sister. I'll take care of you."

"The demons are all around us." Panic filled Madeline's voice as her breath quickened. "We have to run. They'll be back soon."

Madeline tried to get up, but Yasushi knelt, wrapping her in a bear hug, kissing her head. "I know, sister. I'll hide you."

At the sound of Madeline's neck snapping, CC vomited. She knew it would happen but did nothing to stop it.

"Holy Mother of God," Mike muttered, bending to help CC stand.

Emerald put her hand to her mouth muttering something and looked away with fresh tears on her face.

Yasushi continued to hold on to Madeline's body. He hugged her, and then he kissed her head once more before laying her on the ground.

Anthony stood next to CC. She wasn't aware of how he got there. "I've got this," she said and took Yasushi by the hand. "Come on, rev. You helped me when I needed it most. I won't abandon you."

*****

Leigh watched as Stacy tossed up her hands and mumbled, "Look out!" The sedative calmed Stacy enough to sleep, but it did not relieve her from dreaming. Leigh tucked the blanket between the mattress and bed rail and sat down. She knew she should feel exhausted, but too many thoughts raced through her mind to sleep.

Beau came for Barbara around seven. Barbara wanted to stay at Stacy's bedside, but the strain and exhaustion of the day proved too much, and Beau led her away in tears. Carol stayed until nine when her own weariness made her fall asleep in the chair. Leigh sent her home and then called her own husband to let him know she would stay with Stacy tonight. Stacy tried to send her away, but Leigh knew beneath her bravado, fear crept its way through her.

With Stacy finally sleeping, she opened her laptop to work, to focus her mind on anything except for where Kitten might be. Reading Stacy's scene did nothing to improve her mood, so she looked to the pages Kitten had begun. She liked where it was going. It needed a few touch-ups.

8

Reconciliation of Titania and Oberon

"Special Envoy from the Holy Father," Brother Matthew kept repeating, unsure why a special envoy from the Holy Father would visit the Monastery of Christ in the Desert. Many priests visited the monastery—some for the silence, and some for the beer. As they walked along the path, he never realized how loud his sandals were on the stone floor. He found Father Abbot sitting on a bench near the sanctuary, reading. His dark hair shone in the sun, and his gray eyes sparkled as he looked up and smiled at Brother Matthew. When he caught sight of the priest behind Brother Matthew, he stood up, offering his hand. Brother Matthew tried to signal father but failed.

"I have business with one of your lay brothers, father," the priest said and pulled out a letter. "Here are my credentials."

Brother Matthew spoke quickly, "He comes as a Special Envoy from the Holy Father."

"I see that," said Father Abbot, reading the letter. "But I'm not sure you'll get much help from our lay brother, father."

The priest looked at Father Abbot without changing expression. "I may proceed?"

"By all means. Brother Matthew, perhaps you will see Father Manual's luggage."

"I have no plans to stay. Will you show me the way?"

Brother Matthew pinched his lips closed. There was in a hurry, and then there was rude.

The smile on Father Abbot's face remained calm and friendly. "Please follow me."

Brother Matthew watched as they walked along the path toward the contemplative garden. He didn't notice when Brother Mark walked up to him.

"Another guest?"

"No, thank goodness. One of the rudest men I've ever met, even if he is a Special Envoy from the Holy Father."

Brother Mark smiled at his young friend and placed a hand on his shoulder. "Come along. We have work to do, and then you might consider the sin of pride. It often goes both ways."

"Yes, brother." Brother Matthew followed the oldest monk in the monastery back toward the brewery.

Father Abbot stopped at the gate to the contemplative garden. "I will leave you here. He's in there alone, as he is most days."

"Thank you," said Father Manual.

"Father," the abbot said before turning to leave the priest. "He hasn't spoken since he arrived. Whatever trauma he experienced still haunts him."

"Thank you, Father Abbot."

Father Abbot waited but saw the priest would say nothing else. He raised his voice just enough for anyone nearby to hear. "I won't be far away if you need me."

Father Manual walked through the rose garden until he found the man sitting on the bench near the altar of the Madonna. He remembered the man was huge but had forgotten how huge.

"Brother Yasushi, do you remember me? I was once Lieutenant Diggers."

Yasushi made no movement to recognize Father Manual.

"I'm Father Manual now," he walked in front of Yasushi, "Things are happening. The church needs your help."

Yasushi continued to stare at the statue.

"You tried to help me once before, brother. Please. Help me again."

Yasushi stood up and turned around.

Father Manual smiled and stepped in front of Yasushi. "You remember me. Good. Our war with the demons continues, brother. I'm now working with the church. We need you and men like you for the battle that's coming. Will you stand with us?"

If Father Manual intended to say more, he did not get the chance. Yasushi lunged forward with a scream from deep within that shook the leaves and the petals of the roses as he grabbed Father Manual's throat and threw him to the ground.

Father Abbot and Brother Mark arrived before Father Manual registered what was happening and pulled Yasushi off of the priest. Two other monks ran to the garden to help and also reached for Yasushi. Brother Matthew helped Father Manual to his feet.

Father Manual coughed and bent over to catch his breath.

"Come, brother," Father Abbot's voice boomed over the voices of the brothers. "Hail Mary, full of grace, the Lord is with thee."

Yasushi let out another great roar.

""Brother," Father Abbot's voice boomed even louder than Yasushi's. "Hail Mary. Say it."

Quiet filled the contemplative rose garden. Yasushi held his eyes shut and recited the prayer in an audible whisper.

"Take him to his room," Father Abbot nodded to Brother Mark.

"He's mad," spat Father Manual.

"No, only troubled by a great sin. He seldom gives us any trouble. Come inside, father. Let me get you something to drink and help you calm yourself."

Father Manual saw that the abbot did not lead him to the sanctuary or even his office. Instead they went to the reception room. The cool, dark room contrasted to the heat and sun of the gardens. He sat on a bench as the abbot poured him a glass of wine.

"Here, drink this. We had to stop setting out beer, as people came here just for it. We have a tap room for that. Too many wineries around here for people to come here for wine. And if they do want wine, we give them a map of the local wineries."

"There's no mention of Brother Yasushi's mental condition in your files." Father Manual collected himself and his business face returned.

"Brother Yasushi is here to rest, father. His mental condition has never been an issue."

Father Manual lifted his eyebrow. "Never an issue?"

Father Abbot smiled, "Well, perhaps he needs a little extra brotherly love, but we have that in abundant supply here."

"His condition should have been noted. I spent a lot of time tracking him down, Father Abbot. I will mention your lack of cooperation in my report."

Father Abbot poured himself a glass of wine. "If that is what you need to do, then you must do it, father. Brother Yasushi's residency with us has been uneventful but educational."

Father Manual held his wineglass to his lips, then removed it. "How so?"

"His needs are special, so we learn patience and learn to practice discrete observation." Father Abbot smiled at the visiting priest. He pointed up to a large painting over the hearth. "Did you see our painting? It's a Reign original, a donation to the abbey."

Father Manual stood up and stared at the painting. His eyes, still adjusting to the dimness of the reception room, took time to focus on the colors and lines of the painting. He said nothing.

Father Abbot put a hand on his shoulder. "Donated after the arrival of Brother Yasushi. It upsets some people, but I like it. Judith and Holofernes. Very modern, don't you think?"

"How much do you know?" Father Manual turned to face the abbot, rage seethed from the corners of his mouth and shot out of his eyes.

"About what, father? Art? Since the painting arrived, I've learned a good deal. Had to. When I mentioned to our insurance agent a Reign had been donated, she flipped out. I had to learn a great deal about line, form, modern, classical, color, light, dark. It's been an education. Brother Yasushi helps me when he feels like talking."

Father Manual dropped the wineglass on the floor and turned to walk away. "Why isn't the painting listed among the monastery's assets?"

"The bishop thought it best to keep it quiet. If word gets out we have a Reign, we'll be flooded with tourists. And we're a contemplative monastery, father, despite the brewery. I would have to lose the painting just to gain silence."

Father Manual opened the door to leave but turned to look once more at the painting. Familiar eyes looked back at him. The head of a man he knew peeked out of a burlap bag on a silver platter. Its one brown eye reflected a distant light. The other ever-faded blue-gray eye, dull as it was in life, stared at nothing. Even the golden cherub smiling up at the woman wore a familiar face. Father Manual crossed himself and left the monastery.

"I'll be back, Father Abbot, with a doctor. I need Brother Yasushi."

* * * * *

Karol lay like stone on the desert floor. He felt a snake near him, brushing against his body. The occasional scent or whisper of the others watching from the bunker made its way over the breeze to his nose. A bead of sweat etched down his forehead to the bridge of his nose. He remained still like a pebble on the ground.

From behind a boulder in front of a mouth of rock, just inside the shade of a cave, movement. Karol's finger, long ready, pressed the trigger. The bullet, shot true, made its target.

From the small group of men, an instant hush, followed by "hurrah" after Captain Morgan confirmed the kill.

"Smith, go get that rabbit, then give it to cook," Morgan ordered, and a smallish young man with long greasy hair under an old army cap jumped on the four-by-four and roared toward the mound of stone.

"That, gentlemen," said Morgan, "is how it's done. Our enemy doesn't make it easy. They don't prance about for everyone to see them. They know how to hide in the shadows, know when they're being watched. To get them, think like them. Have patience."

Karol dusted himself off. He considered his shot. If he got the head, he'd be pleased. He'd have to wait until Smith got back to know for certain. He listened as Captain Morgan explained how their enemy required a level of stealth they were unused to dealing with, how no matter what training they came to the group with, it wasn't what was needed. But none of these men—women were not allowed in the group—understood what the enemy really was.

He watched Captain Morgan explain the need for patience and give them instructions on where to set up their own mock ambush. Morgan still leaned on his cane, the lines on his face—once prominent in age—now softened into helplessness. Only his eyes, still gray and searing, remained as sharp and piercing as Karol remembered, even if they looked haunted.

Smith arrived with the rabbit. "Perfect, sir," he said, holding up the jackrabbit and smiling the goofy grin he always wore.

Karol took hold of the carcass, examined it, then threw it to the ground. "Shit! Missed the head."

Smith's mouth opened with shock.

"Look at it," Karol spat. "I was aiming for the head. If I don't blow off one of the shits' heads or blow out the heart, they live. You only get one shot. Set me up another trap."

"Yes, sir," Smith replied, unsure whether he should pick up the dead rabbit.

"And stop fucking calling me sir all the time!"

"Yes, ssssssergeant." Smith walked back to the truck where the other trapped jackrabbits waited in the shade.

"You heard that," Morgan shouted at the men. "You get one shot. I don't care how good you think you are. Even the sergeant over there gets no dinner 'til it's done right. You got that?"

"Yes, sir!" They shouted in unison and took the positions around the mound of rocks they had built to house their targets. They would lie out in the hot sun and desert heat until Smith placed all the traps and Morgan released them.

Karol ignored the others as he stretched his neck and twisted his body. He knew how long Smith took to set up. He pissed behind the truck and drank more water. Captain Morgan was always getting on him for not drinking enough water. Captain Morgan made sure everyone followed orders, and if they didn't, Karol pounded the order into them until they obeyed.

A jackrabbit ran across the space between the gunmen and the rocky mound. "Shithole Smith," muttered Karol. Karol didn't like Smith, but he served his purpose. Every group needed someone to fetch and carry. Karol would make Smith pay for losing the rabbit, assuming the captain saw it.

Karol looked up and saw that Diggers had returned and was talking to Morgan. They argued, but they always did. Karol couldn't bring himself to refer to Diggers as father, so called him the priest. Neither the captain nor the priest liked each other, but they got along in front of the troops.

Karol didn't argue with the priest in front of the troops. He wished he could, but both he and the captain owed too much to Diggers and the church. The fiasco in Austin almost cost them their lives and perhaps long jail terms.

Karol often thought about that night. Motoring along the river to the Mugello estate, he could tell the captain was hurting, but he kept going even though they had lost contact with the bulk of their group. He knew now having the full group wouldn't have done any good. En masse, the vamps seemed to exude some darkness, a wall of fear and dread, an inexplicable need to be elsewhere. When the boats pulled up to the dock, that fear and dread almost overwhelmed them. Only Madeline and the captain were strong enough to resist it. Even Karol remembered wanting to turn back.

Madeline was in such a goddamn hurry to get there that night. Only the captain's stern expression and order to move forward allowed him to move ahead. But they were doomed before they reached the gathering.

Madeline raced ahead of them. The captain stood up to cover her. That's when Karol heard a woman's voice shout, "Get down!" Shots were fired. The captain went down. The sounds of flesh being torn and screams of agony replaced gunfire. Just the thought of those sounds still turned his stomach.

Karol had raced to the captain to find him clutching his chest and breathing erratically. The gunshot had put a hole in his shoulder. Karol dragged him back the way they had come, staying low in the grass. Somehow, they moved away from the screaming and burning. He picked up the captain and ran back to the boat. He knew how to bind up the wound, but didn't know what to do about the heart attack. As soon as they were clear of the house, he tossed the cell phones and headed for a public dock. There, he found a public phone and called Diggers, the only person he knew not connected with the night's events. He hoped Diggers could help, and he did.

Together, Karol and the captain transferred from one military hospital to another until the captain was well enough to be without professional care. And then Diggers rented a car for them and sent them here. The facilities were not too primitive, and Karol cared for the captain. As time passed, others arrived, and they trained. It was the captain who first referred to Karol as sergeant, and neither Diggers nor the others questioned the captain's decision.

Smith turned on the light above the mound, signaling the traps were being opened. Karol took up his position, became still like the surrounding stones. He felt the breeze brushing sand against his legs. He smelled the sweat and anticipation of the men near him. From the shadows of the mound of stones, he saw the first flicker of movement. He listened and heard a sigh near him, and then he heard the name: Brother Yasushi.

*****

CC pressed her ear against the rich, dark wood disguising the steel plantation shutters in the living room, listening to the almost silent whoosh as they slid together. As her right hand turned the knob, she pressed her left hand against the shutter to feel the steel bolts slide into place inside the walls. She lifted her face as she stepped away from the shutters, impressed with the steel doors and bolts creating an impregnable wall within the walls of the elegant living room. Not even a car driven at full speed could break through the seemingly normal windows on the outside of the house, and it had been tried.

The antique grandfather clock chimed. *Two thirty in the morning. You should be snug in bed, girl.* Though alone in the house, she tiptoed through the indulgent New Orleans plantation style room with its mahogany rosettes intertwined with deep velvets, brilliant needlepoint, and sparkling silver. No amount of dust rested on the ancient floors or fine, looped carpets that tickled her toes. She floated her hands along the cool wood, allowing her fingers to trace the carved filigree. It wasn't her style. It was elegance and wealth for the sake of elegance and wealth. She turned for a last look at the dimly lit room.

"Too much," she whispered and turned to the grand staircase.

The hairs on her neck pricked. She pulled on the belt of her favorite old robe as though its thin cotton would warm her from the chill racing up her spine. "Anyone here?" she asked, forcing her voice above a whisper.

CC knew the house's secrets and the secrets of its builder and guests. Anyone could be here, but since Hunters fled Austin, few needed the house to rest or heal or conspire. As far as she knew, she and James Earl were the only ones staying at the house, and they only came when the moon was full. The opulent house in the picturesque vineyard of Anthony Mugello wrapped in Hill Country beauty concealed those who needed to hide. His property edged a vast wooded area with streams and caves and more space than people. Here, James Earl could run in peace, and CC slept without fear.

Anthony built the house and vineyard to impress and heal. Everything about the house impressed, from the great double front entry to the French country kitchen decked with the latest espresso machines to the grand staircase. Everything in this house impressed but held too many secrets. Too much blood flowed through the rooms, too much pain hid behind the formality of tradition. Behind the cellar door, behind old, wooden shelves covered with dust hid a massive steel door leading to the safest room ever built. Neither CC nor James Earl would approach the door.

Tonight CC shifted from room to room as shadows slid and turned before her eyes could catch them. She had learned to trust the prick of hairs on her neck and the tingling in her core. Before James Earl left for the evening, they walked through the house, sealing the doors and closing the shutters. It was their routine. She completed her double check of the downstairs rooms—all sealed and locked. And yet, CC knew something was not right, but not right was not the right word. Everything was as it should be.

"Somebody's here." CC said as she stroked the cool, curved mahogany of the stair rail. She laughed. "No one's going to mess with me in Anthony Mugello's house. Relax, CC."

She stepped on each stair as though it might break. This made her laugh. Nothing in Anthony Mugello's house would break without his permission. Her fingers danced along the silky banister, polished to reflect the pin lights scattered along floorboards and stair treads. As she reached the top, she stopped and put her fingers to her nose. A hint of lemon oil registered in her nostrils. "Who cleans the house?"

In the months they had been coming to the house, she never stopped to consider who cleaned the place. "Someone has to."

No one questioned why she and James Earl arrived at the house once a month. The house was always clean, and the kitchen always stocked with simple provisions. At first, neither she nor James Earl wanted to use the house and brought their own supplies, but Cesar chided them. "You're doing me a favor. The vintner doesn't care about the house, he's too concerned with making excellent wine. Anthony's not using it, and I've got too much to do to hang out in the country. You're doing me a favor going out there once a month."

The first time they arrived at the house, she'd been so tired and injured and so awed by the opulence of the place and the threat to their lives, she'd ignored the fundamentals of keeping such a place ready for use. As she and James Earl continued living in Austin and using the Hill Country home as refuge under the full moon, she'd grown accustomed to the often bizarre and quant nature of the house.

And yet, every month James Earl reminded her to be afraid of the place and of him, but she never was. When the moon beamed full and bright, she felt him walking the woods and vineyard, but she never feared him. *So what the hell is bugging me tonight?*

She opened the blinds on the wall over her bed, revealing a view drenched in moonlight and dancing with stars. The vines in full leaf reflected the blue and silver light of the moon on their dark green leaves dampened from a sunset rain. Grapes would soon cover each vine manicured into neat rows. In the distant wooded area, she thought she caught a shadow gliding along the edge of the vineyard. She felt that twinge in her chest telling her James Earl was near. She closed the blinds, not wanting him to see her looking at him.

She shuddered remembering the first time she saw him as a wolf, but on that cold December night, that night when the funeral pyres cast everyone in a golden light and a shining moon and stars and the gunshots and the screaming and the tearing of flesh—Yes, she had seen him as a wolf and she had been afraid. He was beautiful—large, brown, with bloody fangs gleaming in the moonlight. It had been a savage night. He had been savage, but it was that savageness that saved them all.

She bent to smell the single rose sitting on the pushcart holding wine, breads, cheeses, and sweets. The white rose reflected the single reading light over the bed. She poured herself a glass of the sparkling wine. It tickled her nose, sending the corners of her mouth into a grin. There was no note with the gift. She assumed the caretakers left it for them. Or perhaps James Earl put it together, but she shook her head, breathing in the rose's scent. "He's not anywhere near this romantic."

A howl echoed over the vineyard and through the bolted shutters of her room. "Shit! Door," she said. She turned to face the door and froze.

The presence she had felt all evening stood in the doorway, leaning against the frame. Her fear doubled and relaxed at the same time. She held her breath.

"Catherine," said the melodious voice that drifted on night breezes and floated on midnight's shadows. CC knew the voice too well. She was either about to die or—she didn't know.

"I'm glad to see you're still afraid," said Mary. "But tonight you have no reason to be afraid—of me."

CC took a deep breath. She let it out through pinched lips. "I didn't know you'd be here tonight. Had I known—"

"No one ever knows where I'll be."

CC sat on the chair on the table beside the cart. She looked at the figure of the woman she feared more than any other thing in the night. She forced her lips to perk into a smile as she concentrated on preventing her heart from bursting through her chest. Her right hand grasped the lapels of her old robe, pulling them close as her left hand tugged the hem as close to her knees as she could get it. "Do you need an investigator?"

The faintest of a laugh inched its way to CC's ears. CC had no choice but to laugh with it. Her heart returned to its normal rhythm.

"Perhaps," Mary said.

CC's hands moved back and forth from her lapels to her hem. Her foot tapped against the carpet. She opened her mouth to respond, but no sound emerged. Her eyes looked to the sealed shutters. "James Earl," she began, but Mary interrupted.

"Children are missing."

CC focused her eyes on the figure in the doorway. Mary remained indistinct from the shadows surrounding her. Mary was never anything but a shadow, a shadow that was there but wasn't. CC opened her mouth, but words would not emerge.

"I need you to help find the monster destroying them before he kills so many more," Mary said. "I've sent for someone to do the killing. There's no way you could do it."

"If the abductor isn't human—"

"Neither human nor unhuman. He fails in being."

CC widened her eyes. "Are you sure you want me involved? I've met others since settling in town, but I stay away from—"

This time, the laughter from Mary's mouth sprinkled the room with genuine mirth. "You've made a good impression on everyone you've met. They like you, and you understand them. Don't dismiss your skills."

CC leaned back in her chair, balancing on the back two legs. Her eyes stared at the ceiling as she saw nothing in the room. "Neither human nor unhuman. He's killing human children, or you wouldn't want a human involved in the hunt." The front legs of her chair slammed into the floor, muffled by the thick carpet. "You're afraid the police will get involved. That would mean a lot of humans hunting—" CC stopped talking. Her eyes fixed on the shadow that was Mary. "There's been nothing in the news about unusual killings or children missing, so either they don't know or they don't know yet."

"My faith in you is well deserved."

CC nodded her head. Cesar's help in the vineyard's use for James Earl to run in, Anthony's help in getting her investigator's license, even Jenny introducing her to the local vamps made sense now. Mary either wanted or needed a human to help her people.

"You will need to deal with the police and any humans affected by this monster," said Mary. "But be careful, CC. Be afraid of this monster as you have never been afraid of anyone or anything. He's not like us or you. Show no pity, deliver no succor. Imagine your greatest fear, and you'll know what this monster is."

CC watched as Mary's figure dissolved. The speed of her heart increased, and a sweat dripped down her back. A cold finger glided along the side of her face as a hand sat on her shoulder, massaging away a deep knot she didn't know she had before the hand slid down her arm till the hand clasped her hand and a face, pale, indistinct, but beautiful pressed against her face. She felt lips next to hers.

"I like you, CC. You have much to learn, more than your young man. Don't throw away your life. I seek harmony as you do. Everyone will know you're mine."

CC closed her eyes. She forced her chest to open for breath as the finger on her face glided down her neck, under her robe, and circled her breasts. Her heart pounded in her ears as cold lips kissed her lips. Her mouth opened as she breathed in the night, and longing filled her senses. The knot in her stomach she had felt all night dissolved away as the not unwelcome lust surging through her. Her arms and legs wrapped the cold, solid, yet fluid form of Mary as she felt herself lifted and moved. Anxiety of not knowing if she would live through the night shook through her core as fingers slipped her robe open and panties slid away. Her breaths shortened, her lungs gasped for air, and stars filled her eyes from behind closed lids.

Then it was over. She opened her eyes and breathed deep, cleansing breaths. She lay on the bed pulling away the blanket covering her naked, sweating body. From far away, she heard James Earl's long, lonely howl.

"Shit!" she said jumping off the bed and running to the door. It was sealed. She sighed, allowing her shoulders to droop. "Oh, babe," she said, leaning her forehead against the cool, smooth door. "What the hell is going on?"

Mary's presence lingered around her like a waking dream. There was no scent, only the tale of a presence unlooked for. CC made her way to the bathroom and splashed cold water on her face. She examined her face in the mirror. "What did she mean everyone will know you're mine? And what the hell could be so frightening that even a vamp would call it a monster?"

L.K. Latham writes Urban Fantasy and poetry that's about as dark as the chocolate she loves. She spends her days weaving tales of vampires, werewolves, and other creatures known to Dance in the Shadows of the Moon. When not writing, you'll find L.K. baking with chocolate and wine. In the evenings, she rests with a class of bourbon - made in Texas, of course, and waiting for last year's grapes to become this year's wine.

A recovering educator, this native Texas settled in the Austin area with her husband. She enjoys living in Texas as much as she enjoys the wines of Texas, perhaps a bit more than some of its inhabitants, but that doesn't stop her from admiring their spunk and veracity in the face of overwhelming facts.

Join L.K. Latham to receive updates and free short stories in the world of *Midnight Whispers* and beyond at https://lklatham.com

Midnight Bites

Mary Midnight is settled in Austin, but there are others gathering for a few *Midnight Bites*.

Maria ran until her lungs burned and legs trembled. Fatigue slapped her in the face. She wobbled, slipping until her hands grabbed the coarse wood of a lamp pole hiding in the dark. Wrapping herself in the shadows, she filled her lungs with deep, quick breaths. Fear trickled down her back with each drop of sweat. The monster had killed her brother.

She leaned her forehead into the pole as burning embers flowed down her cheeks from her eyes. "Oh, Louis. What did we do?"

A motorcycle puttered past her on the street. Curls like flames tossed in the wind from beneath a helmet. The woman driving the motorcycle didn't see her, but the huge, white dog sitting in the sidecar did. Pink eyes glowed beneath goggles as it passed Maria. The dog barked once.

Maria jumped, afraid of what the dog saw. She ran across the street onto a residential road. Large houses with dark windows watched her run. The top of her foot hit the curb as she jogged between two parked cars to avoid a car driving down the street. She tripped, landing on her hands and knees.

She crawled into the bushes and sat beneath a closed gate. If she pulled her knees to her chin, she could just squeeze into a hole beneath the bushes. Blood oozed from both knees and hands, but top of her foot and ankle throbbed as hundreds of tiny spikes pushed on her muscles. She rubbed her foot with her sore hands.

Footsteps soft and hurried patted in her direction. From beneath the bushes, a young woman, not a girl, close to her own age, jogged along the sidewalk. The girl stopped in front of the gate. The light of her watch lit the girl's face, but Maria couldn't see her face, only the blue light.

"Best time yet," the girl said with pride. "Now, to bed."

The girl walked through the gate. A light from above the front door flashed on. The girl froze, breathing, "Argh! Security light. Who turned that on? Up the tree in back." The girl stepped off the path to the dark side of the house.

Maria twisted her head to look over the bushes. The girl disappeared behind the side of the house.

Maria felt the chill of fear wash over her. "He's near," she whispered.

Maria pushed herself out from under the bushes. She stood ready to run, but her foot would not allow any weight on it. The chill in her heart grew.

She pushed forward, forcing her foot to walk or limp forward. She had to get away. As she hobbled away from the house, she saw the girl climbing into a window on the second floor.

Maria opened her mouth to call for help, but only shook her head. The demon was too close.

Another block, and the streetlights went out. Maria stopped moving, letting the darkness swallow her. Her sore foot surrendered to the pain, and Maria fell to the ground. Tears blocked her vision. A footfall and then another and then the sound of something, close.

Maria pushed herself up with her right arm. *Just move.* She pushed herself forward.

But it was too late. A hand - a claw, cold, hard, grabbed her shoulder, lifting her off the grown. Blackness filled her senses. Putrid, wet breath filled her face. "Where's the others?" the voice, coarse and cruel asked. These were the last words Maria heard before she died.